Into Darkness

Also by J.T. Geissinger

J.T. GEISSINGER

INTO DARKNESS

A NIGHT PROWLER NOVEL

Montlake
Romance

Published by Montlake Romance, Seattle

www.apub.com

Amazon, the Amazon logo, and Montlake Romance are trademarks of Amazon. com, Inc., or its affiliates

ISBN-13: 9781477825549
ISBN-10: 1477825541

Cover design by Inkd Inc

Library of Congress Control Number: 2014907966

Printed in the United States of America

To Jay,
for knowing when to pet the bear, when not to poke it,
and when to let it run off into the woods.

Some say the world will end in fire,
some say in ice.
From what I've tasted of desire
I hold with those who favor fire.
But if I had to perish twice,
I think I know enough of hate
To say that for destruction ice
is also great
And would suffice.

—Robert Frost, "Fire and Ice"

PART ONE

PART ONE

PROLOGUE

The Wall Street Journal, *Wednesday, October 16, 2013*

STOCK MARKETS COLLAPSING AMID DOOMSDAY FEARS

International stock markets are reacting to yesterday's unexplained fire in the sky over the Amazon rainforest in Brazil with massive sell-offs. In the worst single-day decline the Dow Jones industrial average has seen since the infamous Black Monday crash of October 19, 1987, the Dow dropped 4,504 points to finish at 10,664, a loss of 29.7 percent. The SEC has temporarily suspended trading, but top financial gurus warn that without adequate, immediate explanation of the causes of the phenomenon that left approximately one hundred square miles of the rainforest northeast of Manaus burning, the hysteria will only worsen.

Combined with a ground shock that registered 7.3 on the Richter scale, the intense pulse of light was visible as far away as Lima, Peru. One eyewitness described it as an "unearthly" explosion in the atmosphere, and many religious leaders are pointing to end-time biblical prophecies. Exacerbating the public's panic are the uncorroborated reports that Brazil's military launched a massive sortie from the Manaus air force base minutes before the enormous fireball was first seen.

In his speech from the White House yesterday evening, President Obama denied the possibility that a nuclear weapon may have been detonated, in spite of the incredibly powerful electro-magnetic pulse that destroyed satellites, power-supply networks, computers and electrical equipment in Manaus and surrounding areas, an effect consistent with a nuclear explosion.

Information coming from Brazil is virtually nonexistent, but the Federal Emergency Management Agency estimates that the firestorms decimating the rainforest have the potential to create an ecological disaster on a global scale. One of the richest areas of the world in terms of animal and plant diversity, the Amazon, if deforested, could be ground zero for global extinction.

The president is asking for calm amid a growing outcry for answers, but for now the long-term damage to both the environment and global economies remains to be seen.

New Vienna, Austria
16 September, 2027
1:17am IFST
Diary Entry #36

In the dreams, I'm always deaf.

That's what comes first, the velvet silence, the utter lack of sound. It settles over me like the softest of blankets, comforting and warm. When I awake in that silence my dream self—so bold and fearless, so different than I—knows what's coming. She knows exactly what to expect. She welcomes the unnatural lack of noise, my dreaming better half, and she's glad.

She's glad because she's evil.

At least, that's what Father thinks. He's afraid of my other side almost as much as I am. The whipping he gave me this morning is proof enough of that. I didn't *mean* to set the bed on fire, but I was so tired from chores and lessons and the constant effort of *not* touching and *not* speaking and generally pretending to be invisible that I forgot to put my gloves back on after my bath, and, well . . .

Father is going to have to buy me a new bed.

Again.

If only I could be good. If only I could be like the Prefect's daughter Annika, with her shiny curls and sunny smile, or the Inquisitor's daughter Sophie, with her winning manners. But I'm not. I'm weird, and I'm awkward, and all the Annikas and Sophies of the world hate me, though they'd never say it out loud.

They're afraid of me, too.

But we're careful, Father and I. We never give any indication that I might be different. Or at least different in *that* way, the way that could get both of us killed. So far we've been successful in explaining away my gloves and my silence and all the tics of my strange personality as Asperger's and OCD. Hence the need for homeschooling. Hence my obvious lack of social skills. Or friends.

I don't need any friends in those silent, wonderful dreams, though. I don't need anything.

I only need *him*.

Unlike me, the stranger in my dreams is beautiful, more so than anyone I've seen in real life. He's patient, and he's kind, though reeking of danger, and my dreaming self—somehow years older than my actual age of fifteen—is always so glad to see him she goes a little mad. *Magnus*, she greets him silently. With the same resounding silence he answers, *Hope*.

That's a little awkward because Hope isn't my name. But my dream self doesn't care. She throws her arms around this Magnus and kisses him.

He seems to really like it.

I've not been kissed. Though inside I burn brighter than the sun emblem of the Imperial Federation, outside I may as well be Quasimodo for all the attention boys pay me.

But Magnus pays attention. He has eyes as dark as a swan's, and a voice as rich as brown butter, and he looks at me as if I'm something he's been hunting for a long, long time. Something for which he's been waiting.

Magnus. What a name. To be fair, it's not much weirder than my own, but *Magnus*? Sounds like a twentieth-century porn star. Well, whoever this dream stranger is, I know one thing for sure.

He's Aberrant. Like me.

And he's out there. Somewhere, he's out there.

24 January, 2028
3:22am IFST
Diary Entry #154

Today I burned the credit market to the ground.

I didn't mean to do it, but that wretch Annika and her clique of First Form shrews were staring at me and giggling over the BioVite display, and the rage I felt took me completely by surprise. I mean, I should be used to the sneers by now. I *am* used to them. Growing up not only Third Form but also a *weird* Third Form guaranteed that.

But today . . . today I snapped. Big-time.

It wouldn't have happened if I'd kept my glove on to stroke the grocer's cat, as I always do. But today for some reason I was gripped by a violent urge to *feel* something. For once. I needed to touch something other than my own skin when I bathed.

Cinder is a black cat, glossy and plump, with fur like mink. I can't tell you what possessed me to do it, but possess is the right choice of verb because I was as helpless against it as if a demon had slipped inside my body and started pulling strings.

I saw Cinder sitting there between the stacked wooden crates of oranges and the cart of flowers. Inscrutable as the Sphinx, she blinked up at me with her bright-yellow eyes, and, as it always does, a strange recognition crackled between us. She prowled forward. I knelt down. I furtively removed my glove, and stretched out my hand.

And oh, what *bliss*. I closed my eyes and simply luxuriated in the feeling of cool, silken fur as Cinder arched beneath my fingertips, gliding against my hand with a satisfied purr.

Dogs whine and cower when I draw near. Birds shriek, horses whinny and stomp, even crickets fall silent when I pass. But cats are drawn to me and I to them, and Cinder is one of dozens of neighborhood cats I know by name. I love her the way one loves children, or a favorite song. Just her presence makes me happy.

Then I heard the laughter.

I turned and saw the cluster of girls across the way. The heads bent together, the smirks hidden behind hands, the contempt as blinding as sunlight on snow. The effect was that of a struck match tossed on a giant pile of dry kindling. Before I knew what I was doing, I'd shot to my feet, flexed open my gloveless hand, and pushed.

That's what I call it. The "push." It's an outward-bound sensation, no more effortful than an exhalation of breath, but vastly more deadly.

The whole place was in flames in the space of a few seconds. I grabbed Cinder and ran.

I'm still not sure if Annika and her little coven made it out.

I'm not sure if I care.

12 September, 2030
2:19am IFST
Diary Entry #1069

It's my birthday today. At least, the day Father and I celebrate it. I sometimes feel like the baby in that banned book, what was his name? Oh, right: Moses. Found in a basket, just like me. Father would probably be found in a basket chopped into little pieces if the Prefect ever found out we had banned books, but Father is as good at keeping secrets as I am. Better, maybe.

Eighteen years old (near as we can tell), and still never been kissed. Which is probably for the best. God only knows what would happen to the poor boy. Strike that, *Thorne* only knows. *God* is one of those words on the Suppression List that keeps making its way into my diary. Not that anyone will ever read this. I hope. If you are, it means something bad has happened. That thing I've lived in terror of since I was little:

Discovery.

I've been careful since that day I snapped in the market, though. I've been almost perfect. I've learned how to control all my tics. I don't even vanish when I sneeze anymore.

Still having those dreams of Magnus, though. I won't detail how explicit they've gotten, but my older dream self sure is . . . fierce. Just thinking about it makes my face hot.

He's still calling me Hope. I wish he wouldn't do that.

Oh—wait 'til you hear *this*! At Assignations today, I got Hospice Aid. How hilarious is that? I purposely ganked the aptitude tests so I'd be allowed to work with Father in the grow light fields, but the Administrator thought I showed "advanced intuitive capacity," "highly honed observational skills," and a "great propensity for compassion."

Compassion. Ha! If only they knew about the market fire. Even though no one was killed, I was *ecstatic* about Annika's hair burning off.

The joke's on me, though, because now I'll be spending the rest of my days tending to the condemned elderly.

I hate my life.

15 October, 2036
11:37pm IFST
Diary Entry #2553

For the first time in many, many years, I heard the Girl.

I was in Mr. Kirchmann's room, reading to him from *Essays on Enlightenment*—the IF's quarterly propaganda treatise about the glory and necessity of the global unified government—and trying not to grit my teeth too hard as the crusty old goat nodded in agreement to every word I spoke as he lay feebly wheezing in his bed, when suddenly I felt as if a door kicked open inside my head, and someone barged in.

Her presence is electric, and overwhelming. And, if I'm being honest, dark. She's much stronger now than when I last heard her, as a child, and she's much more . . .

Angry. In fact, this Girl is really tweaked. She started shouting straight off, the words tumbling over each other in her rush to get them out.

Hope for fuck's SAKE wake UP get off your sorry ass we NEED you here come and—

And what? I don't know, because I threw up a mental wall and shut her out. I've been cloaking my mind forever—nothing slips in, nothing slips out, it's a simple matter of survival—but when I'm tired, overly emotional, or inattentive, sometimes the cloak gets loose. The doors come unlocked, and the world in all its terrible, greedy enormity comes rushing in.

She comes rushing in. The Girl, whose name I know, from many prior rush-ins, is Honor.

Even from behind the wall I hear her muffled, angry shouts. I retreat, turn the volume down to zero, then she's gone. But the questions remain.

Who is she? What does she want from me? And why, like my dream lover Magnus, does she insist on calling me Hope?

I think it's time Father and I sat down and had a little chat.

Later that night

He said what he always says when I ask questions. "Stop asking so many questions, Lu." Then he went and sat on the porch, and smoked his entire week's tobacco ration while sitting in the dark.

Here's what I know for sure: I can light things on fire. I can get inside people's minds. I can vanish into a cloud of mist, and smell, hear, and feel things others don't. I can move things without touching them, and ~~God~~ Thorne help you if I *do* touch you, because you might find yourself stripped of any special talent you have.

Father found that out the hard way. I accidentally stole his ability to play the piano and speak Czech before he figured it out and started making me wear gloves.

So even if Father won't answer my questions, they all add up to the same thing I've known since I was little.

I'm different. I'm dangerous. I'm almost certainly not human.

And, if I want to stay alive, no one can know.

24 December, 2037
11:37pm IFST
Diary Entry #2987

Father is afraid.

He won't say it, but I smell it on him. Fear smells like something sour and rotting, the same stench of decay I can never wash out of my hair and clothes after work. I overheard him on the telecom with the Prefect tonight, and his voice shook so badly I thought he might cry. When I asked him what was wrong he said "nothing," but he looked guilty. He hates to lie.

An odd misfortune for him, since his entire life is built around doing exactly that.

In other news, I had another "incident."

It wasn't fire this time. It was actually worse, because at least fire is a natural phenomenon. A fire can be started by a million different things; the fire that caused the credit market to burn to the ground, for instance, was thought to have started from faulty wiring in a fan in the butcher's stall. That was the official explanation, anyway. The rumors have never really stopped circulating. But a bunch of knives flying through the air and stopping just before they embed themselves into someone's head . . . well, that's not exactly something that can be explained so easily.

Talk about a red flag.

It was that bastard Cushing's fault. He's always handling the elderly Hospice guests (they're called guests, though everyone, including them, knows they're not allowed to leave) too roughly. I've seen more bruised arms than at Heroin Park. Anyway, I was in the kitchen helping Lars and the staff prepare Thornemas Eve dinner when I happened to glance out the door. The view from the kitchen into the communal dining room is a good one, and there was Cushing, shoving Mrs. Elkins down into a chair so hard she cried out in pain.

Then what did he do? He *pinched* her. He grabbed a fold of papery skin on her upper arm and twisted, hissing at her to *shut the fuck up.*

So, yes. I lost it. Again. Before I could stop myself, I had every knife in the kitchen flying through the air toward that sick bastard's head.

I caught myself before any bodily damage was done, but the sight of an army of knives hovering in midair around Cushing's head, held up by nothing, made Mrs. Elkins faint dead away. Cushing wet his pants. The kitchen staff witnessed the entire thing.

I pretended to be just as horrified and shocked as everyone else, but now there will be an inquiry. The Elimination Campaign will have the Inquisitor out to interview everyone at the Hospice first thing in the evening. Just like six months ago, when I overheard the Hospice Administrator call her guests "cows awaiting the slaughter," and every mirror in the place shattered.

State-sponsored euthanasia is a fact of life in New Vienna, but that doesn't mean I have to like it. Along with rations, sun poisoning, and the televised hangings of Dissenters, frying anyone over seventy-five in the Cinerator™ after a lethal, "humane" dose of SleepSoft-9 is something I'll never quite be able to stomach.

First Formers don't have to worry about growing old, though. Money can buy a lot of luxuries here, as many extra years as you need. In a world run by a corporation only one thing really matters: profit.

Sometimes I wonder how much longer I can survive before the wild, snarling thing inside me breaks free once and for all, and tears this frail and shallow world to shreds.

Thorne help us all if the monster inside me ever gets out.

ONE

December 25, 2037
New Vienna, Austria

Lumina Bohn awoke in the sultry semidarkness to the sound of gunfire.

The sound was off in the distance, a sharp *rat-a-tat* that shattered the eerie quiet of Curfew. She jerked upright on her pallet, heart racing, then held perfectly still, straining her ears, awaiting the final burst.

There was always one more burst.

Through the sooty window across her cramped bedroom glowed the neon beacon of the megascreen, broadcasting the Imperial Federation's tagline, "One World In Harmony," throughout the district. A glance at the slowly rotating screen atop the south tower of what used to be St. Stephen's Cathedral showed the time as 5:17pm IFST. Curfew didn't end for another three quarters of an hour.

As another volley of gunfire rang out, Lu said a silent prayer for the poor soul who'd broken it.

A tap on her bedroom door, then her father's head popped through. *"Liebling? Ist alles in ordnung?"*

He was whispering, the survivalist habit of one long used to hiding. Behind his wire-rimmed spectacles, his brown eyes shone with worry. He knew too well how much she hated the sound of gunfire.

"Yes. I'm fine," Lu lied, noticing how deep the grooves around his mouth had become. His once-dark hair had, overnight it seemed, paled to gray. In his faded dressing gown and house slippers, he reminded her of one of the guests at the Hospice. The thought made her shiver. He still had six more years before they'd have to face that, and Lu tried hard never to think of it.

She tried hard never to think of a great many things.

He switched from German to English. "Can you go back to sleep? You still have a few hours before work."

He looked hopeful, but they both knew she'd never go back to sleep now. Beyond the obvious horror of what gunfire during Curfew meant, there was something darker that prickled her skin and soured her stomach at the sound. Some ancient monster buried deep in her psyche blinked open yellow eyes and lifted its head, hackles raised.

That monster she feared more than anything else, even more than discovery by the Inquisitor.

"No. I think I'll go in early today. We could use the extra credits."

"All right. I'll put the coffee on." Her father swung shut the door, and Lu heard the shuffle of his footsteps all the way down the stairs.

She scrubbed her gloved hands across her face, rose from the bed, and went down the hall into the bathroom they shared. The dying rays of the sun filled their apartment with a dim red light, filtered through the cloud cover, soupy and opaque. She removed the lightweight night gloves, laid them on the ledge above the sink, and stared down at her bare hands.

Tattoos decorated the inside of both wrists. The left showed a birdcage, empty, its wire door cocked open. The right showed a trio of birds in flight, wings spread wide open as they soared. A constellation of tattoos decorated her body, including a quote from *The Bell Jar*, by Sylvia Plath, on her rib cage, the zodiac sign for twins on her right ankle—it spoke to her, for all its meaninglessness to reality; she was a Virgo, not a Gemini—and a fire-breathing dragon curled around her belly button, but the birds were her favorite.

When she was seventeen, she'd read *Lolita* by Nabokov—that one wasn't on the banned list—and a quote from the book had stuck in her mind like a burr, refusing to shake loose. "I talk in a daze, I walk in a maze, I cannot get out, said the starling."

The words had resonated in the deepest level of her heart. Lu understood exactly how that little starling felt. When she pressed her wrists together, seeing her own tattoo starlings fly free, it made her feel a little better.

Keeping a careful eye on the digital water meter on the wall above the tap, she brushed her teeth and washed her face, then combed her fingers through her long, wavy hair and braided it. The single plait fell nearly to her waist. She returned to her room and pulled on the Hospice's standard-issue gray trousers and belted coat over the thin leggings and tank she'd worn to bed, then laced up her favorite pair of boots. The shoe vendor at the market had called them "combat" boots, a name Lu liked. She'd bartered ten water credits for them, a pricey trade but worth it; she spent most of her shift at the Hospice on her feet, and the boots were supremely comfortable, if ugly.

Lu didn't care about pretty exteriors. She knew even the most beautiful things could be worm-eaten on the inside.

A quick check in the cracked mirror above the tiny bureau to make sure her appearance was in order, her usual stuck-out tongue at the reflection of the large red Third Form badge sewn into the lapel, then she made her way down the narrow staircase to the first floor.

Her father was in the kitchen, frowning at a pan of water on the stove. He turned when she came in, held out an empty tin, shrugged an apology. "Forgot to buy more matches. Can't put the coffee on for another half hour. Sorry, *liebling*."

The stove was wood burning, but also had electrical ignition switches, a hybrid necessity in a city where electricity was only available during certain hours. Lu needed neither, but her father had strictly forbidden any hint of *zauber* from her, no matter that they were inside and no one could possibly find out.

"It's all right. I'll get a coffee at work. And I'll pick up some matches on the way home. Anything else we need from the market?"

Looking around the threadbare kitchen, her father made an amused noise she translated to *Is there anything else we* don't *need?* Staring at the nearly empty cupboard shelves, he sighed. "It might be time for me to trade a few more books."

"*No.*" Her emphatic response made her father raise his brows, and Lu shook her head. "I'll ask for extra hours next shift. We're not trading any more of your blacklisted books. It's too dangerous."

Her father chuckled and sent her a warm smile. "I think it's not the danger you're worried about, little bookworm. I think it's which one of your favorites I might trade next."

"Psh." Lu waved the comment away, but he was right. Reading transported her to other worlds so much finer and more interesting than her own. She'd rather give her eyeteeth than give up any more books, no matter how hungry they became.

She crossed to the icebox, yanked open the door, and peered inside. She had to smother the pang of alarm at what little lurked inside. Putting on a bright voice, she said, "Okay. Breakfast. We've got a delicious-looking rind of"—unable to discern the color of the wedge of cheese beneath its layer of fuzzy blue mold, she sniffed—"cheddar. We've got a *very* perky head of cabbage." Her father snorted. The cabbage was decidedly *un*perky. "We've got three cans of BioVite, two FitCakes, and something that looks like it used to be a sausage." She paused. "Or maybe a banana."

Her father peered over her shoulder. "We haven't had fresh fruit in weeks. Whatever that thing is, it's definitely not a banana."

Lu's sigh matched the one her father had made moments earlier. "All right. BioVite or FitCake?"

"Let me get out of my dressing gown before I'm forced to make such a gourmet decision, child." He patted her on the shoulder and began to shuffle from the kitchen. Watching him go, shoulders slumped, hair in disarray, his gait that of a man utterly bereft of hope, Lu felt something inside her chest harden.

As soon as he'd vanished upstairs, she went to the stove, and pulled open the square firebox door. Then she lifted her bare left hand, flexed open her palm, and gave a small push.

The pile of wood inside burst into merry flame.

Lu shut the door, latched it, and stood watching the pan of water on the stovetop until her father returned.

He stopped short in the doorway. Dressed in meticulously clean but worn clothes that included a cardigan with mended elbows, and his trademark black fedora, he looked at the simmering water in the pan, looked at her bare hands, looked into her eyes with a question, with that familiar flare of fear in his own.

"Found a stray match in the cupboard," she lied, turning back to the stove. "You can have coffee with your FitCake. Should make it go down a little easier."

Her father was silent a long while, long enough for the water to boil and Lu to pour it into two mugs, and stir in the dried coffee crystals. When finally she turned and held out a mug to him, he took it with only a murmured word of thanks, not meeting her eyes. They sat down at the kitchen table together and ate their breakfast and drank their coffee, neither one willing to mention the gunfire or the stove fire or all the other unspeakable things that lurched and stomped through the landscape of their lives.

The bells inside the old cathedral began to toll, signaling the end of Curfew.

Her father whispered, "It's Christmas Day."

Lu nodded, surprised as always that his faith was still intact after everything. And that he dared to speak the word *Christmas* aloud. It was just as dangerous as what she'd done with the pan of water.

"Your mother would be proud of you, Lumina."

Startled, Lu glanced up at her father. He stared back at her with unblinking intensity, his eyes bright with unshed tears. "I wish you'd had more time together. I wish the cancer hadn't been quite so aggressive. I know how hard it's been for you, growing up without a mother. Growing up so . . . different." He swallowed and looked away.

"She always called you our little miracle," he said in a strained voice, staring out the small kitchen window into the alley beyond. The view was of the building next door to theirs, identical rows of concrete housing that were nervous looking in the red-dressed twilight. "We wanted a baby so badly, but it never happened. Then one day you came, years after we'd stopped trying. Just . . . out of the blue, there you were." He turned his gaze back to her. "That was the happiest day of my life. Seeing your mother so happy . . . it was the greatest gift I've ever been given."

Lu was aware that her mouth was open. She was aware of a dull roar in her ears, and the feel of her pulse pounding hard through her veins, but she wasn't paying attention to any of that because her father was talking about her mother, something he hadn't done since she'd died when Lu was six years old.

What could this possibly mean?

He reached across the table and grabbed her wrist. "You have to be careful, Lumina," he said with vehemence, his eyes burning hers. "Today, at work. They're going to question everyone, you can't do anything to stand out—"

"The call from the Prefect last night," she guessed.

"Yes."

The hair on her arms prickled. "I can handle the inquiry, you know that. I've always been fine before—"

"It won't just be the Inquisitor this time, Lu." Her father's face had gone a startling waxen gray.

"What do you mean?"

He swallowed. The pause that followed seemed cavernous. "The Grand Minister will be there, too."

All the blood drained from her face. Her father tightened his grip on her wrist.

"No matter what happens, you can't lose your temper. You can't let your control slip. One false move and you'll be collared, then ... then ..."

He couldn't say it, but Lu knew the word he was choking on.

Cleaned.

Killed, only worse, because she'd still be alive, trapped inside a body immobilized by drugs, her marrow harvested from her bones, her stem cells harvested for reengineering. A single Aberrant could provide enough genetic material to make potentially millions in profits from the medicines the Phoenix Corporation created from their captive donors. Rumor had it the donors were kept alive for years; some even said there were donors from decades ago, right after the Flash, zombies in rows staring up at the same patch of ceiling since they were caught.

"I won't go to work," Lu whispered. "We'll run right now. Our bug-out bags are still ready; we have guns, money, papers—"

"No, Lumina." Her father's voice was sad, his eyes even sadder. "I'm too old to run now. I'd only slow you down. You'll have to go by yourself, *liebling*."

"If I run, the first one they'll punish is you! I'm not going anywhere without you!"

It wouldn't be mere punishment, Lu knew. Her father would be made an example of. His death for high treason would be protracted, gruesome, and televised for all the world to see. In the Federation, harboring an Aberrant was a capital crime.

Her father drew a long, labored breath and dropped his gaze to the table. His grip on her wrist loosened. He patted her hand. "If you won't go, the only choice is to try and fool them. But the Grand Minister won't be so easily fooled." His eyes, now full of warning, flashed up to hers. "He knows what to look for. He knows all the signs. Jakob says the man is clever as the devil himself."

Jakob was the leader of the underground church, a man her father admired and trusted. Lu trusted him far less—all zealots struck her as unhinged, whether they were religious, members of the Elimination Campaign, or their Aberrant-loving opponents, the Dissenters—but she had a hunch on this the wild-eyed Jakob was right. The Grand Minister's prowess at sniffing out a hidden Aberrant was legendary. Some said he had a sixth sense for it.

A cold sweat broke out beneath her armpits. "Do I wear my gloves?"

"If you don't, it will look suspicious."

"If I *do*, it will look suspicious!"

Her father nodded sadly. "You have little choice but to try and behave as normally as possible, as if you know nothing. As if you're just like everyone else."

They stared at each other. Lu had been trying to be just like everyone else her entire life. Trying and failing. A thought arrested her. "Why did the Prefect call to warn you?"

A thin smile curved her father's lips. "Not everything is as it seems, *liebling*. The face we show the world isn't always the face we see in the mirror. You of all people should know that."

The revelation hit her like a punch in the gut: The Prefect was a Dissenter. Shocked, she lifted a hand to cover her mouth. Cold and clammy, a flood of guilt for what she'd done all those years ago to Annika at the market flashed over her.

"You're going to be all right," her father assured her, gently patting her arm again. "You're smart, child. Just control your temper, keep your head down, and everything will be all right."

She would keep her head down. But what if the monster inside her wouldn't?

Walking to work, with a second cup of coffee in hand, through the winding, cobblestone streets swamped with pedestrians and bicyclists and the occasional horse-drawn carriage—people thronged the streets immediately after Curfew was lifted as if they'd been spat out of the buildings—Lu tried to calm herself by humming. A habit she'd learned as a child when she'd awoken from a nightmare, she hummed the song her father used to sing to coax her to sleep.

> *Svetlo tve daleko vidi,*
> *Po svete bloudis sirokem,*
> *Divas se v pribytky lidi . . .*

It was from a Czech opera called *Song to the Moon*, about the daughter of a water-goblin who desperately wants to become human after she falls in love with a hunter/prince who frequents the lake in which she lives. She asks the moon to reveal her love to the prince, to awaken him from his dreams so he will come and be with her.

Lu had never seen the moon. Or the stars. Or been in love. All of them existed in the same fairy-tale place as the water-goblin's daughter, imaginary and utterly out of reach.

She glanced up at the sullen sky above, glowering with its usual load of impenetrable oxblood clouds. Hard to believe there was blue somewhere far above, blue like a wide-open eye with a yellow sun hung in the middle of it, blindingly bright. She'd seen pictures in IF-issued history books—*look what was taken from us, look what those Aberrant bioterrorists did!*—and imagined for a moment what that blazing sun might feel like on her face.

Blistering, that's what. Her lips skewed to a wry pucker.

Even through the thick layer of clouds, the sun up in that blue sky beyond was vicious enough to kill during daylight hours. The few Third Formers desperate enough to break Curfew in search of food or water inevitably found that out. Even if they escaped the Peace Guard, the sun showed no mercy. Only after twilight was it safe.

Safe being a relative term.

Still looking at the sky, Lu bumped into something hard. Coffee sloshed from the mug and splattered her face, trickling down her chin and neck.

"*Scheisse*," she muttered, at the same moment someone said, "*Aufpassen!*"

Attention. The word was as hard as a slap against her cheek. When she jerked her head up and looked into the eyes of the person who'd said it, her heart dropped into her stomach.

He was tall, broad, and hawk-nosed, with a cutthroat smile and eyes that never blinked, in the way of a snake. His uniform was crisp, the brass medals on his chest gleamed in the light from the streetlamp. The automatic weapon slung over his shoulder gleamed, too.

"Apologies, *leutnant*," Lu said smoothly, swallowing the acid taste of fear. She adopted a fake smile and a blank expression, a talent she'd cultivated to perfection. "How stupid of me. I was just thinking how wonderful Thornemas Day is; I wasn't looking where I was going." She added brightly, "Can't wait for the fireworks tonight!"

Dieter Gerhardt smiled down at her from his considerable height. Lieutenant of the district's ironically named Peace Guard, he was smug and skin crawlingly familiar, never missing the opportunity to stand a little too close, to stare a little too long. He'd always taken a particular interest in her, and she tried to avoid him at all costs. In spite of his enviable upper Second Form position that had some of the other Third Form girls clamoring for his attention, he scared Lu. She had the unsettling sense that he might at any moment crack open his jaw and eat her alive.

"*Ja,*" he said. Then because of course he would, he lifted his hand and slowly brushed his fingers over her chin, wiping away the coffee.

A flash of anger made her face flush. Lu lowered her lashes to hide the rage in her eyes. Still with her pasted-on smile, she turned her cheek and rubbed her face with her gloved hand. "I must look a mess. Thankfully I didn't get any on you."

Pig. Maggot. *Arschloch!*

"Too bad. Then you might have had to make it up to me."

His trademark cutthroat grin appeared, accompanied by a carnivorous once-over. His gaze lingered on her hips, the swell of her breasts beneath her coat. Her flush deepened. A violent itch bloomed in the palms of her hands.

Her laugh was breezy. "Well, I'm off to work. Happy Thornemas to you." She started to brush past him, but he caught her under her arm. Dieter pulled her closer, his breath sliding down her neck.

"I'll walk with you."

"Oh." *Scheisse!* "Thank you, but you don't have to bother—"

"It's no bother," Dieter said, a hint of hardness in his voice, "as I'm already going that way. And these streets are dangerous for a girl like you."

A girl like me?

He must have sensed the sudden tension in her body, because he laughed, low and pleased, chucking a knuckle under her chin. "Don't worry, *vögelchen*, with me by your side, no one will mess with you. No matter how pretty you are." He gave her braid a firm tug to underscore the word *pretty*, and Lu had to fight hard to resist the urge to scratch his eyes out of his face.

Her smile was sweet, as was her murmur, "*Danke*," though the word tasted bitter in her mouth. With his hand an unwanted presence on the small of her back, a command and a threat wrapped into one, Dieter moved her forward. As they walked side by side down the busy street, people scurried aside, their glances filled with trepidation before they ducked their heads and looked away. Even out of the UV protective over suits they wore during the daylight hours when they hunted, members of the Peace Guard had a certain "I'll gut you" vibe that everyone understood was based entirely on fact.

The guns didn't help, either.

Be calm. Smile. Breathe.

Dieter walked with the unhurried, cocksure stride of one who's used to being obeyed. His hand found its way back under her arm, and his fingers tightened ever so slightly as they walked. He nodded to a few people, said hello to others, but never loosened his grip. Lu had the uncomfortable feeling she was being herded.

It was a silent, ten-minute walk through the tangled lanes of New Vienna to the Hospice. By the time they arrived, her nerves were wound bowstring tight. Her jaw ached with the effort of smiling.

The Hospice building was one of those awful, square brick institutional affairs guaranteed to evoke depression in whomever passed through its doors. Squat and ugly, it sat hulking atop the rise of a low hill, surrounded by brown grass and the occasional withered tree. Glazed windows like dead eyes and finials on the black courtyard gate lent it a sinister air, which today seemed amplified by a thousand thanks to her escort.

Still with that proprietary hand under her arm, Dieter said in an offhand tone, "I'm told the Grand Minister will be visiting tonight. Something about a disturbance. Must be important if the GM himself is coming to check it out." His gaze slid sideways and down, fixing on her.

Dread unfurled in the pit of her stomach. Lu cleared her throat and pretended ignorance. "The Grand Minister? Really? Well, it doesn't surprise me. There've been a few odd incidents over the past months. I hear he's brilliant, though. I'm sure he'll . . ." she cleared her throat again. "I'm sure he'll get to the bottom of it."

Dieter's gaze intensified. He made a sound she might have taken for amusement, but for the total lack of humor in it. "Yes. He will. Nothing ever escapes him." His fingers pressed harder into her arm. His voice lowered an octave. "Nothing."

Lu's heart began a thundering gallop so loud she was sure Dieter would be able to hear it. For a moment she simply stood silently, the foolish smile dying on her lips. She stared straight ahead at the Hospice, her mouth as dry as bone.

In a voice so low Lu nearly missed it over the chatter of a group of passing schoolgirls, Dieter said, "If they bring the ocular scan equipment, you're done for. There's something about the optic nerve that gives it away. They've only recently figured it out. Your contacts won't conceal it."

Lu's heart stopped beating. Her blood froze to ice water inside her veins.

Her contacts were muddy brown, purchased on the black market at an insanely high price. They had no prescription, as her eyesight was beyond the human definition of perfect, but they hadn't been bought to correct any problem with her vision. They'd been bought to conceal the electric, unnatural yellow-green of her irises. She'd worn them as long as she could remember.

Dieter knew. *He knew.*

Her hands began to shake so violently she dropped the empty coffee mug. It shattered at her feet with a sound like a bomb.

Dieter removed his hand from her arm and adopted one of those at ease soldier postures, legs spread shoulder width apart, hands clasped behind his waist. Looking up at the sky, he inhaled deeply the warm evening air. In a more normal tone, he said, "My colonel's old enough to remember when the sky was blue, and winter was cold. Can you believe that? *Cold.* Says it used to snow on Thornemas Day, flakes as big as your thumb." He shook his head, bemused, his attitude casual as if nothing at all had just happened. As if the world itself hadn't just ceased to turn. "Can't say I really believe him, though." Dieter turned his head and looked directly into her eyes. "People make up all kinds of things. Sometimes if they're really good at it, everybody believes them. A really great liar might even convince the entire world his *kuhscheibe* is the truth."

The ground had turned liquid beneath her feet. Lu was poised to run, a scream trapped in her throat. Every nerve in her body hummed with fear, and an odd, animal excitement.

Would it be a relief? To let the mask drop and finally give in to the beast she knew lurked inside her? With a tremor of sick enjoyment, she enjoyed a brief vision of Dieter in flames. Of the entire *city* in flames, and herself standing in the middle of it all, laughing.

Then Dieter leaned close and brushed his lips against her cheek. He whispered into her ear, "The Schottentor gate at the east side of the city, behind the waste treatment plant—you know the one?"

She did. Old Vienna had been a fortress city, surrounded by medieval walls with bastions and gates that had been refortified and put into use to control access into and out of the city when

New Vienna rose from the ashes after the Flash. But why would he mention it?

Dieter didn't wait for her response. "If they figure it out, run. Get your father and go to the gate. Look for the white rabbit. There's always someone on lookout; you can escape that way. Just stay alive. We'll get you out. And whatever happens, *don't let them catch you.*"

He straightened and said in a loud, furious voice, "What a little tease you are, *jungfrau*! You think your shit doesn't stink? Hell if I want a dirty little Third Former like you, anyway!"

Without another word or a glance in her direction, Dieter strode away, back straight, head high, rifle swinging from his shoulder. A pair of men passing by on the sidewalk smirked at her, then moved on.

And Lu was left alone with the shock of comprehension making her reel in disbelief. The world tilted left, slipping dangerously, and in the end it was only the gate of the Hospice that held her up, its iron bars gripped tightly in her fists.

From far, far away, Lumina heard the echo of angry shouting from behind the vast and icy wall she'd erected inside her head.

TWO

The hunter with the scarred face and penetrating dark eyes was perched high atop the street opposite the Hospice, on the crest of the sloped tiled roof of the Palais Hansen Kempinski, a former luxury hotel that now functioned as the IF's media headquarters. Inside, the "news" was manufactured and distributed throughout the federation by a team of reporters on the company payroll, and through the soles of his feet he felt their scurried activity as scant vibrations, smelled their fear and fervor as comingled sour scents on the evening wind.

Some of them actually believed the propaganda they churned out. Most of them were simply too afraid to say they did not.

He watched the young woman leaning on the courtyard gate of the Hospice below with hawklike fixedness. Every sense hummed with the power of her. The elegant, electrical thrill of the energy she emanated was like nothing he'd ever felt. He'd hunted Aberrants for more than twenty of his thirty-six years, and not a single one of them had ever set his nerves alight like this one.

Looking at her, he felt stung. He felt slapped. He felt, for a moment, a jolt of terrifying elation, as if he'd flung himself from the roof and was free-falling through space toward his death.

This was the one he'd been seeking. He'd found her at last.

She pulled herself upright for the first time since her uniformed companion had walked away, and passed a trembling hand over her hair. Even from this distance he saw how hard it shook. He saw the effort it took for her to straighten her shoulders and lift her chin. He longed to see her face, but she had her back to him, and didn't turn, even as she pushed through the gate and walked slowly up the cracked cement path to the Hospice entrance. She removed the glove from her right hand, placed her palm on the scanner beside the front door, then disappeared within the building as the door swung open and shut behind her. The chance to look at her face was lost.

No matter, he thought, rising from his crouch. He'd see her face soon enough. Besides, he already knew what she looked like. He knew everything there was to know about this imposter who called herself Lumina Bohn.

He'd made it his life's mission to do so.

"You're early." Liesel straightened from the kitchen counter, her stout arms dusted in flour up to the elbow. Her expression was surprised, but pleased. The older woman liked her, even if most of the other Hospice workers didn't; the two of them shared a love of silence the gossip-sharing others found off-putting at best, and suspicious at worst.

Round and red-cheeked, with strands of graying hair escaping from her haphazard bun, Liesel was the Hospice pastry cook. As she always did in the evening before first meal, she was preparing the dough for the *apfelstrudel*, the famous dessert the Hospice guests devoured in huge quantity. Dietary restrictions were non-existent in this place, and the guests were allowed to eat and drink to their hearts' content. Sweets and schnapps and fatty foods were served with every meal, and overindulging in all three was heartily encouraged, because no revolt was ever started by a bunch of fat drunkards with digestive trouble.

Also, if one of the guests died sooner than he otherwise might have due to clogged arteries and high cholesterol, so much the better. There was always another citizen who'd aged out ready to fill his bed.

"Need the extra credits," said Lu, taking her place beside Liesel at the long stainless steel counter. She'd already hung her coat in her locker and changed into her white apron. And changed her gloves for a disposable latex pair, perfect for kitchen work but a trifle too thin for Lu's comfort. No push had ever leaked through yet, but she wasn't entirely convinced that would remain the case forever.

Especially today.

The thought caused a tickle in her palms. Lu began immediately to hum.

She and Liesel worked in companionable silence for a moment, rolling, kneading, dusting flour over the dough, until finally Liesel asked, "What's that song you're always humming? It sounds familiar."

"Just something my father used to sing to me. It's from an opera called *Song to the Moon*."

Liesel made a gentle grunt that managed to convey she'd never heard of it. Her grunts were many and varied, one as distinguishable from the other as the notes of a song. She often used them in place of words.

"My mother had a terrible singing voice. Could stun the birds right out of the trees, make them fall dead to the sidewalk."

Lu grimaced, imagining a woman walking along singing while the sky rained dead birds.

"She used to tell me stories instead. At that, she was talented. She was Romanian, my mother, a peasant who married a farmer and had eleven children in twelve years." Liesel shook her head, producing a disbelieving grunt. "Those were the days you could have as many children as you wanted. Can you imagine? No permits? Just breed away like so many rabbits?"

Lu couldn't imagine such a thing. Only two children per married couple were allowed under the IF's birth regulations, and only if the couple could afford it. The wealthy First Form families had no problem paying the birth tax. Everyone else saved or bartered credits or wound up indebted to the government for the remainder of their lives, paying down the astronomical tax through a work program.

And Thorne forbid if you had an "accident." Unplanned, unpermitted children disappeared almost as soon as they were born, raised in State orphanages and ultimately conscripted into the IF's vast, unpaid labor force known as the Drones.

Needless to say, the abortion business thrived in New Vienna.

Liesel said, "Well, there you are. That's how it was before . . ."

Her hesitation was filled with the unspoken terror of the Flash. Of everything it triggered, the wars and turmoil, the food and water shortages, the scorched sky and the barren earth and forever after the lurking stink of death. Though Lu had never known any other sort of life, Liesel was old enough to remember life before the Flash, and to mourn it.

"Anyway, my favorite story was called 'The Hermit's Foundling with the Golden Hair.' It's about, as you might guess, a man who finds a child in a basket on a stream when he goes to fetch some water. A golden-haired child. Just like you."

In the sticky dough, Lumina's hands stilled. The light in the room seemed suddenly too bright.

"It was a boy, in the story, though." A derogatory grunt, as if the sex of the child offended her. Liesel worked the dough between her rough hands. "There was a note attached to the basket with the little baby boy. It said that the child was the illegitimate son of a princess, who'd sent the baby away for fear of her shame being discovered. That story always reminds me of you. Because of the name, I mean, not because your mother was a princess." She laughed, as if the idea was profoundly funny. "Though his was the male version of the name, Lumino."

Liesel brushed a wrist across her forehead to push away a strand of hair, leaving a damp smear of flour behind. "Was your mother Romanian?"

Lu didn't answer. She couldn't; her mouth was too dry. Liesel took her silence as a yes.

"Makes sense, I suppose. Naming you after the Romanian word for light." Liesel's friendly gaze flickered over her. "You're so pale you probably glow in the dark when you take off all your clothes, eh?" Another laugh, and Liesel flipped the dough, punching it down and smoothing more flour over the surface.

Filled with an odd, chilling premonition, Lu whispered, "What happened to the baby?"

"Oh, well, the story was a fairy tale, so of course there were talking lions and dragons and elves, and the boy had to face many trials as he grew, including his father's death, and flight to a new land, and battles of wit and swords. But he was a strong one, that Lumino. He had royal blood, which gave him courage. He never gave up, not even when his enemies killed his—"

"Did you hear the news? The Grand Minister is coming today! Can you believe it? Today, of all the days! We didn't get any of the supplies I ordered because the delivery truck was attacked by those *verdammt* Dissenters, and now there won't be fresh vegetables or those special sausages I wanted! *Scheisse!*"

Lars, Hospice head chef, burst into the kitchen with the heated intensity of high noon. Though small and wiry, with the furtive, darting eyes of a rodent, he possessed the energy of ten men. And the ego of twenty. His diminutive frame was topped with a shock of flaming red hair, in which he took great pride and had a habit of running his fingers through when agitated. Which meant his hands were almost always clenched atop his head.

"I think the Grand Minister will be too busy sniffing out his prey to be worried about *supper*," muttered Lu to the dough, irritated he'd burst in right when Liesel was getting to the best part of the story. She needed to know what happened to that boy. And who had been killed?

"My *schnitzengruben* is legendary, woman!" shrieked Lars, pulling at his hair. "Of *course* he'll want to stay for supper!"

Beside her, Liesel kept her eyes on her work, unaffected by Lars's outburst. "You could make *sauerbraten*. Your recipe for that is legendary, too. And the meat's been marinating long enough; it'll be perfect."

This was Liesel's gentle way of deflecting attention from Lu. She'd done it a thousand times before. But today—maybe because of the shock of finding out Dieter wasn't who she thought he was, or because she was just so, so tired of holding her tongue—Lu spoke up.

"How could it be anything but perfect? It's from *Lars*."

Liesel flashed a warning look in her direction as Lars narrowed his rodent eyes. Lu felt his inspection as a flush of heat on the nape of her neck. He was trying to decide if she was mocking him or not, but she figured ego would win out in the end.

It did. Lars sniffed and made a sound of agreement, lowering his hands to his hips. "You're right. My *sauerbraten* is the best in the district."

"Probably the entire Federation," agreed Liesel, sending Lu a conspiratorial wink. Caught up in planning for the change, Lars didn't notice. He clapped twice and began barking orders.

"Listen up! Finish the *apfelstrudel*, chop the cabbage, make the dumplings, get the *spätzle* ready—"

"And then we'll set the tables with the good lace cloths and the Federation china while you put the finishing touches on the meat," said Lu, turning to give Lars a wide, innocent look over her shoulder. "Don't worry, *herrchen*, we'll make sure everything is smooth as silk for the Grand Minister's visit."

Lars's nose twitched in pleasure, reminding Lu of a happy ferret. He loved it when she called him "master," never recognizing the sarcasm in her tone.

"You better." He brushed past with an imperious lift of his chin. "Because I've heard that son of a bitch is as cold as a witch's tit and twice as ugly. If anything goes wrong with the meal, I'm holding you responsible." He swept from the room just as abruptly as he'd arrived. The scent of cheap cologne lingered behind him in a sour cloud.

Liesel muttered a curse in German. "All the responsibility and none of the benefits. Typical."

"At least we won't have to suffer through another of his 'legendary' batches of *schnitzengruben* today. Last time I thought I'd contracted dysentery."

Liesel grunted.

"And what is that stupid saying, 'cold as a witch's tit'? What does that even mean?" Lu was growing more and more irritated, irked by her earlier premonition of doom inspired by Liesel's story, her father's fraught warning, and the pending visit from the goon squad.

Liesel sighed, and pushed back another flyaway strand of hair from her face. "I don't know, and I don't want to find out."

Liesel began to flatten the kneaded dough into a thin layer with a wooden roller, and Lu followed her lead, realizing with a shiver that she didn't want to find out, either.

Unfortunately, she had a dark, gnawing feeling that she would.

By the time the caravan of sleek black vehicles bearing the Grand Minister and his entourage pulled into the loading dock behind the Hospice on silent wheels, Lu's nerves were as shredded as the red cabbage she'd prepared for the *sauerbraten*.

Like a nest of tumors, tension had been growing in her stomach for hours.

She'd dropped a tray of dumplings, burned her hand on one of the racks in the oven, and snapped at poor Mr. Kirchmann when he'd asked her to read to him during her rounds. She made it up to him by giving him a girly magazine—purloined from her nemesis Cushing's extensive personal collection, which he'd compiled over years of searching the luggage of new arrivals—but she still felt guilty. It wasn't his fault she couldn't get her act together.

It wasn't his fault she had a target on her back.

She wasn't the only one suffering from nerves, though. The entire staff was on edge. To the Hospice guests, a visit from such an infamous character as the Grand Minister was a welcome distraction from their banal daily routine, but fear ran rampant through the kitchen, the laundry, and the administration offices. Fear that if an Aberrant was exposed within the ranks, everyone might be held accountable for harboring the enemy. Two fights had already broken out so far, minor skirmishes where one party accused the other of either being the culprit or having knowledge of who it actually was, and the feeling of hostile scrutiny increased to the point that Lu felt as if she were walking around under a giant, unblinking eye.

That feeling would pale in comparison to the first moment she locked gazes with the Grand Minister.

Cushing saw him first. The orderly had been on lookout since the start of his shift, moving through the halls at double his normal snail's pace, his thick arms swinging by his sides while his eyes darted to and fro, scanning faces and windows with equal intensity. Lu had been avoiding him as she always did, but the moment she heard his shout from near the loading dock doors, she bolted, anxious to get a glimpse of the infamous GM before he entered the building.

Among a chorus of aggravated protests, Lu pushed to the front of the small crowd that had gathered at the wide double doors that led from the interior hallway of the Hospice to the outside dock area where the delivery trucks unloaded their goods. Through the round scratched windows, she saw a group of men in simple, severe black suits garnished with white armbands emblazoned with the IF's sun symbol huddled around the rear of a van that had its back doors open. The men seemed to be trying to remove something from the van, but Lu couldn't make out what it was. She stepped to one side to get a better look, and as she did, found herself staring into a face so familiar she was momentarily paralyzed by déjà vu.

But it couldn't be. She'd never seen this man before in her life.

He, too, wore a simple black suit. More correctly, he wore a jacket and trousers that had been altered to accommodate his two missing legs and one missing arm. He was missing an eye as well—the hole was covered by a black patch, lending him a sinister, villainous air—and he was being carefully lowered by his companions into a waiting wheelchair. He was frail, with wispy white hair and a shrunken chest, the one hand like a skeleton's, yet there was nothing frail about his energy. He looked up and caught sight of her, and Lu took an involuntary step back.

His one eye—blue and cold as an arctic sky—fixed on her with the ferocity of a hungry lion.

She felt pinned in place. She felt, for a moment, that the earth had stopped spinning beneath her feet and she might at any moment shirk the bounds of gravity altogether and go shooting out into space.

Because in that fleeting look, she saw recognition.

Recognition, and rage.

Gasping in shock, Lu spun and flattened her back against the door. She was quickly pushed aside as others surged forward, but her knees wouldn't stop trembling, and she had trouble regaining her balance as she fled back into the kitchen. She looked wildly around for someplace to hide, quickly realizing the stupidity of that plan. The only thing to do, the only possibility for getting out of this situation alive, was to remain calm. Panicking wouldn't help. And if she ran, her father . . .

She wouldn't think about what would happen to her father if she ran.

So she leaned against the stainless steel sink with her eyes squeezed shut until she could breathe again.

Lars pounded down the hallway outside, cursing in German at the staff to get back to their posts. He burst into the kitchen, flailing his arms and shouting.

"Lumina! Lumina, where in the hell—"

He stopped short as he caught sight of her. "Oh. There you are. Where's Liesel?"

Mute, she shook her head, eliciting a dramatic moan from Lars. He thrust his hands into his hair. "Well, *find out*! I've got to finish the *sauerbraten*—"

"Forget the *sauerbraten*!" snapped a female voice. Lu and Lars turned to find the Administrator, grim faced and tense, standing stiffly near the six-burner stove. Mathilda Gruenborn was tall and bone thin, with a schoolmarm's fashion style and a sense of humor that could only be described as missing. At the moment, her pinched face was the exact color as her lumpy sweater: gray.

"You know the protocol: Assemble in the main hall and wait for me there. I'm going to greet the Grand Minister—"

"But the *sauerbraten*!" Lars cried. "If I don't time it just right, the meat will be—"

The Administrator shrieked his name, her face flushing a deep berry red. Lars snapped his mouth shut, lifted his chin, and without another word, marched out of the kitchen. The Administrator breathed loudly for a few seconds, then nodded at Lu, her jaw tight. She spoke through clenched teeth. "You, too, Bohn. Don't make me ask twice."

The itch in Lu's palms, so irritating before, grew now into a hot, throbbing imperative. In an attempt to relieve it, she smoothed her hands down the front of her jacket, a motion which the Administrator mistook as an attempt to straighten any stray wrinkles in the fabric of her coat. She nodded, pleased, then turned and left without another word, leaving Lu to stare after her.

After several moments of heart-pounding silence, Lu walked slowly out to meet her fate.

THREE

The main hall of the Hospice was thick with silk plants and brightly lit in a failed attempt to deflect attention from its startling similarity to an enormous cage. The requisite game tables, craft areas, and "meditation zones" on the second floor competed with the IF-approved library for title of most depressing, while the portrait gallery on the third floor—featuring grim gilt-framed oils of the Federation's top leaders leering down at the guests in the main hall below—beat out everything in terms of sheer creepiness. Above the third floor were the "residences," where Hospice guests would spend their final days in rooms so small one could almost touch both walls when lying in bed.

Trying to look inconspicuous, Lu edged into a corner behind a fake giant philodendron so dusty it made her sneeze.

"Better to be front and center than let them think you're hiding," scolded Liesel softly, coming up behind Lu and taking her arm. "You know what a cat does when it sees the mouse run?"

A question that required no answer. Lu let herself be led away from the comforting cover of the dusty plant to the terrifying center of the room.

Near the entrance and off to the side of the sea of dining tables where guests ate all their meals, the staff had lined up in three rows according to seniority. Administration and managers in front, clerical and support staff behind, then the orderlies with the kitchen and laundry staff. As always, Cushing stood a little apart and ahead of the rest of his line, convinced he shouldn't have to stand with such plebs.

The moment the Administrator entered the main hall with the Grand Minister, Lu's nervous system went into overdrive. With the approaching hum of mechanical wheels, her heart twisted, her breathing increased, all the little hairs on her body stood on end. Every minute detail of the room honed to brilliant, blinding focus, and she felt for a split second as if an animal sleeping just under her skin had awoken, bristling, hissing a warning into her ear.

Enemy! Enemy! Enemy!

Her palms began to itch so violently it was all she could do to stand still. Up on the third floor, one of the paintings lifted briefly from the wall, falling back with a clatter.

Then he was before them. A mangled body, a face full of rage, a white arm band with a brilliant yellow sun emblem, sinister for all its simplicity.

"Good evening," said the Grand Minister in a surprisingly gentle voice, squaring his wheelchair in front of the lines of staff. There was a murmured response, then silence.

Two black-suited men the size of small buildings took positions a few feet behind the wheelchair with their hands clasped behind their backs, legs spread. Their eyes roved over the group with unblinking intensity. A swarm of others lurked in her peripheral vision, moving to guard exits and hallways, to flank the entrance doors. The Administrator stood several feet to the rear of the Grand Minister, her hands clenched to fists at her sides, her face now bleached from gray to white. Lu felt the blood drain from her own cheeks as well.

"Before we begin, I'd like to put your minds at ease about something," said the Grand Minister in his soothing voice, gazing at each person in turn. "You have, no doubt, heard many fantastical stories of my exploits, including, perhaps, the story of how I came to be in this wheelchair, missing a few important body parts. Yes, you don't have to deny it; I know it's true," he chuckled, nodding as he watched the surprised expressions, the questioning, darting eyes. After a moment, he sobered. When he spoke again the faintest tinge of anger colored his voice. "My lifelong fight against the creatures who would kill every one of us if they could has indeed cost me a great deal. But I am not the only one who has paid a dear price, my friends. Each and every one of you has also paid. With your freedom, with your security, with the blood of your family and friends. We've all paid, in one way or another."

Shocked silence. His words edged close to treason. No one dared speak.

"Even to the point of being denied the most powerful and beautiful natural resource of this planet, you have paid." He paused, searching the gathering. "Who among you has ever seen the sun?"

After a moment of breathless quiet, all the older staff members raised their hands. Beside Lu, Liesel's arm lifted slowly, until her hand was high above her head, trembling.

The Grand Minister's voice turned hard. "I was there when it happened, when these filthy animals declared war on the human race. I was at ground zero in the jungles of Brazil on that day twenty-four years ago, and watched it all unfold firsthand." He inhaled a shaky breath, then said vehemently, "*They took our sun.*

The lifeblood of our world. Would you not agree with me that the theft of such a thing is an abomination? That the scorched sky and poisoned atmosphere and the decimation and degradation of life as it had evolved over millions of years is a crime so heinous it can never be forgiven?"

Vigorous head nods, murmurs of agreement. Lu tried to scratch her palms with the tips of her fingers, but couldn't quite manage it while keeping her arms straight at her sides. The itch became almost unbearable, spreading out from her palms, snaking up her arms.

The Grand Minister's face softened. He leaned back in his wheelchair; his hand loosened its grip on the cushioned arm.

"Friends, I'm not here to punish anyone. You've all suffered enough. On the contrary, any assistance given me today will be met not with punishment, but with reward. You may have witnessed things, heard things, perhaps even *hidden* things you thought might cause you or your family trouble if you spoke out. But speaking out will not get you into trouble. You have my word. Anyone who brings something to my attention that leads to the capture of one of these bioterrorists will be well compensated, treated as the patriots they truly are."

The tension easing around her was palpable. Lu thought, *You sneaky son of a bitch.*

She was reminded of something her father often quoted, a line from the French poet Baudelaire. "The devil's best trick is to persuade you he doesn't exist."

Well played, Grand Minister. Well played. Hatred hatched inside of her, foul as a rotten egg. He wasn't fooling her with his soft voice and promises of mercy and reward. She knew a snake when she saw one, even if his poisonous fangs were sheathed.

Upstairs, several of the portraits began to shake, sending a tremor along the walls. The Grand Minister heard the sound and smiled, utterly without warmth.

"So," he said, turning brisk, "I'll meet with each of you in turn, and we shall see if we can get to the bottom of this, and then get out of your proverbial hair." His gaze flicked over the room, searching. Then, horribly, as if magnetized, it settled directly on Lu. His chilling smile grew wider.

"Let's start with *you*."

From behind the pair of dented metal filing cabinets overlaid with a plain slab of stainless steel that served as the Administrator's office desk, the Grand Minister sat in ominous silence, watching Lu as she stood nervously across from him, trying desperately to appear nonchalant.

Failing to appear nonchalant. Her breathing sounded like thunder in her ears.

"Fräulein . . ." the Grand Minister's gaze dropped to the name tag on the lapel of her uniform. "Bohn." His one blue eye gazed into her two brown ones. He seemed to be waiting for a response, so she nodded, and even that small motion felt loaded with guilt. She moistened her lips, waiting.

There were six men in the small office with them, lined against the walls on either side. Four more were posted outside the door. None of them had spoken to her as she'd been led in. None of them had touched her. Every one of them peered at her as if down the sights of a rifle.

All of them bore the faint scent of metal, and a much stronger odor of chemicals, bright as a new penny underneath the other scents of soap and cigarettes and skin.

Guns. Collars. Tranquilizers. The only things they'd need to take her down, and keep her there. When they moved, she heard the muted, musical *chink* of metal on metal as the collars hidden beneath their clothes moved with them.

She shifted her weight from one foot to the other as the Grand Minister watched, his face devoid of emotion.

"I'm informed you were an eyewitness to the incident that occurred yesterday evening."

Lu nodded, trying hard not to blink under his penetrating stare. "And?"

Lu cleared her throat. "It was . . . ah . . . disturbing. Sir."

His nostrils flared slightly, and she wondered if the man could actually *smell* a lie. If so, she was safe for the moment, because the incident *had* been disturbing, even if she'd been the initiator.

The Grand Minister kept staring at her in that inscrutable silence, and she was abruptly more angry than afraid. *He's trying to intimidate me into giving something away.*

But Lu was used to keeping silent. And she hated bullies. She lifted her chin and said nothing.

The faintest hint of a smile curved his bloodless lips, there then gone. "Tell me, Fräulein Bohn," he said, his tone conversational, "how old are you?"

Lu blinked. What an odd question. "Twenty-five, sir."

He made a noise of interest. "Any health problems around your twenty-fifth birthday?"

Now Lu did more than blink. She did an outright double take. "Sir?"

The Grand Minister made a vague gesture with his skeletal hand. "Headaches, strange pains, sudden sickness, things along those lines. Anything out of the usual?"

Lu couldn't help the look of incredulity on her face. This was what he was interested in? Her health? Where was the infamous assassin, the cruel tyrant of lore? It seemed innocent enough, but her senses prickled with the knowledge that this line of questioning was anything but innocent.

"No, sir. Nothing like that," she insisted. "I never get sick."

This piqued his interest, as evidenced by the lift of his brows. "Never? How lucky for you."

Two of the guards shared a fleeting look. Lu's sense that something was definitely wrong ratcheted a notch higher. "I mean . . . I . . . of course . . . the usual colds, that sort of thing, but nothing severe."

This was a blatant lie. Lu had never been sick a day in her life. Not a headache, not a stomachache, not a single cavity. More than once, her father had insisted she take a "sick" day from work to hide that troublesome fact.

"I see," said the Grand Minister, smiling now like the cat that has just devoured the canary. It was one of the most unnerving things Lu had ever seen in her life.

Her stomach began a slow, creeping slide toward her feet.

"And the date and city of your birth?"

There was an employee file open on the desk in front of him in which, Lu knew, all her information was held, including the date and place of her birth, but he ignored it as if it wasn't there.

"September twelfth, twenty-twelve. Vienna. Old Vienna."

He lifted the skeletal hand and stroked one finger slowly along the edge of her file, his thin lips pursed, his expression thoughtful. "So you would have been about . . . thirteen months old at the time of the Flash. An infant."

He said the word *infant* as if it was *bomb* or *plague* or *serial killer*. Lu was mystified.

"Yes."

"And your parents? Their occupations?"

What the hell was this? Why wasn't he asking her about what happened with Cushing last night? What exactly was he getting at? "My father works in the grow light fields. My mother . . . my mother is dead."

"Your father *now* works in the grow light fields," the Grand Minister corrected, his voice as soft as silk. "But he didn't always work there. Did he."

The last part wasn't a question. He was insinuating something, but Lu had no idea what. "Yes, sir, he's always worked in the fields. As long as I can remember, anyway. Ever since I was—"

"An *infant*," he finished quietly, his cold blue gaze meeting hers. Her spine crawled as if a cluster of tarantulas were crawling up it.

"I'm sorry, sir, I don't really know what—"

"Your father was a missionary before the Flash, traveling from country to country, trying to convert people to his faith. Were you aware of that?"

He stared at her accusingly. She stared back, utterly stumped. Her father had pointedly refused to speak of what he did before the Flash. It was one of his "stop asking so many questions, Lu," "the past is just that, Lu" off-limits subjects.

"No. He never mentioned it."

The Grand Minister's brows arched. "Never once, in twenty-five years? Strange, don't you think?"

"Strange," concurred one of the guards flatly, and Lu stiffened.

"Yes, my sources tell me he was quite *religious* back in the day," the Grand Minister said with a sniff of disdain, still fondling her file with an almost reverential touch. "I understand he felt person-ally called by God to spread the word, primarily to the poor and uneducated. In places"—he paused, looking musingly at the ceil-ing—"far off the beaten track."

Her shock at hearing the forbidden word *God* on the Grand Minister's lips was eclipsed by her shock of discovering her father had been a missionary before the Flash.

Or had he? Was this all part of the game?

Beneath the thin latex kitchen gloves she was still wearing, Lu's palms began to sweat. Her fight or flight instincts were screaming *FLEE!* but she was rooted in place, unable to move.

The Grand Minister abruptly turned to one of his guards and said, "Scanner."

From beneath his fitted jacket, the burly guard produced a thin, black device, wireless, about the size of the government-issued data pad on which Lu played IF-approved games, visited IF-approved websites, and read the IF-approved news. This device, however, had an outline of a hand with fingers spread on the display, and Lu sagged with relief.

Fingerprint scanner, not ocular.

The guard set the scanner on the desk in front of her, touched an invisible button to activate it, and stepped away as the screen glowed red.

Without a word, the Grand Minister motioned for Lu to put her hand on the screen.

Proud that her hand wasn't shaking, she slowly peeled the glove from her right hand and laid it on the cool glass of the scanner. There came a soft glow, a line of light moved across the length and breadth of her hand, then a beep sounded, which to her ears seemed almost disappointed. The screen again went black, and Lu stepped away.

"Well, Fräulein Bohn, it appears you have fingerprints. And they match your mainframe profile. Congratulations."

His tone wasn't congratulatory. He and the guard who'd produced the scanner shared a loaded glance, and Lu was seized with the terrifying certainty that he already knew she was wearing synthetic, black market bonded prints to cover her lack of natural ones, and this entire thing was a ruse. A sadistic game, designed for his amusement, to see how long he could frighten her before she'd finally break.

She was already close to breaking. On the console behind him, a pencil skittered across the glass top and rolled off onto the floor, landing with a *plunk* as loud as gunfire in the silent room.

Everyone ignored it.

Slowly, carefully, Lu slid the latex glove into her coat pocket, then stood with both hands hanging loosely at her sides. The Grand Minister watched every movement with the avid attention of a crocodile contemplating a meal.

"Have you ever seen an Aberrant, Fräulein Bohn?" he asked quietly, studying her. "Up close and personal, I mean. In real life."

Lu didn't dare move.

"I must admit, for such vile creatures, they're quite beautiful. Unnaturally so. Every single one of them I've ever encountered, male or female, has a certain . . . otherworldly appeal. It's always puzzled me, how such beauty could conceal such evil." His tone became contemplative. "But I suppose your father might remind me that Lucifer was the most beautiful of all the angels, before he was cast from heaven." His gaze raked her face. After a moment, he said softly, "You've inherited your mother's looks."

Lu's mother had been short and thick-waisted, an olive-skinned brunette. The two of them looked nothing alike.

All at once, Lu understood, and the world fell away beneath her feet.

This man had known her mother. Her *real* mother.

And he knew what Lu was.

Heat rushed to her face, burned hot across her cheekbones. A thrill ran through her body, high and pure and resonating, and with an awful, bellowing battle cry, the monster inside her leapt to its feet.

Lu took a single step backward. Each guard took a single step in. In a coordinated move, they reached inside their jackets.

In a gentle voice, the Grand Minister said, "If you cooperate, you won't be harmed. Your father won't be harmed. The stories of the treatment of Aberrants are greatly exaggerated, urban myths. You'll be kept with others of your kind, kept comfortably and well. You'll never want for anything again." His voice grew even more caressing. He looked at her pleadingly, with grandfatherly concern. "And you can meet your mother—you'd like that, wouldn't you? To meet your birth mother? She's missed you so much."

Lies, all of them, spoken with such ease Lu had to admit that beneath her hatred for this man, she felt a twinge of jealousy. It cost him exactly nothing to produce these smooth untruths, to playact a role. She wished she'd been blessed with such an ability; it would have made her own mask-wearing life much easier.

The funny thing was, knowing she'd finally been discovered wasn't the terrifying experience Lu had always assumed it would be. She felt instead as if a huge weight had been lifted from her shoulders. Though her nerves were stretched taut and adrenaline coursed through her veins, all her fear fell away like a skin she was shedding, until finally there was nothing but acceptance, cold and solid as rock.

Life as she knew it was over.

So be it. If she was being honest with herself, she'd known it would come to this all along. The relief was almost dizzying.

The Schottentor gate, you know the one? We'll get you out. Look for the white rabbit.

Lu reached out with her mind. It was like stretching a rubber band, pulling her awareness across empty space until she came up against a soft resistance. She pushed past it, and with the animal inside her sinking into a killing crouch, said silently into the Grand Minister's head, *I'm going to roast you for those lies, you smug son of a bitch.*

He jerked back in his wheelchair, shock distorting his face, and Lu was suffused with a savage satisfaction.

A smile curved her lips, but she knew it wasn't she who was smiling. It was the animal, eager to feed. Eager for blood. There was a noise in her head, a cry like a thousand roars in the wilderness, an unearthly chorus of gnashing teeth and snapping jaws and hissing. When she took another step back, it was with raised arms, her hands flexed open. A sudden crackle of static electricity sparked through the room, and all the downy hair atop the Grand Minister's head lifted, haloing his face in a cloud of white.

His expression of shock turned to an extremely pleasing one of terror.

"Sorry," Lu said aloud, her smile gone, "but I'm not really the cooperative type."

FOUR

In the split second before the unearthly detonation shattered the quiet and a blast of heated air knocked him off his feet, the hunter on the roof across the street who'd watched Lumina Bohn enter the Hospice sucked in his breath sharply, frozen by the almost sexual pleasure from the burst of power that crackled over his skin. He closed his eyes on a blissful shudder.

Holy mother of God. She's even stronger than—

An orange fireball erupted from the Hospice. It blew out all the windows and destroyed the roof in a fantastic, deafening display that glowed hellish bright against the dark night sky. The shockwave sent him tumbling back, but he quickly recovered, leaping to his feet in a lightning-fast move and steadying himself with a hand gripped around a satellite antennae.

Though this could only be an unmitigated disaster, he felt for a moment the insane urge to laugh. She was so *strong.* Her power, in spite of its terrible fury, was so *refined.*

The urge to laugh quickly fled as people began pouring from the building, screaming.

Some of them were on fire.

He ran with long, even strides across the peak of the roof, never losing his balance, his gaze narrowed on the rain gutter at the opposite end. It had detached, a long length drooping down toward the shorter building adjacent. He leapt on it without hesitation, using his weight and speed to propel him far enough over the alley below that he could drop to the roof of the lower building just as the metal gutter gave way with a groan and buckled. He let go, landed in a crouch, and was up and running again before the ruined length of gutter had even hit the ground.

Sirens screamed from far off in the night. He didn't have much time.

The building he'd landed on was some kind of office complex. He sped over the roof, hurtling skylights and skirting air vents, until he reached the far edge. Looking down, he judged the distance—about one hundred feet from the ground—and, without hesitation, jumped.

He landed soundlessly, his legs accustomed to absorbing the shock of high falls. It only took a moment to reorient, then he was off and running again, darting down an alleyway that led directly to the street and the chaos beyond.

Just as he emerged from between the two buildings, Lumina Bohn flew out the front door of the Hospice, running so fast she was only a streak of painted light against the darkness.

Directly behind her, dodging debris on the ground and the burning chunks of wood and plastic still raining from the sky, a dozen men in black suits followed.

There could only be one place she was headed. The hunter muttered a curse, then set off in pursuit.

"Father!" Lu screamed, bursting through the front door with such force it came unhinged and tore away from the frame with a shriek of crumpling metal. "Father!"

She looked around for him wildly. Not downstairs, not in the kitchen, not in his chair near the front window. She bounded up the stairs, calling his name, knowing it was still a while before his shift in the fields, knowing he'd never go anywhere else. He had to be here. He *had* to be!

She could run faster than any human, but the Grand Minister's men weren't far behind. They only had minutes to get the bug-out bags and leave. Possibly less than minutes. Every second counted, every—

She skidded to a halt outside the doorway of her father's bedroom. Her entire body began to shake, and bile rose in her throat. "No," she whispered, choked and horrified. "*No!*"

He lay still on the floor in the middle of the room, staring at the ceiling, his beloved fedora knocked off his head and tipped over forlornly in the corner. One shoe had been knocked off, too, and even from where she stood she could see the swelling and bruising on his face.

Beneath him on the wood floor glistened a slowly widening pool of blood.

He turned his head, caught sight of her in the doorway, and smiled.

Lu cried out and ran to him, throwing herself to her knees. She embraced him, sobbing into his neck, her pain so great it felt as if her chest would explode from it.

This was her fault. This was all her fault. If only she'd been able to—

"*Liebling*," her father whispered, passing a gentle hand over her hair. Lu looked up through her tears to find him gazing at her with tenderness shining in his eyes, that loving smile still on his face. His voice came very weak, punctuated with a raspy, rattling wheeze. "You mustn't blame yourself. Your mother and I knew exactly what we were doing when we brought you home. We knew the risks."

"No. No. No." It was all she could say. Anguish clogged her throat, tightening around her heart like a vise. Every cell in her body was flush with a horror so profound it had *heft*, so that she felt weighted to the ground, gravity pulling at her harder than it had only moments before. Tears poured down her cheeks, dripping onto his chest, and for the first time she noticed the three perfect, dark holes in the center of his cardigan. Everything smelled of gun smoke and violence.

"I did so many things wrong, raising you. I should have found a way to teach you to hone your gifts, to grow them, instead of making you hide. I never meant to make you feel ashamed of what you are, *liebling*. You have nothing to be ashamed of. I was only afraid." He faltered. When he spoke again, his voice was the barest of sounds, whispering thin. "That is my biggest regret: allowing my fear to rule me. Don't let it rule you, child. Do the thing you are most afraid of. Always ask yourself, 'What would I do if I wasn't afraid?' And then do it. Don't be a coward like I was. Don't be like me."

"Father, please, we need to get you some help, I'll call Jakob—"

He coughed up a vivid spray of blood. Wracked with sobs, Lu clutched his hand and cried harder.

"Never forget, *liebling*," he whispered, his eyelids fluttering closed, "you are one of God's creatures, wondrous and rare. You deserve a place in this world, and so do all those like you. Find your people. Do the thing you are most afraid of. And never forget that I love you. Never . . . never forget . . ."

He fell quiet, and Lu sat in frozen, breathless, disbelieving silence as she watched her father die.

It didn't take long. Mere seconds. His breathing slowed, then stopped. His hands fell slack. One moment he was in the room with her, his presence palpable. The next, she was alone with a corpse.

She rocked back on her heels, threw her head back, and let out a primal, anguished scream.

"Aww," said a voice from the doorway, "is the wee creature upset? Sad to see daddy dearest expire like your water credits?"

She jumped to her feet and whirled to face the door in a single, smooth motion, catching a glimpse of the man who stood there just before she saw a flash of light and heard a thundering *crack*. The noise was accompanied by an odd, whistling burst of hot air. Something hit her in the chest with such force she was thrown back several feet, the wind knocked out of her lungs. She slammed against the wall, cracking her head so hard her teeth clattered and she saw stars, then slumped to the floor, boneless as a rag doll.

Stunned, she looked down. A spreading stain of red was moistening her jacket.

When she looked up again, the man in the doorway was staring at her in clinical curiosity with his head cocked and his lips pursed, as if examining an unusual specimen of bacteria under a laboratory microscope. He stepped into the room, holding a black semiautomatic handgun. With his free hand, he reached into his coat pocket and withdrew a shining silver chain with chunky, interlocking links.

A collar.

"Funny how nobody ever checks behind the bathroom door," he mused, kneeling in front of her to fasten the collar tightly around her neck. The clasp fused shut with a sound like a door being closed. The pain in her chest was so great she could hardly breathe. Her arms didn't seem to be working; she couldn't lift either one of them. Or move her legs.

"Even when they know there's someone in the house, when they can sense something's wrong, they'll search every room, but won't bother with more than a peek into the bathroom." He sighed, as if disappointed her father hadn't put up more of a fight.

Shot, she realized numbly. *He shot me.* She wondered if he'd hit her spinal column, paralyzing her.

But no. Her right hand twitched. She pressed her fingers into the throw rug beneath her, concentrating on its knobby texture, putting all her remaining energy into that one—ungloved—hand.

The man touched a finger to the almost invisible device nestled inside his ear canal. "Target acquired," he said nonchalantly, as if this was something he did every day. He recited the street address to whomever was listening, all the while watching her face. He listened for another moment, then nodded and dropped his hand from his ear, disconnecting.

With the serious, detached expression of a scientist, he gently touched the back of his hand to her face, brushing the slope of her cheekbone with a knuckle. Beyond her pain, she noticed he was handsome, in a cold, carnivorous sort of way. Like a shark.

"Just goes to show you," he mused, examining her skin, her face, her hair, "appearances can really be deceiving."

"Yes," said Lu, reaching up to grasp his wrist. "They sure fuck-ing can."

His eyes widened. This time it was his turn to scream.

Smoke. Heat. Fire, crackling hot. Scalding wind whipping her hair into her eyes, her braid undone, her hands slick with blood, her tears dried to salt on her cheeks. Lu stumbled down the stairs, a maelstrom of burning ash and howling wind surrounding her. Soot clogged her nose and throat, suffocating her. The house groaned—a hollow, echoing baritone as the wood support beams began to collapse—a sound underscored by the high, wavering screams of sirens.

She stumbled from the doorway and fell into the street. Dragging herself to her knees with a gargantuan effort of will that required her to grit her teeth against a tidal wave of pain, she ignored the gaping neighbors, the shouts of alarm and fright, the sound of heavy feet pounding closer.

The Schottentor gate. The white rabbit. We'll get you out.

She didn't bother to look back; she knew the men in black were there. She could judge their distance by the footfalls, their breathing, and the chink of metal beneath their coats, sounds that seemed unnaturally loud to her ears, even above the collapsing inferno of the home where she grew up. It was as if only the most important noises were reaching her ears, picked out and enhanced by some inherent ability she'd never before used, a latent talent designed for situations precisely such as this.

If her hearing was sharper, her agility had been reduced by double the amount.

Her legs were jelly. She didn't know how she was moving, only that she was. That she *had* to. To stay put was to die, or be caged, or something far worse she didn't dare consider. Not now. Now the instinct for self-preservation had kicked into high, powerful gear, and Lu was running for her life.

She made it to the end of the block just as the first of the fire brigade screeched around the corner. Directly behind followed the black-and-yellow Peace Guard vehicles. Flashing lights and sirens and the stench of burning rubber, the babble of voices, the world slipping sideways then righting itself again as she bit down, hard, on the inside of her cheek. She forced herself to keep going even though pain like a spear of fire stabbed through her chest. Her vision faded at the edges. Her body broke out in a cold sweat.

The Schottentor gate. The white rabbit.

She had to make it. She *would* make it.

Gasping, stumbling, she ran blindly, using her sense of smell to avoid places there were people, skirting streetlamps, keeping to the shadows as she went. Even injured and half blinded by pain, she could make it with a bit of luck. She knew how to hide, knew how to melt into darkness, knew all the hidden corners of this city she'd been slinking through all her life. Only a little luck, only a little—

Another set of feet pursued her. Quieter, far more swift than the rest. Up on the rooftops, somewhere—

She glanced up and to her right, catching a flicker of movement, a shadow that vanished as she passed under a footbridge. When she came out on the other side, the shadow was gone.

High above the city on the top of St. Stephen's Cathedral, the message on the district's rotating megascreen had changed from "One World In Harmony" to a flashing red "ABERRANT ALERT," with her name and picture beneath, followed by the words, "Wanted For Murder. Armed And Extremely Dangerous. Notify Peace Guard If Spotted."

Murder. The word sent a sweeping chill of guilt through her.

How many had died at the Hospice?

Liesel. Oh God, Liesel . . .

She ran through a cobweb maze of dirty alleys and cobblestone lanes, gulping warm night air, the city a tintype haze of silver and bronze and glimmering gold around her. She skirted the city center, keeping to the residential areas though it wasn't a direct route. Just as she was sure she would collapse, she spied the ghostly glow of the grow light fields in the distance, illuming the night sky.

The vast tented area where the only fresh vegetables and fruits to be had in New Vienna were grown under mile-long rows of artificial lights was situated on the east bank of the Danube, outside the city walls, surrounded by armed guards and barbed wire. Beyond, where suburbs and schools and shopping centers had once stood, was the uninhabited Wasteland. Legend had it packs of scavengers roamed there, vicious as rabid dogs, but in all his years of working in the fields, her father had never seen them.

Father. An animal sound of anguish tore its way from her throat, and she stumbled and fell.

She knelt in the dirt a moment, panting, crying, until she could finally breathe again. When she stood, she realized with a start she was almost to her destination. The waste treatment plant was only yards ahead, hulking dark behind a chain link fence, its rows upon rows of high windows bright with light, its tall stacks chugging steam into the sky.

Lu limped forward. She couldn't hear her pursuers anymore; had she lost them? No, she realized with dawning horror as she dragged herself across a dark street, just missing getting smashed by a passing electric trolley, mercifully empty of passengers. She couldn't hear them because she couldn't hear *anything.*

The only sound now in her ears was a high, tinny buzzing, and that was all.

We'll get you out. We'll get you out.

Her left leg had gone numb. She dragged it behind her, clinging to the chain link fence, forcing herself forward. It was an eternity. It was a never ending fight, a slog of left foot, right foot, pulling, dragging . . .

Then she saw it, and sobbed in relief: the Schottentor gate.

It was there, just beyond the plant, hidden beneath a tangle of overgrown shrubs, a break in the tall expanse of solid, curving stone that comprised the city wall. It was deserted, dark, one of the lesser gates kept always locked.

With her final dregs of energy, Lu limped past the plant into the dense shadows created by the stand of ancient trees that flanked the wall. Her heart felt as if it was going to give out. Her lungs burned like fire. Her vision was watery, at best, and she knew she had only moments left before she would lose consciousness.

But the rabbit? What, and where, was it?

And who was waiting to help her? Who was watching? There was no one here, no one—

Her gaze fell on a small patch of wall that had been cleared of the dense thicket of vines. There, high above her head, was a crude spray painting, crude but perfectly clear.

A white rabbit. Looking down.

Lu fell and crawled the final few yards, rashing her palms on the sharp gravel, tearing her trousers, skinning her knees. The buzzing in her ears grew to a sound like a hive of angry hornets, but she didn't stop, not even when she thought she saw something move from the corner of her eye, not even when the spear of fire in her chest flared up anew and became not one, but a thousand brilliant points of burning pain.

There was a break in the thicket. A space, no wider than her shoulders, a hidden place where the mess of tangled vines and leaves and overgrown shrubs opened to reveal a passageway. A low black tunnel through the ancient stone, concealed by the mass of old growth. You'd never know it was there unless you were right on top of it, and even then, you might miss it.

A few more feet. Just a few . . . more . . . feet.

A hand reached out and grabbed her.

She tried to fight, but she had nothing left. Pain had leached all the fight from her body, so when the hand became two and flipped her onto her back, she didn't resist. She just gazed mutely up at the man who stared down at her, waiting for him to do whatever it was he was going to do.

He was saying something. She couldn't make it out, and it didn't really matter. All she was interested in was his face. He looked familiar. But no—she would've known him. She would've remembered this face if she'd seen it before.

It was ruined.

The entire right side was deeply scarred, with whole chunks missing and a vicious gouge that ran all the way from one side of his forehead to the opposite cheek. His nose had been broken and never properly fixed, he was missing half an ear, and his chin was notched, not a natural cleft, but as if a piece of flesh had been purposefully cut out.

But he had a superhero's jaw and beautiful soft, dark eyes, in spite of the horror of that face, and Lu found herself smiling up at him. With the last of her strength, she smiled.

What *was* he saying? It was a single word, repeated over and over. She concentrated on his mouth, on his lips—full and surprisingly sensual, a startling disparity against that face—and just before she sank down into the warm, welcoming arms of darkness she realized what it was he was saying.

Hope. He was calling her Hope.

Then, mercifully, there was nothing more.

FIVE

Gentle rocking. Warm wind caressing her face. The hollow, repetitive *plunk* of wood slapping water, a smattering of moisture on her cheek. Lu inhaled and smelled damp earth and river and the musky, pleasing scent of a man, very near.

She'd never smelled anything like him. A lush mix of forest floor and spice and moonlight, his scent was rich, exotic, and tinged with danger, nothing at all like the human men she'd spent her life surrounded by.

Wild, she thought drowsily. *He smells like a wild thing hunting in a nighttime woods.*

She fought to open her heavy lids, swimming up from the blackness that had claimed her . . . how long ago? When her eyes blinked open, she found more darkness, but not quite as opaque. High above, dark shapes moved swiftly past, whispering, a sly rustle, the music of a breeze stirring leaves.

Tree branches, arching gracefully overhead. It was still night, but a faint glow of crimson glimmered on the eastern horizon, promising dawn.

Where am I?

She was so tired. Her body was so, so heavy. And her mouth, God, her mouth was baked to desert dryness.

"Water," she whispered in German, her lids fluttering closed. "Please."

She felt the man's attention snap over, heard his fleet step as he quickly came beside her and knelt down. If he smelled different, he moved differently, too, not even disturbing the air as he passed through it, silent as a ghost.

Then a hand—strong, calloused—cradled her neck.

"Drink."

The soft command was spoken in English. She could tell nothing about him from that one syllable, but understood in spite of the fog in her brain that she was at his complete mercy. Whoever he was, he could do whatever he pleased with her, and she'd be unable to resist.

But his scent . . . it did something to her. It was almost comforting.

She drank greedily from the flask he held to her mouth, too exhausted to examine that ridiculous notion.

When she'd had her fill, she turned her head. He withdrew his hand from beneath her neck. Though she tried again and again, her lids refused to open. She felt his fingers brush her forehead, pause briefly at the pulse beating jaggedly beneath her jaw.

She tried to push out with her mind, to see this stranger's thoughts, determine his intentions, but came up against a solid resistance. It was nothing she'd ever experienced before, smooth and cold, like putting her hand against a dome of ice. She pushed harder, concentrating, without result.

That couldn't be right. She frowned, pushing harder still, searching for a chink, any tiny crack in the ice—

Was that low sound a chuckle? No, not quite. More like a noise of satisfaction, nearer to one of Liesel's grunts.

At the thought of Liesel, Lu's concentration snapped. She whined, high and soft, in the back of her throat. The man shushed her softly, murmuring something in a mellifluous language she didn't know, but somehow, impossibly, understood.

Sittu, heleti. Salamu itti manaz pani.

Sleep, My Lady. You're safe with me.

You're safe with me.

She managed to drag her lids open long enough to see his face above her, a dark, featureless oval, only the shine of his eyes visible. Then, in a brilliant burst of color that flared the night sky into a prism of sapphire and gold and green, the first of the Thornemas Day fireworks erupted in the distance with an echoing *boom*, and his face was illuminated.

One side of his face was illuminated. The smooth, unmangled side.

The rush of recognition felt like stepping off a ledge and free-falling. Like remembering something she'd forgotten, something important, dizzying relief and elation and the startling urge to laugh and cry at once.

"Magnus," she whispered.

His lips parted. His dark eyes grew fierce.

Then the fireworks faded, her lids slid closed, and Lu sank back into the waiting darkness.

When next she awoke, Lu was certain she was dreaming for three reasons. One, she couldn't hear anything. Two, it was cold. Not just cold. *Freezing.* The teeth-chattering, body-shaking, curl-into-a-ball-and-want-to-die kind of cold . . . the kind Lu had never felt in her life.

And three, she was flying.

Pain was still carving molten pathways along her nerve endings, but her mind was slightly clearer, the pressure in her chest slightly less. She was able to lift her head to try to get a better look at her surroundings, but her stomach violently rebelled against that idea, sending the acid bite of bile into the back of her throat. She clenched shut her eyes again, but the one brief glimpse had been enough.

She was lying on her back on an unforgivingly hard surface, covered by a heavy piece of canvas, wedged between a wall and the back of two seats. A man was strapped into one of the seats with his back to her, a pair of headphones over his head, his big hands gripped around a wheel that protruded from a console forested with a million colored buttons and digital gauges. From this angle, he could have been anyone, save for the breadth of his shoulders, the thick, corded muscles of his forearms that showed beneath his rolled up shirtsleeves, and the hatched scars marring his knuckles. There was that hair, too, thick and inky black, its shine like sunlight on water, so different from any she'd seen before.

Never seen sunlight on water, she thought, still groggy. *How would I know?*

In front of him was an expanse of curved glass. Far beyond that in the shimmering distance loomed the jagged peaks of a mountain range, emerald and dusky gray in the morning light.

Which made no sense whatsoever. If it was daylight, everything should be tainted red. Crimson, crimson everywhere, like an endless sea of blood. Even those clouds that wreathed the highest peaks were all wrong. They weren't the roiling, angry thunderheads lurking always over New Vienna, casting bloody shadows over everything below.

These clouds were soft and fluffy, white as goose down. They almost looked cheerful.

Lu opened her eyes again, blinking into the brightness, desperate for another look at those happy clouds. Could they be real?

As if sensing she was awake, the man turned his head to look at her, and Lu saw him in profile.

Not a dream after all. In this light, his scarred face was even more startling.

"We're almost there," said Magnus. His voice sounded scratchy and tinny, as if coming from far away. Why couldn't she hear him right? She lifted a hand to her head and felt a bun of cold metal over her ear; she wore headphones, too.

"Protection. For the noise," he explained, seeing her bewilderment. Those dark, dark eyes met hers, and the snap of connection felt like a plug shoved into a socket.

Electric. Humming. Complete.

He held her gaze for a moment, then turned away, the corners of his lips tugged into a frown.

"Almost where?"

Either Magnus didn't hear or didn't want to respond, because he didn't answer. He didn't turn around again.

SIX

"A PHONE!" screamed the Grand Minister. "BRING ME A FUCKING PHONE!"

For the hundredth time since being dragged from the rubble of the Hospice and lifted to the gurney that had rushed him to the hospital where his badly burned body—what was left of it from all his previous entanglements with the Aberrants—was now being hurtled down a corridor on the way to a surgical suite, his screams were ignored.

Goddamned do-gooders.

He was going to ensure every one of these pieces of shit was strung up and hanged, their corpses left to rot until even the birds weren't interested in their dried remains. The EMTs: hanged. The ambulance driver: hanged. The nurses in the ER: hanged. And every single worthless pile of good-for-nothing crap currently running alongside his squeaky-wheeled gurney: hanged. Or maybe publicly decapitated, then hanged from their ankles until their rotted legs separated from their bodies and their headless, legless torsos fell with the unholy thud of dead meat to the ground.

There would be hell to pay for ignoring his commands.

He'd been spared the total barbecuing suffered by a good portion of his men due to pure luck. The desk he'd been sitting behind in the Hospice Administrator's office had been made of industrial-grade steel, and when the thing calling itself Lumina Bohn had turned the air to fire, a gust of heated wind had preceded the blaze. Fortune had been on his side; he was thrown against the wall, the desk was blown apart, the steel desktop had wedged itself between him and the she-devil, and he'd been saved.

Or at least not altogether roasted, as his men had been.

"PHOOOOOOONE!" the Grand Minister howled, eliciting a kindly cluck of comfort from one of the nurses running alongside his gurney. She patted his shoulder.

"Everything is going to be fine. You're safe now. We'll take care of you," the nurse said gently, patting him again.

This one he'd kill himself.

He continued to scream and thrash all the way down the corridor and into the surgical suite. He screamed as the doctors lifted his body from the gurney to an operating table, screamed as they cut his melted suit from his flesh. Finally, just before someone leaned in to cover his face with an oxygen mask, one of his men burst into the room. He shoved the staff aside, toppling them like so many toy soldiers.

"Escaped!" Hans spat, ignoring the cries of outraged medical personnel around him. "Vanished near the waste treatment plant. She must've had help."

The Grand Minister reached out and curled his hand around the lapel of Hans's jacket, jerking him down with the strength of a much younger man. He'd been badly injured so many times before the pain was like a visit from an old friend, and he welcomed it. Pain kept the mind sharp. Pain reminded him what the stakes were.

Pain was a tool that could harden a man's will, and the Grand Minister's will had been honed to lethal solidity.

"Get me Thorne," he hissed into Hans's face. He was instantly obeyed as Hans withdrew a cell phone from his pocket. While the room fell into shocked silence and stillness at the mention of Thorne's name, Hans hit a button, then held the phone to the Grand Minister's ear.

It rang once. The call was answered, but no greeting came over the line. There was never a greeting. Only that heavy, ominous silence waited, its chill and darkness that of a tomb.

"We've been wrong all along!" he rasped, his throat raw from screaming. "It wasn't that bitch of a Queen of theirs who brought us down in Manaus. *It was her daughter.*"

The silence on the other end of the phone throbbed. Then the man who ruled what remained of the world spoke only two words before he disconnected.

"Find her."

His energy spent, his path now clear, the Grand Minister slumped against the operating table. Hans pocketed the phone, and just before the nurse he was soon going to kill lowered the oxygen mask to his face, he whispered hoarsely to Hans, "New directive. Divert all resources to finding the Aberrant Lumina Bohn. *All* resources!"

A hiss of pressurized air, a murmur of voices, the sensation of weightlessness, then sinking. Then Hans spoke, and the Grand Minister faded into unconsciousness with a savage, satisfied smile on his face.

Hans said, "Already on it, sir. We're getting an intermittent signal from Ritter's collar; he must have tagged her at the father's house before she escaped. If the signal holds, we'll have her in a matter of hours."

SEVEN

"You're saying she burned the house *after* she was collared? Is that possible?"

"It's the only explanation. There's no way the mog from Enforcement survived the fire long enough to tag her. The entire building was in flames in seconds. It was the same at the Hospice. He shot her, collared her, *then* she lit him up."

"But that would mean . . ."

"Yes. Especially since she was able to scan me after the collar was already on. The technology doesn't seem to have any effect on her at all. For that matter, neither do the flames. She came out of both buildings totally unscathed. Not even a singed hair. And the reports I'm getting indicate the only burn injuries at the Hospice were the GM and his men. The other injuries were all secondary, caused by shattered glass or other objects propelled in the initial explosion. It's almost as if her Gift is . . . sentient."

A pause. Then the first speaker, a woman, said to the second, "Well, look who we're talking about here. If Honor's any indication, anything's possible."

An even longer pause. Finally, reluctantly, the second speaker, a man, replied. "That's exactly what I'm worried about." The voices fell silent, and only the faraway music of water dancing over stone remained.

Lu opened her eyes.

She was in a dim, cool chamber with smooth, rounded stone walls, lit only by a few candles sputtering in niches that cast flickering shadows over everything. There was no furniture save the feather mattress beneath her and a small wood table nearby. The air smelled like damp rock, hot wax, and creatures who weren't human, and the sound of running water was underscored by a constant, melancholy drip that seemed to be coming from . . . She looked up.

Hanging from the ceiling directly above loomed a forest of long, sharp teeth.

Lu bolted upright, rolled to one side, and became tangled in the mess of heavy blankets that were wrapped around her. She fought them off and got her feet beneath her, but failed at the effort to stand when she sank deep into the mattress, pillowy and insubstantial as clouds. Off-balance, she pitched forward. Just before she fell flat on her face, she was caught by a pair of strong, steadying hands.

Breathless, her palms erupting with heat, Lu looked up into the face of the man who'd caught her.

Eyes like dark chocolate, rimmed in a thicket of long black lashes. The beautiful bone structure, the full, luscious lips. The face of an angel, mauled by the devil's claws.

"They're just stalactites," Magnus said gruffly, his fingers gripping her arms a little too hard. "Water drips through the limestone and leaves deposits that over time form a hanging cone. They're not dangerous."

Lu stared at him, her heart still pounding. *Stalactites. Not dangerous.* She couldn't get her mind wrapped around the idea that the ceiling teeth weren't going to chomp down on her; in all her reading and homeschooling she'd never encountered the word.

The candles all around the room flared bright, sputtering and popping in their niches, a tune that corresponded with the itch in her palms. His tone drier, Magnus added, "Please don't light me on fire. I'd prefer not to look any worse than I already do."

For a long, frozen moment they stared at one another, until Lu released a breath that felt as if it had been punched from her lungs. She threw her arms around his shoulders and buried her face in his neck. "Magnus!" she whispered, her voice choked.

God, it's really you!

He reacted as if he'd been slapped.

He stiffened, dropped his hands to his sides and recoiled. "Don't touch me!" he snarled. He leapt to his feet, eyes flashing with fury, and turned away, every movement jerky and awkward. He stalked out of an arched stone doorway a few meters away, leaving her staring after him in shock.

"Note to self: Magnus has personal space issues," Lu muttered, oddly crushed by his reaction. They'd been intimate, in every way that two people could be! Well, without actually *being* intimate, that is. Physically.

Then a terrible thought arrested her; had her dreams been only one-sided? Had he not actually participated in them, the way she had, all the kissing and touching and . . . the rest? For some reason she'd always assumed the dreams were as real to him as they were to her, two minds touching across time and space, but maybe the encounters had all been in her own head?

But no, he'd come for her—he'd found her! He *knew* her, just as she knew him, she'd seen it in his eyes when she'd first said his name. That telling flare of emotion, quickly smothered, but definitely there.

Then what could it be?

She sucked in a breath, horrified by the thought that maybe he wasn't joking when he asked her not to light him on fire. Could he think she would hurt him? Could he be . . . *afraid* of her?

Lu looked down at her ungloved hands in horror. Of course he was afraid of her. He'd seen exactly what she was capable of.

She suffered a moment of excruciating shame, so familiar from all the years of odd looks and whispers behind hands.

"Don't take it personally. He's had a few rough decades," said a low, cultured voice from the doorway.

Lu looked up. There with crossed arms and a slight smile stood one of the most beautiful women she'd ever seen.

Tall and curvy with a mass of long, dark hair she wore in a loose ponytail over one shoulder, the woman was what her father would have called a "*kiefer auftakt.*" Jaw dropper. She wore tight leather pants, a belted, finely cut tunic of wool, and knee-high boots, all of it black. Though a slight softness of jaw, laugh lines at the corners of her electric-green eyes, and strands of silver threaded through her hair suggested she was somewhere in her early fifties, she was stunning. All easy grace and regal bearing, with a face a master artist would have loved to reproduce on canvas with oils or carve into marble.

She exuded that wild, nighttime scent like Magnus did, only hers was sweeter, more brown sugar than spice. But her eyes held the same sharpness, the coiled tension in her limbs, the same animal readiness. As beautiful as she was, everything about her screamed *Danger*!

Clearly, she wasn't human.

In response to Lu's gaping inspection of her, the woman raised her brows.

"Sorry," said Lu, realizing how rude she was being. "You're just . . . unexpected."

The woman's smile vanished. She smoothed a hand over her hair. "I know. I look a mess." She looked down at herself, and her expression soured. "Twenty-six years and I'm still missing my wardrobe at Sommerley." She sighed and once again looked at Lu. With a shrug, she said, "Well. One does what one must. Keep calm, carry on, and be grateful some other female learned how to weave and sew or I'd be wearing nothing but a fur pelt, because there's no way in hell *I'm* doing anything so domesticated."

Lu was stumped for a reply.

"Morgan." She approached with an outstretched hand, and stood waiting while Lu rose unsteadily to her feet. They shook hands—Lu tentatively, because she never touched without gloves—and Morgan nodded. It felt as if something had been decided.

"How's it feeling?" Morgan jerked her chin toward Lu's chest.

With a gasp, Lu remembered. Her hands flew to her chest and she looked down, tugging aside the Hospice jacket she still wore, pushing aside the tank . . .

Nothing. There were bloodstains on the shirt and jacket, bits of flaky dried blood still clung to her skin, but other than that, there didn't seem to be a scratch on her. And, she noticed for the first time since awakening, she felt no pain at all.

She stared at Morgan. "I don't understand. I was shot. I know I didn't imagine that."

"Of course you didn't imagine it," replied Morgan gravely. "And those weren't just any bullets you were hit with; judging by the way you reacted, you were shot with a special T."

In response to Lu's blank look, Morgan said, "Toxin-laced ammunition. Powerful nerve agents, specifically. Anyone else would have been completely incapacitated for weeks." Her smile was bitter. "They make those just for us." Her gaze dropped to Lu's neck, and her eyes darkened. "That will have to come off."

Lu touched the cool metal links of the collar around her neck, but she was much more interested in what Morgan had just said. "Wait—why am I okay then? Did I have surgery? How did I heal so fast? Did you take the bullet out?"

As they had before, Morgan's brows arched, two dark quirks that managed to convey she thought Lu's questions were more than slightly absurd. "No, ducky. *You* took the bullet out. In a manner of speaking, of course."

The two of them stared at one another in silence for a moment that stretched itself out until it was as cavernous as the room. The candles that had settled down after Magnus had stalked out suddenly flared up again, responding to the rising heat in Lu's palms. She said quietly, "Okay, Morgan. I have questions."

Morgan's eyes didn't miss the way Lu's hands had squeezed to fists, or the sudden brightening in the chamber, but she merely nodded, watching her. Waiting.

If she was afraid, she was hiding it well.

Lu said carefully, "You're an Aberrant, yes?"

Morgan's eyes flashed. "I am most certainly *not*! There's not a damn thing aberrant about me!" She paused to consider. "Well, I'm British so that's not entirely true, we do have our little peccadillos." She paused again, the blaze in her eyes undimmed. "But if what you're really asking is am I human, the answer is resoundingly *no*."

Lu digested that in silence, realizing she'd again been unintentionally rude. *Another note to self: Other Abs don't like to be called Abs. Good to know.*

"How long have I been here, wherever here is?"

"Southern Wales. And about twelve hours."

Wales. Lu saw a pre-Flash encyclopedia picture in her head,

rolling green forests and craggy mountain peaks and crystal lakes tucked into valleys between.

"How did I get here?"

"Helicopter. Well, Magnus had to take you down the Danube out of the city in a coracle first to avoid the antiaircraft missiles, but you flew out somewhere between Bratislava and Budapest. I don't know exactly where, but it would have been somewhere remote. The countryside is safer; surveillance is concentrated on the big cities."

Coracle and helicopter were more words Lu wasn't familiar with, but she guessed by context the first was some kind of small boat, and she knew what flying was because her father had once, after too many glasses of *eiswein*, mourned the loss of the freedom to travel between countries by air. The IF controlled all air traffic, and there were no longer any passenger flights anywhere. Only military or government planes were ever aloft.

Your father was a missionary before the Flash, traveling from country to country, trying to convert people to his faith. Were you aware of that?

Lu swallowed around the fist in her throat the thought of her father produced. She wouldn't allow herself to cry in front of Morgan. She'd save that for later, when she was alone.

"What day is it?"

"December twenty-sixth."

So from the time she was shot to now, no more than twenty-four hours had elapsed. Which meant that she'd been shot with some kind of super bullet and healed without a trace of injury in a day, a feat that, judging by Morgan's tone and description, was highly unusual, even for Abs.

And what did she mean by, "*you* took the bullet out"? What could Lu possibly have done to remove a poison bullet while unconscious?

She could get those answers later, but right now there was one critical thing Lu had to determine in order to decide what she was going to do next.

Holding perfectly still, her attention honed on every tic and blink and telling twitch of Morgan's muscles, Lu said, "My father died in my arms yesterday. I have no home, no friends, and I'm most likely the target of an international manhunt. I can honestly say I don't care if I die because I have absolutely nothing to live for, so if you brought me here for something I'm not going to like, I promise you this: I won't hesitate to kill you or anyone else who tries to hurt me. I won't go down without a fight."

They stared at one another while drop after drop of water fell with a melancholy *plink* from one of the longest stalactites above to a small pool on the cave floor below.

"So. Tell me, Morgan. Are we going to be friends or not?"

The oddest thing happened then. Morgan's eyes misted, a little furrow appeared between her brows. She gave a small shake of her head, and her expression softened until Lu would have sworn what she was seeing was pride.

"You won't remember me, of course," Morgan whispered. "You were just a baby. But I never forgot you. I prayed every day, *every bloody day* that we'd find you. And we finally did. And Christ on a cracker if you aren't *just* like her, all piss and vinegar and a giant set of steel balls."

All the little hairs on Lu's arms stood on end.

Just like who?

Morgan sniffed. Her eyes were bright with unshed tears. She said, "I'm your godmother, pet. Yours and your sister's. Welcome home."

EIGHT

Godmother. Sister. Home. Those words crashed around the inside of Lu's skull, pulverizing her ability to hold any other thought. For a moment her vision wavered, the edges of everything blurred, and she realized it was because of the moisture swimming in her eyes.

"And here I thought *yesterday* was eventful," said Lu, numb with shock.

Morgan swiped at her eyes and gave Lu a brilliant smile. "Oh, thank heavens! How I've missed sarcasm! There's a serious lack of snark in this colony, ducky. Everyone's as dry as a nun's snatch."

With that unappetizing visual, Morgan crushed her into a hug.

After a moment in which Lu stood there stiffly with her arms at her sides, still dumbfounded, Morgan suggested, "Pretend I'm Magnus. You didn't seem to have any trouble figuring out how to get your arms around him."

Lu felt as if she were having an out of body experience as she slowly wrapped her arms around Morgan's waist. She closed her eyes, rested her head on Morgan's shoulder, and marveled at the insanity of life. *One minute you're being chased by assassins, the next you're trading hugs with your new fairy godmother.*

It was a testament to the sheer strength of the survival instinct that more people didn't eat a bullet for breakfast.

She said, "Hopefully you'll like it more than he did."

"Oh, he liked it well enough." Morgan pulled away and smiled, smoothing a stray hair away from Lu's forehead with a motherly touch. "He stabbed the last poor bastard who tried to hug him, so barking and running away with his tail between his legs is a big improvement."

"Stabbed?" Lu repeated, incredulous. Even to someone with a lifelong no-touching policy, that seemed a little much.

Morgan's smile turned wry. "He isn't exactly what you'd call touchy-feely."

No kidding.

Lu took a deep, calming breath. "I'm sorry I said I'd kill you. I mean I guess I would have, but . . . now that I know you're my godmother, it seems a little . . . aggressive."

Morgan waved it off, saying, "Oh, pet, if I had fivepence for every time someone's threatened my life, I'd be a bloody billionaire."

Pence: another unknown word. Were they like credits? Uncomfortable, Lu shifted her weight from foot to foot. She'd never felt stupid before, but coming up against the obvious limitations of her knowledge made her feel exactly that.

Examining her expression, Morgan said softly, "There's a lot of people who are really eager to meet you. But there's no rush; you can stay here and rest for as long as you like, get your bearings. Get cleaned up, have a bath. I'll send some fresh clothes and food in—"

"No," said Lu abruptly, filled with an eagerness and hope she hadn't felt in years. "I want to meet everyone. I want to know everything. I want to do it now."

Morgan's face did that softening thing again. She shook her head, swallowing. "Well, then," she said, her voice catching, a little tremble in her lower lip, "onward and upward!"

And she took Lu by the arm and led her out of the room.

Across the vast, echoing space that comprised the main cavern of the caves the last surviving *Ikati* called their home, Magnus watched as Morgan led her new charge from the chamber she'd awoken in toward the low passageway that connected the private living areas to the community and meeting areas.

He'd lingered in the shadows of a massive flowstone formation after he'd left her room, hoping to catch his breath before heading to the Assembly. But try as he might he couldn't get his heart to stop drumming against his ribs, or ease the trembling in his hands. Every inhalation was a ragged echo in the darkness.

She'd wrecked him. She'd left him totally undone, and all it had taken was the momentary press of her fully clothed body against his.

He flexed his hands open and leaned against the cool stone, hanging his head, closing his eyes against the memory of her face just before she'd whispered his name. Relief had shone in her eyes, huge and real and so sweet it stunned him.

No one looked at him like that. Ever. Hardly anyone but a few of the Assembly dared to even look him straight in the eye.

Not that he blamed them. His temper was as ugly as his face. As ugly as the memory of the things that made him unable to bear the touch of another living being.

But if he was being totally honest with himself, he'd have to admit what had really done him in was the *absence* of something. Something he would've recognized from his fevered dreams, dreams that had taunted him and tempted him and driven him to night-sweat agony for years.

Dreams that had fueled an obsession, in which a golden-haired temptress was always the star.

Desire.

Hope, siren of his dreams, looked at him with eyes so burning with desire he could hardly breathe. They were so real, those dreams, so lucid and tantalizing he always awoke with a groan, the sheets drenched, his hand sticky with his seed, his body still shuddering from his release.

Lumina Bohn looked at him the way a homeless animal looks at someone who's just given it a bed and a snack, and withheld an expected kick: with gratitude.

"Can't blame her either," he whispered to no one and nothing, eyes squeezed shut in the dark. In fact it was he who should be grateful to her for deigning to look upon him at all. If his face made *him* sick to his stomach, it had to be a thousand times worse for someone used to gazing at only perfection in the mirror.

Magnus shoved away from the wall and stood still for a moment in the dark. Then, determined there would be no more slips of control, he squared his shoulders, turned, and followed the faint, familiar and oh-so-torturous scent of his own personal demon through the twisting stone corridors of the caves that he called home.

"Before the Flash this place was a national park," Morgan explained, seeing Lu's questioning glances at the rusted iron handrails that lined the pathway on which they walked. There were railings like it bolted to many of the tunnel walls that branched off into darkness, and other evidence the caves and passageways weren't merely the work of nature came in the form of stairways carved into stone, old electrical lines strung with cobwebs that snaked between dark bulbs, main corridors that were paved, and the occasional crumbling bit of scaffolding. The ancient scent of humans still lingered here, too, and a spike of pain shot through Lu's stomach.

Father.

She swallowed, blinking away tears, forcing her voice to sound normal. "How well protected are you here? Is there a nearby town? Can you be sure it's safe?"

Morgan made a noise that was both proud and somehow sad. "Nothing can get at us here. The old entrance is now underwater, and we blocked all other access except a small portal that was never mapped by them."

Them equaled humans. It was the first time in her life Lu had been on the other side of that slightly derogatory pronoun.

"As for nearby settlements, well, pretty much the entire United Kingdom is a ghost town. The British government refused to cooperate with the Phoenix Corporation when it began taking everything over—Queen Elizabeth never did fancy Americans, you know—and the islands were basically cut off. Thorne gave a thirty-day evacuation order, and anyone who didn't cooperate . . . well, they were just left to starve. No food or supplies were allowed in, the electricity was shut off, the entire population was plunged right back into the middle ages. Virtually no one had survival skills, and that was when Thorne still had the isotope clouds here so nothing could be grown, so," she shrugged, "it was total chaos. After a few years, pretty much all the humans had fled, been starved out, or killed in the rioting—"

"Isotope clouds?"

Morgan gave her a look. "Sorry. I forgot you've been living in an alternate reality your entire life. Those red clouds you're so used to seeing lurking over New Vienna?"

Lu nodded.

"They're manufactured."

Lu stopped dead in her tracks. "Manufactured!" she repeated in disbelief. The word echoed off the cave walls and faded to silence. "Why? How is that possible?"

Morgan shrugged again, a move heavy with pathos. "Science. Humans engineered powered flight, created nuclear technology, and sent unmanned craft into deep space, you think a few poisonous clouds circling the planet would be a challenge? They're not exactly stupid, in spite of all their stupidity. As for why, well, population control requires creativity. You can't achieve world domination and shape general opinion with some leaflets and a few dazzling speeches. You need really heavy-hitting propaganda, the kind people can't argue with. The more in-your-face and damaging to your opponent, the better. Tangible stuff. Visible stuff." Her voice soured. "Like clouds the color of blood that change life-supporting beams of sunshine into burning rays of death."

Lu felt choked with hatred. All her life, she'd heard what vile bioterrorists Aberrants were, what dangerous traitors, what *evil*. And the truth was that the supposed proof of their evil was manufactured by the very people crying the loudest for their heads?

"So the Flash must have been them, too," Lu said, anger quickening her blood. "The destruction of the rainforest in Brazil, the unexplained lights in the sky, the earthquake, the fire . . . that had to be them, too! That was all part of Thorne's plan for world domination, wasn't it?"

Morgan's expression changed to one that looked suspiciously close to pity. She pursed her lips as if carefully choosing her words, then with a one-shouldered shrug that seemed to imply *what the hell, she'll find out sooner or later*, said quietly, "No, pet, that wasn't them. That was all you."

Lu froze in openmouthed horror. "*Me?*"

"That's not entirely accurate," purred a voice from the shadows behind her. Lu whirled around, searching the darkness, her senses stinging and surging with a weird recognition.

From behind the curve of a giant boulder several paces away, a woman appeared. Dressed in head-to-toe pristine white, she was blonde, pale, and utterly feral. She eased onto the path with a cat-like silence, her movements deliberate, her large, luminous eyes shining eerily bright.

Lu exhaled a breath that felt like fire.

Looking at this stranger was like looking in a mirror. The long, wavy hair, the slightly pointed chin, the forehead tipped with a widow's peak, the tiny mole above the arch of the left brow.

The idea she'd been cloned sidled up and lingered beside her, unspeakably uncanny.

The woman smiled, but it didn't touch her eyes. She said, "You had a little help, didn't you, sis?"

There was an awkward pause. Then Morgan, sounding irritated, said, "Hope, this is Honor. Your twin sister."

Honor. The Girl in her dreams. The Girl who was always so angry. Whom she'd managed, almost completely, to block. Her *twin*. Lu couldn't think of a single coherent response. She said numbly, "My name isn't Hope."

A voice inside her head replied, *Actually, flamethrower, it is.*

Honor's cold smile grew wider.

NINE

Before Lu had a chance to process anything beyond her own shock, Honor's gaze honed in on the collar around her neck.

"Honor," warned Morgan, just as the metal around Lu's throat began to freeze.

It happened so fast. As cold became frost became ice, the collar crackled . . . and shrunk. Lu felt a stabbing pain against her carotid artery, and instinct kicked in.

She lifted her arms and flexed open her palms, aiming at Honor.

When the ball of fire cleared, with a roar and the acrid smell of burning fabric, Morgan was crouched on the ground with her arms flung over her head, coughing, the sleeves of her tunic singed and smoking. Honor was standing with her hands on her hips, glaring at Lu with those predatory eyes, completely unscathed.

"Overreact much?" she snapped.

The collar popped off with a muted *tink!* and fell in one solid, frozen chunk to the ground at Lu's feet, where it promptly shattered to pieces.

Lu stumbled back, hands clutching her throat. "Did you just try to *strangle* me?" she shouted, livid.

Honor's response was a roll of her eyes and an exaggerated sigh. "And they say *I'm* melodramatic."

"What the hell is going on here?"

The growled question came from Magnus, who'd appeared as if from nowhere. He helped Morgan to her feet. Lu noticed he didn't take her hands, but grasped her under the arms, stepping away as soon as she was standing.

Honor lifted her chin, examining Lu with a disapproving curl of her lip that managed to make her appear even more menacing. "Someone apparently has some *trust* problems."

"Honor took Hope by surprise, that's all," said Morgan before Lu could spit a retort.

Honor said coldly, "I had to get that thing off of her—"

"By *shrinking* it?" Lu hissed.

"Metal contracts when it freezes—"

"You might have taken that into consideration, seeing as how it was around my *throat*—"

"I wouldn't have hurt you!"

"Easy to say *now*!"

"Stop!" Magnus thundered, stepping between them.

Lu and Honor fell silent. Vibrating anger, Magnus looked back and forth between them, his dark eyes flashing fire. He was quiet a moment, controlling himself, then he said in a low voice, "Honor. She doesn't know you. She doesn't know your Gifts. She doesn't know any of us." His burning gaze cut to Lu. A muscle in his jaw began to flex, over and over.

Expressionless, Honor sent Magnus a long, searching look. The temperature of the air dropped sharply, sending a creeping frost that bloomed white down the mossed stone walls. She looked back at Lu.

With the icy weightlessness and silence of falling snow, Honor's voice whispered inside Lu's head, the words meant for her alone.

I wouldn't have hurt you, flamethrower. Obviously you can't say the same for me.

Damn. This close, keeping Honor out of her head was proving to be nearly impossible.

They stared at one another, bristling, until Honor turned and vanished back into the shadows. The darkness engulfed her as if she'd been swallowed.

After a tense moment, Morgan said to Magnus, "She won't like it."

Magnus ran a hand through his hair, exhaling hard. "I'm not taking sides."

"Really? Because that's exactly what it looked like you were doing. At least she'll think it was."

"I'm just trying to keep the peace," said Magnus between gritted teeth.

"Ha!" Morgan inspected her singed tunic sleeves. "That's like trying to stop a volcano from erupting and a tornado from chewing up a trailer park. Where the girls are concerned, I think it's a much safer bet to just find shelter and wait out the storm."

"I'm so sorry," Lu said, ashamed and unsettled by the whole encounter. "It's just . . . the shock. Of everything. Are you all right?"

Morgan, ever aplomb as Lu was quickly finding out, waved off her concern. "Right as rain. I hated this jacket anyway. And you being a bit out of sorts is certainly understandable, pet, under the circumstances. Don't worry about it."

"Are *you* all right?" Magnus, quiet but still intense, directed this to Lu. Their eyes met, and she had to look away because she felt naked under his gaze. She knelt and picked up a broken piece of the collar. It was coldest thing she'd ever held in her hands.

"So Honor can freeze things?" Lu flipped the frosted metal from one palm to another because to keep it in one spot too long would have caused an ice burn. Hairline cracks covered the metal in webs; the silver had blackened in spots.

Morgan chuckled softly, then sobered. Lu looked up to find Morgan staring at her with that little furrow between her brows. "Just out of curiosity, pet . . . how much have you been able to explore your Gifts?"

Lu looked from Morgan to Magnus. His eyes were dark, unreadable. She stood.

"I haven't. I couldn't. My entire life I've been trying to pretend I don't have any. I was just trying to be unnoticed. Trying to fit in. To be normal . . . like humans."

With a small shake of his head, Magnus murmured, "Pearls before swine."

Heat crept across Lu's cheeks.

Do not give what is holy to dogs, and do not throw your pearls before swine, or they will trample them under their feet, and turn and tear you to pieces.

It was a verse from that most infamous of banned books: the human Bible. The book her father so loved, and spent hours reading, the curtains drawn, his face rapt, his lips moving soundlessly over the words.

"Oh," said Morgan, sounding more than a little mysterious, her lips curved to a Mona Lisa smile, "this is going to be *so* much fun."

She and Magnus shared a look. If she didn't already know Magnus was about as unsmiling as anyone could get, Lu would have sworn she saw a small, upward curve to his lips, there then instantly gone.

He said, "We can get started tomorrow. Right now there are a dozen Assembly members fidgeting in their chairs waiting for me."

"Us," Morgan corrected, but without rancor. He sent her a sidelong look. She said, "Oh, I know, they can't start without *you*, but I'm sure everyone is much more interested in meeting the guest of honor today." She waved him on. "We're right behind."

"Ladies first." His tone was calm, but tension tightened his shoulders. He didn't seem to appreciate Morgan's breezy dismissal, but she shrugged that off, too, leaving Lu to wonder if there was anyone this formidable woman feared. Even Lu already had a healthy respect for the temper she could see, barely leashed, simmering under Magnus's careful control.

Morgan raised her brows at Magnus. She turned to Lu. "I'm sorry, do you see any *ladies* present? Because all I see are a couple of badass birds who could really use a—"

"Morgan!" Magnus's shout echoed off the stone.

Morgan sent Lu a wicked smile, then said to him, "You *do* make for easy pickings, ducky. You know I can't resist."

Along with flared nostrils and hands that had curled to fists, that muscle began to flex in Magnus's jaw. He said slowly, "Do not. Make me tell your husband. You're being incendiary. *Again.*"

Morgan pressed her lips together. Lu saw it was because she was trying to bite back a smile. "*Moi?*" She pointed at Lu and said innocently, "I'm not the incendiary one." Then without waiting for an answer, she knelt, gingerly scooped up the broken remains of the collar and announced, "I'll take this over to Beckett. See you at the Assembly in two shakes."

And she was off.

Magnus watched her go, muttering to himself, "How the hell Xander puts up with it, I'll never know." He raked a hand through his hair again, something he seemed to do when disturbed—which Lu guessed meant he did it frequently. "You should be resting. I'll bring you something to eat, clean clothes."

"No."

Magnus turned to her, startled at the bluntness of her answer, and, judging by his glower, none too pleased another female was being disagreeable.

"Morgan said everyone wanted to meet me. And I want to meet them." She paused a beat. "Besides, I'm not hungry. And I can rest when I'm dead."

She thought she saw it again, that fleeting amusement. But he was apparently so good at quashing anything except growls and scowls she really wasn't sure if she'd imagined it. His face was wiped swiftly clean of any traces of emotion.

"All right," he said, "come with—"

"First explain something to me."

He'd been turning away, but snapped back in place as if pulled, his lips thinned to a line.

That muscle in his jaw is certainly getting a workout.

"Morgan just told me something—several things actually—I'm finding a little hard to process."

"Such as?"

"Mainly that *I* might have been the cause of the Flash. That can't really be true . . . can it?"

He considered her in stony silence for what seemed an eternity. Finally he said, "We can discuss this later. Right now I have to—"

"Was I?" Lu stepped closer, her voice rising. She took another step toward him when he didn't answer, and he twitched, as if tensing to run.

"Was I somehow the cause?" She'd emphasized each word, moving even closer, until finally they were almost nose to nose. She had to look up to meet his eyes. This close they were as warm and rich as melted chocolate, though their expression fluctuated between anger, alarm, and a strange, raw ambivalence.

I'm not going to light you up, she wanted to say, seeing how uncomfortable he was. Instead she repeated herself when he refused to answer.

"Magnus. Tell me. Was I somehow the cause of the Flash?"

He swallowed. His gaze drifted to her mouth, then he blinked and turned his head, staring off into the darkness. He said, "There's no *somehow* about it."

No. Oh God, *no*.

The room seemed to tilt, sliding sideways from center, a slipping spin that had her stomach flip-flopping like a dying fish. She heard Magnus say her name, saw him reach for her with the alarm in his eyes turning now to wide-eyed panic as the whole world came crashing down over her ears.

Wars. Death. The destruction of an entire planet.

Because of me.

A part of her dove into full-blown, indignant, there's-no-way-in-hell denial. But another part—a darker part, the part where the animal lurked—believed it. Fully and immediately, she grasped the thing that had always made her father so afraid.

She wasn't just a monster.

She was pure evil.

Magnus caught her as she stumbled back, sagging against the wall as if her knees wouldn't support her. Her eyes were still open, half-lidded and blank, so he knew she hadn't fainted, at least not in the traditional sense of the word. She'd simply *stopped*. Stopped breathing, stopped responding, stopped looking at him as if he was holding a life preserver and she was in the middle of the ocean, drowning.

He'd just taken that life preserver and flung it off the other side of the boat, right into the hungry maw of a shark.

"Hope! Hope, talk to me!"

The pulse in her neck fluttered wildly. Her face had blanched ghostly white. She blinked once, then put her hands over her face and moaned. It was a low, wretched sound he recognized as one of a creature whose soul was in cinders.

He'd made that sound himself, too often to count.

His hands were gripped around her arms before he could think, and he eased her to the floor. "Just breathe. Just sit here a minute and breathe, *heleti*."

She'd begun to tremble violently. She put her head on her knees, hiding. She said to herself, "The Romanian word for light," then laughed a low, ugly laugh, a sound utterly devoid of humor. It might have been the most hopeless noise he'd ever heard. She lifted her head and stared at him with eyes that were huge and dark, still wearing those brown contacts that to his keen vision were so obviously fake.

"My name isn't Hope. It's Lumina. Which is the Romanian word for light. Because I caused the Flash." That ugly laugh made another appearance, now accompanied by a manic glint in her eyes. "My parents had a really depraved sense of humor."

"No," he said softly, kneeling in front of her and still holding her arms, fighting the rise of panic and the urge to flee that always accompanied being too close. He pushed both emotions away and concentrated on her. On what she needed from him right now.

"No," he said again. "Your name isn't Lumina. You aren't in the human world anymore; you don't have to keep your human name. You'll never again have to hide who you are, or what you can do. You'll never again have to pretend. And you'll never again be alone, do you understand? We're your family here—"

"I *had* a family," she said vehemently, her trembling growing worse. "They're dead."

"They weren't your Blood—"

"It's not about blood!" she cried, stiffening. "Family is who takes care of you, who sacrifices for you, who would take a bullet to keep you safe!" Her face contorted; she was trying not to cry. "There're more powerful things than *blood*!"

Magnus gazed at her, feeling all her rage and pain and confusion, wishing he had the right words to help her. Wishing he wasn't so broken, so he could simply take her in his arms and comfort her, one lost soul to another, no questions asked. But he knew from hard experience that wishful thinking was nothing but a waste of time. He *was* broken, and had little to offer except the truth. So he simply spoke it.

"There is nothing in this world more powerful than your Blood. Not a single thing."

She just stared at him, lips pinched to a *don't-cry* grimace, eyes fierce with unshed tears. Even like this, in dirty clothes with uncombed hair, with an unwashed face and her features twisted in anguish, he thought she was the most painfully exquisite thing he'd ever seen. Honor had the same face, the same body, but it was Hope's spirit that elevated her from merely pretty to perfect. That— literal—fire she possessed lit her up from the inside so she glowed.

"Tell me."

Her voice was ragged, the emotion behind it raw. Magnus inhaled a slow breath, debating. He quickly decided that not only did she deserve to know, but in her shoes, he'd demand it, too.

"You are Hope Catherine Moore McLoughlin. Your grandfather, Charles, known to humans as the Earl of Normanton, was, in his time, the most powerful our kind had ever seen. He was called the Skinwalker, able to Shift into any form, any element, any thing or even idea. I understand he particularly enjoyed being a crow, a butterfly, and a cold wind." His voice turned wry. "Maybe that's where Honor gets it."

Hope's eyes widened. Her lips parted. She stared at him, rapt.

"Your mother inherited her father's abilities. Though her own mother was human, Jenna—"

"My mother's name was Jenna?" Hope said, her voice small. "And she was . . . half-human?"

He nodded. "She was even more powerful than her father. And you and Honor are even more powerful than her."

She processed that a moment. "Is her grave here, in Wales? Is she buried nearby?"

She leaned forward. The scent of her hair and skin filled his nose, and his mouth went dry. His heart contracted with a horrible, acute *ache*, and he had to resist the urge to jump up and run or smash his mouth against hers and kiss her.

For God's sake, keep it together, Magnus!

He dropped his hands from her arms, tucked them under his armpits, and rocked back onto his heels. He said gruffly, "No. She's not buried nearby."

Her face fell. She sagged back. "Oh."

"No, I mean, she's not buried at all."

She blinked at him, confused, and he realized he was making a mess of the whole explanation. He carefully chose his next words.

"She's not buried because she's not *dead*, Hope. Your mother is very much alive."

TEN

Morgan made her way through the dim tunnels quickly, not needing light to navigate the corridors she knew so well. Like all her kind she could see in the dark, but even if she hadn't been able to, she'd lived in this chilled palace of ancient stone and flowing water for over two decades. She could navigate the twists and turns with her eyes closed.

In spite of the damp that made her bones ache and the lack of natural light, she loved it. The caves of Ogof Ffynnon Ddu, over three hundred meters deep and sixty kilometers long, featured roaring rivers, thundering waterfalls, and vast columns of glistening limestone, formed as stalactites and stalagmites grew together after millennia of longing from above and below. Cave shrimp, pale as bone, scurried in the rocky beds of pools, fish swam aplenty in the underground lakes, and an entire ecosystem of subterranean plant and animal life abounded on which to feed.

And there was music. Hauntingly beautiful, the song of water—running and dripping and flowing all around—underscored all her days and nights with the loveliest melodies. For Morgan, a woman once blessed with considerable wealth and cursed with a fetish for beautiful things, this music was the only thing of true beauty left in her life.

Well, that and her husband, Xander. She smiled, wondering how long it would take to turn his growls of anger when he heard she'd been smart to the Alpha—again—into purrs of contentment when she snuggled against him and said she was ever-so-sorry.

Ten seconds. Tops.

One of the many things she adored about her husband was his inability to stay mad at her. You'd think a man who'd once been the tribe's most fearsome assassin, the famed "Wrath of God" himself, would have a little more fortitude in the face of a few feminine wiles. But Xander's fury melted like snow in sunlight with nothing more than a kiss from his wife.

And because of *her* inability to stay out of trouble, Morgan spent a lot of time kissing him.

That wasn't the only reason, of course. Xander was an excellent kisser.

"Knew I'd find you here, kiddo," she called as she stepped through an egg-shaped opening in the stone, cradling Hope's frosted collar in her cupped hands.

In stark contrast to the rest of the caves, this room was illuminated by a soft, ambient light that almost perfectly mimicked the warm glow of a summer sunrise. It seemed to emanate from the walls themselves, but its source was the young man seated behind a sturdy wooden bench strewn with every kind of electronic device in various states of assembly. He was staring through a lighted magnifying glass, and didn't look up when she came in.

"Auntie M," he said with exaggerated patience, "I am no longer a 'kiddo.' I am a grown man. Allow me to demonstrate." Still without looking up, he flexed both arms, causing a pair of spectacular biceps to bulge from his short-sleeved shirt.

"Beckett, really," she sighed. "Muscles might impress your little groupies, but I happen to know from personal experience there's much more to being a man than a pair of big guns."

Beckett looked up from his work and grinned. The light in the room grew brighter. "*Vast* personal experience, no doubt."

Morgan attempted an outraged expression, but found herself grinning back at him instead. "Cheeky bastard! Don't let your uncle hear you talking to me like that, or he might just tear off one of those big arms of yours and beat you over the head with it."

"What?"

He pretended innocence, and Morgan could see exactly why all the young girls—and most of the older ones, too—swooned in his presence. He had long, curling lashes, eyes the exact color of new grass, adorable dimples, perfect teeth, and golden, always-tousled hair. Along with a quarterback's body and a pirate's swagger, he was utterly charming. And bright. And one of her favorite people in the world.

Beckett said, "I'm sure the poor man *knew* he was marrying a man-eater—"

"Goddess, I think you meant to say." She rounded the desk and presented her cheek for a kiss. He obliged, and she gave him an arch look. "And I'll have you know I was *quite* the virgin when I married your uncle. Completely untouched!"

He grimaced. "Way too much info. And, if I know you at all, a complete fabrication."

"Well, if you're going to insult me I won't give you your present," she said lightly, perching on the edge of his desk.

The room was cramped with makeshift tables covered in a haphazard sprawl of wires, the innards of computers, broken monitors, boxes of mobile phones, data pads both working and not, and a jumble of other unidentifiable electronic flotsam. One wall was covered in old maps, the opposite wall displayed posters of World War II bombers, muscle cars, Amelia Earhart, and the odd pinup girl. Then there was the clock collection. Stacked in old milk crates in a teetering column that nearly reached the ceiling, hundreds of old clocks ticked out the minutes and hours, all of them set to pre-IF, global standard time for New York City, which Beckett insisted was the center of the civilized world before the Flash.

His obsession with pre-Flash memorabilia was eclipsed only by his fascination with electronics from all eras and countries. Some of it he'd scavenged from abandoned homes and offices in the surrounding countryside, and some if it came from much farther afield; when Magnus went hunting, he never failed to bring something back for Beckett's collection, pilfered from some lab or locked building.

Magnus's Gifts rendered things like locks, and even walls, obsolete.

"Present?" Beckett perked up like a dog when it hears the word *treat*, his eyes alight. "What present? What is it?"

Another reason to love him: He was easy to please. Morgan stretched out her arms, opened her palms, and said, "You're welcome."

He went still, eyes widening. "No way."

Morgan laughed. "Way. Take it, will you, it's freezing my hands!"

"On the glass, on the glass!" He swatted aside the tiny silver chip beneath the lighted microscope as if it were a fly. "Here!"

Morgan gingerly deposited the heavy chunks onto the lighted glass base of the microscope and sat back, watching Beckett with an affectionate smile. He leaned down to peer at it. Beneath the glass, the light ticked up several degrees, though he hadn't touched any dial or switch.

"Whoa," he breathed, "this is totally new technology. There are all kinds of code embedded in the links, and is that . . . what is that?" A bubble of light the size of Morgan's wedding band hovered over a jagged spot on the edge of a broken link, illuming the blackened metal from both sides. He made an interested grunt. "I've never seen that on any of the other collars."

"No doubt they're improving all the time," muttered Morgan sourly.

Careful not to touch it with his fingers, Beckett used a pair of wooden tongs to rotate the broken collar. The bubble of light followed the move. "Why is it frozen?" He tapped a link. "Honor?"

"Mmm." Beckett's Gift fascinated her no end. What must it be like to be a power source all your own? She thought she'd probably use it to create an age-defying diffuse glow around her face, then wondered absently if she could bribe him to follow her around, doing just that. She touched her cheek, considering.

"So Magnus is back."

"That he is."

Beckett looked up expectantly, as if just realizing what that meant. "And?"

A swell of emotion rose inside her, huge and bright, and for a moment she couldn't answer. Half her lifetime of searching, and finally, *finally* they'd succeeded. Morgan still didn't quite believe it was real.

She said simply, "Mission accomplished."

A new light appeared in his eyes. A new tension sharpened his face. "I want to meet her."

Morgan recognized that look. It was a version of the expression Magnus got whenever Hope's name was mentioned, from the time he'd been a much younger man, with an unscathed face and a soul untouched by darkness. He'd never even met Hope, so it made no sense whatsoever, but each and every time someone said her name, Magnus's eyes would grow darker and hotter, his face flush with something that looked—before he could stifle it—suspiciously like longing.

And here was Beckett doing the same thing. Morgan sincerely hoped every unmated male in this colony wasn't going to start fighting over her goddaughter. *Then again*, she thought, brightening, *we haven't had a proper suitor challenge around here in ages.*

God knew Honor wasn't going to be helping that situation along anytime soon, prickly ice queen that she was.

"You will. Just not right now; she's on her way to meet the Assembly. Which is where I should be going, incidentally." She stood. "I'll see you—"

He stood also, abandoning the collar. "On her way to the Assembly? How long has she been here?"

"Hours, ducky. She's been asleep—"

"And I'm just now finding out? Why doesn't anybody tell me anything around here?" He seemed really aggravated. He stared at her, awaiting an answer.

"Because, dear boy, you spend most of your time hunched over this table, fiddling with your computers and sending encoded messages all over the world—"

"Planning is a necessity when you're trying to overthrow a totalitarian regime—"

"—which doesn't allow for much in the way of *conversation*. Your groupies might love you, but they've learned by now not to come knocking when the lab lights are on. Hence your lack of knowledge on the comings and goings of new—and quite lovely, I might add—persons."

The *treats* and *presents* look returned to his face. He crossed his arms over his chest. Trying to seem nonchalant and utterly failing, he drawled, "So. She's pretty then."

Drily, Morgan said, "She looks exactly like her sister, Beckett. She's more than pretty."

His lips twisted. "So she's *scary* pretty."

"When I said she was lovely, I wasn't talking about her face."

Now he looked confused. "So she's . . . nice?"

Morgan considered that. "If by 'nice' you mean she's the type of girl who's afraid to say what's on her mind, or ask for what she wants, or wouldn't tell you when you're being an asshole because she might bruise your delicate ego, then, no. She's not nice." A smile lit her face. "She's *un*nice. In fact, she's decidedly wicked."

Eyes sparkling, he looked at her a beat. "Sounds interesting."

Her smile slowly faded. She exhaled a heavy sigh. "She's more like her mother than I ever would have guessed, knowing her twin. Hope has that same rebellious streak as her mother, that same fearlessness. Yet she's much more . . ." she searched for a word, inspecting her singed sleeve. "I don't know. Fragile, maybe. Sensitive. Jenna was always so self-contained. So self-*assured*. Hope seems like the kind of girl who could slay a dragon to save a village if she had to, but would cry herself to sleep later, wondering if the beast had a family who would mourn."

Beckett lowered his brows. "So she's manic-depressive."

"Oh, for God's sake!" Morgan threw up her hands. "She's *disoriented*, is what she is! As you would be, too, if you were shot and collared and woke up in a strange place with strange people. So do me a favor when you meet her: be kind." She turned to leave.

Beckett's voice climbed a notch. "*Shot*?"

Without turning, Morgan said over her shoulder, "Believe me, pet, that's the *least* terrible thing that's happened to that poor girl recently."

She headed toward the Assembly room, leaving the normally sunny Beckett behind to brood.

Lu stared at Magnus with the kind of silence one reserves for funerals, and discussions with medical professionals about that large, inoperable tumor they've just discovered in your brain.

"My mother is alive," she repeated disbelievingly. Magnus nodded, watching her warily, it seemed, for any unusual outbursts. Like a giant ball of fire, for instance. But she felt nothing but that pervasive, numbing shock. She wondered if that was her brain's defense mechanism, deciding quickly that she preferred numbness to howling fits. At least it was less embarrassing.

A godmother. A sister. And now a mother—all alive.

"When do I meet her?"

Magnus hesitated. "She's not here."

"Where is she, then? Can I go to her?"

More awkward silence. Then: "The thing is . . . we don't know exactly where your mother is." He added firmly, "But she's definitely alive."

Lu blinked at him, more confused than ever. "How do you know she's alive if you don't know where she is?"

"Because of Honor's Gift."

When she just waited him out, he added, "Telepathy."

"They . . . talk to one another? Like that?"

When he nodded, nausea made her stomach lurch, and she covered her mouth with her hand. She'd been blocking Honor for years, blocking everyone's thoughts for years because she'd learned the only way to survive was to shut the world out, to act "normal." The probability that she'd also inadvertently been blocking her own mother made her feel sick. She shook her head, trying to clear it enough to make sense of what he was telling her.

"So does that mean she doesn't *want* Honor to know where she is, or . . ."

Anger flickered across his features, darkening his eyes, thinning his lips, and suddenly she knew exactly what it meant.

Horrified, Lu breathed, "She's a prisoner!"

His expression was a tortured mix of grief, guilt, and fury. He looked away, as if he couldn't meet her eyes, and she took his silence as affirmation.

All the stories she'd ever heard about how Abs were abused in government-run detention centers slammed into her head and became a whirling vortex of horror inside her skull. She whispered, "For how long?"

He seemed reluctant to answer, and she thought his teeth were in danger of shattering with all the grinding of his jaw.

"Magnus—*how long*?"

"Since the Flash."

Oh dear God. For decades, her mother had been locked up, probably experimented on, probably *tortured*—

Lu squeezed shut her eyes, forcing herself to remain calm though all she wanted to do was succumb to the sobs trapped inside her chest. She saw the Grand Minister's face just before she threw up her hands at the Hospice, remembered the words he'd said that she'd been so convinced were lies.

And you can meet your mother—you'd like that wouldn't you? To meet your birth mother? She's missed you so much.

Lu wanted to vomit. Her voice shaking, she said, "And my birth father?"

Magnus exhaled heavily, as if he'd been holding his breath. "We don't know where he is either. Or if he's . . ."

Alive. He didn't say it, but the unspoken word hung there.

"Honor can't talk to him, and your mother doesn't know his whereabouts. They were separated . . . in the . . . battle . . ."

She began to hyperventilate. Trying hard to concentrate on the sound of water rushing over some far-off streambed, she thought if only she could stay focused on that sound, she might be able to banish the images in her head. The terrible, bloody images—

"Hope." Magnus's voice was soft, but beneath it she heard the edge. "Your mother is unharmed. She's a prisoner, yes, but apparently a well-treated one. And I'm going to find her. If Leander is alive, I'll find him, too. It's what I do. Find our people, what's left of them. And bring them back to live here. We're trying to rebuild, one at a time. There's not many of us left, but . . . it's something. It's a start. I give you my word: *I. Will. Find. Them.* No matter how long it takes me. No matter the cost. I'll bring them back to you. Or I'll die trying."

She opened her eyes and looked at him. Every muscle in his face showed his strain and fatigue, his eyes, so dark and intense, showed her his sincerity. She didn't know if what he was promising was possible, but she knew he believed what he was telling her. And that, at least, was something.

In that moment, she began to trust him. Whatever else he was, Magnus was a man who would rather die than not honor his word, and that made her breathe just the tiniest bit easier. Even if it was short-lived, he'd just given her some peace of mind.

And he found me, she thought, studying his face. So maybe it really is possible.

After a long while, she said, "I think I might need a drink. Or four."

That seemed to soften the hard lines around his mouth, which is what she'd hoped for.

"You're in luck. Jack makes potato vodka that will rot your guts but will definitely put you right in the head. At least until you go blind from drinking it."

"Jack?"

"You'll meet her at the Assembly meeting."

"Jack's a she?"

His lips twitched. Was he trying not to smile?

"That she is." He stood, helping her up by the arm. Lu leaned on him heavily, more shaky than she'd realized, and he steadied her, his eyes worried though his posture was stiff. *Because I'm too close*, she realized. She sighed and stepped away, noting how the tension left his body when she did.

She sighed again, scrubbing her hands over her face. Time for a change of subject.

"Do you have any gloves here? Even if they're thin, I just . . ." she stared at her hands. "I feel naked without them. I've been wearing them my whole life. And after what happened back there with Honor I'm not sure it's safe for me to walk around without them." She thought of Morgan's singed jacket. "Honor wasn't hurt, but someone else could be."

His brows knit. "Gloves can control your Gift?"

"I don't really know how it works," she admitted quietly. "Just that I don't have accidents when I wear gloves."

"Ah, yes. Your 'accidents.' That's how I knew where to find you, incidentally."

When Lu looked at him, startled, he said, "The fire at the credit market. That was my first clue where to look."

Seeing the confusion on her face, he said, "Just like the IF does, we monitor GlobeNet for any kind of suspicious activity that might indicate one of us living undercover." His face hardened. "And we try to get to them first."

GlobeNet was the Imperial Federation's international spynet, which surveilled all citizens and communications and distributed the "news."

So technology had brought him to her. Not those wonderful, delicious dreams, which now that she thought about it, probably *were* only one-sided. She knew she had Gifts she didn't understand; perhaps dreaming about people she'd meet was one of them. She'd never met her birth mother or father in those dreams, though. Or her sister. Or her godmother.

Only him. A very *different* him, unscarred and smiling, full of lightness and life.

So . . . just like the rest of her life, her dreams of Magnus had been a lie.

Lu tried to feel nothing but her newly found numbness, but all sorts of other emotions were leaking through. Fun, lovely things like foolishness. Misery. Despair.

New Vienna. City of her childhood, city of dreams. All her life had been nothing but dreams. And here, finally, was reality.

Boy, did it suck.

"Are you sure you want to go to this Assembly meeting, Hope? You look pale."

The concern in his voice and eyes was genuine, but now Lu realized it for what it was: brotherly. "Yes," she answered dully, turning away. "And I told you before, my name's Lumina."

I'm the monster who broke the world.

ELEVEN

Everyone had been milling around, talking quietly in small groups, until Magnus and Hope—*Lumina*, he corrected himself—were about ten meters from the entrance to the cave where the Assembly regularly gathered. He knew it wasn't only their footsteps echoing on the stone that had cut off the conversation so abruptly.

It was Lu. Her presence was electric, as tangible and shocking as a hand slapping his face.

Walking beside him, she was pale and silent, her lips set to a grim line. He thought she looked slightly ill, and had to fight the urge to pick her up and carry her back to her bedchamber. That urge was simultaneously fighting the urge to get as far away from her as possible, because he also had another—and very powerful—urge to kiss her. *More* than kiss her, but he wasn't allowing himself to dwell on that.

That would come later, when he was alone in bed.

He felt his control unraveling, each and every second he stood by her side. To be honest, he felt a little ill himself. He had no idea how he'd manage to live in the same vicinity with this woman, the siren of his dreams.

It probably would involve a lot more trips to search for lost kin.

They entered the cave. This one was high ceilinged, with a spectacular display of mustard-colored stalactites bristling from above. He'd chosen it as the Assembly place because it was quiet, dry, and away from the main population; with a species that could hear a flutter of wings and determine without sight if it was lark or crow or pigeon, one had to take precautions.

"Friends," said Magnus into the expectant hush. "As you can see, fortune has favored us."

He watched them watch her, saw their amazement, their gladness, their relief.

And beneath it all, their fear.

His chest tightened, seeing that. Though they had good reason to be afraid, he hoped Lumina didn't notice. He turned to her. "My Lady, may I present the members of the Assembly to you?"

She looked at him askance, clearly baffled by the title and the formality. He had to press his lips together to keep from smiling. He led her forward, his fingertips just grazing her elbow, and the introductions began.

He wondered what they must look like to her as each was called, coming forward to curtsy or give a slight, respectful bow. There was Xander, Morgan's husband, black clad and bulging with both muscles and weapons, swords strapped to his back, knives on his belt and boots. An assassin, he normally had that assassin's flat killer gaze, his eyes glowing amber, but when he looked at Lumina there was only kindness there.

Next came Christian, still tall and handsome as he'd always been at close to sixty, with his wife, Ember, a shyly smiling, petite brunette. Lu stared at the woman, astonished to find a human in this place.

She wasn't the only one.

Jacqueline, known as Jack, came next. Her red hair was as fiery as her personality, befitting the woman who'd founded the Dissenter movement. Once a famous reporter in the disbanded United States, she now headed the small but ferocious group of humans dedicated to overthrowing the IF's rule and living peacefully with the *Ikati,* otherwise known as Aberrants.

Jack's husband was the very *non*human Hawk. Former Alpha of the Manaus colony that had been destroyed in Brazil—ground zero of the Flash—his mixed feelings for Lumina were clear as he stepped forward with a glower. Dark-haired and brawny, he was close in age to both Christian and his half brother Xander. Like the other two males, he still had all the potency and magnetism of his youth.

"My Lady," he said curtly. He stepped back, lips thinned. Lu shot Magnus a worried glance, but he just nodded and continued with the introductions.

Demetrius and Eliana were next. Originally from the Roman colony that had been abandoned after the Flash due to security concerns, they were the most feral of the group. Both of them were clad in their usual black leather ensembles, complete with trench coats and matching guns strapped to their thighs and waists. At over six and a half feet, Demetrius stood the tallest of all the males, his shaved head, brow piercings, and neck tattoos lending him a sinister air, but only when he wasn't looking at his wife. Lithe and porcelain-skinned, with choppy black hair dyed mostly blue, Eliana was adored by her warrior husband, and it showed in his every glance.

"*Salutem, domina,*" Eliana murmured. Lumina started, and Magnus caught her eye.

"I didn't know I spoke Latin, too," she said under her breath.

Too?

A fine sheen of frost began to form on the walls, blossoming with a crackling whisper as the temperature in the cave simultaneously dropped. Magnus turned just in time to see Honor glide silently into the room.

"You weren't going to start without me, were you?"

Though he knew she was teasing—because Honor never cared to attend an Assembly meeting—not a hint of a smile touched her lips or eyes. Which, Magnus reasoned, was a good sign. If Honor smiled it would be such a momentous occasion the Earth's axis might shift, disrupting gravity and launching them all into outer space.

A frozen heart was the only thing the two of them had in common.

"Thank you for coming," he said, inclining his head. Surprisingly, he wasn't being ironic; he actually *was* thankful she'd come. He hoped Honor and her sister might eventually grow close. Lord knew Honor could use some thawing, and Lumina . . .

He glanced back at her, concerned. She was trying valiantly to cover it, but he sensed how much it cost her to stand here, acting normal. Maybe if she and Honor spent some time together, got to know one another—

"Oh, I wouldn't miss this for the *world*," Honor said, staring hard at Lumina. While everyone else tensed, the twins sized each other up in hostile silence.

Okay, maybe "grow close" was overreaching. Maybe "not murder each other" was a better goal.

Magnus gestured to the large round table surrounded by chairs on the opposite side of the cave. "Let's sit."

Honor said, "Dear sister and I have a few things to work out first." She looked around, her frosty gaze sliding over the gathering. "Everybody might want to clear out for a bit, until we come to an understanding."

Without even looking at Lumina, he felt her bristle. The air temperature spiked; the candles in iron braziers along the walls flared up with a hiss.

Shit. Can anyone say "disaster of epic proportion"? He stepped between the two women, eliciting a low growl of displeasure from Honor.

"*Move*, Seeker," she said, deadly soft. "Or I'll make you move."

"I'm the Alpha of this colony, Honor." He controlled his tone, though all he wanted to do was wring her neck. Not that he'd survive the attempt. Not that he cared. "I'm responsible for the safety of everyone here. And you know I can't guarantee anyone's safety if you get upset."

Her eyes were the permafrost of ancient tundra, where ice never thawed and life refused to grow. By her sides, her hands flexed open, fingers twitching as if they longed to wrap around his neck. "Yes, you're the Alpha. Congratulations on being the proud owner of a *dick*."

Her voice dripped acid contempt. The answering growl that rumbled through his chest was pure reflex; he really despised it when Honor went all man-hater on him.

With a sneer, she added, "And I'm not upset. Not yet. But if you don't get out of the way in the next five seconds, I will be. And we all know what happens then."

They stared at one another, seething, until a soft voice broke their stalemate.

"You know what I hate more than anything in the world?" Lumina stepped out from behind him. She faced Honor with her shoulders back, grim determination on her face. Magnus felt a rush of admiration for her, which was quickly swallowed by panic. She had no idea what she was doing—and Honor had had a lifetime to practice her Gifts.

Her extremely *deadly* Gifts.

"Bullies," Lu finished quietly, staring Honor down. "And that's exactly what you are, isn't it? You're nothing but a big fat bully."

The harsh intakes of breath from the Assembly were loud in the silence of the cave. For a moment, Honor looked stunned, which left *him* stunned; was she . . . hurt?

"No," Honor whispered, shaking her head. "That's not . . . I'm not . . ."

"Yes, you are," Lumina insisted, stepping closer to her sister while everyone else in the room began to edge away. Christian pulled Ember against his chest, Demetrius stepped in front of Eliana, Hawk yanked Jacqueline to his side. Xander merely shook his head and muttered, "Women."

"You tried to choke me the minute we met. Why, because you didn't want any competition? You liked being the strongest one? The most powerful? So that everyone else has to do whatever you say or face the consequences?"

Honor's mouth dropped open. She looked crushed. Lost.

Between Magnus's fear at what might be imminent and his anxiety for Lumina's safety, lurked his astonishment that someone—finally—had gotten Honor to show any kind of emotion. He'd known her since she was born, and had never seen her be anything but . . . cold.

Okay, angry, too, but mostly just cold.

Lumina stepped closer to her sister, until they stood just a few feet apart. "That's it, isn't it? You like being feared." She tilted her head, examining Honor with a shrewd eye. "You know who that reminds me of?"

Don't say it, Magnus thought. *Dear God, please do not say—*

"Sebastian Thorne."

As Honor stiffened, the air in the room went frigid. Ice formed in crackling long fingers along the walls. The group behind Magnus took another few steps back.

"Well," said Honor in a furious whisper, "at least I'm not a *coward*!"

Lumina flushed, looking as if she'd been slapped. "What did you just call me?"

She'd said it slowly, enunciating every word, and Magnus knew that if he didn't intervene quickly all their lives were in peril. He said, "Ladies, this really isn't the time or the place for—"

"Butt out!" Honor and Lumina yelled in unison, and a low tremor rumbled through the floor.

Behind him, Ember squeaked in terror. Magnus held still, calculating the time and distance it would take him to get to Lumina. With his Gifts, he could get her to safety, unseen, at least giving her a chance to escape aboveground and get a head start before Honor came looking for her. His own head would be on the chopping block for it, but there was no way he was about to let Honor hurt Lumina.

So you've chosen sides after all. Apparently one of your Gifts is Epic Stupidity.

"I said you're a *coward*," snarled Honor, her mouth skewed in the identical don't-cry grimace he'd seen on Lumina so recently. "You'd rather hide out and pretend to be something you're not than be with your own kind!"

"That's a lie! I never knew where you were! I never knew who I was!"

"Because you wouldn't let me! You blocked me every single time I tried to reach you!"

"I was just trying to live my life! I was doing the best I could! I was just trying to fit in, to be normal, and not get *killed* in the process!"

They'd drawn closer to each other as if magnetized. The low rumble in the ground amplified. Around the table, the chairs rattled. A fine dusting of grit drifted down from the ceiling above, and a candelabra near the entrance toppled over, falling with a clatter to the stone.

Christian warned, "Magnus."

"Lumina. Honor. Please." Magnus eased closer to them. They ignored him, staring at each other with blatant hostility, rigid and silent, fire and ice, opposite sides of the same coin. "You can sort out your differences later, after you've both had a chance to—".

"Not get killed?" Honor repeated with an ugly laugh. "Are you *kidding* me? That's what you've been afraid of? That's what kept you living like a scared little mouse, hiding under the baseboards? Your fear of *getting killed*?"

Her voice had risen to a shout. Magnus knew his time was up; he had to act now, or risk Lumina's life. He inhaled, feeling his muscles relax into the loose readiness they always held before battle, feeling his mind sharpen, all his senses honed to the task at hand. When he exhaled, his breath frosted out in front of his face in a plume of pearlescent white.

Honor said, "Time for a reality check, little mouse."

And because his senses were so heightened, he sensed rather than saw the sword that flew through the air toward Lumina, wrenched from its sheath on Xander's back by an invisible force. It parted the air with the barest, sinister *hiss*.

He moved to leap in front of its path, but too late.

The sword punched through the space between Lumina's shoulder blades with a loud, sickening crunch of bone, burying itself to the hilt.

Everyone else in the room gasped, or shouted, or cried out in horror, including him. But Lumina only stared at Honor with parted lips, her eyes bulged wide, her face disbelieving. The blade that protruded through her breastbone spurted blood in a fast-flowing gush onto the floor.

Lumina staggered forward a step. Calmly, Honor reached out and steadied her. Then in one swift move she pulled the sword from her sister's back and tossed it aside. It skidded over the floor with the racket of metal striking stone, rocked once, and came to a standstill.

Magnus caught Lumina as she fell. He eased her to the cold floor, horror permeating every cell in his body. His mind refused to accept what he was seeing, refused to accept the impossibility that Honor had just murdered her own sister, the woman he'd spent half a lifetime searching for.

The woman he'd spent half a lifetime dreaming of.

He looked up at Honor. She stood staring dispassionately down, her white clothing splattered with a lurid spray of crimson, while Lumina lay warm and still in his arms. He growled—a savage, threatening sound that reverberated off the walls—but Honor's only reaction was the slightest flicker in the depths of her eyes. Her anger seemed to be cooling in degrees, keeping time with the blood pulsing from the gash on her sister's sternum. She knelt down, watching Lumina's face, intently watching the light drain from her eyes.

Lumina's lids fluttered shut. Her breath rattled to a stop, then she fell perfectly still.

Magnus had never hated anyone in his life as much as he hated Honor in that moment. His hatred was a thing inside his chest, a pressure, a volcanic heat—

"Don't get your panties in a wad, Seeker," Honor muttered, shooting him an icy glare. "I know what I'm doing. Demonstrations are always more effective than conversations. Have a little faith, will you?"

What?

Honor reached out, and lightly slapped Lumina's cheek. When that produced no response, she tugged—not gently—on a lock of her sister's hair. "Hey. Drama queen. Get over yourself. We've got work to do."

There was a long, terrible silence. Lumina's blood was splashed on his hands, his clothing, all over the stone beneath his knees. He was finding it hard to breathe, hard to think, but he knew beyond his fury and panic and crushing sense of loss—was that even rational, to mourn for a woman he didn't know?—that he was missing something. Something Honor obviously knew, but he didn't.

Something that caused a faint glimmer of hope to flare in his chest.

It was at that moment that Lumina coughed. Her body was wracked by a deep shudder. She sucked in a ragged breath, and opened her eyes.

Lumina stared up at Honor with a frown of confusion, and Magnus's heart skidded to a dead stop inside his chest.

With the single most satisfied smile Magnus had ever seen, Honor said, "Happy birthday, Sunshine. Welcome to the first day of the rest of your life."

Gasping, Lumina touched her chest. She yanked down the collar of her blood-soaked shirt, and stared; the gash that had been pumping blood only seconds before had entirely vanished.

She looked up at Magnus, and he waited to hear what she would say with his heart now pounding like a jackhammer in his chest.

Her lips quirked. On a faint, exhausted sigh, she said, "So, about that drink . . ."

PART TWO

PART TWO

TWELVE

The clipped footsteps that echoed down the corridor leading to the lone cell on the bottom floor of the prison were measured and precise, as regular as the mechanical tick of a time bomb counting down the seconds until doom into the silence.

Four. Three. Two. One.

Never hurried. Never slow. Never a single alteration in pace over all the years the slight, stooped man with silver hair and dead eyes had visited. Just that slow, rehearsed, bride-down-the-aisle-wedding-march approach, joyless and inevitable as death.

Ticktock. Ticktock. Ticktock.

The woman lying in wait for the man with the precise footsteps couldn't stop the bitter smile that curved the outer corner of her lips. *Thursday again*, she thought. *Nothing if not predictable.*

His appearance was the only way she knew which day of the week it was. No clocks or calendars decorated the walls—nothing, in fact, decorated the walls—but once at the beginning of her incarceration, he'd let it slip on his way out that he'd be back to see her next Thursday. From then on she hadn't needed a calendar to tell her what the day was; she had one in her head.

Today marked the thirteen hundredth Thursday she'd spent in this cell.

From the simple cot that folded down from the wall, she rose to a sitting position and thrust her bare feet into a pair of cotton slippers. Her plain white shift was of the same material, and had no zipper or even a single button. It was one piece, sleeveless, and fell just above her knees. Her captors had never even given her underwear, and she still couldn't decide if they thought she might somehow be able to use a bra and panties as weapons, if it was a psychological tactic designed to make her feel vulnerable, or if it was simply spite.

Her gut voted for spite.

She folded her hands in her lap, closed her eyes, and inhaled. Listening. Scenting the air. Even three state-of-the-art airlocks and a perfectly seamless lead box couldn't contain every single atom of nitrogen and oxygen, and a few was all she needed.

Sweat. A stronger odor of smoke than usual. Stress phero-mones, sickly sweet like overripe fruit.

Hmm. Doctor Evil's agitated today.

She hoped someone close to him had died. Painfully.

She lowered herself to the floor and began to do pushups, partly because it was her routine to exercise upon awakening, but mostly because she knew Dr. Evil absolutely *hated* to be forced to wait for her heart rate to return to normal before he could perform his unwelcome task.

By the time he'd passed through the final airlock and entered her cell, she was up to thirty-six. He stopped and waited by the door, silently watching, as she continued from thirty-seven to one hundred, counting aloud because that really annoyed him, too.

He wasn't the only one watching. She was always watched, monitored by camera and audio, her every move recorded. She'd long ago become accustomed to it; all sense of modesty had fled along with her sanity, and she didn't mind that they watched when she ate and slept and showered, watched when she went to the toilet, watched when she cleaned the blood from her thighs when she had her period because tampons had been refused. She even let them watch when she touched herself in bed, because an orgasm was the single thing of luxury or pleasure in her life. And she hoped whoever was watching was disgusted by it, and by her.

It was a small sort of rebellion, but it was all she had.

When she was done with her pushups, she rose and faced the man.

He didn't look pleased, which was no surprise. The surprise was that he was empty-handed.

He waited for her to speak. When she didn't he said, "No exam today, madam."

He always called her that. He was an evil little fucker, but she had to admit, his manners were impeccable.

She stayed silent, enjoying the look of irritation that flickered over his face. No doubt he'd hoped she'd weep with joy, or thank him, or even have the decency to look relieved.

Instead she kept her expression as bland as her cotton shift, and waited. She'd become an expert at that, and knew that almost anything you needed to know could be determined by watching, waiting, and keeping your mouth shut.

In her mind, she imagined crushing his sternum with her teeth, ripping his heart from his chest, and devouring the still-pumping organ while he looked on in helpless horror. It brought a faint smile to her face.

"This way, please." He gestured to the airlock. The door slid open with a near-silent *siss* of pressurized air, and her flat expression vanished along with her determination not to speak.

"*Out*? Why? What's happening?"

Dr. Evil said, "The Chairman has sent for you," and she knew from both his tone and the spike in his heartbeat what a bad idea he thought it.

Explains all the extra cigarettes he's smoked in the last few hours. She wondered just how long and how vigorously he'd argued against allowing their most valuable prisoner out of her cell.

But what did the Chairman want? Why, after all these years, would he summon her?

This was one case where waiting and watching wouldn't help; she'd have to go and find out.

But first a bit of fun.

Faster than he could move or scream or even blink, she crossed the room and was at his side, smiling. "Well, we don't want to keep the Chairman waiting, do we?" she breathed into his face, and gently laid her hand on his arm. Beneath his starched lab coat, it shook.

"Harm me and you only harm yourself, you know that, madam," said Dr. Evil, his eyes wide and terrified, his voice doing no better than his arm. In fact, his whole body was shaking.

How many years had it been since she'd attacked him? She didn't remember exactly; a decade at least. Maybe two. With the collar someone had fitted around her throat when she'd been unconscious when first brought to this facility, she couldn't Shift, and therefore was far less of a threat, but she still had her speed and her strength, which had been enough to beat him bloody on more than one occasion.

So long ago, though. He probably thought since she was past fifty now and had been docile as a lamb for years, all the fight had been leached out of her. He probably thought the memory of what they did to her when she acted out or disobeyed had weakened her will, that perhaps the all-too-vivid recollections of billy clubs and stun guns and high-voltage electrodes against her temples had been an effective deterrent.

Wrong.

"I know," she said lightly, "but at least this time it will be worth it." She placed her hands on either side of his head.

It took only a single sharp twist, and it was done. Dr. Evil slid to the floor, tongue protruding, eyes still wide and terrified.

His shaking, however, had stopped.

Twenty-five years of needles, poking, and invasive examinations by this man, ended with a flick of her wrists. Wondering who they'd send as a replacement, she calmly went and sat on the bed.

A disembodied male voice came over an invisible speaker. "Subject. Lie face down on the floor and put your hands behind your back."

Subject. Not prisoner or citizen or even her own name. *Subject* was meant to remind her that she was property, a thing owned by people more powerful than she, a lowly peasant beholden to a sovereign under the theory of the divine right of kings.

She wasn't a peasant, though. She was a Queen, no matter what they called her.

She did as she was told. In a few moments, through the airlocks filed a team of hulking men with rifles. Dressed in combat black, they wore face shields, gloves, and boots, so not a single inch of skin was visible. Not even their eyes were visible behind the mirrored shields.

While the others kept their gun sights trained on her, one of them put a knee to her back and cuffed her. He hauled her to her feet. Without a word—and, curiously, without a glance at the body on the floor—he shoved her ahead of him into the first airlock. Four men stepped in behind them, and the doors slid shut.

A *whoosh* of suction from above, that same *siss* of pressurized air when the rear doors had closed, and another set of doors in front of her opened. A rifle poked into the small of her back, which she took as an invitation to step forward.

Once through all three airlocks, she stood blinking in a long, bright, sterile corridor. More of the black-clad men with rifles lined either side, down its entire length. She said loudly into the silence, "Not a great plan, boys, lining up on both sides. How many do you think would be killed in a cross fire?"

This caused more than a few of the men along the walls to shift their weight from one booted foot to the other.

"Move," said the guard with the gun at her back, and so, more curious than anything, she did.

The room the guards led her to required a long elevator trip, but the ride was so smooth and swift she couldn't tell whether it went up or down. Another lighted corridor, another row of men with guns, a short stairway carpeted in plush, ivory wool, and then she stood before a set of polished wood doors. The doors opened, and she looked in.

The room was big, but the time she'd spent in her cell made it seem cavernous. Decorated in muted tones of ivory and gold, the furniture, carpeting, draperies, and silk-paneled walls were all of the finest quality, which her eyes, so long denied anything of beauty, drank in.

A guard uncuffed her, and said, "In."

She stepped forward a few feet, then stopped, shucked off the cotton slippers, and went on, stifling a moan at the silky decadence of the carpet against her bare soles. The doors closed behind her with a quiet *snick*.

The main room opened to another: a formal dining room, complete with a glittering crystal chandelier. Beyond that was a gleaming kitchen she didn't approach; she turned instead the other direction and found a master suite right out of *Architectural Digest*. A curving staircase led her to the second floor, where the dramatic strains of Bach's Toccata and Fugue in D Minor for organ playing through wall speakers teased a wry smile to her lips.

Phantom of the Opera music. Someone had a sense of humor.

She recognized the Monet above the fireplace, the Renoir above the sofa in the sitting area, the exquisite little bronze Degas ballerina on a lighted stand against one wall. A profusion of white roses scented every room, bursting from vases of bone china and marble, and after so many years of smelling nothing but antiseptic and dead air and the sour human smells of the man who came to visit her on Thursdays, the lush perfume of fresh flowers was so welcome she had to stand still for a moment, inhaling greedily, drunk with the unexpected pleasure of it.

She'd had money once, a great deal of it, and knew that every piece of art and furniture in this place had been carefully selected by someone with a vast amount of wealth, and perhaps an even greater sense of style.

But it was the view that really moved her.

One entire wall of the second floor was composed of windows, floor-to-ceiling glass that showcased in the most brilliant, stunning detail the long white strip of sand and the glimmering ocean that loomed beyond. The sky was ablaze with purple, lavender, and crimson, the most spectacular sunset she'd ever seen. As she watched, a pod of dolphins broke the surface of a cresting wave, sailed weightlessly for a heartbeat, then sliced back into the water, disappearing without a trace.

The sight made moisture well in her eyes. She'd swum as a dolphin only once, but it had been one of the greatest joys of her life.

Where on Earth was this place?

Behind her, someone said, "I knew you lived by the beach when you were a young woman. Venice, wasn't it?"

She whirled around, stunned that she'd been so engrossed she hadn't even heard anyone enter. There stood a man, tall, slender and sophisticated in a beautifully cut suit of deepest royal blue.

"Jenna," he said warmly, his voice a rich, seductive baritone, "I've wanted to meet you in person for so long."

He was neither handsome nor ugly, but rather . . . *interesting*, with the kind of features that wouldn't stand alone well under close examination—his nose was too long, his lips too thin, his hairline asymmetrical—but when brought together managed a pleasing, oddly trust-inspiring harmony. It brought to mind a respected newscaster, or a beloved character actor rather than a movie star. He was slightly stoop-shouldered, and his close-cropped pale hair and veined hands belied the age his smooth facial skin tried to hide, but he exuded the robustness and vitality of a far younger man.

You're seventy if you're a day, thought Jenna. Vain bastard.

The color of his suit perfectly matched his eyes. She wondered if it was intentional.

"Funny," she said, "I would have thought you'd choose the word *torture* instead of *meet*."

He ignored that and moved closer with a slow, easy stride that telegraphed he had no fear of her. He didn't smell of fear, either. Surprisingly.

"Technology," he said as he searched her face, correctly guessing her thoughts. "There are as many things in this suite that can kill you in an instant, if I deem it, as there are flowers in that vase." He gestured to a nearby urn dripping roses.

"Only ninety-seven? In all this space?" She looked around. "I'd think you'd want a little more coverage per square foot."

The man frowned at the vase. "There should be one hundred roses in that vase. In every vase." He didn't seem at all surprised that she was able to calculate the exact number in a passing glance.

"Guess the florist miscounted. Are you going to chop off his head? Or just stick him with a few electrodes and turn up the juice?"

Her withering tone didn't rile him. Instead, he offered her an apologetic smile. It actually looked sincere. "I regret the necessity of using force on you, Jenna. I'm not a violent man. But you must admit, it was only when you yourself provoked it."

"Strange how I wouldn't like being a prisoner. It's such a wonderful way to spend one's life."

Was that smile of his now *admiring*? He lowered his head and looked at her through his lashes, something she'd only ever known simpering heroines in romance novels to do. "He said you were a spitfire," he murmured, and she grimaced at the thought of Dr. Evil describing her that way. It sounded much too . . . chummy. And grossly familiar.

He shook his head. "Please forgive me. I haven't properly introduced myself. I'm Sebastian Thorne." He had the nerve to proffer his hand.

Jenna said quietly, "I know who you are. And I'm sure you realize I can easily crush your hand if I wanted to. Or a whole lot of other things I doubt you'd appreciate having crushed." She managed not to glance at his crotch, but only just.

Without lowering his arm, he said, "Yes, my associate now cooling on the floor of your cell is proof enough of that. However, you'd be dead before you could do any real damage to me. And I think you're going to want to stay alive to hear my proposition."

Still not afraid, just calm, cool, confident. She almost envied him his composure; she herself was feeling the first stirrings of an array of unpleasant emotions. He didn't seem to care one whit she'd murdered his associate. Another "subject," no doubt.

"You can't really think I would shake the hand of my arch enemy."

His brows pulled together. He lowered his arm, looking—the *asshole!*—wounded.

"There's no need for us to be enemies, Jenna. In fact, I'd like to think we can become good friends." He walked slowly to the windows, and clasped his hands behind his back as he contemplated the view. His tone offhand, he said, "As Leander and I have become."

Everything inside her ground to a halt.

Leander! *Leander*! *Leander*! It began slapping against the inside of her skull, that name so long unspoken aloud, the name of the man she loved more than anything else in the world, and always would, regardless that she hadn't seen him since she came to this place. He'd been ripped from her arms in that hellhole jungle in Brazil, both of them wounded and no longer able to fight, and she hadn't seen him since.

He was here, somewhere nearby? And had been, all this time? And—she swallowed back the acid taste of bile in her throat— Sebastian Thorne and he were *friends*?

It was a trick. A lie. It had to be.

Only the thing was . . . he didn't smell like he was lying. Everything in his posture and scent and bodily functions said he was telling the truth.

Very slowly, Jenna lowered herself to a nearby chair, just looking at Thorne. Waiting silently, while the animal inside her screamed for blood.

Still to the windows, he said, "One of my Enforcement operatives in New Prague captured one of your kind three weeks ago. Name of Alejandro Luna." He turned his head and peered at her, his blue eyes as fathomless as the deepest reaches of space. "You know him."

She did. Once the Alpha of the Brazil colony, Alejandro had been bested by his half-brother Hawk in a ritual power challenge. Alejandro disappeared into the jungle in shame just days before the attack by Thorne's men, and she never knew what had happened to him.

"He was quite the fount of information, that one," Thorne added with a faint, knowing smile, making Jenna's skin prickle with dread.

She'd met Alejandro a lifetime ago when she'd gone to Sommerley in search of answers about her father's disappearance. She hadn't known what she was then, had only had her dead mother's cryptic warnings of "If they ever find you, run," as a guide. She'd been living in the human world with a human mother back in the days when all that meant was that she was different, not marked for death. In the days when what she wanted more than anything else in the world was to solve the mystery of what had happened to her father, and had followed a beautiful stranger named Leander all the way to England to find the answer. Alejandro had visited them there, as had the Alphas of the other colonies, as they tried to determine if she was friend or foe.

So yes, she knew him. And he knew her.

He knew *all* about her.

Thorne said softly, "Tell me the locations of the rest of the *Ikati*, and you and Leander will be reunited. You can live here," he swept out his arm, "in luxury and peace for the rest of your lives. With your daughters."

Her heartbeat, loud as thunder. Tremors in her arms and legs, her mouth as dry as bone.

"We already know the whereabouts of one of your daughters. Lumina, she calls herself. She's incredibly powerful, that one. Blew up a good portion of New Vienna the other day. She escaped, but we're tracking her." His gaze flicked to the collar around Jenna's neck. He met her eyes again. "It's only a matter of time. But you can expedite that process, because you know exactly where she is, don't you? And where your other daughter is. And where each and every single *Ikati* on the face of this Earth is, right at this very moment." His voice had grown softer and softer, until his final words were so hushed they were nothing but a breath of air past his lips.

"Don't you."

It wasn't a question. It was a statement of fact, because one of her many Gifts was that of Sight, and it allowed her to not only See inside people's minds with a touch, but also to locate any living creature anywhere who had even a small percentage of *Ikati* Blood flowing through his or her veins.

Without the collar, she could See. With it, she was blind.

"You're lying," she said in a tremulous voice, watching him, smelling him, looking for any tic or tell that what he was saying was false.

There was none.

"I believe you can ascertain perfectly well if I'm lying or not," he answered, still with that intimate whisper. "My offer is genuine. When Alejandro told us what you could do, I had this suite constructed in less than two weeks. Everything you can ever need is here; most anything you desire will be provided to you, you have only to ask. Your freedom will be restricted, of course, but I had my engineers design this interactive data screen specifically with you in mind. I call it the Oracle. It's operated solely by voice; just tell it what you'd like to see and you can go anywhere in the world." Without taking his gaze from her, he raised his voice and said, "Phuket."

On the screens she'd thought were windows, a crystalline lagoon appeared, dotted with colorful canoes. Beach, sand, craggy cliffs covered with trees, fluffy white clouds freckling the sky.

"Fiji."

A sun-bleached dock stretched over blue water. A thatched hut sat empty on the sand off in the distance. More fluffy clouds.

Thorne smiled. "It's all pre-Flash imagery, of course. We had to really dig deep to recover all the data. It works for any spot on Earth, but since you grew up near the beach . . ." He shrugged. The casual smugness of it made her want to kill him so badly she had to bite her lip, hard, to distract herself.

Because what if—*what if*—what he'd said before was actually true? About Leander? About the girls?

Jenna closed her eyes, fighting hard to maintain her control. She didn't want this man to see her fall to pieces. She stayed like that for a silent count of ten, until Thorne said something that made her open her eyes.

"Your daughter is lovely, Jenna. She obviously gets that from you." He reached inside his jacket, withdrew an envelope and stood there fingering it, staring down at her with a predatory light in his gaze. "Would you like to see a picture of her?"

A sob stuck in the back of her throat. She raised a hand and covered her mouth, afraid of what would come out. A sudden hot prick of tears flooded her eyes.

"Here," he said softly, and removed a photograph from the envelope. He held it out between two fingers, and, for the first time in twenty-five years, Jenna broke down and cried.

The camera had caught the image of a young woman running. Her arms and legs were bent in a way that suggested she was moving fast, and at the exact moment of the shot, neither of her feet was touching the ground. Her hair—long, braided—streamed out behind her in a blurred streak of gold. Her face was turned toward the camera, suggesting she'd been just about to look over her shoulder, and Thorne was right: She was lovely. Lovely and fierce, because Jenna knew deep in her guts that this picture had been snapped when she was being chased, but there wasn't a trace of fear in her eyes. If anything, she looked almost exhilarated.

Her baby. A grown woman now.

All those years, lost.

"It was taken by surveillance cameras so the quality is a little poor, but there are others." He removed another photo from the envelope. This one was posed, official-looking, featuring a slightly younger looking version of the girl in the first photo staring directly into the camera.

"This is from her work identification badge. That's how we discovered her; she didn't seem to be able to keep her . . . powers until control." His voice grew as gentle as his eyes. "Tell me where the *Ikati* are hiding, Jenna, and I promise you I will return your daughters to you. Unharmed."

Fury flashed over her, scalding hot, and Jenna's face burned beneath the stream of tears. He'd stolen so much from her—husband, children, family, home—the most precious things in any woman's life, including years that could never be retrieved. And why?

Simply because he could.

She stood, not caring about her tears, the way her hands were shaking, or the way her voice broke when she vowed, "Someday I'm going to end your life, Sebastian Thorne. For every year you've taken from me, for everything you've done, one day I'll watch the light go out of your eyes and then I'll spit on your corpse. I will *never* cooperate with you."

He slid the photos back into the envelope. He placed the envelope back into his coat pocket. He turned to the Oracle. "Bring up subject four-nine-eight-six."

The wall of glass flashed black, then showed the interior of a cell exactly like the one she'd just left. A man reclined on the folding cot, his back against the wall, a leg folded beneath him, the other stretched out to the floor. Bare-chested and barefoot, lean and leonine, he was reading a book. Thick black hair brushed his broad shoulders, a week's worth of beard shaded his jaw. The image appeared to be static, the man held so still, but then he turned a page of his book and Jenna fell to her knees on the plush ivory carpet and let out a scream of anguish so primal and raw Sebastian Thorne took a few steps back in alarm.

She sobbed, "Oh God—*Leander*!"

"You can put your family back together, Jenna," said Thorne urgently. "Just tell me what I want to know and he'll be transferred here immediately. As soon as we have your daughters, they'll be brought here as well."

Violent sobs wracked her body. She hugged herself, rocking, crying, unable to look away from the image on the screen.

Alive. He was alive! The love of her life and the father of her children was *alive*!

Or was he? Could this be another trick?

"How do I know that's even him? This video could be years old! He could be dead by now!"

Thorne nodded. "Fair enough." To the Oracle he directed, "Bidirectional audio on." There was a short burst of static, then he said to the screen, "Good morning, Leander," and the man in the video jerked up his head.

He carefully laid aside his book. "Thorne."

The tone, pitched low and commanding, the British accent evident even in the single word he'd spoken; she'd know that voice anywhere.

Jenna couldn't breathe. Her lungs refused to do their work. She only stared at the screen, her mouth open, her face wet, her body frozen in place.

Thorne said, "I have someone here who'd like to speak with you," and looked at Jenna.

She tried to form a sentence. She tried to think of the words that could convey the depths of her agony and wretchedness and longing, but in the end she came up with only one.

"Love."

It was a hoarse whisper, but it was enough.

Leander leapt from the bed, his face transformed from wary to tormented, craving, disbelieving. "Jenna! Jenna!"

Thorne said, "Bidirectional audio off," and Leander's voice went silent, though she could see he was still calling out her name. She closed her eyes and bowed her head to block out the image of him stalking wildly around the cell, mutely shouting at the ceiling and walls.

"Why now?" she whispered. "After all this time . . . why now?"

She heard Thorne move to the other side of the room. He sat in a chair, crossed his legs. "Because now the Phoenix Corporation is approximately fifteen days away from replicating the specific aspects of your DNA that we've so successfully used in our patented medicines."

When she raised her head and looked at him, he was smiling blandly at her, hands folded in his lap.

"Now, my dear lady, we don't really need you at all. This entire facility can be shut down. And all four thousand nine hundred eighty-seven subjects in it can be terminated."

Her lips parted, but no sound came out. On the screen behind Thorne, Leander upended a table, shredded the book, tore the thin mattress from the folding cot and ripped it to pieces in his bare hands.

"You can't save them, but you can save yourself, and your daughters. And," he glanced at the Oracle, watched for a moment as Leander took the single metal chair in the room and began slamming it against a wall, over and over, until it crumpled in his hands, "you can save him." He turned his gaze to her again. "But if you don't tell me where the rest of your kind are hiding, I will kill your entire family, and I'll make you watch while I do. Then, of course, I'll kill you."

I thought you said you weren't violent.

She didn't realize she'd spoken aloud until he answered her, explaining as one would to a child. "It's a figure of speech. When I say 'I'll kill you,' I'm referring to one of my minions, of course."

He actually calls them minions, she thought, stupefied. But he was still talking.

"I prefer to leave such distasteful things to hired specialists. Like another associate of mine you might recall: a certain legless, one-armed zealot named Two? You're right; you wouldn't know him by that name. He was promoted from Thirteen when he successfully captured you. Everyone in the Corporation has a number indicating his status in the hierarchy; I find that much more straightforward than titles. He's also known in the Corporation as Agent Doe, or simply the Doctor, but the general public know him as the Grand Minister. He's a former German special forces soldier whose mother was mauled to death in front of his face when he was a child by a tiger at the circus." He shuddered. "Can you imagine? Well, it certainly explains his pathological hatred of cats. His loss, my gain. And so it goes with life."

This didn't make sense. What was she missing? She knelt before him silently, awaiting the explanation she knew would be forthcoming. And because he was carefully watching every emotion that played over her face, it was.

"You can't imagine the cost and effort I've invested over the years into capturing your people, Jenna. If you give me the location of the remaining free Aberrants, I'll no longer have to expend energy chasing them down. My ultimate goal will be complete."

"Ultimate goal," she repeated, trying not to look at the screen, her heart flayed open inside her chest.

His trustworthy newscaster face broke into a grin. "The extermination of your entire species." He let that sink in a moment, then added, "But in exchange for pointing me in the direction of the rest of your wayward kin, I'm willing to let you and your immediate family live out the rest of your natural lives together, here. I think it's the least I can do for your helping me achieve my goal."

Her mind was splitting apart. The earth was lurching to and fro beneath her. Everything in the room was on the brink of exploding into pieces. "How would you know I was telling you the truth? How would you know I wasn't holding something back, letting a few of them go, pretending to give you what you want?"

"Oh, that." He waved a hand dismissively. "Rest assured the Phoenix Corporation has the technology for making sure a subject is telling us the truth, the whole truth, and nothing but the truth. Your friend Alejandro can attest to that." He paused. "If he were still alive, that is."

Jenna whispered, "And how do I know you'll keep your end of the bargain? That you'll bring my family to me if I do tell you what you want to know . . . that you'll keep us alive longer than even a day?"

His smile faded. He gazed at her in contemplative silence for a moment. "I wasn't always a businessman, Jenna. I didn't always want to rule the world. I had a family once upon a time. A wife, a daughter, both of whom I loved very much." His face clouded. "They were taken from me by a simple fault of human biology. A rare neurological disorder my daughter inherited from my wife. We're so frail, humanity. So many things can go wrong with a body. So many diseases can rob us of our lives. Even a wrong step off a curb can spell disaster; the tiniest jolt to the head, applied in just the right spot, can end us altogether!"

He seemed outraged by the thought. He looked at her and his gaze grew fierce. "But *you* . . . you're different. You're not plagued by disease. Viruses, bacteria, fungus, sickness, you're immune to them all. You heal faster, you age slower. Your strength, speed, and agility are vastly superior to ours, you have powers we've never even imagined." He sat forward in his chair, rested his elbows on his thighs, and threaded his fingers together. "I'm man enough to admit that your species is, for all intents and purposes, better than mine.

But I'm also intelligent enough to foresee the inevitable decline of humanity inherent in that reality. It's the most powerful universal law of them all: survival of the fittest. Even though we vastly outnumber you, evolution would eventually win. The *Ikati* would claw their way up to the top of the food chain."

He leaned back. "Unless, of course, one of the species on a lower rung took them out before they could."

Her laugh sounded insane, even to her own ears. "And so Sebastian Thorne single-handedly saves the human race."

He shrugged, unapologetic. "Yes. Well, with help from the minions, of course."

"That still doesn't answer my question; how do I know you'll keep your end of the bargain?"

He seemed pleased she was considering it.

Was she considering it? Was she only buying a few more precious seconds with Leander, even if he couldn't see or hear her? What was she doing? She didn't know. The universe was imploding inside her mind. All the stars were blinking out.

"I didn't get to where I am in life by burning bridges, Jenna. I keep my promises. But beyond that . . . as I said before, I think you can tell when someone's lying. I think with all your enhanced senses you just *know*. So look at my face. Look into my eyes. Listen to my voice."

He leaned forward again, and this time his newscaster smile didn't make an appearance. Solemnly, he said, "I promise you I will reunite you with your family, and allow you to live here in this suite, unharmed, in peace, for the remainder of all of your lives. If you or your husband die before your children, they will be left alone until they die of natural causes, or old age, however it is you normally die. You will never again want for anything; only the freedom to leave these rooms will be denied."

He spoke the truth, or at least he ardently believed what he was saying.

And all she had to do to hold Leander and her children in her arms again was condemn each and every one of her species aside from them to death.

Her silence displeased him. He said, "Perhaps I can help you make up your mind." In a quick, elegant motion, he snapped his fingers.

Behind him, the Oracle showed a swarm of guards enter Leander's cell. They surrounded him, threw him down, began to beat him with fists and boots and billy clubs. He fought back—*still so strong*—but there were so many of them, and only one of him, and she knew it wouldn't be long before they beat him to death.

The snarl of fury that ripped from her throat echoed through the room. She jumped to her feet and lunged at Thorne.

Jenna was frozen mid-lunge by a stinging pain in her arm that instantly paralyzed her. The room slipped sideways, and as she looked in horror down at the tiny silver dart sticking out of her bicep, she heard him say in a reasonable manner, "Why don't I give you a few days to think about it. I'll even be generous, and wait a week." He smiled, and Jenna had never seen anything as soulless. "After that, the exterminations begin." He pointed to the Oracle. "Beginning with *him*."

Then the floor came up hard to catch her, and all the world went black.

THIRTEEN

The sound that slipped between Lumina's chapped lips was a combination *kill me* groan and weak *give me water* plea for help. She sat up in bed, hand to her forehead, and concentrated on keeping the contents of her stomach down.

Memories of last night and Jack's potent potato vodka came back with strobe light, gut-lurching clarity. The *kill me* groan enjoyed an encore.

"You're awake."

Lu glanced up to see Magnus leaning against the arched doorway of her bedchamber, watching her with an expression both concerned and strangely intense.

How long has he been there?

"Unfortunately, yes. *Ugh.*" She swallowed what felt like a mouthful of garbage and stuck out her tongue, repulsed by the taste in her mouth. She fought the unwelcome feeling she might not want to know exactly what had happened during the last few hours of her day yesterday, which at this point were engulfed in a black, throbbing fog of hurt.

Magnus pushed away from the wall and walked closer. "I told you that was rotgut vodka."

Her answering groan made him chuckle. If she hadn't been in so much pain, she would have done a double take and stared; it was the first time she'd heard him make a happy sound.

She liked it. She wanted to hear him do it again.

"Excuse me, but *you're* the one who suggested it. You said, and I quote, 'It will put you right in the head.' Which would only make sense if by *right* you meant dementia? Or maybe a coma?"

As she'd hoped, Lu was rewarded with that chuckle. Low, deep, and wonderfully masculine, it sent a little thrill through her body, which unfortunately made her want to lean over and retch. She grimaced, cradling her stomach.

"I suppose I should've given you better warning. Jack is Irish on both parents' sides; they don't make alcohol for the faint of heart."

"Or the faint of stomach, either." Lu rubbed slow circles over her belly, eying the glossy fur coverlet on the bed, worried it might soon be ruined. She'd never had a hangover before in her life, and could imagine few things worse.

All right, she *could* imagine a few things worse, but not self-inflicted things.

"Is it really that bad?" Magnus crossed the room and stood over the bed, looking down at her with his brows pulled together, all traces of humor vanished. "Are you going to be sick?"

Lu had to slowly inhale and exhale a few times before she could answer. "I think so." She nodded, which made the room lurch in a really bad way. "Uh-oh."

In a swift, sudden movement, Magnus knelt beside the bed. He said, "Look at me."

She did, and found him staring at her in intense concentration.

He didn't move, touch her, or say anything else, but her queasy stomach and pounding head abruptly settled, and the fatigue, dry mouth, and allover body aches that accompanied them were just as suddenly gone, too. From one second to the next, she went from feeling sick to feeling great.

"Huh," said Lu. "Okay, *that's* weird."

Magnus just stared at her. She swallowed, stretched her neck one way then the other, and sat up straighter, inhaling a deep breath.

He said, "How do you feel now?" and she slanted him a look.

"You did something." Her soft accusation didn't faze him. Strangely, though, he'd begun to turn a little . . . green. Realization hit her like a thunderbolt, and Lu gasped. "Magnus!"

He winced, closed his eyes. "Not so loud, please." He pinched the bridge of his nose between two fingers, making a grumble of distress in his throat.

"You . . . you take away pain? That's your *Gift*?"

His full lips twisted. He cracked open an eye and looked at her. He said, "One of them. This particular one has a few unfortunate side effects," then his face crumpled. "Jesus, woman, exactly how *much* did you drink last night?"

Lu swung her legs over the side of the bed, wanting to touch him but knowing he wouldn't want her to, wanting to comfort him but not knowing how. "Magnus, you didn't have to do that! It's *my* fault, you shouldn't have to—"

"I'm sorry, am I interrupting something?"

The young man standing in her bedchamber door was about her age, broad, blond, and ridiculously good-looking, with a soft glow around his head that seemed to be coming from behind him. He looked between her and Magnus, a little unsure, but Magnus shoved himself to his feet and growled, "No, Beckett. I was just leaving."

Lu begged, "Magnus, please, wait—"

"I brought these for you," he said gruffly, and dropped two

pairs of gloves on the small table beside her bed. He turned and strode stiffly from the room without looking back before she could ask him again to stay.

As Magnus brushed past him in the doorway, Beckett grinned at him, flashing a dimple in his cheek.

In response, Magnus growled.

Beckett didn't seem to mind. He turned his attention to Lu and held out the bundle he carried in his arms. "My aunt asked me to bring you these. She said badass chicks deserve badass threads." His rakish grin deepened. "I couldn't agree more."

"Your aunt?" She craned her neck to see around him, but Magnus was gone. How could she thank him for what he'd done for her? Especially if he kept running away?

"Morgan. Well, she's not technically my aunt, but we're tight. I've called her that since I was a kid." He noted the confused expression on her face. "Oh, shit, sorry, where are my manners?" He bowed from the waist, then straightened and said formally, "Beckett McLoughlin, at your service, My Lady. It's my sincere pleasure to make your acquaintance. Welcome."

McLoughlin. That was one of the names Magnus had called her: Hope Catherine Moore McLoughlin. She looked at Beckett, intrigued by a new possibility.

"So we're related? Are you my . . . brother?"

For a moment Beckett looked appalled. "No! I mean . . ." he cleared his throat, rearranging his expression to one slightly more composed. "My father and your father are brothers. You met my parents at the Assembly meeting. Ember and Christian? He's my dad."

"Oh. So we're cousins, then!"

Beckett seemed to have some kind of a problem with her being related to him, because his look soured. He said grudgingly, "Well, *technically*. Yes."

She didn't understand the subtext here, but without the

hangover clouding her mind and wreaking havoc with her body, Lu suddenly remembered the event that had caused her to want to get so blindly drunk.

She'd died, and been resurrected.

Correction: She'd been *killed*, and been resurrected.

Payback's gonna be a bitch, Honor, she thought angrily. Then with a flash of horror: *Am I a zombie now?*

Looking at her expression, Beckett's face fell. "I'll just leave these for you—"

"I'm sorry, it's not you. It's not you at all. I just . . ." She stared at his expectant expression, feeling competing urges to laugh, cry, and dive deep into bed, pull the covers over her head, and never reemerge. She blurted, "I died yesterday, Beckett. *Twice.*"

He considered her, his expression serious. "I know." He paused a beat, then broke into another of his seemingly endless supply of grins. "Is that *awesome*, or what?"

Lu ran her hands over her hair, realizing there wasn't a mirror in this room, and she had no idea what she looked like. Was her skin zombie gray? No, her hands and arms were the normal color. She had to assume her face looked normal, too. She put her hand over her heart; still beating.

"May I?" Beckett gestured to the clothing in his arms, and glanced at the end of her bed. Why someone hadn't thought to put a chair or a dresser in the room, she had no idea.

She nodded, and he came forward and laid the clothes at the foot of the bed. He retreated to the door, keeping his eyes to the ground, not turning but instead walking backward, until he was again at the arched entrance.

Finally he looked up at her, smiling as if he'd just won a million water credits. His teeth were spectacularly white.

"If you're up for it, a bunch of us are going hunting topside later. You're welcome to join in."

Lu's brain closed around the word *topside* with an almost audible snap. She pictured the cloud-wreathed peaks she'd seen on the flight here, she pictured emerald forests and cool, shady glens. But there was another word he'd spoken, a word that made her mouth water and her blood quicken in the most wonderful way.

"Hunting?"

"There's only so much fish you can eat," he said with a laugh. "Topside there's rabbit and birds and even red deer." He laughed again, this one softer. "Though I pretty much always let the deer get away."

"Why's that?"

His eyes shone in the low light. "Because it's the chase I love. If a deer gives me a wonderful chase, I give the deer its life in return. I let it go." He shrugged, a little sheepishly it seemed. "But I figure it's a fair trade."

Knowing she was missing something again, Lu frowned at him, but he was backing out the door.

"So, are you in?"

His expression was so hopeful she couldn't deny him. "Sure. It's a date."

His eyes darkened. "A date," he repeated softly, holding her gaze. Then he abruptly turned and left.

On his way back to the small, dark cave where he slept—he couldn't even call it *home* because that would imply some kind of warm, pleasant space filled with good memories—Magnus ran into Morgan, hurrying through the cool passageway with a large bundle of towels in her arms.

"Oh! Magnus! I'm glad to see you; I was just going to take these to Hope and show her where the bathing pool is. Will you please help me—"

"Lumina," he said through gritted teeth, his stomach threatening to crawl into his throat and out through his mouth. "She likes to be called Lumina."

Morgan stopped and peered at him. "Are you all right? You don't look so good."

The reminder of how he looked was extremely unwelcome. Especially in light of the way Lumina had gazed in wide-eyed wonder at the dazzling, Day-Glo Beckett, he of the perfect face and perfect . . . everything else. The memory made him angry, and a low, hostile growl rumbled through his chest.

Morgan rolled her eyes. "I meant your *color*, Magnus. It's somewhere between battleship gray and moss green. What's wrong?"

My face. My soul. My life. Aloud he said, "I have a hangover."

Morgan stared at him, comprehension dawning in her eyes. "Oh, ducky," she said gently, "that was really sweet of you."

He clenched his teeth harder. "Morgan. About the pet name thing. I'm the Alpha; calling me 'pet,' 'ducky,' and 'luv,' is disrespectful and undermines my authority. Cut it out."

She said defensively, "It's not disrespectful, it's affectionate! And I don't call you those names in front of anyone else—"

"You called me 'ducky' in front of Lumina just yesterday!"

She stopped to consider it. "Did I? Hmm." Her look sharpened. "Which bothers you more: that I did it, or that I did it in front of *her*?"

He exhaled hard. The rumbling noise in his chest grew louder.

Morgan looked pleased with herself. "That's what I thought. But don't worry, I won't let it slip again. In front of *anyone*."

She began to brush past him but he stopped her with a sharp, "Wait."

Morgan turned with lifted brows, surprised by his tone.

Voice lowered, he said, "I assume you heard about what happened during the Assembly last night."

She'd missed Honor's little "demonstration." Immediately after-ward, the meeting had ended before it had even begun, as everyone fled to their respective chambers to whisper and conjecture. Except for Jack, who'd nervously over-served Lumina the infamous vodka while she stared in numb silence at the wall, and Hawk, who stood watching Lumina from one corner of the room with a face as stormy as a hurricane. As for himself, he'd made good use of the heavy bag he'd found in an abandoned gym on one long-ago search trip, and dragged all the way back to the colony so he had something to do with his fists other than beat them against the walls.

He used to do that a lot.

Morgan said, "Oh. That."

"Well?"

She stared back at him, defiant. "Well what?"

"Did you know?"

There followed a weighted silence. Finally Morgan relented. "I suspected. *We* suspected; Xander was there, too, when Caesar was killed. It was during an Assembly meeting." She released a soft breath, and some of her defiance went with it. "Everyone else who was at that meeting was lost."

Lost meant one of two things: killed in the battle that followed the Flash, or captured, as the Queen had been. Magnus had been a mere eleven years old that day. He'd lost his entire family, had watched both his parents fall from gunfire as the hidden enemy shot from the trees. Leander had been shot, too, and badly wounded, and Jenna had had to make the most terrible choice a wife and mother could make.

Who to save: Her husband? Or her children?

Magnus knew this part of the story because he'd seen it with his own eyes. Crouched low in the underbrush, terrified and not knowing whether to run or pick up a weapon and fight, he'd seen Jenna give one of her babies to Morgan, who, protected by Xander, ran. Then Jenna Shifted to an enormous white dragon, picked up her other baby gently in her teeth by its little onesie, and flew away, leaving Leander lying motionless on the ground.

Magnus had no idea how much time passed, but the dragon returned and took shape again as a woman. She crouched on the ground by her husband, cradling his head, crying, whispering something into his ear that Magnus couldn't hear.

Before Jenna could turn to dragon again and spirit Leander away, she, too, was shot. Then a knot of booted, armed men had collared them both, and dragged them into the trees.

Chaos, never ending. The jungle burned, gunfire rang out, the stench of smoke and gasoline permeated the air in fuming clouds that choked him. Hundreds of military aircraft had been plucked from the sky and lay in broken pieces between the trees, their ragged metal guts spilling out a gruesome slew of bodies.

There had been a ground assault, too. A very effective one: Corpses had lain bent and broken everywhere, festooning the earth and trees like hideous ornaments.

"What did you see? What happened at the meeting?" Magnus stepped even closer, staring down into her face, his heart pounding inside his chest.

"What did I see?" she repeated softly. Her gaze turned distant. "I saw two infant girls end the life of a madman. From firsthand experience, I know that insanity runs in Caesar's family; all the men of his Bloodline were touched by it. But he was born with something far more sinister than a garden-variety crazy streak. Something that made him invincible. Untouchable. Something that made any wound heal, no matter how it was caused." Her voice darkened. "He'd died a hundred times before the final time in that jungle. And the only difference was the girls."

Her faraway look cleared, and she gazed at Magnus with a burning intensity in her eyes. "That's why Jenna was able to let Hope and

Honor go; she knew they'd be all right. She knew they could take care of themselves. Even though they were just little babies, their mother knew those children would never be in any real danger."

All the hair on Magnus's nape rose. He whispered, "Because she knew they couldn't die."

Morgan nodded. "They stole Caesar's Gift. Then they lit him on fire without even touching him, and he burned to death, right before my eyes. He'd come to kill us all, and the only reason he wasn't able to was Hope and Honor. They saved my life, Magnus. And the life of my husband. If it wasn't for them, I wouldn't be standing in front of you right now."

Stunned, Magnus whispered, "*Stole* it from him? How?"

From beneath the load in her arms, Morgan slipped free a hand, and held it aloft.

Understanding hit Magnus like a ton of bricks; that was really why Lumina had asked him for the gloves. But, no—Honor never wore gloves. And why . . .

"So Honor's known, all these years? She knows she's . . ." He could barely bring himself to say the word, it sounded so impossible. "Immortal?"

"We never spoke of it. But from what I understand about what happened between her and Lumina yesterday, there wasn't a doubt in Honor's mind that plunging that sword through her sister's back would cause no permanent harm. So she must know. And I suspect that has a great deal to do with her attitude, as well."

His brows pulled to a frown, and Morgan's expression softened.

"How would you feel, Magnus, knowing you were going to outlive every single person you loved . . . over and over again? Knowing that to get close only guaranteed you pain? Knowing that even *if* you someday tired of life, if you'd lived a thousand years and couldn't stand a single minute any longer, there was nothing you could do about it?"

The enormity of it stole his breath. He stood there in the dim corridor with the sound of dripping water like cannon fire in his ears as he thought about—really thought about—what it would be like.

Morgan said, "I don't know about you, but I wouldn't like it. In fact, I think I'd feel *cursed*. The thing that makes life so precious is that it's fleeting. Take that away, and life becomes like visiting your in-laws; just one more irritating obligation you really wish you could get out of, but can't."

"You're right," he admitted. "That's got to be the worst thing I've ever heard."

"Remember that the next time you're tempted to snarl at Honor," Morgan gently admonished.

"Snarl? I don't *snarl*!" His shout echoed down the corridor, and Morgan lifted an eyebrow, smiling.

Magnus said, "Okay. Conversation over. A man can only stand being wrong so many times in a one-minute span." He turned and began to walk away.

Morgan's laugh followed him. "Now you know how my husband feels!"

Magnus felt a deep wave of sympathy for Xander, which was quickly overtaken by a pressing need to get horizontal; Lumina's hangover had given him a respite for a few minutes while he talked with Morgan, but judging by the pounding in his temples, and the strange noises emitting from his stomach, his time was up.

He strode through the shifting shadows toward his cave, his mind a tangle, his stomach in knots, his head feeling as if it weighed a thousand pounds, completely unaware of the blinking red glow that had begun to emanate from Beckett's darkened lab on the other side of the colony.

FOURTEEN

The bath was sublime. Cold, but sublime.

Morgan had taken Lu to a breathtakingly lovely pool, fed by a fast-running stream that dropped into a waterfall. The water was so clear she could see the silver glint of minnows swimming near the rocky bottom, and after Morgan left her so she could have some privacy, Lu floated on her back, staring up at the constellation of stalactites on the shadowy ceiling high above, pondering all that had happened in the last few days.

Then, alone in the cool, echoing dark, she finally allowed herself to cry.

She had to eventually get out of the water to do it because the sobs were too strong, wracking her body until she could hardly breathe. She sat on a rock, wrapped in one of the soft towels Morgan had given her, with her arms wrapped around her knees, wretched and homesick and soul-bruised, letting it all go.

"I'm sorry, Father." Her whisper carried over the water, bouncing softly off the cave walls until it died under the rush of the waterfall. "I'm so sorry. I love you."

Though Magnus had said her birth mother was alive, and her birth father might possibly be as well, her heart was broken. The man who'd raised her had died because he'd taken her in, protected her, and sacrificed for her. He'd been killed *because of her.*

I'll never let that happen again. Even if it meant never getting close to another living soul, she wasn't going to be the cause of anyone else's death. From now on, she would take care of herself.

She might, however, do a little killing of her own. The memory of the Grand Minister's cruel, sneering face flashed before her eyes, and her hands clenched.

The can't-die thing might prove to be useful.

The thought of what else it might prove to be was too much for her to consider. And she took a little solace in the fact that at least there was one other person she knew who was afflicted with the same thing: Honor.

Frigid, sword-wielding, Bitch of the Universe Honor.

She dressed in the clothes Morgan had left for her and headed out, determined to have a cozy little one-on-one chat with her sister. But she was quickly intercepted by Beckett and a group of a half dozen other young people, trailing behind him like admiring puppies.

Even the three guys looked at Beckett as if he were some kind of luminary. It could have had something to do with the soft yellow light emanating from his head.

"Hi!" Beckett enthused, flashing his thousand-watt smile. "We were just headed out; you're coming, right?"

Before she could answer, Beckett said, "Oh, sorry! My bad manners again." He began introducing the group, pointing each one out in turn, the guys first. "Sean, Dash, Oz, Kali, North, and Sayer."

If Lumina's own name hadn't been so strange, she might have felt the impulse to question each about the origins of his or her name, but she only nodded at them, receiving a mix of hesitant smiles and looks of outright intimidation in return.

She guessed they'd all heard about what happened last night with Honor.

Wonderful.

Sidestepping the awkward silence that had descended, Lu asked, "Um, Beckett? What's up with . . . that?" She gestured to his head.

"My Gleam, you mean?" As he spoke, the sunbeam glimmer around his head spread to his entire body, until the air all around him was aglow. She had to admit it was a pretty spectacular Gift. And she wasn't the only one who thought so; two of the girls actually sighed. "Yeah, it comes in handy around these dark caves." He shrugged, but Lu could tell he was pleased she'd mentioned it.

In light of her recent vow not to get close to anyone, she made a mental note not to mention it again. She didn't want Beckett getting the wrong idea.

She said, "I bet. Anyway, have you seen Honor? I need to talk to her."

He blinked in surprise at the change of subject, and Lu wondered how often someone turned the conversation away from him. Never, judging by the way everyone else was blinking in surprise at her, too.

"Uh . . . yeah. She's already topside." He seemed disoriented for a beat, then straightened his shoulders. "I'll take you to her, okay?"

His self-confident, charming smile was back, and though she guessed it was the exact same smile he sent in every girl's direction, Lu had to admit it was pretty irresistible. She smiled back. "Great. Thanks."

Then she and Mr. Gleam and his fan club began the long, winding ascent through the caves to the surface.

"Holy . . ."

It was the only word that came to mind.

The view that greeted Lu when she emerged from the gloom of the caves into the brilliance of the day was the single most spectacular thing she'd seen in her life.

Color, everywhere. So much color it stung her eyes. The gently sloping hillside where she now stood gaping was carpeted in emerald, and dotted with the darker forest green of trees. The sky was blazing, enamel blue, the clouds so white they shone like pearls. Even the air smelled like a color: green. Lush, verdant, and rich with life. Off in the distance, the moors teemed with wildflowers, lavender and sapphire and pink, and a gentle gray-blue mist rose from the peaks of the faraway mountains.

But none of that compared with the glory of the sun. She'd never imagined such a color could exist. Pictures couldn't do the blinding golden-yellow-white-diamond of it justice.

Lu closed her eyes and tilted back her head, basking in the most profound pleasure she'd ever felt: sunlight on her face.

"Feels good, doesn't it?"

Even without opening her eyes, she recognized Magnus's voice. And his scent. He'd approached so quietly she hadn't heard him, and briefly wondered if that was another of his Gifts: Utter Silence.

"Good doesn't even come close." She was whispering, not wanting to break the spell. "An orgasm doesn't feel this amazing."

The minute the words were out of her mouth, she wanted to swallow them back. *Idiot! What were you thinking?* Heat spread across her cheeks to her ears, and it wasn't from the sun. She opened her eyes, cleared her throat, and quickly changed the subject. "You didn't let me properly thank you earlier, about the hangover thing. So . . . thank you. I can't tell you how much I appreciate it. Are you feeling any better?"

She chanced a glance at him. He wore a black jacket with a hood that partially obscured his face, but what she could see of it was, if possible, flushed an even deeper red than hers.

"No." His tone was gruff, the word a clipped syllable. He wouldn't look at her. Instead, he was paying close attention to a nearby clump of bluebells nodding cheerfully in the sun.

"Why aren't you resting, then? I could barely sit up in bed earlier, how are you even—"

"I heard you'd come up. I wanted to be here. To keep an eye out."

An eye out? Lu scanned the landscape with new dread. "Morgan said we were safe here."

He finally turned his head and looked at her. The color still hadn't left his cheeks, leaving the scarred side of his face blotchy, ruddy beneath the snarl of pale scar tissue. "*Safe* is a relative term. There are all kinds of ways to get into trouble." He glanced away, and his gaze fell on Beckett and his group, who'd given her a moment alone and were waiting at a respectful distance by a nearby stand of pines.

Beckett was looking back at them without his trademark smile. "You don't like him?"

That eloquent muscle in Magnus's jaw jumped. "I didn't say that."

"No, but judging by that death glare you're shooting him, I'm making an educated guess."

The bluebells were now subjected to the death glare. He said, "In case you haven't noticed, this is my normal expression."

"Oh, I've noticed." This earned her a sharp glance, which she didn't wilt under. "But this *particular* look is more severe than most. It's borderline murderous. If I didn't know better, I'd think you were planning on committing a violent act against Glowlight Gary over there."

Magnus crossed his arms over his chest and looked into the distance. In profile, he was truly magnificent; the unscarred side of his face was all perfect planes and angles, high cheekbones and full lips and the serious slash of his brows. She wondered if he'd stood on her right side on purpose, and felt her heart give a little twinge of . . . what? Empathy? Is that what made her suddenly want to wind her arms around his shoulders and press herself against him?

Yes, she told herself firmly. *It's only empathy. And you are a terrible liar.*

"Should I infer from your little nickname for Beckett that you haven't been sucked into the bottomless chasm of his charm yet?"

The bitterness in Magnus's tone stunned her. As did the final word he'd spoken: *yet.* He fully assumed she'd be looking at Beckett the way Kali, North, and Sayer looked at him. The way everyone probably looked at him: googly-eyed and drooling.

"Nah. I could never be interested in a man prettier than me. My ego's way too fragile."

She'd been joking, her tone light, but he turned and looked her fully in the face with an intensity even more surprising than his obvious dislike of Beckett. He said vehemently, "There isn't a person who's ever lived who's prettier than you."

Her heart did a funny little flip. No one had ever said anything remotely similar to her. She'd never thought of herself as pretty, only as different, dangerous, an outsider who was worth more dead than alive. To everyone else but her parents, she'd been a *thing.*

To everyone else but her parents . . . and the Magnus of her dreams.

She said, "Thank you. That might be the first compliment anyone's ever paid me."

To which Magnus replied, "That's because people are fucking morons."

His posture held the same rigidity it always did when he spoke to her, his face the same hard, closed lines. But his eyes burned dark with raw emotion, and for a split second she almost recognized her dream lover.

Then something vast hurtled by overhead with a powerful whoosh of cold air, darkening the sky, and Lu ducked down with a scream.

In mere seconds it was gone, and she looked up and saw what had passed. She saw, but she didn't believe.

There making a slow banking turn in the sky, skimming the underbellies of the clouds and leaving a swirling trail in its wake, was a dragon.

Pure white, with silver-tipped wings and silver barbs along its tail, it was enormous but elegant, moving gracefully with powerful thrusts of its wings. Even from this distance she could see the creature's vivid yellow-green eyes, the long, silky white mane along its neck, its muzzle full of razor-sharp teeth.

Magnus exhaled with a sound that was frustrated and aggravated in equal measure. He muttered, "Your sister has a real flare for the melodramatic."

Lu rose, her gaze fixed on the horizon and the creature flying closer. Making, it appeared, a beeline in their direction. "Honor . . . that's . . . I don't . . ." She shook her head, too blank to respond.

Magnus had moved several steps away. He glanced at her, everything about his face and eyes now guarded, closed down. He said, "I suppose this would be as good a time as any for you to try it as well."

"Try it?" Lu repeated, barely able to form the words as she watched the dragon fly closer and closer, its muzzle curling back in what looked like a grin.

"Flying, Lumina."

Her head snapped around and she gaped at him. "*What?*"

He said, "From what I've seen, the flying itself is the easy part. It's the landings that'll give you some trouble."

Then he walked away, and Lu was left standing alone as her sister the dragon began to descend.

FIFTEEN

Magnus had been right: Landing was a problem. The white dragon barreled down toward Lu, its wings pumping a furious backbeat as it attempted to slow itself. Legs out, talons extended, fangs bared, it made such a terrifying picture that Lu's first and only thought was to bolt.

Lucky she did, because the dragon landed with a thunderous, ground-shaking *boom* in the exact spot she'd just been standing.

Crouched a few yards away, Lumina was pelted with clods of dirt and tufts of dislodged grass. She stood, brushing muck from the new outfit Morgan had given her, and stalked back to the dragon.

"Are you crazy?" she shouted at it. "What is your problem with me?"

The dragon folded its wings, shook back its mane from its face, and fixed her in its feral yellow-green gaze. With a derisive snort, it exhaled a chuff of white vapor and rose to its full height. Its powerful tail flicked out from behind it, lashing dangerously close to Lu's legs.

Lu crossed her arms and straightened her spine. "I'm not afraid of you, and you only have yourself to thank for—"

The dragon opened its mouth and exhaled again, this time with a powerful blast of blue frosted air so cold it burned like fire.

When the air cleared, Lu was unscathed. Unfortunately, she was also naked. Her clothes had frozen solid, then been shorn away in tiny bits of scintillating fabric that floated gently down from the sky like snowflakes. Only her boots remained intact, and they were crusted in ice.

She felt all the eyes on her. She felt with acute humiliation the chill of the slight breeze on her naked stomach, buttocks, and thighs, the warmth of the sun on her shoulders. And from the corner of her vision she saw Magnus running toward her, tearing off his jacket and shirt.

The shirt off his back, she thought. *That's really sweet.* Then she stalked over to the dragon and punched it in the face.

That was the first moment of what would become the most amazing hour of her life.

The dragon reacted by snapping its head to the side, but toward Lu, instead of away. It caught her in the ribcage and tossed her into the air where she sailed, spinning with her arms and legs flung wide, until it caught her on the back of an outstretched wing. Its pale flesh was tough but smooth, pearlescent in the sunlight, exuding heat, and as she stared down at the pattern of interlocking scales, she thought in grudging admiration, *It's actually kind of beautiful.*

Then with a flick of its wing, the dragon sent Lu sailing into the air once again. She flew over its back and landed on the opposite wing with an audible *oof*!

Panting, she looked up to find the dragon staring at her over its shoulder, its long neck craned back, an expression in its reptilian eyes that was . . . smug.

It was *toying* with her.

Something inside of her just snapped.

Lu didn't know exactly how it happened, but one minute she was screaming in impotent rage, pounding her fists on the unyielding hide of the dragon wing so hard her wrist popped, the next she was fifty feet in the air, looking down on the creature from above.

In an instant, everything was different. *She* was different. She inhaled, and felt the suck of air into massive lungs, smelled mice and voles and rabbits deep beneath the earth, tasted the sweet, ripe bite of an apple from some faraway, unseen tree on her tongue. She exhaled and from her mouth came a plume of smoke intermingled with an orange blaze of fire, and it was then that she realized what she'd done.

She'd Shifted. To dragon.

Holy. Shit!

And the most astonishing thing—aside from the sensation of wind beneath her wings, and the expressions on the faces of the group of people staring up at her wide-eyed and frozen from below—was that it was effortless. She knew she must be pumping her wings, but it felt as if she were standing still, floating, not flying. It felt as if feet and hands were things she'd learned how to use, cumbersome things in another cumbersome body, but wings and talons and smoke and fire were the way she was really meant to be.

As if she was, finally, wearing the right skin.

She banked and flew away with no more effort than a thought: *left*. Another, *higher*, and she'd punched through the damp, clinging density of the cloud cover. She bared her fangs, exulting in the sting of cold wind on her muzzle, the moisture beading mirrored drops along her mane, the wind a roaring *hiss* in her ears, and kept going.

Then she sliced through the top of the clouds like a scythe, and all was silent and still, the sky an endless sheer curtain of sapphire above.

Honor appeared a heartbeat later, winging around her in a loose spiral, grinning that beastly grin. *Like I told Magnus*, came the voice inside Lu's mind, *demonstrations are always more effective than conversations.*

With that, Lu understood.

Are you always going to be this much of a pain in my ass? she answered back, flipping over to fly upside down, staring in awe at the vast nothingness of the atmosphere, stretching vapor thin and crystalline above. She noticed her wings were vermilion, the barbs along her tail and her talons a gleaming, beautiful gold.

That's what older sisters are for, came the wry retort as Honor executed a breathtaking rolling dive, sunlight shining off her scales in blinding winks of silver. Lu righted herself and chased after Honor, finding a cold gust of wind that carried her closer.

Older? We're twins!

I'm older by three minutes, baby sister. And a whole lot wiser. By the way, you hit like a girl. We'll work on that.

Lu was momentarily too busy admiring how lean and strong Honor was as she flew to be angry. Her shape wasn't the bulky, monstrous one she'd seen dragons depicted as having in old fairy tales. She was lithe and elegant, every movement a poem of economy, every stroke of her wings filled with grace. Up here in the heavens her sister was as luminous as a star, and, for the first time since meeting her, Lu felt a swelling rush of affection for this alabaster doppelganger with whom she shared nothing in common but her face.

Or so she'd thought. Watching Honor now, Lu had the distinct feeling there was so much more to her than that icy, aloof front she presented to the world.

I don't know about wiser, but I'll buy older, Lu thought. *You really should think about investing in a good nighttime moisturizer, sister dear.*

The two dragons grinned at one another. Then in a move that to an observer would have looked perfectly coordinated, they pumped their wings and glided higher into the glimmering solitude of the morning sky.

"So she *is* as Gifted as Honor," breathed Dash, so named for his Gift. Even in a colony of creatures that were preternaturally fast, his ability to run from one place to another, unseen because he moved so quickly, was unusual.

Standing beside Dash, Beckett said with authority, "No." Everyone looked at him, including Magnus. Their eyes met, and Beckett said, "Hope is more Gifted."

Magnus knew it was true, but it was the proprietary tone that riled him. Was *meant* to rile him. "She likes to be called Lumina," he growled, staring at Beckett without blinking long enough that the younger man flushed and looked away.

"What do you mean, *more* Gifted?" asked Oz, cracking his knuckles and straining his neck to catch a glimpse of the two dragons, high up in the sky. His real name was Liam, but his affinity for the ancient heavy metal band Black Sabbath and its dove-decapitating lead singer, Ozzy Osbourne, had earned him the moniker. Beckett had hacked into the database of a pre-Flash rock-and-roll station once and made the mistake of letting Liam browse the MP3 files. The rest was history. Magnus couldn't count how many times the strains of "The Wizard" and "Paranoid" had blasted through the caves.

Now gazing into the heavens, Beckett said, "Just what I said. Hope is stronger. I can feel it."

I'll just bet you can, thought Magnus, and enjoyed a fleeting image of himself bashing Beckett's perfect head into the large rock several feet behind him.

The group sensed his anger, and began to look nervous, which was wise; things tended to bleed when Magnus got angry. Though he was Alpha and they should have respected him simply for being more Gifted than the rest of the tribe—with the exception of Honor and now Lumina—it was his temper that really kept everyone in check. If only he could keep *himself* in check.

The heavy bag could only take so many beatings before Magnus needed other outlets.

But he didn't need a fight now. What he needed was to burn the image of a gloriously naked Lumina from his mind.

His heart had stopped when he'd seen her standing there wreathed in vapor, her pale skin gleaming in the sunlight, pieces of her ruined clothing drifting like frozen confetti all around her. Unfortunately, he wasn't the only one; Beckett, Dash, and Oz had all gone bug-eyed, too.

But only Beckett had lit up like a sunrise, bathing them all in a burst of evanescence that felt dirty for all its shiny brightness.

He was really starting to hate that kid.

Magnus had never before been touched by jealousy's cold green fingers, but he wasn't going to lie to himself about it; irrational as it was, jealousy was the correct term for the emotion eating a hole in his guts and burning like acid through his veins. Along with a host of other emotions, he felt protective of Lumina, and he couldn't stand that look in Beckett's eyes. That possessive, greedy look.

The one he was sure was identical to his own.

She's better off with the pretty boy than with a busted-up bastard like you, whispered a little voice of reason inside his head.

With an ache inside his chest that felt carnivorous, Magnus watched the two dragons soar for another moment, wishing with all that was left of his mangled heart that he was even half the man he used to be. Half might have been enough to offer, enough to have allowed him some self-respect. But he wasn't that man, even by half. He was a ghost. An angry poltergeist, haunting the ruins of his former life.

He wasn't worthy. Not of her.

Without another word to the group, Magnus turned and walked away.

Honor led, and Lumina followed. For an hour they flew together, far above steaming fields and a sprinkling of deserted, crumbling villages, past the spidery, pale veins of empty roads, the horizon bleeding into a purple curve where earth met sky ahead. The wind was a roar when they changed directions, but when they rode along with it, letting it carry them aloft like untethered kites, there was the most beautiful stillness, and for the first time she could remember, Lu felt peace.

As she flew, her mind kept returning to the memory of Magnus running toward her, tearing his jacket and shirt off, his expression a mix of cold fury and hot intensity, his chest, arms, and stomach completely bare.

He was muscular, well-formed, but far too lean for a man his size. Every muscle was visible beneath his skin, every vein in his arms was outlined in stark relief. She wanted to cook him a meal, and sit and watch him eat it. She wanted to feed him from her fingers, and watch that dark heat always smoldering in his eyes flare into a blaze.

She wanted to run her hands over every scar on his body, pressing soft kisses to each one with her lips.

It was bad, whatever had hurt him. From waist to face his right side was a mess, and she knew the hooded jacket he wore over his shirt was due to shame from his appearance. But he hadn't even hesitated to bare himself so he could cover her. He hadn't thought of himself.

Suddenly needing to see him again, Lu said to Honor, *I'm getting tired. Let's go back.*

Honor peered at her with slitted eyes, a wingspan away. If she suspected that was only partly true, she didn't let on. Instead, she banked and Lu followed, and soon they were headed toward a grove of trees close to the entrance to the caves.

They landed near a rocky outcropping with such a total lack of grace both of them were laughing when they Shifted back to human form. Honor touched down first, gouging a deep, ragged furrow in the earth behind her, and Lu came in too fast and executed the most awkward belly flop, accompanied by a face plant directly into the dirt. In the trees nearby, a flock of swallows rose in a sudden tangle of quicksilver into the sky.

"I wish I had a camera so you could see the look on your face." Honor had Shifted back to woman and was walking toward a small pile of clothing atop a rock. She dressed quickly, still chuckling, and gestured to what she hadn't donned. "These are for you; I thought you might be needing something to wear, and we're the same size, so . . ."

Lu was cold, and feeling self-conscious at her nudity, even though it was only her and Honor in the clearing, so she pulled on the clothing Honor had brought as fast as she could. "Thanks. By the way, do your clothes have some kind of heat protectant or something?"

"No. Why?"

Lu shrugged, cinching the belted white jacket around her waist. It matched the white trousers, an exact replica of Honor's outfit. She pulled on a pair of white boots, wondering if Honor realized no one would be able to tell them apart. And if that's what she'd intended. "Because your clothes weren't burned when I . . . uh . . . you know, in the cave yesterday. And Morgan's were. And mine were, too, this morning when you decided to cold-roast me in front of everyone." Her voice soured. "Thanks for that, by the way. Now everyone and his brother knows what I look like naked."

Honor smirked. "You shouldn't have punched me. And in answer to your question, you just don't know how to control your Gifts yet. At least consciously; I'm sure if you hadn't liked Morgan, much more than her clothing would have been burned with her standing so close to you when you lost it in the cave yesterday."

Lu frowned, confused. "Okay, but I still don't get how your clothes weren't affected, and ours were."

They turned and started to pick their way up the small hill of granite. The entrance to the caves was on the other side, along with Beckett and his group. Lu hadn't seen Magnus anywhere when she and Honor were making their descent, and wondered if he'd returned to the caves.

Honor just sent her a mysterious smile and said, "It's just a matter of awareness, of focus. With practice, you'll be able to protect whatever you want from the effects of the Gifts."

That sounded interesting. They walked a while in silence while Lu pondered it. "By the way, how did you know getting me angry would make me Shift?"

"The first time I Shifted I was angry, too. I figured if it worked for me, it would work for you."

"Really? What happened?"

In response to Lu's question, Honor's face flushed. Keeping her gaze averted, she said simply, "I saw something I didn't like."

Lu got the distinct feeling this was a topic of great importance for getting a better idea of what made Honor tick. Trying for an offhand tone, she asked, "Nothing too serious, I hope?"

They'd reached the crest of the hill, and Honor scanned the landscape below with a sharp eye. Her gaze fell on Beckett, playfully chasing Sayer around the trunk of a tree, and her lips thinned.

"Not really, in the scheme of things. But to my ten-year-old self, it felt like the end of the world. The end of *my* world, anyway."

Lu sensed the anger and pain behind those words, and knew instinctively Beckett was the cause. Taking a risk, she asked tentatively, "Does he know?"

Honor's head whipped around, and she glared at her. "Even if he did, he wouldn't care," she hissed, two blotches of color staining her cheeks. "He doesn't care about anything but himself!"

They stared at one another a moment, Lu watching as Honor struggled to compose herself. "But you care about him," she said. "Don't you?"

The ice was back in Honor's eyes. The stone beneath their feet crackled with a thin gloss of frost. "Don't ever say that to me again."

Lu reached out for her sister's arm. "Honor—"

"Shut your trap, Hope!" She shrugged off her touch, stepping back.

"Stop calling me Hope, will you? My name's Lumina—"

Honor shouted, "You can call yourself Puff the Magic Dragon if you want, but it doesn't change the fact that your name is HOPE!"

"Fine," sighed Lu, tired of this. Would they always be fighting? "Please refer to me as Puff the Magic Dragon from now on. And I'll call you Smaug."

Honor's icy glare narrowed. "What the hell is a Smaug?"

Lu folded her arms across her chest. "Ever read *The Hobbit*? No? Well, Smaug is the dragon in the story, described as 'a most specially greedy, strong and wicked wyrm.' I think it's appropriate."

Honor's eyes widened. Her voice rising, she said, "A worm? Did you just call me a *worm*?"

Lu was just about to retort, "Don't forget the greedy and wicked part!" but a faint, odd noise distracted her. She looked to the sky, listening hard.

"What is that?"

Honor heard it, too, her gaze fixed on the horizon. "I don't know. Nothing good, though." She stepped closer, pressing her shoulder against Lu's, the argument forgotten.

They stood there together in breathless, rigid silence for a moment, every sense open, their ears straining to filter out the wind whispering through branches, the birds singing in the trees, and Beckett's faint laughter, a teasing echo that had the blood again rising in Honor's cheeks.

The steady *whop-whop-whop* of blades cutting through air, the mechanical noise of gravity being beaten into submission . . . Lu knew that sound.

Together, Lu and Honor whispered, "Helicopter!"

They shared a look of horrified comprehension, then bounded down the hill at a flat-out run.

SIXTEEN

By the time they reached Beckett and the rest of his group, they'd all heard the helicopter, too. They stood in the long shadows of the pines, faces upturned, tense and silent. Magnus was nowhere to be seen.

Sayer, the petite, raven-haired girl Beckett had been chasing around the tree, said nervously, "We should get back into the caves."

Beckett nodded, still looking at the sky. "Yes, you should. Take Kali and North with you. Dash and Oz, make sure the girls get inside, and let everyone know we've got Enforcement on our tails. Get battle ready."

"*Enforcement?*" whispered a horrified North. She was taller than Kali and Sayer, just a few inches shy of Beckett's height, with almond-shaped green eyes that dominated her face. "How do you know it's Enforcement?"

"Who else would it be?" said Beckett, then pointed suddenly, his face hard. "I was right; look."

Cresting a jagged black range of mountains in the distance was a trio of black helicopters. They turned, following the line of the peaks, and even from where she stood, Lu could see the bright yellow sun emblem painted on their sides.

"But how?" cried North.

"My collar," Lu whispered, reaching up to touch her throat. "There must have been a tracking device in it."

A ripple of panic went through the group. Suddenly Magnus appeared as if from nowhere, stepping out from behind the massive trunk of a nearby tree. He said, "Everyone follow me," and began to stride quickly toward the entrance to the caves, a small, black opening in the side of the hill.

But he was brought up short when Honor said, "That won't be necessary."

Everyone turned to look at her, but she was still staring at those helicopters, drawing inexorably closer.

"There's only three of them." She glanced at Lu with an odd, wild gleam in her eyes.

Magnus walked slowly back, and stood in front of them. "You're right. It's a scouting party," he said. "If they were sure we were here, they'd have sent an entire battalion."

"They'll have thermal imaging cameras," interjected Oz, sounding even more nervous than Sayer had. "If they do a ground scan—"

"They're not going to get that far," said Honor softly, still looking at Lu. "Are they, sis?"

Everyone fell quiet, looking back and forth between the two of them, and Lu had a bad feeling about what Honor might mean. She said, "If these three go off grid, the IF will know something happened. They'll just send more."

Honor didn't even blink. "Yep. But it will take them a while because they won't be sure what caused them to go offline. Could be weather interference, could be an equipment malfunction, could be a million different things. The IF will wait awhile before they send another search party, maybe even a few days. Whereas if they get infrared readings on close to a thousand warm bodies living in the caves of Ogof Ffynnon Ddu, the entire Federation will converge on this island faster than you can say, 'Smaug is obviously the smartest dragon.'" She paused for a beat. "And the prettiest."

Her stomach knotting as she watched the helicopters fly closer, Lu asked quietly, "So what do we do?"

Honor replied with one of her cold, cold smiles, sending a shiver of dread down Lu's spine. "What we do best."

"Which is?"

A sudden, freezing wind whipped through the trees with such force it bowed their highest branches. Honor's chilling smile grew wider. "Wreck shit."

Magnus said, "Beckett, get back to your lab and destroy that collar. And take everyone with you."

Looking at Honor with a strange, conflicted expression, Beckett replied, "I'm not leaving."

"It wasn't a request!" snarled Magnus, stepping closer to Beckett. "Get everyone inside and take care of that collar! *Now!*"

Beckett's nostrils flared as he stared hard at Magnus. The two men stood chest to chest, Magnus standing a few inches taller, but Beckett broader in the shoulders, until Sayer took Beckett's hand and tugged at it.

"Beck. C'mon." She shot a worried glance at Magnus, then gave another, sharper, tug on Beckett's hand.

"You should listen to Magnus," said Honor softly, staring at the sky, the wind whipping her hair into a cloud of glinting gold around her shoulders. "He knows firsthand how things tend to go a little sideways when my sister and I lose our tempers." She flicked a glance at Sayer, then at Beckett, then at their joined hands. Her gaze returned to Beckett's face, and she said, harder, "I don't want anyone to get hurt."

A flicker of emotion darkened Beckett's eyes, and for a moment he and Honor just gazed at one another. Then he said quietly, "Someone always gets hurt when you're involved, Honor." He turned his back and dragged Sayer away by the hand, and the rest of the group followed him, setting off for the entrance to the caves at a trot.

As Honor watched them go, a low rumble of thunder echoed through the hills in the distance. The wind grew stronger. A roiling black mass of thunderclouds appeared in the sky, crackling with hellish purple veins of lightning.

"Is that *you*?" Lu whispered to Honor, watching the sky darken in fascination.

"You should see me when I'm PMSing," Honor replied in the same hard tone she'd used with Beckett. She'd finally stopped watching him when he and his group disappeared into the caves. "Which is pretty much all the time," she added, which made Magnus snort.

"Go inside, Seeker," said Honor. She took Lu's hand and held it tightly.

"Not a chance in hell, Ice Queen," he replied in a tone that clearly broadcasted how serious he was. He came and stood beside Lu, and she looked up at him, into those dark, beguiling eyes. Holding her gaze, he murmured, "I wouldn't miss this for the world."

Honor said, "Suit yourself. But don't blame me for your bruises."

Magnus glanced at Honor, frowning.

That's when the first of the hail began to fall, hurtling down from the sky with such force the golf ball–sized chunks of ice bounced high off the ground with a sound like the clatter of hooves.

"Control, this is Tango Aztec two-niner-six-four Alpha, over."

"Go ahead, Tango."

"We're experiencing severe weather conditions en route to target. Request permission to land until flight conditions are more favorable, over."

A crackle of static. "Describe your situation, Tango. Control is getting interference with your readouts."

Interference? The helicopter pilot and his copilot shared a glance.

"Tail wind at twenty-eight knots, low visibility due to heavy fog, temperature currently at—" No. That couldn't be right. The pilot frowned at the digital readout; according to his instrument, the outside temperature had dropped thirty degrees in the last minute.

"Tango, repeat your last transmission, please, we're having trouble with your signal."

The pilot knew the temperature gauge was malfunctioning. It had to be, because at the rate it was dropping, the fuel lines would ice up—

Bam! Bam! Bam! The pilot started in his seat, shocked by the enormous white balls raining down on the windshield.

On the console, a red warning light blinked on at the same time an alarm shrilly sounded. There immediately followed a grinding, hollow groan from the rotors, and a violent shudder shook the cabin.

"Oh, shit!" shouted the copilot.

Control called over the com again, but the words were garbled, lost beneath the howling of the wind and the blinding crackle of a jagged fork of lightning that exploded in the dark sky not ten meters in front of the aircraft.

Now truly panicked, the pilot engaged the anti-ice system, but his instrument panel lit up like a Thornemas tree with a barrage of warning lights, madly blinking red and yellow. The gyroscope spun wildly, the vertical speed indicator lurched, the torque meter went off the charts.

The rotors stalled. The copilot screamed, louder even than the wind. Then with a jolt that flattened the pilot's stomach up under his lungs, the helicopter dropped like a rock from the sky.

"This one's dead, too." Lumina covered her mouth with the back of her hand. She turned away from the mangled body of the man who had been thrown clear from the smoking wreckage of one of the helicopters, and stood with her eyes closed, dragging fresh air into her lungs, her lips pressed together, blood quickly draining from her face.

As it had drained from the man's body to stain his frayed uniform, and darken the grass.

"Wreck shit," Honor had said, and that is precisely what had happened. All three of the IF helicopters had gone down in the storm, and everyone on board was killed.

Lu had felt such a thrill of power to stand there beside her sister, to wield such awful force. Especially on her enemies, the same group who'd murdered her father, the same bunch of mindless disciples of Thorne who wanted nothing more than to see her caged, or dead. It had made her blood sing. It had made her nearly dizzy with wicked glee.

But then, oh then in the quiet aftermath, witnessing the carnage she had wrought . . . what intense disgust she'd felt. What black, encompassing revulsion.

At herself.

Lu knew people died in war. It was a simple, incontrovertible fact that lives ended when battles began. But a thing known in theory is much different when experienced firsthand. Believing in an eye for an eye is all well and good, until you're forced to stand in front of your enemy's face and pluck that offending eye out of its socket with your own fingers. Then revenge loses some of its charm.

"It had to be done," Magnus said.

Lu opened her eyes to find him standing just a few feet away, watching her with strain clear in his face, his posture. She hated to see that worry on him, but even worse than his worry was a new thing lurking beneath, a thing that hooded his eyes and curved his lips and shoved an icy splinter of panic into her heart: admiration.

She didn't want to be admired for this . . . *butchery.*

"Let's get back to the caves," said Honor. "We need to make a plan for what we're going to do next." She seemed utterly unaffected by the sight of dead bodies, or that she'd helped make them that way, and Lu wasn't sure if she was envious, or disappointed. How could Honor feel nothing, witnessing this? How could she stand there dusting off her hands like nothing had just happened?

Her thoughts were interrupted when a low, wretched moan came from the only helicopter they hadn't inspected yet, lying on its flank about thirty meters away in a shallow depression between a stand of trees and several large boulders.

Lu whirled around and stared at it in horror. "Someone's still alive!"

Grimly, Magnus said, "Apparently so." From within his jacket, he withdrew a knife with a long, curved blade that gathered the light into a sinister sheen along its edge.

"No—God! Magnus, just . . . *don't.*" He'd been about to head in the direction of the moan, but Lu stepped in front of him, blocking his path.

"We can't afford the luxury of mercy, Lumina. There are too many lives at risk to leave any loose ends untied."

"They're not loose ends, they're people!" She answered before she even had a chance to edit the words, or think about why mercy might mean so much to her now when only minutes before she'd been so bloodthirsty.

One of his dark brows arched. "No, they're hunters. Hunters who wouldn't hesitate to slit your throat if the situation was reversed."

"Just . . . wait. He might . . . go . . . on his own."

Magnus watched her closely for a moment, his gaze turned assessing. "Do you really think one more, or one less, makes a difference to anyone, anywhere? You think someone is keeping score? That there's an old man with white hair in the sky looking down and making hash marks next to your name in a book, and that someday you'll have to answer for every one?"

Lu was taken aback by the hardness in his tone, his total lack of compunction. She stared at him with a flame of anger constricting her throat. "If you're asking if I believe in God, the answer is yes! I don't think God is an old man who lives in the sky, but I *do* think it makes a difference in the universe, or whatever you want to call it, every time you cause suffering!"

He looked, oddly, as if she'd slapped him. It lasted only a second before he regained his composure, the strange pain that had so briefly flared in his eyes now snuffed out.

"This was self-protection, Lumina, not premeditated murder. Those are two completely different things. You and Honor just saved a thousand lives—"

"By taking a dozen!"

"You *cannot* be sentimental—"

"Well I am!" she cried, her eyes filling with moisture. "I know you're right, it had to be done, but screw you if you think I'm not going to feel bad about it!" She looked at Honor. "And screw *both* of you for not feeling bad about it, too!"

Nauseated, her heart pounding, Lu turned and headed toward the helicopter without a glance behind.

Like the other two, it was a shambles of crumpled metal. Only one of its two rotors was still attached, bent and deeply gouged, with electrical wiring spraying out like severed veins. The tail had sheared in half on impact, and the tail rotor had separated with such force it was embedded in the trunk of a nearby tree, sticking out at a crazy angle. Wreckage was strewn all over the ground. Piles of black metal spat flames, smoke and gasoline fumes wafted in pungent gray and iridescent coils through the air.

Unlike the others, this helicopter wasn't surrounded by bodies.

From inside, the moan came again, fainter this time.

Lu froze, her chest tight, feeling as if she might be sick. The impulse to run away was almost overwhelming, but holding her in place was an equally strong desire to lay eyes on this stranger, this person who'd been sent to . . .

Sent to what, exactly? A pulse of heat went through her body like a wave, and Lu knew with absolute certainty that she had to get to whoever was making those awful moans, before he stopped making them.

Because he was more valuable to her alive than dead.

She closed the final distance to the helicopter in a few long strides, then looked in.

She recoiled with a gasp.

The inside of the helicopter looked painted in blood. It was everywhere: on the ceiling, the floors, the seats, the instrument panel, dripping down the walls in gory, long streaks. There had been four men strapped inside, two in front, two in back . . . and they were all still strapped in. But they'd been crushed, almost as if an invisible, giant hand had seized them, and squeezed. Their skin had burst like overripe fruit.

By some miracle, the pilot was conscious. Barely.

Fighting down a throatful of bitter bile, Lu yanked on the pilot's dented door, and swung it open. His eyelids fluttered. He turned his head a fraction of an inch, and saw her. Lu noticed his eyes were the color of an ancient pair of denim trousers her father had owned: the palest, softest blue.

"You," he whispered in German. He wheezed, and a red bubble appeared at the corner of his mouth.

"Y-you know me?" Lu whispered back. Her hand on the door shook so hard it rattled the frame.

His eyes glazed. He nodded.

Of course; the entire Federation must know what she looked like. Her picture would have been plastered everywhere, just like it was in New Vienna, on the megascreen. By now, the image of her face would have been distributed around the entire world. What was left of it.

Lu pushed that realization aside to focus on what she needed from the pilot. She could see she didn't have much time. Without another word, she reached out, and gently touched his face.

She stood like that for a long, silent moment, concentrating, not knowing exactly how this worked, only that it did. The pilot looked back at her without alarm or fear, just that glaze of agony in his eyes, the light behind them rapidly fading. With the faintest of whispers, he said, "Prettier than your picture, girl." His mouth turned up on one side, then he closed his eyes and died.

Lu dropped her hand from his face. She stared at him, her body wracked with tremors, her soul in the darkest place it had ever been, a bottomless pit of burning ashes and howling windstorms and boiling lakes of blood.

She let the door swing shut. She turned, finding Magnus and Hope waiting for her where she'd left them, watching. Then she moved forward as if in a dream, not even flinching when the helicopter exploded into flame and a writhing ball of orange fire engulfed everything around it, including her.

SEVENTEEN

"Are you going to tell us what this is all about?" asked Beckett gently, looking over Lu's shoulder as she drew in bold, broad strokes across the standing black chalkboard erected in a corner of his lab.

She didn't respond. Magnus watched, fascinated, from the back of the lab while she carried on with the drawing. Her slender arm moved ceaselessly, outlining the shape of a tall, wide cylinder, with a hollow core and identical levels, spaced evenly from top to bottom. On the three floors nearest the top, she drew a series of oblique shapes flaring out from the hollow center in a spoked pattern, like a spider's web. The other levels she partitioned into dozens upon dozens of small squares. The lowest level she shaded all in red, holding the chalk on its side for greater coverage. When she finished, she stood staring at the object on the board with her hands propped on her hips, silent.

Then she threw the chalk at the board so hard it shattered into dust.

Magnus shared a weighted look with Christian and Xander, both of whom stood near the opposite wall. They were joined by Morgan, Demetrius, Jack, Hawk, and Ember, while Honor stood alone, arms crossed and silent, by Beckett's collection of clocks stacked in crates.

Lumina hadn't spoken a word since they'd returned from topside. Magnus had watched her, pale and trembling, emerge from the wall of flame that had engulfed the helicopter, and had been momentarily surprised by the realization that she'd somehow retained all her clothing, unlike earlier with her encounter with Honor. But then she'd strode past him without even a glance, her eyes dark, pupils dilated. He'd sensed her fury like a thousand tiny pinpricks on his skin.

After what she'd said to him just before going to the helicopter, Magnus had assumed her fury had been directed at him. Watching her now, he wasn't quite so sure.

"What is that you've drawn, Lumina?" he said into the hush.

She unclenched her hands from her hair and turned slowly, looking around the group. "That's the Imperial Federation's international headquarters, which also functions as a maximum security prison." She paused a beat. When she spoke again, her voice shook with fury. "Which is where they're keeping my parents, and four thousand nine hundred eighty-seven others."

The gathering was stunned into silence. Then Honor said with hushed awe from her place alone by the clocks, "You took the pilot's memory."

Lumina's gaze cut to her sister, and Magnus had never before in his life felt someone exude such pure, unadulterated rage. "All those medicines the Phoenix Corporation makes? All those profits that support the IF, and that bastard Sebastian Thorne and his empire? *They're made from us.* I'd heard all the rumors, but the reality is so much . . . what the IF does to them . . . it's . . ."

She broke off with a choked cry of rage. Magnus pushed away from the wall, propelled by an almost violent urge to take her into his arms and say or do anything to soothe her, to take that anguished expression from her face. He crossed the room in several long strides. "Lumina. Look at me."

She did, and Magnus watched as her face cleared, the pain in her eyes replaced by calm, at the exact rate his own calm was being replaced by sickening, overwhelming, vicious rage.

"No!" Lumina stepped closer, understanding dawning in her eyes. "No, don't you *dare!*" She reached out and shoved him in the chest.

She was strong, and he was unprepared, and her push sent him staggering back a few paces before he recovered himself. She closed the few steps between them quickly until she stood mere inches away, staring up into his eyes, solemn and so beautiful it distracted him for a moment from the furor burning through his veins.

"Give it back."

He'd been angry before many, many times in his life, but Magnus hadn't felt this particular, rabid brand of rage. He felt as if the emotion he'd taken from Lumina was so blindingly hot and encompassing it was the equivalent of standing on the surface of the sun. He couldn't stop his hands from shaking, or his nostrils flaring, or the way every one of his muscles had tensed.

Her gaze still locked on his, Lumina said, "It's not yours. It's mine. Give it back."

Everyone else in the room was watching them, arrested by this little melodrama and momentarily distracted from the reason they were here in the first place.

Magnus growled, "No."

She stepped even closer, and he had to restrain himself from recoiling. Not because he didn't want her so near, or because he didn't like the looks that were flying back and forth between the others, the obvious surprise that he'd allowed her to get so close, but because it was all he could do to resist the urge to reach out and grab her, and pull her hard against his chest.

Desire for her pounded through him, so strong he could hardly breathe.

"Magnus," Lumina said solemnly, "thank you. I know what you're trying to do, and I appreciate it, I really do, but I need that feeling you took away because it's going to help me get through this. It's going to help me deal with what I have to do next. Without that anger, I'm just going to be so sad I'll want to slit my wrists, so I'm asking you please to *give it back*."

Shaking with her fury and his own wretched desire, Magnus hoarsely said, "I can't stand to see you suffer, Lumina. Not if there's anything I can do about it. I'm sorry, but the answer is no."

She looked at him a long, silent moment. She released a quiet breath. Then she said softly, "All right. Have it your way. But just remember: You brought this on yourself."

Then she rose up on her toes and kissed him.

It was exactly as he remembered from a thousand beautiful dreams. No—it was better. Her lips like velvet, the soft, languorous stroke of her tongue against his. The fever that crackled through him, burning, her scent flaming hot in his nose, the lush warmth of her body. All of it conspired to wipe every thought from his mind, every hesitation and the final shred of his will, so that he closed his eyes, crushed her against him, and kissed her back so hard he bent her back from the waist.

The collective gasp from the gathered group barely registered in his consciousness. Because now Lumina wound her arms around his shoulders, moaning into his mouth. An erection charged to life between his legs.

He had no idea how long the kiss lasted; time had lost all meaning. Then there was a change from one moment to the next, a loss of the warmth of her mouth, a withdrawal of her body heat, and he opened his eyes to find a roomful of shocked *Ikati* and one very pissed off Lumina.

Wordlessly, she snapped, *Now we're even.* With her thoughts echoing in his mind, Magnus realized with horror that she'd reclaimed more than just her own pain.

She'd taken the one thing that kept him sane.

She returned to the chalk drawing, leaving everyone gaping in her wake.

"We need to find this structure. It's massive, so it shouldn't be too hard. Beckett, since you seem to be the resident computer genius, do you have any current maps of the IF?"

Beckett looked exactly as electrocuted as Magnus felt. He stammered, "I . . . uh . . . that is . . ." He shook his head to clear it, then straightened his shoulders and continued on, a little more in control. "Let's find out."

From his cluttered desk, he retrieved a small, handheld device and pointed it at the map Lumina had drawn. With a click and a sound like crickets chirping, a ray of translucent red light scanned the board from top to bottom, then disappeared as quickly as it had appeared. Beckett plugged the device into a larger one, about the size and shape of a shoebox, and a three-dimensional rendering of Lumina's drawing flickered to life, floating in the middle of the room like a disembodied spirit.

"Specular holography imager," Beckett explained, walking around the perimeter of the wavering image. It was rendered in a brilliant royal blue, except for the bottom layer, which pulsed vivid red, corresponding to the red in Lumina's drawing. She drew closer to it, as if pulled by an invisible lure, her gaze trained on that pulsing band of red.

"That son of a bitch," she whispered. She glanced at Honor. Something unspoken passed between them, but Magnus caught a whisper of it, because Lumina had stripped him of the mental shield he'd worked so hard to develop over so many years.

That's where they keep her.

Into a keyboard wired to the shoebox, Beckett typed something. He waited a moment, examining the rapidly scrolling text that appeared on an adjacent computer screen. "There's nothing shaped like this on any of the system maps. Which, if it really is IF headquarters, makes sense: They wouldn't want anyone to be able to access it."

"A hidden file, then," said Christian, stepping forward to examine the image. "Or another closed system you can't access."

Sounding insulted, Beckett said, "There isn't a system I can't access."

"Well, everything that's built needs plans, blueprints," interjected Xander, absently combing his fingers through Morgan's long hair. They stood side by side on the opposite side of the cave, so close they looked fused together, and Magnus didn't want to know where Morgan's left hand was, her arm completely hidden behind Xander's large back. Morgan caught Magnus's eye, and sent him a wink, which he responded to with a glower. Which, naturally, made her smile.

"Maybe it's pre-Flash," suggested Demetrius in his deep, gravelly voice.

Beside him, Eliana nodded. "They could even have converted another existing facility. Something old . . ."

"But there's nothing this particular size or shape on the maps, and whether it was pre-Flash or not, it would show up—"

"You know what it looks like to me?" interrupted Jack. She drew away from Hawk's side, and came up to the image, examining it from top to bottom. "A silo. Like one of those towers you'd see across the Midwest in the disbanded United States, steel structures filled with grain or coal in the ag belt."

Magnus considered it. Then it hit him. "But not all silos in the US were above ground. And not all of them were agricultural." Everyone looked at him. "Ever heard of the Atlas missile program?"

"Shit," breathed Beckett. "You're right. It could be a bunker!"

"Underground?" Honor stepped forward as everyone else was, coming to get a closer look. "You think this thing could be underground?"

"That would definitely explain why it wouldn't show up on the modeling maps," said Beckett, nodding. "They're all aerial based: topography, buildings, that sort of thing, built out from the pre-Flash earth-mapping computer programs. There's an associated sub-program that identifies all the known underground structures, like sewers, subway systems, catacombs. But if, like Magnus suggests, this is a government-built structure constructed as part of a national defense plan, the blueprints would never have been made public."

"Or been catalogued electronically," added Ember, beside Christian, her fingers threaded through his. "The Atlas missile program was decommissioned in the 1960s, long before the creation of the World Wide Web, or the rise of information technology. Those blueprints were most likely stored in hard copies deep inside some secret government vault."

"So we're looking at the disbanded US, then?" Beckett was beginning to sound excited.

"Not necessarily, son," said Christian. "Many pre-Flash governments had missile programs. Russia, China, Iran, France, Germany . . . there were dozens. Maybe more."

"So it could be anywhere. We have no idea where to start looking," said Morgan, sounding deflated.

"Actually we do." Everyone turned to look at Lumina. "The helicopter pilot was born in the same city he worked. He raised his . . ." she swallowed, pausing a moment to steady her voice. "He raised his family in the same place. The same place I believe this structure is located, although I couldn't tell for sure from his memory . . . he died before . . ." She paused again. "I don't know exactly *where* this thing is, but I think I know the city it's in."

"Where?" said Magnus.

Lumina looked at him, her expression registering fury, anguish, and, worst of all, self-recrimination. With a telling tremble in her voice, she asked him, "What's the worst place in the world it could possibly be?"

No one else understood her, but Magnus grasped her meaning instantly, even before she sent her thoughts directly into his mind.

She was right there. My entire life, my mother was right there, and I didn't know it. Her eyes filled with tears.

With his heart aching for her, Magnus said into the hungry silence, "New Vienna."

Slowly, Lumina nodded, her eyes burning his. "I have to save her, Magnus. I have to go back."

His gaze never leaving hers, Magnus shook his head. "No." He stepped forward, the space between them charged. "*I* have to go back. You'll be recognized immediately—"

"I'm not going to just sit here and wait—"

"That's exactly what you're going to do—"

"She's *my* mother—"

"It's *my* responsibility!"

They'd moved closer and closer while they spoke, drawn as if by an invisible magnet, eyes locked together. He felt all the other eyes on them, he felt the tension in the room, but all he could think about was Lumina, her anguished face and voice, what he could do to take away her pain.

Finally they stood once again mere inches apart, staring each other down. Into the uncomfortable silence, someone in the room coughed.

Always the hard way with you, she said into his head, examining his determined expression.

Before he could form a reply, she said aloud, "Fine. We'll go together."

EIGHTEEN

Almost another full day passed before Lumina and Magnus set out on their journey back to New Vienna, and in that time he managed to avoid speaking directly to her, preferring instead to communicate his plans and directions in the presence of others so that she would overhear and be informed, deftly sidestepping the need for one-on-one conversation.

It was as if her kiss had changed something between them. As if he'd erected defenses even higher and more fortified than those he'd had before. He wasn't even looking at her.

Though she knew she could communicate with him by speaking right into his mind, Lumina avoided doing it, sensing his need for privacy. She was well-practiced in blocking stray thoughts, so it was no great challenge, but the temptation was great.

As was the temptation to kiss him again.

If he smelled enticing, he'd tasted even better, and Lumina found her gaze straying over and over to his mouth. Those full, sensual lips became a sort of beacon, drawing her attention any time he came near. When he spoke, she was mesmerized, just watching them move, sometimes losing the shape of the words altogether so that she was left with a kind of muted pleasure, his teeth and lips and tongue moving silently while she lost herself in the memory of how he'd tasted. Of the way he'd reacted when she touched her mouth to his. Of the need she'd felt surge through him, into her, another memory she lingered on in her private moments, the ache of his unfulfilled desire.

Her own desire for him was huge, real, and frightening.

She'd promised herself she'd never get close again, she'd never again risk another person's safety for her sake, and she'd meant it. But every moment she spent near him became a kind of torture, because no matter how hard she tried to block it out, the animal inside her knew what she really wanted, and was far less self-controlled.

The animal inside her was greedy, a writhing, hissing beast that demanded satisfaction.

Lu knew that kiss had been a touchstone. It had changed them both. For better or worse remained to be seen.

" . . . approach through the southern Czech border," Magnus was now saying to Demetrius and Hawk, both of whom were intently studying the holographic map Beckett had projected above the center of the rectangular Assembly table. Beckett had been dismissed after setting it up, not only because the Assembly was always held in closed session, but also because Lu could tell he was getting on Magnus's last nerve. Beckett had been shadowing him, dogged as a bloodhound, insisting he should accompany them on their trip, regaling Magnus with reason after reason why he'd be an asset in their quest to extract Lumina and Honor's mother from the IF prison.

Magnus, naturally, had flatly refused. *Flatly* meaning with a bite as friendly as a crocodile's.

"Why not go in the way you came out?" asked Hawk, frowning at the map.

"I never take the same route twice. Too risky. Especially now: Enforcement's offering a huge reward for any eyewitness information from Thornemas Day."

"Christmas Day," Lu softly corrected from her seat at the far end of the table. Demetrius and Hawk looked at her. Magnus's head angled in her direction, but he didn't lift his gaze from the map. He wore the hooded black jacket again, so his face was cast in shadow, but she noted his shoulders, just slightly, tensed.

You think there's an old man with white hair in the sky looking down and making hash marks next to your name in a book?

His words came back to haunt her. She wondered, looking at his stiffening posture, if they haunted him, too.

She wondered, for the hundredth time, what had happened to him to make him so . . . *him*.

He went on as if she hadn't spoken. "I think we'll have to leave the copter as soon as we cross the Channel and continue on foot; security will have been significantly stepped up. Patrols will be tighter, including air patrols. Beckett's intel suggests that anywhere east of Antwerp and south of Amsterdam will be rough going."

"But that's exactly where you're headed!" protested Demetrius, drawing a line with his finger from the English Channel to New Vienna.

His voice grim, Magnus said, "Correct."

"There's another way you could get in. One that doesn't require a helicopter."

This from Honor, who sat beside Lu with her trademark pissed-off expression. They'd had an epic argument about the pros and cons of her staying to guard the colony versus joining Magnus and Lu on their hunt as she'd wanted to, and eventually—after a

small earthquake that dislodged quite a few of the older, larger stalactites from the cave roof—she'd relented.

Barely.

Now she glanced Lu's way, with a small, knowing smile on her
lips.

"No," said Magnus, with enough volume that it echoed off the
walls.

"Forget it," said Lu simultaneously. The thought of flying over
Europe as a dragon with Magnus straddling her back held all kinds
of weird connotations.

Honor shrugged, then began inspecting her fingernails with
interest. *Coward.*

Call me that one more time, thought Lu, reddening, *and the next
time we see Beckett, I'll roast off all your clothes.*

Honor inhaled a sharp breath, and glared at her.

Lu glared back. *Yes. I figured out how to do it. Don't test me.*

You are such a bitch!

Call the kettle black much, pot?

Stop it!

This new, unexpected voice brought Lu up short. She looked at
Magnus, who looked back at her with steel in his eyes, the first time
he'd made eye contact with her since their kiss. Beside her, Honor
glanced back and forth between the two of them with narrowed eyes.

What? Honor asked suspiciously, and that's when Lu realized
her sister couldn't hear Magnus. His voice was for her, and her alone,
which made her strangely satisfied. And more than a little confused.

Nothing. Lu lowered her gaze to the tabletop, gnawing the
inside of her cheek.

"Jack, can you set us up with some of your people? We'll need
at least five nights' lodging, maybe six, on our way into the city."
Magnus continued aloud, his voice controlled, his attention back
on the map, as if nothing at all had happened. Lu might have

wondered at his control if two of the words he'd just spoken hadn't jumped up and seized her around the neck.

Five. Nights.

The tabletop became incredibly fascinating. She examined every minute scratch and chip and flow of the grain, willing herself not to linger on those words, or on their meaning, or on the myriad possibilities that lay therein. Beneath the convenient cover of her hair, her ears grew hot.

"You got it," replied Jack. "And for the way out? I assume you'll want different places?"

Magnus paused before he spoke, so long that Lu glanced up at him. "We'll cross that bridge when we get to it," he said darkly. His gaze flicked to hers. Finding her staring back at him, he turned his head away, but not before she saw the strange resignation in his eyes. Something about it made her skin crawl.

Carefully, she raised one mental wall, and lowered another, unsure if this exercise would work.

What is it, Magnus?

His lips thinned. Beside her, Honor showed no sign she'd heard Lu's question, so Lu kept her face carefully neutral, her gaze in the middle distance, focused on nothing.

I really wish you wouldn't do that, came Magnus's curt response, his face still turned away.

Lu's ears burned hotter. *Tell me what's bothering you and I promise I won't do it again.*

Jack said, "All right. I'll get on it. I should have names and addresses for you within a few hours." Among murmured goodbyes, she and Hawk left the Assembly room, leaving Demetrius in all his shaved-head, leather-bound, tattooed glory standing in silent contemplation of the map.

It bothers me that you can do it at all.

Lu sent Magnus a sidelong look. *That's not an answer.*

If you had any respect for me, Lumina, it would be the only answer you'd need.

Both the words and the acidity of his tone floored her. Her face went bright red. Mortified, she flung up a wall between them, shutting him out.

"You'll need clothes," said Honor quietly, not looking at her. "You can take whatever of mine you need." She seemed unusually subdued. Somber, even. "And we should test your Gifts, at least a little more before you go. We should practice. We don't even know if you can—"

"There's no time," said Magnus. "As soon as Jack has those names for us, we're gone. Every minute we stay here is one more minute we risk the lives of everyone in that prison. And everyone here." His eyes cut to Lu's. He seemed about to say more, but then he turned to Demetrius and spoke in a lowered voice. "Anything you need to tell me?"

A subtle change overtook the big male. It was nothing sudden, nothing huge, but a look crept over his strong features, an odd expression Lu recognized as the same one that had so changed Magnus's face only moments before.

Resignation.

He shared a glance with Magnus, fleeting but indelibly dark, almost *sad*, and Lu's stomach twinged with foreboding.

Demetrius straightened. Crossed his bulging arms over his chest. Stared hard at the map, as if it had personally offended him, his square chin jutted out like a dare. He muttered, "Cogs in the machine, Seeker, all of us. You know it as well as I."

Magnus jerked his head toward Lu and Honor, his brows quirked as if he were asking a silent question, and Demetrius shook his head.

Whatever that exchange meant, it definitely held meaning for Magnus, because he closed his eyes for the briefest of moments, then nodded, as if satisfied.

Only he wasn't smiling.

He adopted the same pose as Demetrius, arms crossed, legs spread, and Lu and Honor were treated to the sight of two big, handsome males glowering down their noses at them. "Have you told Jenna we're coming?" asked Magnus, looking at Honor.

She tensed. Lu looked at her, sensing her sister's worry.

"She's not answering me. Not since yesterday."

Lu sat up straighter. "Has that ever happened before?"

Honor shook her head, threaded a lock of her hair between her fingers, and began to nibble it. If Lu hadn't been so filled with new anxiety about what their mother's silence might mean, she would have smiled; she'd only stopped chewing on the ends of her hair when she began wearing it in a braid a few years ago.

She laid a hand on Honor's arm and gave it a reassuring squeeze. *Everything is going to be okay.*

Honor nodded, but didn't reply. She stood. "Are we done here?"

Magnus and Demetrius shared a look. It was Magnus who answered. "We leave as soon as Jack has those names, Lumina. Get a bag ready. But pack light; whatever you bring you'll have to carry."

Lu nodded.

"And one more thing."

She looked up at him. Magnus was looking back at her with an expression of dispassion, his face closed off again. But beneath the shadows of his hood, his eyes were aglow, intent and unblinking.

"Your hair."

Lu reached up and touched her head. "What about it?"

"It's too . . . distinctive. We'll get you another pair of contacts to replace the ones you lost when you Shifted, but you need to do something with your hair so it won't be so noticeable. Dye it. Hide it under a hat. Something."

Honor said, "I know what to do."

"Oh. Okay," said Lu, rising from her chair. She brightened. "I've always wanted to be a redhead."

"Not *red*." Magnus still wasn't blinking. His gaze burned the air between them like a lit fuse. "*Less* distinctive, Lumina."

Honor reached out and took Lu's hand, gently pulling. "I said I know what to do, Seeker. You worry about getting in and out safely, and leave the beauty regimens to me."

With that, she led Lu away, leaving Magnus and Demetrius staring after them in silence.

Magnus waited until Lumina and Honor's footsteps had faded before he spoke, and even then he kept his voice low. "I don't want to know the details. I don't believe a man should know how he's going to die. No good could come of that. I only want to know one thing: Will she see it?"

He didn't turn and look at Demetrius, because he knew how difficult this was for him. His Gift of Foresight had, more often than not, been a terrible burden for him. The knowledge came to him in dreams, but those dreams were almost always nightmares. He'd known his home colony in Rome would be invaded. He'd known his two best friends would refuse to leave with everyone else, and would die defending it. Magnus assumed Demetrius also knew the hour and method of his own death, and his wife Eliana's. On the scale of horrible things, that was right up there with knowing you were *never* going to die. So he didn't look at the hulking male who'd become as close a friend as Magnus had had in the last twenty years; he just waited.

"Yes. Lumina will be there when it happens." Demetrius's voice was filled with sorrow.

Magnus cursed. "But she'll be unharmed? She'll get her mother out of that prison? They'll escape?"

"I'm sorry, brother. I don't know the outcome. The Dream was . . . incomplete."

Magnus cursed again, louder.

"There's something else, though. I don't know how to explain it."

Now Magnus did look at Demetrius, because the tone in his voice changed. Gone was the sorrow, replaced by agitation, or frustration.

"What is it?"

Demetrius glanced at him. His eyes were the color of polished obsidian. His brows pulled together, and the three small silver rings in his eyebrow glinted in the low light. "She'll be different, afterward. She won't be the same woman she is now. In fact, she won't *be* Lumina anymore at all."

"What the hell does that mean? How could she not be herself?"

Demetrius exhaled a heavy breath, passing a hand over his face. "All I know is that Lumina won't exist anymore, not in the way she does now."

Magnus whirled around and faced Demetrius. "You said she would survive! You intimated it, when I asked if there was anything you needed to tell me, you shook your head no—"

"She'll live," Demetrius insisted, his voice growing louder to match Magnus's. "But she *won't* be Lumina. I don't know how to better explain it, Magnus. I don't know what the Dreams mean, I only know what they show me!"

Magnus was breathing hard, his hands clenched to fists at his side. "But she *will* live. You're sure of that, at least?"

Demetrius nodded, and the steel band that had tightened around Magnus's chest loosened a degree. "All right," he said, mollified. "If that's the best we've got, I'll take it." He turned to leave.

From behind him, Demetrius said quietly, "You can change it, you know."

Magnus stopped, listening.

"The future isn't set in stone. Every action, every decision, creates a new path. You don't have to walk into this situation, knowing what you now know. We can find another way."

Magnus turned slowly and looked at Demetrius. "Fate's going to have her way with all of us, D. If I sidestep now, it's just a delay. You'll have another Dream another night, and find out how I die a different way. Am I right?"

Demetrius lifted his chin, his gaze steady and penetrating. He said nothing.

"I made Lumina a promise that I'd bring her parents back to her, or die trying. There's nothing in this world that could change my mind, not even knowing that at least half of that promise is guaranteed to come true. I'm a tool, Demetrius. I'm an instrument. And every breath I've ever taken in my life has been leading me to this." He paused, and for a long moment the two looked at one another. With quiet reverence, Magnus added, "Dying for her will be the best thing I've ever done. It's what I'm meant for. It's my destiny, Demetrius. And I welcome it."

Then he turned and walked away.

NINETEEN

Honor's room—*cave*, Lu kept reminding herself—was well away from the warren of others they'd passed on their way through the cool, echoing passageways that led from the Assembly chamber. The shadowed beauty of the place enthralled her; soaring ceilings and secret corners and whispers teased along stone walls, the scent of water and moss, air so deathly still it felt entombed.

It was magical. She loved it, in the way a prisoner long held under lock and key loves his first glimpse of open sky. She felt safe and secure in this enchanted underground city.

But, most of all, she felt *free.*

"It's not half as wonderful as you think it is," muttered Honor, sweeping regally into her rooms beneath a low, carved archway of stone. She'd installed thick white curtains on either side of the entrance, plush and sound dampening, so that when she released the tasseled ties that held them back, the velvet panels fell together with a swish and a billow, and the sound of flowing water from beyond was instantly muffled.

"If you'd spent your entire life sleeping in a bedroom the size of your sitting area, you might disagree," Lu said, eyeing the sumptuous white divan flanked by a pair of fat, snowy armchairs that surrounded a low grate of glowing embers sending up feathers of orange ash into the air. The entire room was sumptuous, outfitted all in white, from the furniture to the draperies to the rugs underfoot, and Lu wondered briefly why her sister insisted on having no color in anything she owned, from her clothes to her décor.

Everything in Honor's world was bleached as bone. Colorless. Bloodless. Even her dragon form was pallid as the full moon.

Honor sniffed, clearly disagreeing with Lu's assessment. Moving to her bed, an elaborate, four-poster affair of downy pillows and gauzy curtains and white fur throws, she stripped off her jacket, casually tossing it atop the coverlet. Her boots followed, thrown one after another over her shoulder to land in hollow thumps against the stone floor, then she padded barefoot back to where Lu stood near the entrance.

She held out her hand. "C'mon. There's not much time."

Lu followed as her sister towed her past the bed, around a gnarled column of stone into an adjacent chamber. It was a bathroom of sorts, though there was no shower or bath. But there was a vanity with a mirror, lighted by small, flickering votives set into niches into the stone, and Honor pushed her down onto the small padded bench before it. She stood behind Lu, gathered her loose hair into her hands, and began to work the strands into a braid.

"Funny," Honor said after a moment, her voice neutral, "that we'd both wear our hair this long, even though we'd never met." Her eyes met Lu's in the mirror, and Lu glimpsed the pain her sister tried to hide behind her bland looks and flavorless tones, her hard and frigid persona.

She reached up and grasped one of Honor's wrists. "We're coming back," she said, her voice quiet but vehement. "You know that, right? We're going to bring her back . . . and if . . . ." She couldn't bring herself to say the word *father*, so she just said, "if Leander is there, we'll bring him back, too."

Honor stood still for a moment, eyes downcast, her face a shade paler than bone. She worked her wrist free from Lu's grip, and her fingers began slowly to thread through Lu's hair.

"Honor," Lu said, her throat constricting. "Please. Say you know we'll come back."

For the first time since she'd met her sister, Lu saw an emotion other than anger. *Raw* emotion, laid bare and unapologetic. Her face twisted, her voice shook with the force of it.

"You want me to lie to you so you'll feel better? Well, sorry, but the answer's *no*." Her fingers tugged at Lu's hair, jerking her head back as she wound the strands together. She kept her eyes on her work. "I *don't* know that you'll come back. I don't know *anything*. And neither do *you*."

Tug. Yank. Lu's head jerked to and fro.

"All these 'Gifts,' all these 'talents,' all this 'power,' and still we're just as helpless as a pair of bunny rabbits being chased by a pack of wolves!" Honor's voice rose in perfect counterpoint to the rising shaking in her hands, in her body. The mirror affixed to the wall skittered a few inches left, and Lu's heartbeat jumped with it.

"But Magnus—"

"Magnus is good at what he does. He's never failed one of his retrieval missions, but there's a first time for everything. Did you catch that little exchange between him and Demetrius?"

"Yeah, what was that all about?"

Honor made a sound of disgust. "Demetrius dreams the future. It's his Gift."

Lu bolted upright. "So they already know how this plays out!"

Honor pulled her back by her shoulders, and continued braiding the long strands. "D's Foresight isn't an exact science. And it's sporadic; he didn't know Magnus would find you, for instance. But he saw *something*." Her eyes met Lu's in the mirror. "'We're all cogs in the machine?' Could he be any more cryptic?"

Lu knew Magnus wouldn't tell her what their exchange had meant, even if she begged. She also knew she couldn't eavesdrop on his thoughts, not only because that was wrong, but also because he'd sense her and shut down. She decided she'd just have to figure something out, because she desperately wanted to know what he and Demetrius knew.

"Magnus wouldn't let me come along if Demetrius had Dreamt I'd get hurt."

"Like I said, his Dreams aren't an exact science. Sometimes they're bits and pieces, a puzzle that has to be deciphered, not a picture fully developed. And if you get hurt, you'll heal." Honor's voice lowered. Gained a new, darker edge. "No. Getting hurt isn't the worst thing that could happen."

She tied a small elastic band around the end of Lu's braid, and stepped back to inspect it. Lu wondered why she'd bothered to braid it when she was supposed to be doing something to make it look different, but then Honor said something that snapped her back to cold, hard reality.

"Consider for a minute what happens if they catch you."

Even though she'd thought the same thing, hearing it aloud was like a slap in the face. "They won't."

Honor's snort was derisive. In the mirror, her expression was a contradiction of pain and worry, confusion and resignation, and Lu felt something shifting in her, a profound change swelling to the surface faster than Honor could contain it. Suddenly, her face was transfigured by misery.

"Don't be so sure. Overconfidence is an excellent way to screw up. Because if you get too complacent and they *do* catch you, you'll be spending the rest of eternity in a sealed cell!"

In one swift, smooth motion, Honor unsheathed a small knife she had hidden at her waist, pulled Lu's braid taut, and sliced it cleanly off only an inch away from her exposed neck. Her shorn hair fell forward around her face in a short, perfect bob.

Lu leapt from the chair and whirled around, her hands lifting to her head, her eyes wide and disbelieving. Honor just stood there with her long, severed braid dangling from her hand like a beheaded snake. She was breathing hard, eyes glittering, hands trembling at her sides.

"Don't get caught," she said, the words ragged, harsh. "I only just found you. I can't lose you again."

Then she dropped both the knife and the severed braid, and pulled Lu into a hard hug, sobbing.

Lu couldn't help it. She started to laugh.

She wrapped her arms around her crying sister and laughed. "You crazy, unstable, psycho *witch*!"

Honor sobbed harder, hugging Lu so tight she could hardly breathe.

Morgan's voice, hesitant, came from behind the drawn entrance curtains. "Ducks? Everything all right?"

Honor pushed Lu away, angrily wiping tears from her face, and left Lu by the vanity while she began to pace like a caged animal in front of the smoldering fire in the sitting area in the adjacent room. "Fine!" she yelled. "Everything's just peachy friggin' keen!"

You really don't deal with emotions well, sweetie, Lu thought. Honor's answering shout reverberated inside her head.

SHUT! UP!

"Morgan, come in," said Lu, hurrying to the other room. When Morgan stepped through the curtains and saw her, she clapped a hand over her mouth, staring.

"I know, right?" Lu fingered a lock of her hair. Without all the weight, her head felt as if it were floating above her shoulders, light as air. She had to admit she liked the feeling, though she felt unduly exposed, her neck bare to the cool air, her nape naked. She also had to admit she *wanted* to be angry with Honor for doing something so drastic, but wasn't.

She got it now. She had her sister's number. That hardcore, badass act wasn't fooling her anymore. Beneath that icy façade was just a girl who felt everything a little too much, and didn't know how to handle it.

Morgan's gaze flicked to the floor in front of the vanity. She saw the knife and the braid, glanced over at Honor, then looked back at Lu. "Well," she said, her composure recovered, "it suits you. Now you look like Princess Di."

"Who?"

Morgan waved a hand, stepping into the room. "Never mind. Listen, I came to talk to you about something." She hesitated, then amended, "Actually I came to offer you something."

"Let's sit," suggested Lu, her curiosity piqued by the tone of Morgan's voice. She gestured toward the sofa and chairs Honor still paced around, but Morgan shook her head.

"I'll only stay a moment, I know you're getting ready to leave. There's just . . ."

Her lovely face clouded, and Lu's heart rate spiked. "What? What's wrong?"

"No," she said gently, taking Lu's hands. "Pet, there's nothing wrong." She laughed softly, shaking her head. "Besides everything, of course." She glanced down at their joined hands, inhaled a deliberate breath, then quietly said, "I want you to have it."

"Have what?" asked Lu, perplexed.

Morgan lifted her eyes and fixed Lu in her green, green stare. "My Gift."

A beat of astonished silence followed this declaration as Lu and Honor stared at Morgan, processing what she'd said.

"No," Lu said, but Morgan was already shaking her head.

"You don't even know what it is yet. And believe me when I say it can come in incredibly handy."

Lu withdrew her hands, crossing her arms over her chest. "It's kind of you to offer, really, but—"

"Take it," Honor cut in suddenly. Lu turned, and found Honor staring at her with fierce, frozen intent, her cheeks still wet. "Morgan's right: Her Gift is amazing. And much more subtle than ours. It's perfect for what you're about to do. Take it. Drain her."

Drain her? Lu felt vaguely insulted. "I'm not some kind of vampire—"

"Yes," Honor interrupted, her voice hard, "you *are*."

Lu opened her mouth to protest, but then she thought of the pilot's memory. She thought of Magnus's mental shield. She thought of how she'd learned to play the piano, and fluently speak the several languages she'd never once studied.

She tucked her bare hands under her armpits, and turned away from Morgan, her cheeks heating in embarrassment. "I don't want to be this weird . . . *collector*."

"Her Gift of Suggestion is one of the best." Honor's voice still rang with that hard edge, but now also held a pleading undertone. "Anyone would kill to have it—"

"If it's so special, you take it!"

"I can't!"

It hung there in the air, throbbing with import, tapering away into silence while Lu and Honor stared at one another and Morgan waited in quiet stillness near the door.

"I don't have that Gift," said Honor, her voice soft. "Believe me, I've tested it. I've tried. I can't do what you can do."

"But . . . Caesar . . ." Morgan floundered, at a loss for words, staring at Honor, obviously struggling to understand.

Honor slowly shook her head. "That wasn't me. That was Hope."

Morgan's eyes had gone wide. She whispered, "So *Hope* took Caesar's Gift of Immortality . . ."

"And then we killed him," finished Honor, her voice hollow.

A tingle of horror swept up Lu's spine. "Killed him?" she repeated slowly.

Seeing her expression, Honor said, "You've never heard of Caesar?"

Lu shook her head.

Morgan came closer, her expression dark. "He was a murderer. He was one of us, but he wanted to rule the world, and he slaughtered a lot of high-profile humans in his quest for power. And he planned to kill your parents, and you, though you were just little babies—"

"Why would he want to kill *us*?" Lu looked back and forth between Morgan and Honor.

Morgan said, "Because your mother was the Queen."

Lu just stared at her, speechless.

"She still is, in fact. But once Caesar found out he was Gifted with Immortality, he plotted to kill her, and take over the entire world, *Ikati* and human both. We'd lived in secrecy and silence for thousands of years, hidden in small colonies like this one, but Caesar decided he was done with all that. It was he who betrayed us to Sebastian Thorne. It was he who started the war between our two species. His insanity is the reason behind *every* terrible thing that's befallen us in the last twenty-five years, and there's not a day that's gone by that I don't give thanks that that son of a bitch is dead."

A log settled lower in the grate. The fire sighed and released a knot of orange sparks. And inside of Lu, memory was knitting together with abrupt concrescence, like fingers interlacing, or a key fitting into a well-oiled lock.

She asked, "It was the day before the Flash, wasn't it? When Caesar tried to kill us?"

Morgan looked startled. "How did you know?"

There were pictures in Lu's mind, a series of images she'd carried with her for as long as she could remember. The images had always seemed nonsensical, a collage of unrelated items, like photos pasted into a scrapbook: a snapshot of a man with black hair and midnight eyes, standing atop the crenellated tower of a crumbling kasbah in the desert, staring up at the star-dusted sky; the same man clutching a tiny baby to his chest in a strangely elegant tree house in the darkest heart of a jungle, his face twisted with rage; a long, wavering line of pinprick lights that weren't stars twinkling on the morning horizon; a soundless flight over a landscape of emerald green, bisected by the sinuous black twist of a sluggish river; a charming house surrounded by flowers on the edge of a small village, its front door painted yellow.

The sky a blazing pulse of color, flashing scarlet to orange to brilliant, blinding white.

Lu had always assumed these pictures were things she'd conjured from the imaginary worlds she visited in books, or perhaps remnants of long-ago dreams, or random snippets of forgotten songs, her mind creating images from read or spoken words. But now she saw the pictures for what they really were: memories.

Only not her own. Her mother's. She'd stolen them from her.

Lu crossed slowly to the white duvet, sank into its plump, welcome cushions, and stared into the fire.

"Pet? Are you all right?"

Numb with recognition, Lu whispered, "Of course. Why wouldn't I be? Seeing as how I just realized that the first time I killed a man, *I was barely more than one year old*."

"*We*," said Honor. She sat beside her on the sofa, took her hand, and squeezed it. "We did it. Together. And Morgan is right: He deserved it. I'd kill him again if I could."

A sound worked its way from Lu's throat. It was part laugh, part choke, part cry of disbelief. She thought of the helicopter pilot, that red bubble at the corner of his mouth, and had to close her eyes to contain the tears that pricked beneath her lids.

How many more people will I kill in my lifetime? Is that what I am? A murderer, like Caesar?

No, came Honor's firm reply. *You're a warrior. Like me. And sometimes warriors get their hands bloody, but the difference is that a murderer kills because he wants to. A warrior only kills when he has to, to protect himself, or the ones he loves.*

Lu opened her eyes and gazed at her sister, whose mouth had curved into a smile.

Or, in our case, to protect the ones she loves.

Morgan sat on Lu's other side. She took Lu's chin firmly in hand and forced her to meet her eyes. "You will *not* feel guilty for what you did. I won't allow it. Guilt and shame are wasted emotions, only ever useful for what they can teach us. Learn what you can, then let the rest go, because if you allow guilt to sink its claws in you, you'll never be free of it."

"The only people who don't feel guilt when they've done something wrong are *bad* people," Lu countered.

"That's correct. And you do feel bad, which proves you're not one of those people. But I'm telling you now that guilt is only a half step away from fear, and if you allow yourself to wallow in guilt, fear will follow on its heels and eventually you'll find yourself paralyzed. Don't let either one dictate how you'll live your life." She smiled, releasing Lu's chin. "I never have, and Lord knows there are a million reasons I could've."

Lu sat for a moment in silence, absorbing Morgan's words, until Honor spoke again.

"You need to get your head straight about this."

Lu looked at her sister, and found her staring back at her with her usual freezing intensity. Her tears had dried. Her armor had been donned.

"There's always a price to be paid for freedom. That price is blood. It's ugly, it's tragic, but it's reality. We didn't start this fight, but we have to be willing to engage, and fight back. We have to do what it takes to protect ourselves, or we all die. The strong either protect the weak, or devour them. You and I are strong. So was Caesar. He chose the second path, and we chose the first. Can you see the difference?"

With her fierce sister on one side, and her fiery godmother on the other, Lu experienced a moment of profound calm, like the breathless stillness in the eye of a storm. She'd never felt so centered, or so suddenly sure of what she had to do. She thought perhaps it was the kindness of denial—ignorance was definitely bliss, in her experience—or maybe mass hysteria on a smaller scale, the effective mindwashing of two talented salespeople, but their words touched a chord deep inside her, and her shame was unexpectedly replaced by . . . well, if not pride then at least satisfaction.

Honor was right. If they wanted to, she and her sister could wreak the kind of havoc on the planet that would be nothing short of biblical. And who could stop them?

But they didn't want that. For all their differences, they wanted the same thing.

Peace. Freedom. And most of all . . .

"I want you to promise me something." Lu leaned in close to Honor, staring her deep in the eyes.

She seemed slightly taken aback by Lu's sudden change of demeanor. "Which is?"

"Tell Beckett how you feel about him."

Honor and Morgan both said, "What?" at the same time, only Honor's voice was an octave higher. And much louder.

"No matter what happens after I leave, whether I make it back or not, I want to know that you're not going to go on like this for the rest of your life. I want you to tell Beckett how you feel about him, because I think there might be something there. If I have to be courageous, you do, too."

Morgan's eyes were wide as she searched Honor's face. "You and *Beckett*?"

Honor ignored Morgan, concentrating instead on stabbing Lu with daggers of withering fury using her eyes. "I am *so* going to kill you," she said, her voice dangerously low.

Lu smiled. "Yeah. Let me know how that works out for you. Besides," she said, tugging on a strand of her sister's long mane, "you deserved it. And Morgan, thanks for the offer, but I'm not taking your Gift. I think it's time I learned how to use all of mine."

She rose, fluffed her shorn hair, crossed the room to the pair of large dressers where she suspected Honor kept all her clothes, and began to dig through the drawers for something to wear on her perilous, ill-planned, and possibly ill-fated return to New Vienna.

PART THREE

TWENTY

They left with the last of the light. As the helicopter rose into the sky and the crowd that had gathered on the moors to see them off grew smaller and smaller, the emerald valley darkened to sapphire and smoke-purple shadows, gloomy twilight colors that perfectly reflected Lumina's mood.

She watched the sun sink behind the jagged peaks of the mountains in the west, wondering if she'd ever see that particular sight again. Shaking off her sense of doom, she turned to Magnus in the pilot's seat beside her.

"How long will it take to cross the Channel?"

"Not long," he replied without glancing in her direction. He offered nothing more.

She waited, hoping her silence would prompt something from him—anything—but he acted as if he were alone on the flight, flicking switches and checking readouts, adjusting his headphones, taking up most of the space in the small cockpit with his oversized frame. Lu felt small and insignificant beside him, but most of all, *worst* of all, ignored.

He hadn't wanted her help on this trip. She'd insisted, and they both knew her powers would be a significant asset, but that didn't mean he had to like it.

Judging by his body language, the way he kept his gaze averted, and the tension rolling off him in waves, he didn't like it at all.

Or maybe what he really hadn't liked was that kiss.

She dropped her gaze to her hands, turned her wrists over and inspected her empty birdcage and starling tattoos. It had been stupid, taking that kiss. A rash impulse better ignored. But every time she looked at him she saw a million fevered dreams, and the echo of longing eating its way through her chest grew larger with every passing minute. The longing had a new companion in humiliation; everyone saw how he'd begun avoiding her. She felt the speculation that surrounded them, the curiosity, and understood those were two of the last things on Earth a man like Magnus would want.

Evidently his way of dealing with unwanted attention was to become even more closed and tightly wound than before. If that was even possible.

His withdrawal left her feeling off-balance, like something familiar and right had been pulled askew, two planets yanked out of their proper orbits. She wouldn't speak to him in his thoughts again—he'd made it perfectly clear how he felt about *that*—and he obviously had little inclination to speak to her aloud, so all she could do was stew, wonder, and try to blot out the memory of the exotic, night-spice taste of the man who was, quite literally, the man of her dreams.

Lu stifled her sigh, and turned her attention to the view.

Mile after mile of rolling moors and wild peat land, a range of craggy mountains and the unexpected surprise of a lake nestled between two peaks, its surface black and mirror smooth, reflecting back the rising moon. Abandoned villages one after another, connected by arteries of roads upon which nothing moved. The villages grew larger, closer together, until all at once Lu realized that they were no longer villages, but suburbs.

London loomed large and black in the distance.

Fascinated, she pressed her face to the window, her breath frosting the glass. In minutes they'd reached it. The city sprawled vast and eerie as a dream beneath them, cloaked in a restless, low-lying fog that crept in whorls and eddies around the edges of everything. There was the Thames and the Tower Bridge, Westminster palace and Big Ben, the huge, unmoving wheel of the London Eye, all familiar sights from her father's history lessons. In the moonlight, it was beautiful, a ghost city in a landscape of haze and starlight, utterly unmoving and dark.

Not a single light shone from a single window. Nothing stirred but the fog.

She looked closer into those unmoving streets, and saw the remains of burned-out cars, heaping piles of garbage, red double-decker buses overturned at intersections to block a way in or out. Windows were broken everywhere. Storefronts were boarded. Abandoned vehicles littered every lane and boulevard and bridge, haphazard as toys left over from children's playtime. London was no longer a city; it was a graveyard.

Anger blossomed inside her again, ugly and huge.

"How they must have suffered," Lu whispered to the glass. "How horrible it must have been."

"No more than what you've suffered. Or I."

Startled out of her reverie, Lu looked at Magnus. He didn't meet her eyes, but judging by the expression on his face he already regretted speaking. She turned away, pretending not to feel his relief when she did. Pretending not to wonder exactly what it was that he'd suffered.

She'd asked Morgan about it, just before she'd hugged her good-bye, and hadn't gotten a satisfactory answer.

"I have something I need to ask you."

Morgan's manicured brows arched. "Which is?"

"Magnus. What happened to him?"

"His face, you mean," Morgan said. "The scars."

"No, I . . . I mean yes, I guess so, but not specifically. More like, what happened to make him so . . ."

"Moody? Surly? Unapproachable?"

Lu nodded, biting her lip, and Morgan, being Morgan, instantly guessed the meaning behind this line of questioning.

"Oh, dear, does someone have a soft spot for her gallant rescuer?"

"Maybe," answered Lu softly, looking at the ground. "But it's less like a soft spot and more like . . ."

"A painful ache?"

When Lu glanced up, Morgan was staring back at her with affection, and clear understanding, in her eyes.

Lu nodded again, equally embarrassed and relieved. "And I can't figure out what I should do about that, if anything. He seems like he just wants to be left alone. Like he can't stand the company of others. And I know how much he hates to be touched. He's like a feral animal. He's so . . . rough."

Morgan chuckled, then smoothed a hand over Lu's hair, a twinkle in her emerald eyes.

"A diamond in the rough is still a diamond, pet. One just has to know how to handle it to bring out all the facets of its beauty. Only with a pair of gentle, loving hands can it be polished to perfection. Men are the exact same way."

That was it. Morgan hadn't told her what had happened to Magnus to make him so feral. To scar his face and body. She'd simply smiled a Mona Lisa smile and suggested that Lu treat Magnus the same way she'd treat a cornered animal: gently, and with extreme care.

Gently. She looked again at her bare hands, then from the pocket of her jacket—courtesy of Honor's closet—Lu withdrew one of the pairs of gloves Magnus had given her, and pulled them on.

They touched down in the wilderness between Calais and Boulogne-sur-Mer in France. It was an old-growth forest, dense with towering trees that were perfect for concealment, and far enough away from civilization to be safe from the Peace Guard, Enforcement, or electronic surveillance. They'd encounter those problems soon enough, but for now Magnus was satisfied of their safety.

Safety being a relative term; he was as much in danger of losing himself completely as he always was around Lumina.

She was quiet and careful, following his lead without speaking as he jumped out of the helicopter, hoisted his small pack onto his back, and began to head north toward the rendezvous point where Jack had indicated her people would pick them up. They'd be staying their first night in one of dozens of safe houses the Dissenters operated in France, but they'd have to hurry to make it through the forest in time; the people who were meeting them would wait only fifteen minutes, no more. If Magnus missed this first pickup, he and Lu would be spending the night walking.

And when daybreak came, they'd have to find shelter or die. Already the thin clouds overhead were tainted that ominous, poisonous red. Farther inland, the clouds grew thicker, the color more opaque.

He needn't have worried. Lumina was as swift as she was silent, and had no trouble keeping up with him as he navigated through the dark forest toward the access road. The road used to function as the initial route from the ports of the seafront to the interior cities, but now was as abandoned as London had been. There was no more international commerce, no shipping or exports, no trade between nations at all. There were only large, self-supporting cities existing like dystopian oases in the middle of the vast desert of the remains of the world, and the Phoenix Corporation controlled them, as they did everything else.

Even the clouds.

They broke through the tree line and the road was there, two lanes of cracked asphalt just beyond a shallow ditch choked with brambles and weeds. On the other side of the road, a deer stood frozen—nose twitching, ears pricked forward, black eyes shining in terror. A second passed, then she bounded off into the woods, her tail a flash of white against the darkness.

"Oh," breathed Lu, amazed, watching it go. "I've never seen one of those before. Only in books."

Magnus had grown up in the Amazon. He'd seen every kind of bird and reptile and mammal—had, in fact, *eaten* all of them—and couldn't imagine growing up as she had, confined to a city with no access to the natural world. She was an animal, as were they all, and she needed animal outlets.

He was arrested by that thought. She'd said she'd never had a chance to practice her Gifts, spending all her energy on trying to be "normal," and had only just yesterday Shifted for the first time . . .

"Do you know what the *Ikati* actually are, Lumina?"

She didn't turn to look at him, and really, could he blame her? He knew he'd been acting on the far side of sullen and testy, but keeping her at a safe arm's length had become of paramount importance to him. After that kiss, after everything that itched and throbbed between them, after the revelation about his own, imminent demise . . . Magnus was taking no chances.

He was going to die. Soon. He couldn't—*wouldn't*—be so selfish as to take what he wanted from her, which was much, much more than just another kiss.

"What do you mean?" Her brows pulled together in confusion.

"You, Honor, and your mother are the only living *Ikati* who can Shift to something else than our original form . . . you know that, right?"

Now she did look at him, and that familiar snap of connection made his blood sizzle in his veins.

"Original form?"

He couldn't help it. His own hand betrayed him. Before he could think, he reached out and lightly touched a lock of her hair. It was like silk between his fingers. When he spoke again, his voice was husky. "This body is a clever disguise. We learned to look human millennia ago as a survival mechanism, but this isn't what we are."

Her hand lifted, then stilled in the air, just inches from his, as if she'd been about to touch him but stopped herself. "What are we then? Will you show me?"

Her voice was lowered to match his own, the softest throaty purr, and it was all he could do not to take her into his arms and give in to all the wild thrashing inside him, the burning and the need. Instead, he only gave a curt, wordless nod, dropped his hand and turned away.

After a moment, she turned away, too. Then, mercifully, from off in the distance came the low, electric drone of engines. Together they waited for Jack's friends in silence, the space between them raw.

Inola Hart was not at all what Magnus had been expecting.

She was about Jack and Morgan's age, elegant and severe with her dark hair pulled to a tight chignon at the nape of her neck, which served perfectly to highlight the angular attractiveness of her face. Sloe-eyed, tall, with nut-brown skin and a commanding air that suggested she was used to ordering people around, Nola, as she'd instructed they call her, seemed the kind of woman who'd be equally at home in a ballroom or on a battlefield.

Magnus decided he liked her immediately.

The young man she introduced as her nephew, James, however, Magnus *disliked* immediately, primarily due to the way he couldn't stop ogling Lumina.

Magnus grudgingly admitted that James tried to be circumspect about it, but from the first moment he'd pulled off his motorcycle helmet, his eyes had gone straight to Lumina's face, and stayed glued there. When they weren't blinking in admiration at her body, that is, which was on spectacular display in one of the tight-fitting warrior chick costumes Honor favored. She'd dyed it black, at least, so she didn't stick out like a spotlight, but the stretchy, figure-molding material left little to the imagination.

"Good for ease of movement," Honor had said breezily in response to his bug-eyed look when Lumina first emerged from the caves to meet him at the helicopter, and if he hadn't known better, he'd almost have thought Honor was smirking.

"James, take Lumina. I'll take Magnus," Nola said, about to don her helmet.

"No," Magnus said firmly, stepping forward. He stared at James. "I'll take Lumina. You and James can ride together, Nola."

James held his hands up in a surrendering gesture. "Whatever works for you, man. I'm easy." He dismounted the bike—sleek and black, one of the newest electric models—and ambled over to Nola, who was watching this exchange closely.

Her gaze flicked between him and Lumina. "We've got about an hour's ride ahead of us. If either of you need to take care of business, do it now. Unless it's a dire emergency, we won't stop again until we get home."

"I'd rather get started now," said Lumina.

Magnus agreed. He mounted the bike, handed Lu the helmet from the peg on the back seat, then donned the extra one Nola handed over. He slid his small shoulder pack around to the front, giving Lumina room, and she swung her leg over the seat and climbed on.

Her arms slid around his waist. Her chest pressed against his back. The weight of her settled against him, firm and plush and agonizing. And, as Magnus depressed the ignition button and felt the bike hum to life beneath them, he said a prayer for strength to a god he knew did not exist, because he'd never answered a single prayer before.

TWENTY-ONE

The safe house was in a small town near the Belgian border. The house itself was distinctly European, with a steep mansard roofline and charming shutters, but beyond that, the planned community offered zero in the way of diversity or interest. The town might have been anywhere. Like London, it was entirely devoid of life.

Except for the pair of black motorcycles that had traversed its roads.

Surprisingly well-preserved roads they were, too, except for the occasional ragged crack or pothole. The bigger problem was the rotting husks of abandoned cars, but the motorcycles had maneuvered around them handily, and Magnus was again impressed with Nola. From what Jack had told him, he gathered that Nola was the person Jack trusted most in the world, aside from Hawk. She and Nola had been best friends in their lives before the Flash—Jack, a reporter for the *New York Times* and Nola, an attorney for the United Nations—and Nola had proven herself unwaveringly loyal.

When Jack had founded the Dissenter movement, Nola was the first one on board.

Travelling through an unlit, uninhabited town at night was always eerie, but Magnus was accustomed to it. By the time they reached the safe house he should have been feeling more relaxed. They'd landed easily, made the rendezvous, made good time over the highway without encountering any trouble. Only he didn't feel relaxed. With Lu's body so tightly fused to his, her thighs around his hips, her arms clinging to his waist, Magnus felt like he might explode in frustration.

Not for one second, however, did he regret not letting her ride with James.

They cut the engines, dismounted, pulled off their helmets. Nola led them around the side of the darkened house, through a wooden gate that groaned open on rusted hinges. Magnus expected a normal suburban backyard, but instead found himself looking at a small, shed-like building on a slab of concrete, surrounded by nothing but a wide expanse of dirt. Nola led them to the shed, and lifted a hinged door, revealing an empty interior.

"Bring the bike in," she instructed over her shoulder. "There's just room enough for the four of us."

He did as he was told, eyeing Nola speculatively, but she simply shut the hinged door behind them, looked to make sure no one was within a few inches of the walls, then pulled a cord hanging from the ceiling.

With a jolt, the cement floor below their feet began slowly to descend.

Lu jumped, but Magnus had to chuckle. "You're full of all kinds of surprises, aren't you, Nola?"

Lu flashed him a look he couldn't decipher, quickly recovering to adopt a bored expression. Nola shrugged, smiling. "Every woman is full of surprises, much to man's great horror or delight. A woman only has to surprise a man once to find out what he's made of." Her smile deepened. "And whether or not he's worth her while."

"What about you, Lumina?" prompted James. "I'll bet you're full of surprises."

Lu sent him a sideways, penetrating stare. "You have no idea."

The way they looked at each other made Magnus's chest tighten. He had to curl his hands to fists to stop them from curling around James's throat.

After a short descent during which James stared at Lu, Lu stared at Nola, and Nola stared at the walls crawling upward, the platform came to rest at the end of a short, dark tunnel. At the far end a pair of lanterns flanked a closed door.

"Leave the bikes here." Nola rolled her motorcycle a few feet into the tunnel, kicking down the stand. Magnus parked his bike behind hers, and the four of them proceeded to the door.

It was steel, reinforced with rebar through the concrete on either side. Magnus noted the small black eye of a camera mounted to the ceiling. "How do you have electricity so far from the cities?"

Nola waved impatiently to the camera. "We siphon it from the grid, but we have a few generators for emergencies, too."

"Siphon it from the grid? And the IF doesn't notice that?"

Nola looked at him over her shoulder, her expression amused. "If they did, we wouldn't be having this conversation, now would we?"

Full of surprises, indeed, he thought admiringly. Lumina stiffened. He glanced at her, but she wasn't looking at him, focusing instead on the door, which had opened.

In the doorway stood an ancient man, the oldest living person Magnus had seen in many years. He had to be close to one hundred, if not beyond. His hair was long and white, braided in two plaits that fell below his shoulders. He was olive-skinned, like Nola and James, but his was papery as parchment, and deeply lined. Also like

Nola and James, he had dark, almond-shaped eyes, pronounced cheekbones, and a proud stoicism that hinted at Indian ancestry.

Though elderly, his posture was straight and sure, his gaze clear. And his voice, when he spoke, was strong and commanding.

"*Ulihelsidi. Osadatsu?*"

Nola squeezed the old man's arm. "All good, Grandfather. *Ositsu*. No problems."

He nodded, eyeing each of the group in turn, then moved aside to let them in. Like James, he paid particular attention to Lumina, and Magnus had to swallow the growl rising in his throat.

The old man looked at him, his eyes sharp and assessing. Then his face creased into a smile. He said something to Nola in that language of theirs, and she laughed.

"What?" snapped Magnus.

"Grandfather says your lion roars so loud the moon can even hear it."

Well, thought Magnus, relaxing, *at least he got the genus right*. "I'll take that as a compliment."

"Oh, believe me, it is. If he didn't like you, he would have called you a dung beetle. Or worse."

"Grandfather can tell everything about a person as soon as he meets him," explained James to Lumina as they proceeded down a short corridor, then a flight of stairs. "He has the Spirit Eye."

"Spirit Eye?" Lumina repeated, looking with interest at James.

Following behind the two of them, Magnus had to resist the violent urge to trip James and send him sprawling to the floor, and scolded himself for being so petty and ridiculous. He noticed Nola's grandfather was looking more and more pleased.

"It's a Native American—"

The old man interrupted James with a sharp correction in his language.

"Sorry, Grandfather. It's a *First Nation* belief. The Spirit Eye lets you see into a person's soul."

"Sounds like an amazing Gift," murmured Lu. The old man replied, and as Nola led the group through another door into a small antechamber that opened to a large, tri-level living area, she translated.

"He says it's almost as good as Dreamwalking."

Magnus sucked in his breath. Lu stopped dead in her tracks. Nola and James proceeded forward, James to a bank of monitors and computer equipment glowing blue and green along one wall, Nola toward a kitchen on the opposite side of the floor. The old man moved past them, smiling like the Sphinx.

Lu kept her gaze fixed on the old man as he joined Nola in the kitchen and lowered himself into a chair around a square wooden table. He picked up a book—real paper, real pages, a cracked, gilt-lettered spine—and began to read, ignoring everyone.

Lu glanced at Magnus, her expression fraught, but neither one of them spoke.

"You must be hungry," called Nola from the kitchen. "The bedrooms are on the second floor; yours is last on the left. When you've settled in, come get something to eat, and then we'll talk."

She began to bustle around the kitchen, making preparations for a meal, while Magnus stood looking at her in dawning horror, realizing he'd never asked Jack about sleeping arrangements.

Dear God . . . were he and Lumina going to be sleeping in the same *room*?

Lumina moved past him, walking stiffly toward the stairs, and he knew they were about to find out.

"I'll take the floor," he and Lumina said at the same time, staring at the twin-sized bed.

Magnus moved past her into the small room, dropping his pack on the wood dresser. The room was sparsely furnished but clean, with an adjacent bathroom. He did a quick inspection, then turned back to Lu, still unmoving in the doorway. She looked pale.

"*You're* taking the bed. I'm sure there's a couch downstairs I can sleep on."

"I don't snore," she muttered, dropping her own pack beside his on the dresser. Magnus frowned, wondering at the tone of insult in her voice. Surely she didn't think—

"Everything copacetic?" James appeared in the doorway, bright eyed and bushy tailed, and Magnus enjoyed the image of the dark-haired man sailing through the air, screaming, after he'd tossed him over the second-floor railing.

"Fine," he answered, teeth gritted. "Thank you."

Lu asked, "James, do you have a couch downstairs? Magnus and I—"

"Are very happy with the room," he cut in. He was surprised how easy it was to speak through clenched teeth. Probably it had to do with his vast experience in the area. "Again, *thank you.*"

He spoke the words with just enough hostile emphasis that James's smile faltered. He cleared his throat, then cleared out with a salute and an awkward, "Great. Awesome. 'Bye."

When he'd gone, Lu said, "Why don't you like him? He seems perfectly nice."

No, he seemed perfectly obnoxious, and, worse, perfectly enamored. There was no way in hell Magnus was going to chance letting Lumina sleep unguarded with that hound sniffing around. Without answering, he removed his jacket and threw it on the chair, then stood there with his hands on his hips, glaring at nothing.

The sound of bedsprings squeaking made him turn. Lumina was perched on the edge of the bed, back ramrod straight, lips pressed together, face the color of a ripe tomato.

"What?" he asked.

"Is this how it's going to be now? You seething and ignoring me because I forced you to take me along? I just want to prepare myself so I don't expect anything. Like, a normal conversation."

The sarcasm in her tone announced her anger better than shouting would have. Magnus ran a hand through his hair, trying to get his jealousy under control. Trying, for once, to think rationally where Lumina was concerned. "I'm not angry because of that."

Her back stiffened. "Oh." She shook her head, laughed a short, humorless laugh. "Right. I should have known." She stood, moving as if a steel bar had been implanted in her spine. "Well, you don't have to worry; it won't happen again. You have my word."

"What are you talking about?"

She turned her head so he saw her in profile. But she didn't look at him. And her face was still that troubling shade of red.

"Touch you. Kiss you. I-I won't do that again." She paused, then said in an angry rush, "I'll leave that to *Nola*," and bolted to the door.

Lumina was fast, but he was faster. Magnus reached her just before she passed the threshold, took hold of her arm, slammed shut the door, and pushed her—less gently than he should have, he realized as her eyes widened in alarm—against it.

He stared down at her, one hand on her arm and the other braced against the door. Their noses were inches apart.

"I'll ask you again, and I want an honest answer," he said gruffly. "What are you talking about, Lumina?"

She moistened her lips, and he almost groaned. This close, the scent of her skin and hair, the warmth of her body, conspired to strip every rational thought from his mind. A tremor ran through her arm and it was all he could do not to lean in and cover her mouth with his.

"You like her," Lumina whispered, staring into his eyes. "Nola. You like her."

He blinked, confused. "What's not to like? She's obviously intelligent, resourceful, loyal . . . she's putting her own safety at stake to help us . . ." He trailed off because Lumina's lips twisted. She looked away, breaking their eye contact, and refused to look at him when he asked her to. So he took her chin in his hand and forced her to look at him, and they stood there like that for several long seconds, just gazing at each other, until it hit him like a shock of cold water poured over his head.

"You're *jealous*?" he whispered, astonished.

She didn't deny it, which was just as shocking as her jealousy. Her cheeks burned, but she just stood looking at him silently, her chest rising and falling with short, erratic breaths.

He'd never before in his life been tested as cruelly as this. With his hand on her face and their bodies so close and now *this*, this impossible, beautiful, maddening thing . . .

She was jealous over him. *She* was jealous over *him*.

He closed his eyes and muttered a curse.

Lumina said softly, "Please let me go." The humiliation in her voice drove a stake through his heart. He opened his eyes to find her expression frozen, her lashes swept down to hide her eyes. The knowledge that she assumed his curse was some kind of rejection was even worse than the knowledge that it was, perhaps, the best possible scenario for them both.

Fate had just handed him the perfect opportunity to drive a permanent wedge between them.

He could keep himself safe from the awful temptation of having her so near. He could keep her safe from the colossal mistake of wasting emotion on a worthless recipient, and, worse, one who wouldn't live to see the next full moon. If he could just force himself to let her assumption stand uncontested . . . if he only had the strength of will to deny himself the one thing he wanted more than anything else he'd wanted in his miserable life . . .

For her. Do it for her.

In the end, she decided for him.

Lumina shook off his hand from her face, twisted out from his grip on her arm, and opened the bedroom door. Without another word, she left the room, and Magnus sank to his knees and hid his face in his hands as he listened to the sound of her short, hard footsteps echoing down the hall.

TWENTY-TWO

Dinner was as enjoyable as having all the skin on her body flayed off with a knife. A rusty knife. *Slowly.*

Lumina listened to James's cheerful prattle, answered Nola's questions about the health and happiness of Jack and Hawk, and suffered the friendly-but-intense scrutiny of the old man everyone simply called Grandfather, all while robotically shoveling food into her mouth, aware on some level she needed to keep up her energy, so she chewed and swallowed, tasting nothing at all.

Her mind was stuck on instant replay. The look on Magnus's face when he'd realized she was jealous was . . . it was . . .

Horrified.

And now, so was she. Horrified, humiliated, and ashamed of the depth of her own stupidity.

His expression hadn't been the worst thing, however. Oh no. That honor was reserved for the way he seemed to have grown calmer in reverse proportion to her mortification. Almost as if her jealousy had made him . . . *relax*.

Miserable bastard.

"This is excellent stew, Nola," said the bastard between mouthfuls, his second helping so far. Judging by the way he was shoveling it down without pause, a third helping was in his immediate future. "What's the meat?"

Meat? Lu frowned at her steaming bowl of rich brown broth. She'd thought those delicious chunks were some sort of exotic vegetable. She hadn't eaten meat in . . . well, years probably. She and her father hadn't been able to afford it.

Nola, sitting beside Magnus at the table, offered him another slice of bread. He accepted it with a grateful nod, and she answered, "Venison."

Scheisse, she was eating Bambi. Lu nearly spit out her mouthful of stew, but remembered in time these people were helping her on her quest to save her mother. She swallowed, trying not to grimace too obviously. The taste of innocent murdered creature, however, lingered unfortunately on her tongue, which prompted a feeling of sentimentality for the tasteless-as-cardboard BioVite and FitCakes she'd grown up eating.

Magnus said, "Delicious. You the hunter in the family, James?"

So now he was being *friendly* to James. This man's moods gave her whiplash.

James laughed unselfconsciously. Like Beckett, he had a gift for laughter, and because it was so genuine and such a welcome sound in her state of misery, Lu smiled at him. She wished she could laugh like that.

"That would be a big, fat *no*," said James, smiling back at Lu. "If I were the hunter-gatherer around here, we'd all starve to death in days. I'm more the nerd type. Nola, on the other hand, can track an animal like it was wearing a flashing target on its back." His smile faded. He shrugged, looking down at his bowl of stew. "I know we need to eat, but . . . I just couldn't stand to kill anything. I'd feel too bad about it. Guess I'm kind of a sentimental sap that way."

Lu said, "I like it that you're sentimental. And you're *not* a sap. No one should ever feel good about killing, even if it's life or death."

James beamed at her. On the opposite side of the table, Magnus froze, *un*beaming, his spoon halfway to his mouth.

Nola said sourly, "Compassion is right up there with love on the list of things that can kill you in this world."

Grandfather said something, his voice soft but firm. After a moment, Nola translated, sounding chastened, her gaze on her food.

"He says 'Love and compassion are necessities, not luxuries. Without them humanity can't survive.'"

The old man and Lu looked at one another, and she felt as if an invisible hand had reached out and squeezed her heart. "Is that a First Nation saying?"

To Lu's surprise, the old man answered in perfect English.

"I wish we could take credit for it, but the Dalai Lama said that." He laid his wrinkled hand on the book he'd been reading, which lay on the table beside his bowl of stew. "He's one of my favorites. The Great Spirit moved through him like wind over water; he was very wise. But a terrible dresser."

After a beat of surprised silence, Lu laughed. James joined her, the old man sent her a toothy grin, even Magnus cracked a smile. Nola rolled her eyes and sighed.

After that, the conversation rolled smoothly. Lu found out that Grandfather, James, and Nola were Cherokee, one of many minority groups from the disbanded United States who'd fled to Europe after the Flash when the US suspended the Constitution and the Bill of Rights. The Federal Emergency Management Agency set up detainment camps for Dissenters and suspected "enemies of the state," and they'd seen the writing on the wall. Hoping Europe would be better, they'd settled first in London.

"Which, as we all know, turned out to be a total disaster," said James, who relayed that he was only eight years old at the time. Nola was his mother's sister, who'd been killed in the chaos, as his father had been.

Lu grew uncomfortable at this talk of death, her guilt at being the instigator of the Flash rising like bile to leave a sour taste in her mouth, until Nola said something that jarred her.

". . . Thorne took full advantage. He was just looking for the right opportunity to start his war. The Flash gave him the perfect stepping-off point."

Lu sat up straighter. "What do you mean?"

"Sebastian Thorne was trying to orchestrate conflict for years before the Flash. He knew that nothing unifies people like war, or a common enemy. He also knew that war creates incredible pockets of opportunity for those willing to do anything in the grab for power. And what he wanted, ultimately, was power. On a global scale. So he took the isolated incident of the Flash, and with clever manipulation and propaganda, turned it into a coup of every government on the planet."

In response to Lu's blank expression, Nola explained patiently, "Look, the Flash caused instability, but the world had seen a lot worse before that. Stock markets would've recovered, things would've eventually settled down. But Thorne started dropping bombs and pointing fingers. He was already an influential man, even then—a very *rich* man—who'd been stockpiling weapons all over the place. So when the missiles started flying from Iran and Russia and the United States, everyone blamed everyone else, and it devolved rapidly from there. In the space of a few weeks, everything collapsed. The entire world was chaos. And out of the ashes rose Sebastian Thorne and his oh-so-ironically named Phoenix Corporation, swooping in to save the day."

Lu sat back in her chair, stunned. "If this is common knowledge, why doesn't everyone rebel? Why hasn't someone tried to get to him before?"

"I never said it was common knowledge." Nola rose to clear the empty bowls. "The Dissenters know it, of course, but to everyone else Sebastian Thorne is the man who single-handedly saved the world."

James amended wryly, "And then made its entire population captive dependents."

"Even the strongest people eventually grow to love their chains," said Grandfather. His warm gaze met Lu's. The hint of a smile touched his lips. "Unlike wild animals, who can never be tamed, no matter how long they're kept in captivity."

But you already know that, don't you, Tsulahisanvhi?

He was still gazing at her with that scant, clever smile as her jaw dropped.

How did you know you could talk to me this way?

Grandfather's smile deepened. *Old people know a great many things the young aren't interested in.*

I'm interested, Lu thought firmly. *And frankly I'm not that young.*

Grandfather shrugged, pulling a face. *Everything's relative. When you get to be my age, a midlife crisis looks about the same as a toddler's tantrum, which looks about the same as early onset dementia.*

Midlife crisis? I'm only twenty-five!

In my day, twenty-five was midlife. Especially for a woman. Strike that—twenty-five would've been an old maid. The medicine man of our tribe would've prescribed a strong tea of boiled bull testicles and tomcat urine to clear away all those cobwebs and tumbleweeds in your uterus so you could maybe still attract a man and have a family.

Lu scowled at him. *Good thing I wasn't born in your day, then. By the way, it must've been exciting when fire was first discovered, right? And when the wheel was invented? Those must've been good times!*

Grandfather grinned, lighting his entire face. *Ah,* Tsulahisanvhi. *You don't disappoint.*

There was that word again. Su-la-he-SAN-vee. Frustrated with the silent conversation, Lumina said aloud, "Hey, James? What does *Tsulahisanvhi* mean?"

Into the kitchen sink Nola dropped the bowls with a clatter, turning to stare.

Sounding more than a little confused, James said slowly, "Uh, well, I'm not such an expert with the Cherokee language, but I think it means . . . Resurrected One."

Silence reigned, until Nola broke it, her voice cutting. "Where did you hear that word, Lumina?"

"Oh, I think I read it in some old, moldy, irritating book," she answered lightly, watching with aggravation as the smile on the old man's face grew bright as the sun.

Okay, Grandfather. We need to talk. And it's not about the dust bunnies in my uterus.

I'll tell you whatever you want to know, little dragon, but first you have to find me.

Lu's scowl deepened with her confusion. *Find you? You're sitting right across from me!*

Grandfather rose from the table, looking down from his considerable height. To everyone there, but looking at Lu, he said, "My bones cry out for bed. It's time for me to go to sleep."

Which is where you'll find me . . . if you can.

He winked, turned, and walked slowly away from the table, leaving Lu gaping at his broad, retreating back.

Magnus had been watching her and Grandfather during their silent conversation with the unblinking stare of a predator, his gaze darting back and forth between them, quick as light. "Lumina?" His query was low, tense, filled with something darker than concern. Lu quashed the tiny seed of hope that took root in her heart in response to his worried tone, and avoided his eyes.

"I just realized I'm tired, too. Thank you for dinner, Nola. James, it's been wonderful meeting you." She rose. To Magnus she sent a curt, businesslike nod. "And now if you'll all excuse me, I'm off to bed. Goodnight."

She left, pretending not to feel the stabbing pain in her heart at the look she saw pass between Nola and Magnus as she went.

She didn't know how this worked, and was beginning to get frustrated.

Lying on her back on the twin bed, wearing a T-shirt she'd found in one of the bedroom's dresser drawers because she hadn't thought to bring a nightgown, Lu stared up at the dark ceiling. She'd tried counting backward from one hundred. She'd tried counting sheep. She'd even tried deep breathing exercises, which did nothing except make the room spin. Now she was trying to remember something she'd once read about progressive relaxation of the muscles, but the events of the past few days were whirling round and round inside her head, fighting each other for the spotlight. Sleep seemed as elusive as a smile from Magnus.

Magnus. With a groan, Lu turned on her side and stared at the wall.

She heard him downstairs, talking with Nola and James, their voices muffled, indistinct. She knew she could've picked out the words if she'd wanted to, but the low, rumbling tone of his voice was soothing to her agitated state, and anyway she probably didn't want to know what they were saying.

She definitely didn't want to know if Magnus was looking at Nola in that admiring way he'd looked at her before.

Lu knew it was ridiculous. She had no claim on him. They had no history, except the one she'd made up in her own mind. The knowledge didn't make her feel any better, because in the deepest, darkest corner of her heart, she felt as if he were already hers. As if he'd always been, and always would be.

Ridiculous.

She sighed and closed her eyes, resigned to a long, sleepless night of tossing the sheets.

And then.

She was standing in an enormous field of waist-high grain, the breeze rippling waves over its golden surface. The sun shone bright overhead. A lone hawk soared high, high up in the clear cerulean sky. The scene was beautiful, peaceful, and utterly silent.

Little dragon.

Lu turned. There behind her stood a handsome young man. His long, dark hair was braided in two plaits that hung halfway down his chest, his brown eyes shone with welcome. He was tall and his bearing was proud, and she recognized him at once.

Grandfather!

Edward Fastwater, he corrected with a grin. *Otherwise known as Running Bear.*

But you're so . . . young!

He laughed, without noise, his head thrown back, white teeth glinting in the sunlight. *The soul doesn't age the way the body does, little dragon.*

Lu looked around, marveling at the endless, restless field of grain. Black hills jutted into the horizon. In the far distance, a lazy column of smoke twined up from the chimney of a lone house. *Where are we?*

He moved closer, his palms open, skimming the heads of the grain. *Near where I grew up. I visit here often.*

She turned her face to the sun, watching the hawk soar on an updraft of wind. *It's beautiful.*

For a moment, his face darkened. His warm eyes grew serious. *The world was a very beautiful place, once. It can be again, but only with great sacrifice.*

Lu looked at him sharply, arrested by the word. *Sacrifice?*

He regarded her, still with that somberness, the wind stirring his braids around his shoulders. *All of nature is checks and balances, little dragon. When the scale swings too far one way, it's inevitable that it will turn and swing the other. For every day, there's a night. For every winter, a spring. For every gift . . . a price.*

A rush of cold wind tossed Lu's hair into her eyes. She felt a change in the air, a sense of pressure, a gathering and a girding up, as if the sky and field and the earth itself tensed in expectation. Then in the sky above the black hills appeared two spots of brilliant, glinting white, moving fast as falling stars.

What is that?

Young Grandfather turned, scanning the horizon. His face cleared. *Ah. Your sister is on a Dreamwalk, too.*

I don't understand. What's happening? How is this possible?

Her confusion was met with a gentle smile. *All you seek can be found in this way. Focus your mind. Open your spirit. And look. Remember, there's nothing that can elude you here. You knew this as a child. You must relearn it as a grown woman.*

Lu watched the spots of white grow closer, and closer still. But they weren't spots at all; they had wings and tails and long, elegant necks . . .

They were dragons.

She recognized Honor, lithe and swift. But the dragon beside her was, if possible, even more beautiful. Large and magnificent, its wingspan was enormous, its power undeniable. They soared nearer, gloriously pearlescent in the sunlight, then passed overhead with monstrous grace, the drafts of their wing beats flattening the grain. They didn't look down or seem to notice her, and Lu watched with an ache in her heart as they flew away, growing smaller until they disappeared altogether.

Is that . . .

Yes, answered young Grandfather. *You're touching the edges of Honor's Dream. Tonight she visits your mother.*

Why did she never visit me? All the years we were separated, I only Dreamt of . . .

Young Grandfather smiled at her again. *Dreamwalkers go where their souls are called, to the places—and people—most dear to them. Your sister tried to visit you many times, but you wouldn't allow her in.*

Lu was swamped with regret. How many years she'd thrown away, hiding, when all she had to do was open herself and she would've found the sister she'd never known. The sister who'd tried, over and over, to come in.

I've wasted so much time.

Time doesn't exist here, little dragon.

A thought made Lu frown. *I never knew Magnus, before he rescued me in New Vienna. Why would I Dream of him, and not someone else? Why would I visit him, of all the people in the world?*

She turned and looked at young Grandfather, so tall and straight, his smile so gentle. *The soul seeks its mate. Its journey isn't complete until it finds its missing half that will make it whole.*

Soul mates? No—that's not possible. Soul mates don't exist.

He laughed his silent laugh again, his eyes laughing along with him. *Everything with a name exists.*

I don't believe it!

Unlike Tinkerbell, true love doesn't need you to believe in it in order to exist. His eyes twinkled mischievously. *Neither do dragons.*

Lu stood unmoving in the silent field of dream wheat, gazing at the dream man, feeling all her dream emotions exactly as if she were awake. Her logical mind fought his words, but they affected her, for all her effort to remain untouched. There was only one, tiny problem.

He doesn't want me, Grandfather. We can't be two halves of a whole if one of the halves doesn't like the other one.

He reached out and laid a hand on her shoulder. It was warm, so strangely concrete and real. *Are men so different where you're from?*

Her dream blush was real, too. She looked into the distance, watching the wheat ripple and flow. *I don't have much experience in that department.*

Young Grandfather patted her shoulder consolingly. *A piece of advice, then: Listen to a man most carefully when he's silent. Words can lie, but silence always speaks from the heart.*

The hand on her shoulder that had felt so real suddenly lightened, its grip less firm. Lu looked over at young Grandfather, and for a moment he shimmered and went translucent, then solidified again.

It's time for me to go, little dragon.

Go? Go where?

He looked past her, into the field, and Lu followed his gaze. There in the distance stood a woman. Dark-haired and lovely, dressed in an old-fashioned gown, she held the hand of a young child. They were smiling at him. Waiting.

When Lu turned back, he was shimmering again. This time it took longer for him to coalesce. His face, beaming, was full and clear, but his body wavered in and out of focus. The field of wheat shone and undulated behind him like an endless rolling sea.

I've waited as long as I could to meet you, and I'm so glad I did. Remember all I've told you. And remember what your father told you, as well.

Lu stood there, dumbstruck.

For one final time, young Grandfather spoke. *Do the thing you're most afraid of.*

Then he was gone.

TWENTY-THREE

Lu awoke in quiet darkness, her neck damp with sweat, sheets rucked in tangled disarray around her legs. Her body ached as if she'd been running for a long time, but her mind was clear and still. She stared up at the ceiling for a moment, awed yet strangely calm. It seemed her capacity for accepting the impossible or insane had grown in accordance with all the insanities life tossed her way, and for that she was grateful.

Otherwise she'd definitely be crazy by now.

She stretched beneath the sheets, stomach growling, then scrubbed her hands over her face. Ready to face whatever new drama the day would unfold, she sat up, but froze as she realized she wasn't in the room alone.

There on the floor beside the bed slept Magnus.

On his back, legs crossed at the ankle, hands folded at his waist, fully dressed, not even a pillow to cushion his head. She examined his expression and found it, even in sleep, tense. What could make someone look so wary while sleeping? What did he dream of?

Or whom?

Lu's breath hitched, but she pushed her jealousy ruthlessly aside. It was time for her to focus on getting into New Vienna safely, and getting her parents out of that prison. Worrying about Magnus's possible feelings for their elegant host—older than he by a good ten, fifteen years, but who knew what his preferences were?—served only to aggravate her.

Carefully, trying to be as slow and silent as possible, Lu eased her legs over the edge of the bed, and set her feet on the floor. She stood, holding her breath, tiptoeing away—

A big hand shot out and grabbed her ankle.

Magnus jerked upright. Lu lost her balance and flopped awkwardly onto the mattress. Then they were staring at one another with identical expressions of surprise, confusion, and worry.

"What's wrong?"

Lu gritted her teeth and closed her eyes. They really had to stop saying the exact same thing at the exact same time; it was getting weird.

She opened her eyes and tried again. "Hi. How are you?"

He stared back at her as if he wasn't entirely convinced he was awake. His dark brows pulled together. His gaze darted around the room, scanning for danger.

"Well, hello to you, too, Lumina! I'm great, and how are *you*?" she said, more than a little sarcastically. Sarcasm was practically a given when you were mocking someone else's silence while he had a kung fu death grip on your leg. Magnus's only response was to tighten his grip on her ankle.

"So . . . has my leg offended you in some way? Or is this some kind of *Ikati* wake-up greeting I'm not familiar with?"

Magnus frowned at her. Then his gaze slid to her bare ankle, wrapped in his warm, rough hand, and he snatched his hand away as if her skin burned him. "Sorry. Reflex."

Lu arched her brows. "That's some reflex. I'd hate to see what you do when someone sneezes. Reflexively punch him in the face?"

He didn't answer, concentrating instead on getting to his feet, turning his back, and gathering his figurative armor. She felt his withdrawal like the tide going out, a swift, inexorable retraction. Suddenly weary in spite of just awakening, she sighed. Loudly, apparently, because Magnus turned and looked at her, his dark eyes cool and guarded.

"I wonder what time it is," she said, avoiding his eyes to look around the room. There was no clock, and it was still dark outside, so she had no idea how long she'd been asleep. Magnus, however, answered with confidence as if he'd just looked at his wristwatch. The one he wasn't wearing.

"Just before dawn. We'll have to wait out the day before we get on the road again . . ." His gaze dropped to her legs, and his expression transformed from cold to something else. Something that looked suspiciously like anger. He growled, "What are you *wearing*?"

Lu looked down at herself. Realizing the T-shirt wasn't exactly doing a stellar job of covering her bare thighs, she tugged at the hem. Heat rose in her cheeks. "I dunno. Night stuff."

"Night stuff," he repeated stiffly, his eyes unblinking. He swallowed.

"You told me to pack light," she said defensively. "I found this in one of the drawers."

"That's a man's shirt."

Lu looked down at the shirt. It was a perfectly innocuous white short-sleeved T-shirt, utterly ordinary. It probably belonged to James. "So?"

His face grew more and more ruddy, his lips thinned to a pale line. Against his tanned skin, both his scars and the thin line of his lips stood out, and Lu thought she'd never seen him look quite so on edge. "So . . . nothing. It's just . . . short. Just . . . get dressed, all right?" He turned away again, and Lu had the startling thought that it might be in order to hide.

From her.

Because she wasn't fully dressed.

And there was that hope again, pushing up its stupid, green, cheerful leaves in the dark soil of her heart. Aggravating! Not helpful! But what to do about it? *Ignore it, that's what*, Lu told herself, determined.

Inconveniently, her determination was sidelined by two things. "Do the thing you're most afraid of," and "Silence always speaks from the heart."

Crap. Fine, then. Here goes nothing.

Ignoring the fact that she probably had hideous morning breath and her hair was sticking up around her head in spiky, unattractive clumps, Lu rose slowly from the bed, and went to stand directly in front of Magnus. He looked at her, startled, eyes widening, his cool composure cracking as fast as two hands clapping. He waited, watching her watching him, vibrating tension, until finally he couldn't stand it anymore and snapped, "What?"

Lu almost felt sorry for him. Almost.

"I'd like to ask you a question."

His nostrils flared. He nervously licked his lips. "No."

"You don't even know what it is yet! Just hear me out. If the answer is still no, then fine. I'll never ask again."

Her logic seemed to stump him, because there was no pithy comeback, no reply at all. Just that full-body tension and those dark, dark eyes, wary and undeniably heated.

"Okay, so here it is." She tilted her head and looked up at him, watching carefully for any telling change her words might evoke. "Have I ever visited you in your dreams?"

Watching the cascade of emotion that poured over Magnus's face while he struggled for words, Lu thought, *Whoever said silence is golden was a freaking genius.*

First, shock. Then a flash of something that was either embarrassment or chagrin that turned his face white, as if he'd been caught doing something bad. The color swept back in high spots over his cheekbones with the arrival of what looked like indignation. Then followed, in quick succession, longing, desire, and acute despair.

Then his face emptied, as if wiped clean by an invisible hand. He said, "What a strange question."

Not a no, not a yes, just a simple deflection. Which didn't matter because he'd told her everything she needed to know in his fraught silence, and everything that had happened between them in all her years of dreaming came back to her in a huge, burning rush, like a wave of lava crashing over her. Her lips parted on the only word that came to mind.

"Magnus."

It was a whisper. It was a plea, soft and ardent, a plea for him to admit aloud what he'd just admitted in his silence. She wanted to hear him say it, to speak the words, *Yes, I've made love to you a hundred times, yes, I loved every glorious minute of it, yes, I want to do it again right now, yes, you're the only one and will always be, yes, yes, yes, yes, YES!*

He said none of those things. He said nothing at all. Everything was there between them, bright as danger, electric and pulsing and true, but he held his tongue and Lu held hers, and they only stared into each other's eyes, a new question burning the pit of her stomach like a swallowed sun.

What is this feeling? This violent, gut-wrenching ache?

She might've said it aloud, but a noise shattered their connection. It was a high, keening wail from somewhere nearby.

Magnus reacted instantly. He turned and bolted from the room, shouting over his shoulder, "Put some clothes on!"

Lu dressed faster than she'd ever dressed in her life. In mere seconds she followed in the direction he'd gone, her heart pounding, hands shaking with adrenaline. She found him standing down the hallway, outside another bedroom, its door open to reveal the scene inside.

Nola was kneeling on the floor beside the bed, crying and holding the hand of Grandfather, who lay peacefully in spite of all the noise she was making. James stood behind her with his hand on her shoulder, watching Grandfather with a look of grim resignation.

Magnus murmured, "He's gone?"

James glanced at them and nodded.

It's time for me to go, little dragon.

All the tiny hairs on Lu's body stood on end. She raised a shaking hand to her mouth, stepping back with a cry.

Nola lifted her head and looked right at Lu. Her face was streaked with tears. She said, "I had this awful dream where he came to tell me good-bye, and I woke up so scared I had to come check on him. And when I did, he . . . he just wouldn't wake up. He was lying here, like he is now, his hands folded over his chest, holding this."

She held up a trembling fistful of wheat. "Where would he have gotten this?"

Everyone looked at Lu, as if they knew she already knew the answer. Which she did.

Lu lowered her hand from her mouth, took a deep breath, and whispered, "In the field near where he grew up. I was there with him, last night."

All the air went out of the room. No one moved. No one spoke. Only Grandfather looked peaceful, a small smile playing at the corners of his lips.

"He . . . he asked me to find him, to Dreamwalk with him, and I did. My sister and mother were there, and we talked, and then there was another woman . . . she was waiting for him . . . and he said he had to go . . ."

She stopped speaking because she realized she was babbling, and also because Nola's face had bleached to the color of bone. She released Grandfather's hand and slowly stood, her eyes as wide open as they would go.

"What woman?" she whispered.

"I-I don't know. She had dark hair. She was young, pretty, wearing a long flowered dress and a lot of silver bangles on one wrist. And she had a child with her . . ."

From Nola's throat came a strangled sound. Her expression was tortured. "A child?"

Lu whispered, "A boy. About seven, eight years old."

Nola's throat worked, but no sound came out, and Lu felt the compulsion to keep speaking, to try and explain the unexplainable. To do *something* to ease that terrible look on Nola's face.

"They were waiting for him. They were happy, smiling. And he was happy to go . . . to go be with them . . . he'd only been waiting for me, and now that we'd met he could . . . he could . . ."

She couldn't get it out. Her own throat was closing; tears began to slide down her cheeks. Then Nola broke down and sobbed into James's chest. He held her, looking over her head at Lu with an expression she couldn't decipher.

"Nola's grandmother was killed in a car accident many years ago," he said. "Her son James was in the car with her; he was eight at the time. I was named after him."

There was a winch tightening in degrees around her chest. Her heart began to pound like it was trying to claw its way out of her chest. "I'm sorry," Lu whispered, her voice cracking. "I'm so sorry."

"It's not your fault. You've done nothing wrong." Magnus stepped closer to her, gazing down at her with his own indecipherable expression. She looked up, pleading at him with her eyes. She needed his arms around her, needed the comfort she knew he could give, needed to hear him say it again, that it wasn't her fault. She just needed . . . *him*.

So she closed the small distance between them, wrapped her arms around his broad shoulders, and buried her face in his neck.

He stiffened, but didn't pull away. There was a breathless moment she was certain he would, but then—oh miracle—his arms came up hard to encircle her. He lowered his mouth to her ear. "It's all right," he whispered, his deep voice the softest, gentlest stroke of sound. "It's all right: I've got you."

I've got you. It broke the final shred of her restraint. She sobbed, her body wracked with a shudder. Both sobs and shudders kept coming, and soon Magnus was stroking her hair, murmuring comforting words she followed the shape but not the substance of, letting his voice wash over her, his heat warm her, his strength support her, until she was crying in earnest, letting everything out. He picked her up in his arms and carried her back to their bedroom. He closed the door behind them with his foot, and gently laid her on the bed.

He went to the bathroom and ran a washcloth under cold water, and brought it back to her with a box of tissues that he set on the little table beside the bed. Then he wiped her face with the cloth and dried it with the tissues, and made her blow her nose.

"Who knew you'd be such an ugly crier?" he whispered, brushing the hair from her forehead. He gazed down at her with such tenderness it almost made her break out in a fresh round of tears.

"I don't ugly cry," she sniffled, not believing it for a minute because she could feel the way her face had distorted, but not insulted because she knew he was teasing. *Hoped* he was teasing.

"You're right. You don't ugly anything. You couldn't be ugly if you tried."

The way he said it was so sweet, such softness from such a hard man, that Lu forgot for a moment all her hesitations and the walls he'd erected between them, and reached out to touch his face.

He snatched her hand with lightning speed, curling his fingers around her wrist. He held it suspended in the air between them, the look of softness in his eyes from seconds before replaced by an icy, furious look that might have made Honor proud.

"Don't."

It was all he said, but Lu felt the pathos behind it, the years and years of suffering and self-hatred. She felt it, and her heart wept for him, for whatever burden he carried, and wouldn't share.

"Please let me touch you," she begged.

The fury in his eyes was matched in his voice, though he kept it low. "You've touched me more than any other living thing in the last twenty years. That should be enough."

Was he talking about *physically* touching, or something else? She couldn't tell. She didn't care. "It's *not* enough, Magnus. I want more. I want more of you."

Her words affected him. His eyes flashed, the hand around her wrist began to shake. He said hoarsely, "Why would you want me? I've got half a face!"

"That doesn't make you half a man!"

He loomed over her, pressing her back against the bed, capturing her other wrist now and pinning both over her head against the pillow. He was angry and his anger was shaking him, sending tremors through his chest and arms, flooding his face and neck with color.

"You don't know what you're saying! You have no idea what kind of man I am, or the things I've done, or the things I'm capable of! *You don't know anything about me at all!*"

He made a sound that was part growl, part wretched cry, his teeth bared, his eyes wild. He looked for a moment like an animal, and Lu remembered that Morgan had wisely advised her how to treat a wild animal: gently.

So as gently as she could, Lu told him the truth.

She looked deep into his eyes and said, "I know that underneath all your sharp bristles, you're kind, loyal, and honorable. You're smart, and capable, and there's nothing you wouldn't do to protect the colony, including sacrificing your own life. So that makes you selfless, and the most courageous person I've ever known. And I know that even though you're all these wonderful things, you don't think you deserve even the smallest happiness. You punish yourself as much as you can, you deny yourself any kind of pleasure, even *smiling*, and whatever it was that happened to make you that way, you can't forgive yourself. Or you won't. Either way, you hate yourself, Magnus. And knowing that breaks my heart."

His expression was stunned; his eyes registered the depth of his anguish. He turned his face away and moved as if to withdraw, his grip loosening on her wrists, but Lu reached out and gently placed her hands on either side of his face, turning him back to her and holding him there.

"I won't bring it up again. Not because I don't want to know, but because it's obvious you don't want to talk about it, and I don't want to have anything to do with giving you more pain than you already have." Her voice grew smaller. "And I won't say this again either, but you should know that I think you're beautiful, Magnus. I've always thought you were the most beautiful thing I've ever seen."

"*Look* at me! I'm *not* beautiful!" he hissed, his voice strangled, his body frozen above her.

"You are to me."

He made a sound low in his throat and closed his eyes. Because he wasn't moving away and he'd allowed her to keep her hands on his face, Lu took a chance and did the thing she'd been wanting to do since she'd first done it in Beckett's lab, in front of everyone.

She kissed him.

But she didn't start with his mouth; she wanted to show him with her actions what she'd said to him in words. So—slowly, gently, easing forward—she stretched toward him, brushing her lips against his scarred cheek.

He sucked in a breath. Lu froze, expecting him to bolt. When he didn't, she closed her eyes, inhaling his scent deep into her lungs. Then she lightly rubbed her cheek against his, and leaned in farther to nuzzle her nose into the soft, warm spot just beneath his earlobe. There she pressed another kiss. A tremor ran through him at the touch of her lips against his skin.

He said her name, the barest whisper of sound, as she ran her mouth along his jaw. The stubble from his unshaven face tickled her lips. His hands dug into the sheets on either side of her head, bunching the fabric in his fists.

She slid her hands from his cheeks into the soft thickness of his hair and kissed the other side of his face, his closed eyelids, the bridge of his nose, slowly working her way back to the other side, then down to his neck, to the scars that puckered beneath his jawline. She kissed those, too. His pulse throbbed wildly against her lips. He exhaled, a soft groan that sent a spike of desire all the way through her.

"Please."

His voice was low and wretched, filled with terrible longing and pain. Lu didn't know if he was asking her to stop or to go on, so she gently pulled his head down and fitted her mouth to his.

He moaned into her mouth. Lu thrilled at the sound of it, every nerve ending tinglingly alive. He sank his hands into her hair, adjusted his weight atop her so his pelvis pressed down against hers, and kissed her back, ferociously.

She loved it. The solid weight and heat of him, the scent of his skin, his taste. The way he couldn't get enough of her mouth, his tongue invading, demanding, his fingers tightening in her hair as his erection dug into her belly, almost painfully hard.

He pulled back to gasp, "We can't–I can't—" but Lu flexed her pelvis against his and cut him off with another kiss. It went on and on, wild and deep, and would have almost surely led somewhere her body desperately wanted to go had it not been for the sudden, muffled sounds that broke them apart and left them staring at each other, panting and shocked.

The sounds were unmistakable, ones they both recognized:

Gunshots.

TWENTY-FOUR

They leapt from the bed. Magnus threw open the door, and the two of them bounded into the hallway, calling out for Nola and James.

"Here!" called James from downstairs, and they quickly went to the first floor.

Nola and James stood in front of the wall of computer screens, watching images of the exterior of the property in black and white; the front and back yards of the house, up and down the street, the entrance to the shed. It was there a group of six men stood with rifles pointed at the door.

At least, Lu *assumed* they were men. They had two legs and two arms, but that's where the resemblance to anything human ended. Each wore an obviously handmade suit of armor cobbled together from an odd collection of metal parts, all of it spray-painted matte black. Only their boots, gloves, and ragged-edged capes were fabric, but what made them look so otherworldly was their headgear. Helmets soldered together with garish seams sported face masks from which dangled foot-long rubber tubes that ended with blocky canisters fashioned to look like skulls or eagles or bears. Some sprouted feathers atop, others were rimmed with claws. All had a pair of soulless-looking glass eyes staring out, reflecting back the lightening sky in glints that made them appear to wink in sinister welcome.

"Scavs," said James grimly, zooming the picture in with a dial on one of the keyboards. "They must've followed us in."

Lu was fascinated in spite of the danger. She'd heard of these wandering groups of survivors who lived outside the cities, scavenging what they could from abandoned homes and stores. Legend had it they'd mutated from exposure to the sun, but it was impossible to determine if this group was mutated, or suffered from nothing more deadly than a seriously impaired fashion sense.

The biggest one, a hulk with a pair of enormous bat ears on his helmet, whom Lu assumed was the leader from his I'm-in-charge-here stance, cocked his rifle and shot another round into the shed door. The handle promptly exploded into a fine spray of dust, leaving a gaping hole.

"So much for that reinforced door," Nola muttered.

"I suppose I should deal with this," said Lu. Her stomach sank at the thought of what "dealing" with it entailed. Before she could utter another word, however, Magnus snorted.

She glanced at him, surprised. With a dour expression he said, "Hold your horses, Wonder Woman." He glanced away from the camera to meet her eyes, and Lu could have sworn she saw a twinkle of humor there. "I think I can handle this one on my own."

He turned and left the room without further comment. After a minute, she said to Nola and James, "Hold my horses?"

"It basically means don't get ahead of yourself." Nola winced as she watched the scav leader lift his big leg and kick the shed door down. "And the subtext was something along the lines of, 'Please don't emasculate me in front of company, sweetheart.'"

Sweetheart? Lu's cheeks flamed. Nola turned and gave her a look. "What? You think I can't tell when a man's in love?"

Lu almost choked on her own tongue with the force of her denial. "*Love!* He's not—he doesn't—"

"Of course he does," Nola scoffed, waving a hand to indicate how ridiculous Lu was being. "And so do you. It's all over you both."

Lu was silent, reeling. Examining her stunned expression, Nola asked, "Not too many boyfriends in your past?"

Lu avoided that question, put a hand to her head, and quietly said, "I actually thought he liked you."

"Of course he likes me. What's not to like?" Nola countered without an ounce of self-consciousness. "But he doesn't like me in *that* way, sweetie. You've got that all locked up. Oh, shit." Her attention was glued to the screen that showed the interior of the shed, and it became immediately apparent what had her cursing.

The Scavs had figured out how to operate the elevator.

Magnus waited until he heard the elevator lurch to a stop, and the clank of metal chain announce the inner door was being lifted. Unseen behind the wall, he waited until he heard the Scavs move past him down the dimly lit tunnel toward the steel door that led into Nola's hidden underground compound. Then he placed his palms flat against the wall and concentrated.

Cement began to disappear beneath his hands, flaking away silently in waves that left a growing mound of stone dust at his feet.

His Gift of turning solid matter into dust with a touch was the one that had earned him the spot as Alpha of the Wales colony. Though it didn't work on flesh and the range was limited to whatever he could touch, it had incredible applications, including digging all those perfectly shaped sleeping chambers in the rock. But it wasn't his favorite Gift, or the most effective.

Or the deadliest.

He tunneled silently through the wall between the elevator shaft and the door, then stood in the low light, watching the Scavs assess their next move.

He licked his lips, not even realizing he did it, still tasting the soft sweetness of Lumina's mouth. He hoped she wasn't watching the cameras, because what he was about to do wasn't going to be pleasant. And though she said she knew him, had even—unbelievably—said she thought him beautiful, she didn't know him like this.

He didn't want her to know him like this. But life is a bitch, *and* a slut, because she screws everyone. He stepped forward on silent feet.

"Steel," grunted the bear-headed Scav to the big one with the bat ears.

Looking into the small black eye of the camera on the ceiling, Bat Ears tapped the nose of his rifle against the door. "Yoo-hoo! Anybody home?" he called in falsetto. His companions snickered.

A disembodied voice answered over a hidden speaker. "Nobody here but us chickens."

Nola, sounding bored. Magnus smiled grimly: She definitely didn't scare easily. He crept a few feet closer, the curdled stench of unwashed skin wrinkling his nose.

Bear Head whispered with reverence, "A *woman*!" The other four began to shift their weight and mutter, but Bat Ears fell perfectly still, his air of jaunty humor vanished. He gazed into the camera a long, silent moment, then removed his helmet.

Big mistake.

It was a peculiarity of Magnus's Gift that he had to be looking directly into the eyes of his victim for it to work. That meant close quarters, which sometimes meant close calls, if those victims happened to be armed, as these six were. So instead of a direct assault, Magnus often had to resort to guerrilla tactics.

It was guerrilla fighters, after all, who'd perfected the art of the surprise ambush.

The *invisible* ambush.

Magnus gathered the shadows around him, and closed the last few feet between him and the armed group of thugs.

"What . . . where'd he go?" James stared in confusion at the black-and-white video display. Where only a second ago Magnus had stood, sneaking down the hallway like a burglar—actually it was closer to swaggering down the hallway like a pirate—now there was only blank space.

"Jack said he was special," Nola whispered, her gaze glued to the screen. "I have a feeling we're about to find out exactly what that means."

Standing just behind them both, Lu watched in awe as chaos ensued.

The man who'd removed his helmet to stare into the camera had a gaunt face, matted black hair, and black eyes that hinted at depths of violence that made her skin crawl. One second he was glaring into the camera as if he were going to eat it, the next he whirled around with a shout. His five companions froze, and stood unmoving as their leader clapped his hands on either side of his head and began, loudly, to scream.

He fell to his knees, then to the floor, writhing and screaming in agony. The other Scavs began to shout over each other, panicked.

"What the hell?"

"Luter! What's wrong?"

"It's poison! The air is poisoned!"

"Nothing's showing on the readout, idiot!"

"Then *what the fuck* is wrong with him?"

The leader continued to roll and shriek, only now his nose was copiously bleeding. As were his ears. His helmet lay discarded on the floor beside him, blank-eyed and grotesque. He began to sob and beg.

"Please! Make it stop! Make it stop! OhGodJesusMotherMary-pleasefuckingmakeitstop!"

A tingle of horror swept up Lu's spine. She knew with chilling, bone-deep certainty that whatever was happening to this man, Magnus was the cause. Remembering what he'd said to her in the bedroom, her chill grew deeper.

You have no idea what kind of man I am, or the things I've done, or the things I'm capable of.

The man on the ground coughed up an extravagant amount of blood. Lu jumped, hand to her mouth, watching wide-eyed as two of the other men's helmets were wrenched from their heads by an invisible force and tossed aside. They, too, fell to the floor screaming.

The other three made a run for the elevator.

They didn't get far. All three were thrown to the ground within seconds, their helmets removed and thrown away, their screams rising in horrible harmony with the others. Their noses began to spray blood. Their screams were punctuated by wet, bloody coughs, and Lu knew what was coming next.

Magnus! No!

Instantly, the men stopped screaming.

An awful silence ensued, broken only by low groans and the sound of pained wheezing. The men rocked on the floor, clutching their heads, curled into fetal positions. The leader, the one who'd been afflicted first, crawled slowly to his knees and sat back on his haunches. He touched his face, shook his head as if to clear his vision.

"Today's your lucky day, Scav. Any other time and I would've ended your sorry life without a second thought," said a low voice, a growl from the semidarkness that wasn't attached to anything visible. Wherever Magnus was, he must've been close to the leader, because the man cowered at the sound of his voice.

"Please!" he entreated in a ragged whisper. "We were just looking for food!"

His hands flew to his head again. He began, shrilly, to scream.

It was over as quickly as it had started. The man fell forward onto his hands, gasping for breath.

"I don't like liars. You should know that up front. I *also* don't like repeating myself, so I'm only going to say this once: Leave, and never come near here again. Next time, I won't be so forgiving."

Then it seemed all the men were released from the grip of agony that held them. One by one, they staggered to their feet, grunting and groaning, wiping blood from their faces, their eyes wild and disoriented. The leader found his helmet and stumbled down the tunnel toward the others, and one by one the rest retrieved their headgear. They fell into the elevator, collapsing to the floor.

The door closed. The elevator creaked to life. Then there was only an empty tunnel festooned with bloodstains, and a tall, smooth-edged hole in one wall.

Something glinted oddly in the dim light. A sly glimmer began to coalesce into a solid form. Then Magnus appeared, looking up into the camera, his face as cold as stone. He looked a long, long time, and Lu knew he knew she was watching, and waiting for her to pronounce judgment against him.

When she remained silent, still stunned by what she'd seen, his voice, broken and raw, spoke into her head.

Not so beautiful now, am I?

He turned on his heel and strode away.

TWENTY-FIVE

For a person who'd grown up in a society where the elderly were murdered with a lethal dose of chemicals, then incinerated and disposed of along with the trash, Lu found Cherokee burial customs exotic, foreign, and hauntingly beautiful.

First, Nola washed Grandfather's body with water and boiled willow root. Then she anointed him with lavender oil to cleanse his body of impurities. She sang a lament on her knees beside his bed, while James performed purification rituals for the house. They then gathered all Grandfather's belongings, wrapped his body in a shroud, and sang more lamentations until the day had passed and darkness again overtook the sky.

Then they went outside, dug a hole, and buried him in the yard with his head facing west. His clothing, favorite books, jewelry, old photographs, and wedding ring were buried with him.

During all of it Lu fought back tears. Her own father had escaped the injection of SleepSoft-9 and the Cinerator™, but in the end he'd burned anyway. There was no grave for her to visit when they reached New Vienna. No evidence existed that he'd ever been alive at all. There was only a place in her heart that would forever remain empty, and her memory of him, the gentle, faithful man who'd raised a foundling child and paid the ultimate price for his kindness.

Though she'd been surrounded by death almost her entire life, Lu felt that her father's and Nola's grandfather's deaths were connected, as their dying advice to her was connected, as she herself was connected to something larger and unseen. The weight of her destiny loomed heavy, and if she was being honest with herself, she wasn't sure she was capable of rising to the occasion.

This rescue plan she'd concocted wasn't exactly foolproof. What if she failed?

Magnus spoke quietly from behind her. "It's time."

Lu had been staring at the computer screens, lost in thought, her eyes focused on the image of the mound of freshly dug dirt in the yard, but now she turned and looked at him. His eyes held that cold, remote look again, which told her in no uncertain terms that this morning's interlude in the bedroom hadn't been the breakthrough she'd hoped it was.

Her heart sank. *Fool.*

She was a fool to think she could change a man so damaged. She was a fool to believe there could be anything good or happy in her future. She was a fool to believe in the power of love.

There was no love in this world. There was only death, and darkness.

"I'm ready," she answered, her voice empty. She turned back to the screens.

He hesitated a moment before moving away. He said a few words of condolence and thanks to James and Nola, accepted two canteens of water and small packages of wrapped food for their packs, then wished them both farewell.

"The bikes only hold a six-hour charge, so don't take any detours on the way to your next stop," cautioned Nola in a quiet voice. "All your stops on the way to the city should have chargers, but once you get to New Vienna, you'll have to ditch the bikes altogether; they're not registered. It'll raise a flag."

"Will you stay here?" Magnus asked. He left unsaid any words of caution about the Scavs, but his concern was implied in his tone.

James said, "My guess is we're safe for a while, at least. They won't be in any hurry to come back. We'll be careful, don't worry about us. Just . . ." He faltered, and Lu turned to find him looking at her. "You guys be careful, too."

"We will. Thank you for everything, both of you." Lu crossed and gave Nola a hard hug, then hugged James. When she withdrew, James squeezed her hand, then dropped it and went to the kitchen, busying himself with tidying up. Nola walked them to the door.

"There's something you should have." Nola handed Lu a small envelope with her name written on the outside in a masculine scrawl. Curious, Lu looked inside: There at the bottom glittered a gold chain with a pendant. She tipped the envelope and the necklace, cool and heavy, slid into the palm of her hand.

The pendant was in the shape of a dragon. Wings spread, tail curled, mouth open as if about to spew fire. It had tiny rubies for eyes, and it was the exact same dragon that Lu had tattooed on her stomach. She gasped.

Nola said, "Aside from his wedding ring, that was Grandfather's favorite piece of jewelry. He was never without it. I found it inside the book on his nightstand, in that envelope with your name." Nola paused, drawing a steadying breath. When she looked into Lu's eyes, her own were moist. "There's an inscription on the back. I looked it up. It's Aristotle. Maybe it means something to you?"

With shaking hands, Lu turned over the pendant. In a whisper, she read aloud the words inscribed there.

"Hope is the dream of a waking man."

The three of them stood there in silence, until Magnus finally spoke.

"She certainly is."

Their eyes met. Without another word, he turned and opened the heavy steel door, and melted into the darkness of the tunnel.

"Lumina." Nola's voice was soft, filled with a hesitation that dragged Lu's attention back from the fading sound of Magnus's footsteps.

"Yes?"

"I just want to say . . . thank you."

"For what?"

Nola swallowed, looking down at the necklace in Lu's hands. She seemed to be fighting for words. "So many terrible things have happened to me in my life. I've . . . it's never been easy for me. Even when I was a little girl." She laughed a low, husky laugh, filled with dark humor. "*Especially* then. There were countless days when I would have gladly killed myself, if only I'd had the courage." She hesitated, then glanced up. "But today I found something I lost long ago."

Lu waited silently.

Nola said, "Hope."

"I . . . I'm sorry. I don't understand."

"I never really believed in anything . . . after. You know. *Life.* But now . . . what you saw, with Grandfather . . ." Nola's eyes misted, and she reached out and clasped Lu's shoulder. "Grandfather used to tell me, 'There is no death, only a change of worlds.' I never believed that. Until today. Until you. And now I have a reason to keep pushing forward through this nightmare existence. I have the only thing a person really needs in order to survive: hope."

Lu's stomach roiled with nausea, her heartbeat skittered and tripped. She looked down at the necklace in her hand. "Please don't put me on a pedestal; I'm no hero, Nola. I'm actually more of a dysfunctional mess. And I'm sorry to say this because you've been kind to me, and I don't want to seem like an ungrateful jerk, but . . ." She met Nola's eyes, and knew her own were bleak. "It might have only been a dream. His last dream. And not . . . what you think it is."

"Maybe," Nola admitted. "But maybe not. And that's where the hope part comes in." She wrapped her arms around Lu's shoulders and hugged her, swift and tight. Then she pushed her away, all sentimentality replaced by that commanding side Lu had begun to think of as the General. "Off with you, then! And don't forget what I said about the range on those bikes."

She gave Lu a gentle shove toward the door. Lu pocketed the necklace, nodding, and turned to leave, but Nola's voice made her turn back one final time.

"Something else Grandfather used to say, Lumina."

"What's that?" Lu watched a smile hatch over Nola's face.

"Those who have one foot in the canoe, and one foot in the boat, are going to fall into the water."

Lu blinked at her, nonplussed. "I can honestly say I have no idea what that means."

Nola's smile grew wider. "It means a divided heart is destined for failure. So plant your ass in the canoe, let go of doubt, and paddle like a motherfucker. It's the only way to get where you need to go."

Then she pushed shut the door.

Three days of round-the-clock pampering and the best medical care available on the planet had not improved the Grand Minister's mood one iota.

"Idiot! *Schwachkopf*! *Kretén*!" he screamed at the young nurse who'd come to change his bandages and apply fresh salve to his red, weeping skin.

The doctor standing calmly on the other side of the Grand Minister's bed assumed his insults were hurled in three languages in order to make sure there was no doubt of his displeasure. As if his manner and tone weren't enough.

"Please try to remain calm," said Dr. Petrov in his practiced, soothing voice. He'd dealt with nearly every kind of human sickness in his long career, and considered himself a particular expert in diseases of the mind; it was obvious to him that the Grand Minister was a lunatic. Of the raving variety. But such a fact, stated aloud, would ensure the swift removal of his head—or something even more cherished—so Dr. Petrov only smiled his bland smile and kept the damning evaluation to himself.

"Calm!" shouted the Grand Minister. His face turned an interesting shade of plum. His lone blue eye bulged, threatening to pop from its hollow socket. "You expect me to remain calm when I've just found out you've been slathering me in goo made from THOSE DISGUSTING ANIMALS?"

Dr. Petrov adjusted his spectacles, trying to communicate with his eyes to the frightened nurse that she should ready another syringe of tranquilizer. They'd already used several on their patient since he'd awoken yesterday and had promptly started screaming.

"That *goo*, as you call it, has literally saved your skin, my dear Grand Minister. Had we not applied the Neoderma, you certainly would have died by now. You suffered third-degree burns over seventy percent of your body, charred skin, blistering, shock, and deep tissue damage, and the medication was necessary to—"

With surprising strength, the Grand Minister grabbed Dr. Petrov's arm and yanked, pulling him down to the bed. The clipboard he'd been holding flew from his hands and fell with a clatter to the white tile floor, the papers attached to it fluttering like dry leaves in a breeze. He stared at the Grand Minister in wide-eyed shock.

"I would rather *die* than be defiled with that shit you call 'medication,'" he snarled into Dr. Petrov's face, spraying spittle. "Do you hear me, imbecile? I would. Rather. *Die!*"

Appalled, Dr. Petrov extricated himself from the unnaturally strong grip of the Grand Minister, and straightened, motioning to the nurse. He smoothed his hands over his hair, and down the front of his white coat. With as much dignity as he could muster after having been momentarily overpowered and practically assaulted by a one-eyed, one-armed, no-legged patient, he said, "While you are under my care it is my obligation to ensure you do *not*, in fact, die, Grand Minister . . . but once you're released, you're free to do as you wish. In the interim, we will continue the Neoderma therapy, and any other courses of treatment I deem necessary, including the CellRenu you've been receiving intravenously, which is helping to repair the damage to your lungs and air passages from inhaling smoke and superheated air."

The Grand Minister fell silent, staring agog at the bag of clear liquid dangling from a metal hook beside his bed. The plastic tube that snaked down from it ended with a steel cannula embedded in a vein in the back of his hand. Dr. Petrov took the opportunity to snap his fingers, and the nurse darted forward, the syringe held ready in her pale, trembling hand.

"You're injecting me with . . . them?" the Grand Minister whispered, his face a mask of horror. "You're putting their poison in my *blood*?"

Dr. Petrov cared nothing for politics. He didn't care about ideologies, either, except when it came to honoring his Hippocratic oath. And he had a secret thought, which he hardly even dared admit to himself, that the "disgusting animals" from which all the astonishing medicines of the last quarter century were made were far less disgusting than many of the people he knew. Like his assessment of the mental state of the Grand Minister, Dr. Petrov kept this dangerous opinion in the dark, quiet basement of his mind, where it would never see the red light of day.

"It's not poison, sir. It's *medicine*," sniffed Dr. Petrov. He nodded to the nurse, and, with his help and after much flailing and cursing on the part of the Grand Minister, she succeeded in plunging the needle into the vein in the crook of his spindly arm. They watched as he struggled to keep his eyes open, and failed. His limbs grew lax, and he quickly drifted into a drugged sleep.

The doctor and his nurse shared a smile and the tenuous relief of two soldiers who'd just dodged a hail of bullets. There would be another volley as soon as the Grand Minister awoke again, but for now, thankfully, they could enjoy some needed, if short-lived, peace.

"Well." Dr. Petrov straightened his glasses and smoothed his lab coat again. He was surprised to find his palms were sweaty. "Nothing like a little wrestling match to get the blood going, eh, nurse?"

She gave an exaggerated eye roll, exhaled a shaky breath, and chuckled. "I have to admit, Doctor, this one gives new meaning to the words *pain in the ass.*" She chuckled again, then clapped a hand over her mouth, realizing what she'd just said. And about *whom.*

"It's all right," said Dr. Petrov, keeping his voice low. "I couldn't agree more. Just be careful you don't let that slip again in front of anyone else." He rounded the end of the bed, patted her shoulder, and watched with pleasure as a blush spread across her cheekbones.

"Yes, Doctor."

"So," he said, turning brisk. "What do we have up next?"

The nurse bent, retrieving his lost clipboard from the floor. He followed her from the room to the nurses' station just outside and tried not to admire the alluring twitch in her hips as she walked; he was a married man, after all. His fidelity was less about adoration for his wife, of which he had little, and more about pragmatism, of which he had a lot; the grass was never greener on the other side of the fence, he knew, only a different shade of green than the one on your own. And probably riddled with gopher holes you'd twist your ankle in, and thorny burrs that would cling to your socks. No sense disrupting your entire life to graze in new pastures when those same pastures would look downright dull once you'd been grazing in them a few months or years down the road.

Some men claimed variety was the spice of life, but Dr. Petrov knew that particular spice only led to diarrhea.

From the station counter, the nurse picked up the data pad with the rounds log and ran a finger down its list of contents, perusing with pursed lips. Something about her face was different, but Dr. Petrov couldn't put a finger on it. Less makeup, perhaps? Her skin definitely had a glow he hadn't noticed before.

"Four-ten fell out of bed again. Minor contusions, nothing pressing. Five-sixteen needed an additional two pints of B positive, and is stable. Five-thirty-one is complaining of chest pain, but his tests are all negative . . . oh, here's one." She brightened. "The patient in six-oh-two who came in last month is awake, and asking for a doctor—"

"Six-oh-two? Talking? Are you sure?" He was positive the nurse was mistaken; that particular patient had been involved in an accident at the waste treatment plant that had left him comatose, with zero brain activity. For him to be awake would be nothing short of a miracle. Dr. Petrov had seen too much in his time to believe in those.

"Yes," said the nurse, looking up from the data pad. "Six-oh-two. He's just finishing his supper now, I believe."

"He's *eating*?" Dr. Petrov was astonished.

The nurse shrugged. "Said he was starving. Asked for steak."

Now Dr. Petrov was *more* than astonished, though he couldn't think of the word that would properly convey the depths of his shock. Patients awakening after experiencing severe brain trauma were disoriented, mute, as weak as newborn lambs. And after a prolonged coma, they often couldn't speak until months had passed and they'd relearned a variety of forgotten skills, including language. For this patient to be cognizant, hungry, and demanding a meal went beyond miracle territory and straight into . . .

The hair on the back of his neck prickling, Dr. Petrov slowly turned and stared down the long, sterile corridor toward room six-zero-two. "Nurse," he said slowly, "pull his history for me."

"Certainly, Doctor." With a few swipes and taps on the device, she had it, and handed the pad over.

Male, aged twenty-nine, admitted mid-November after a head injury caused by a high fall. No response to pain stimulus, no verbal or motor responses, brain injury classified as severe. For all intents and purposes, he was as "alive" as a zucchini. His medical history indicated general good health prior to the accident, with the exception of diabetes which he'd had since childhood. It was being managed by a daily dose of . . .

Now all the tiny hairs on Dr. Petrov's arms stood on end. He looked deeper into the patient's history to confirm that he had, for the last twenty years, been taking Glucaphase, a once-daily pill manufactured—as all drugs were—by the Phoenix Corporation.

He'd seen a patient only yesterday who claimed her eczema was cured after going on mesalamine for ulcerative colitis. And last week another patient who'd been scheduled for open-heart surgery to correct an atrioventricular canal defect he'd had since birth had insisted on a final round of tests because, as he put it, "I suddenly feel finer than a frog hair split three ways."

Those final round of tests showed a man in perfect health. His heart had mysteriously healed.

He'd been taking a drug for migraines from the Phoenix Corporation for six months.

"Doctor? Are you all right?"

With the feeling he'd been staring at something huge and obvious and looking right through it, Dr. Petrov slowly set the data pad back on the counter. He looked at the nurse. He said, "Have you done something with your hair? You look . . . different."

The nurse, blushing, reached up and touched her head. "Oh! Thank you, Doctor. No, my hair is the same. But I'm not wearing my glasses, maybe that's it."

Yes, that was it. She'd worn an elegant little pair of gold glasses since he'd known her. Without them, her face looked younger, brighter. "Got contacts, have you?"

She laughed self-consciously. "No. Funny thing is, I just haven't seemed to need my glasses anymore. Last week I realized I hadn't been wearing them all day, and was getting around fine. Which is strange because I had terrible vision, but . . . it just sort of . . . fixed itself." She shrugged, still self-conscious. "Not that I'm complaining!"

The buzzing from the ceiling lights seemed suddenly a thundering racket in his ears. "What a stroke of luck," he said to the nurse, feeling as if someone had just pulled the wool from over his eyes to reveal a new and quite monstrous landscape. "Tell me, nurse, are you by chance taking any kind of medication?"

The nurse blinked at him, surprised. "No, Doctor. Nothing."

A little of the tightening in Dr. Petrov's chest eased. "You're sure? Nothing?"

"I'm sure. I hate taking pills; I have problems swallowing them."

"What about injections? Inhalants? Sublingual drops?"

The nurse was beginning to look nervous. "Doctor, I don't get sick. You know that; I've never missed a day of work. And I don't have any health problems. You could say I'm as healthy as a horse."

Coincidence, then. Dr. Petrov was beginning to feel a bit better, until the nurse added one final thing.

"Well, except for that time of the month."

The doctor froze, staring at his attractive young nurse, who was now looking back at him sheepishly.

"I get terrible cramps the first day of my cycle, so I just started taking Femistrin a few months ago. They're these tiny little pills, so I can get them down without too much trouble."

"I see," replied the doctor, from somewhere far outside himself. And see he did, but in the clarity of this sudden understanding came the knowledge that revealing what he had just deduced would bring him nothing but trouble, most likely of the fatal sort. So because Dr. Petrov was, above all things, a practical man, he shut his mouth, gave the nurse his best bland, doctorly smile, and dropped the subject.

As he went about the rest of his day, a small, secret part of him marveled at the way Man continually underestimated the subversive, creative genius of Mother Nature.

He wondered what She had in store for the human race next.

TWENTY-SIX

It was a five-hour ride to Lu and Magnus's next stop, through a dark wasteland of empty roads, skeletal trees in rotted forests, and sluggish black rivers, their banks clogged with decaying trash. Lu had never been outside New Vienna, and was horrified at what the Earth had become, littered with the corpse of civilization. Everything was abandoned, the towns and streets and sky, and her sense of loneliness and despair was crushing.

How could the world ever be made new again?

The idea had taken root: this hopeless world made new. She'd only just admitted it to herself, and was mentally trying it on like a new dress to see if it fit. It bunched and puckered in places, scratchy and too tight, but the more she dwelled on the thought of a different sort of world as they rode, the more stubborn the thought became, until she eventually realized it was more than a possibility.

It was an inevitability. In its current form, the world was unsustainable. Left so long neglected, it would eventually perish, and so would the ragged dregs of life that still inhabited it.

Lu didn't want the world to die. She wanted it to be, as she'd been, *resurrected*.

Her plan to this point had only revolved around getting her mother and father out of the IF's prison, but as she and Magnus navigated through the charred ruins of Europe, the plan seemed too small in scope. She could rescue her parents, possibly even set free the other prisoners, but what then? Where could they go? Where could they hide where they wouldn't be hunted? And if she were to free them, how would all those prisoners survive in a world designed specifically to destroy them?

No. Rescue couldn't be the ultimate goal.

The ultimate goal needed to be the death of Sebastian Thorne.

The problem was, Lu had no idea how she might go about it. How could she get to him? Where the hell did the man even live?

Another dilemma: Killing Thorne wouldn't be self-defense. It would be murder. Premeditated. First degree. That little detail was giving her already raw conscience hissy fits.

"We're off at the next exit," came Magnus's voice through the ear bud in her helmet. He was ahead of her by a few yards, as he'd been the entire trip since they'd left Nola's, navigating a safe path through roads and highways that were more than occasionally strewn with obstacles. She pulled up beside him and he glanced over. Through the helmet's shield she saw his eyes, glossed with fatigue, and she wondered how much he'd slept last night, on his back on the floor beside her bed.

As he pulled his gaze away and returned to his place ahead of her, Lu wondered if either of them would ever enjoy a good night's sleep again.

When finally they reached their destination, a small cabin tucked away deep in the German wilderness somewhere between New Frankfurt and Nuremberg, she was exhausted, too, as much from the wild careenings of her mind as from the journey.

Their hosts, a gray-haired couple in their late sixties who spoke only hushed, hesitant German, were as different from Nola and James as day from night. Words were few and supper was served without ceremony. Lu realized, watching them skitter about the small cabin like creatures of prey in a nighttime woods, that they were terrified. Of what they were risking, harboring her and Magnus. Of what might happen to them if they were caught.

If courage could be defined as the ability to do the thing that scares you most, these people were giants of bravery.

"*Wir in ihrer schuld sind*," Lu said quietly to the woman after the supper dishes were cleared and she'd shown Lu to the cramped bedroom she and Magnus would be sharing. Another twin bed stared back mockingly at her from the middle of it.

The woman shook her head, then looked her in the eye. "No," she answered in German. "The debt is ours. Had mankind been wise enough to stand up for what was right all those years ago, we wouldn't be in the position we're in now. The minute we turned our backs on you, we turned our backs on ourselves. That's why we joined the Dissenters." Her eyes were overbright. Her mouth was pinched. She looked as if she hadn't truly slept in years. "There is only one way out of the fire, child, and that is to walk through it. But the Lord promises that if we have faith, we shall not be burned. And my faith could move mountains."

Lu's throat tightened. This woman reminded her so much of her father and Liesel it was like a spear through her heart. "*Danke*," she whispered. On impulse, she threw her arms around the woman, and squeezed her into a hug.

She froze, but quickly recovered, even chuckling after a moment and patting Lu on the back. When she pulled away, some of the fear had left her face. She gave Lu a gentle, tentative smile, pinching her cheek like a grandmother. "I'll give you pastries to take with you in the morning; you need some meat on these skinny bones. In the meantime, sleep. And sweet dreams, child. You deserve them."

"You, too," Lu murmured. The woman left on silent, slippered feet, and she and Magnus were alone.

"You like her," he said, staring out the lone window in the room where he'd stationed himself since they'd been shown in. Like all the windows, it sported blackout shades, but he'd pushed them aside to peer into the night.

"I like anyone who offers me pastries." She tossed her small pack on the bed, sat on the edge of the mattress, and pulled off her boots, throwing them into a corner. "Or who's willing to stick out her neck for what she believes in."

Magnus turned from the window, letting the shade snap back in place. She felt his gaze like two hot hands on her back, but refused to turn and meet it. Though everything was left to be said, also nothing was, and she didn't have the energy for either. Avoidance seemed the best course of action. "You had the floor last night, so you should take the bed—"

"Shut up," he said mildly. Startled, Lu turned and looked at him. There was a mischievous glint in his eye, and she realized he'd said it on purpose to make her look at him. She raised her brows and gave him a look, which he waved off with an imperious flick of his wrist.

"You're still the girl, and I'm still the guy. I'll take the floor."

"Excuse me, mister sexist, but I'm a *woman*, not a girl. Additionally, my gender has absolutely no bearing on our sleeping arrangements—"

"Shut up," he said again, this time with a quirk to his lips that looked suspiciously close to a smile. "*Woman*."

Lu studied him a moment. "Just out of curiosity, are you bipolar?"

"I've definitely been called worse." He sat on a chair opposite the bed and pulled off his own boots, tossing them aside in the exact offhand manner she'd done only moments before. Lu couldn't decide which was more disturbing: the sight of his bare feet, strong and oddly sexy against the wood floor, or this new lightheartedness that had come over him without any seeming cause. She wanted to ask him about it, but was afraid the question might chase away his good mood, so she made a noncommittal noise and went to use the bathroom.

When she emerged, Magnus was on his back on the floor with his hands beneath his head. His eyes were closed.

"At least take the pillow," Lu protested, stepping around him to the bed. She pulled the pillow from it, dropped it onto his face, then jumped under the covers just in time to hear his growl.

The pillow came flying over the bed, this time landing on her own face.

"Stubborn much?" she muttered, wrestling it aside. She stuffed it under her head and stared up at the ceiling, realizing she was still fully clothed. That wouldn't make for a comfortable night's sleep. As surreptitiously as possible, she unzipped her jacket, slid the trousers down her legs, and kicked both out from under the covers so they slithered to the floor on the opposite side from where Magnus lay.

After a quiet moment, he said, "Was that your attempt at being stealthy?"

Lu's cheeks burned. Even in darkness, she felt exposed. "Some people can't sleep *dressed*, Magnus."

"I took my boots off," he said, perfectly reasonable, and Lu smiled in the dark.

"The things that make you smile," he said to himself, a hint of laughter warming his voice.

"How did you know I was smiling?"

Another quiet moment. Then, all laughter gone, he whispered, "The air feels lighter. And . . . so does my heart."

It sat there between them. Such a small thing, but it felt immense and dangerous, as if he'd admitted to murder, or plotting a government coup. It also felt fragile as a soap bubble floating on a breeze. She wanted to capture that bubble in her hand and stare at it awhile, before it burst.

Lu whispered, "Magnus?"

He waited, not answering. The silence was deafening. Her heartbeat went jagged, and she knew he could sense that, as well as he could sense her longing and her wretchedness, the hole that had always been inside of her that nothing seemed to fill, except him. Lu swallowed the words she wanted to say, a litany of *I need you I want you I think I've loved you my whole life*, and said other, less perilous, words instead.

"What you said before, about what the *Ikati* really are. Our true form. Will you . . . will you show me?"

A quiet inhalation. "Now?"

His voice was gentle, a little unsure, and his hesitation worked on her like a reverse spell, releasing her own doubt so she sat up in bed with sudden, ravenous confidence. She looked down at him. He looked back at her, his eyes shining mercury bright in the darkness.

"Yes. Now."

Slowly, he sat up from the floor. Then he stood, holding her gaze, those silvery cat's eyes flashing. He removed his jacket, then dragged his shirt over his head and let it fall, so that finally he stood before her bare-chested and magnificent, in spite of the snarl of scar tissue that marked all the skin on his right side. Or maybe even because of it.

His hands went to the top button of his trousers, and Lu couldn't look away. Even if she'd wanted to, she couldn't.

She needn't have worried, however, because before Magnus's

fingers had undone a single button, his hands and arms and chest had begun to glow softly, and the room was bathed in light.

It only took a few moments. He went from solid to beautifully amorphous, a man-sized shape of curling gray mist and tiny pinpricks of dancing lights, until the Magnus that had just stood before her had entirely transformed into a ruffling, shimmering cloud of vapor. His trousers slid empty to the floor and lay there, leaking air.

Lu jumped from the bed, clapping and squealing, bobbing up and down on her toes. "Yes! That's amazing! I used to vanish when I sneezed before I learned how to control it, but this is—"

She fell still and silent because the beautiful cloud of vapor began to swirl around her in a sinuous coil, drifting over and around her whole body, slipping like living silk against her skin.

"Oh," she breathed, lowering her arms as they were gently surrounded by mist. The mist trailed down her legs and Lu became acutely aware that she wore only her panties and a camisole. A tremor passed through her body, and the soft cloud contracted slightly around her, as if in an embrace.

Lu closed her eyes. She said his name, the barest whisper of sound between her lips. Feeling him like this was intimate and intensely sexual, so much so that a surge of heat passed over her, heat and desire, hardening her nipples and sending a spike of pleasure straight down between her legs.

The cloud of mist withdrew. She was left bereft, trembling, undone.

Then the mist changed again, drawing in on itself to coalesce into another form, not man or mist, or anything she would have ever imagined in all her wildest dreams.

A huge, powerful body, rippling with muscles. Four legs and sharp fangs and a long, sinuous tail, almond eyes glowing phosphorescent green against a wedge-shaped head covered in glossy black fur. As was the rest of him.

A panther. The most incredible, impossible thing Lu had ever seen. Shock leached the strength from her legs, and she sank to the mattress.

The animal stalked slowly toward her, a low rumbling purr vibrating through its chest. In disbelief, Lu began softly to laugh. He stopped a foot away, watching her with those preternatural eyes. He was feral and unnaturally large, towering over her and looking as if he was about to devour her whole with that set of impressive teeth.

"Well," whispered Lu when her laughter had faded. "Aren't you a pretty kitty."

His snout wrinkled, curling back to reveal razor-sharp canines. Lu sensed how dangerous he was in this form, far more dangerous and perhaps less rational than in human form. But she wasn't afraid of him; she was fascinated. She reached out and tentatively brushed her fingers against his cheek, and oh, what exquisite plush softness, like the finest mink.

His whiskers twitched. The rumble deep in his chest grew louder. His eyes closed, just longer than a blink.

"Is this okay?" Lu slid her fingers along his jaw, rubbing softly, then scratched him behind the ear. He tilted his big head into her hand, allowing it, but slanted her a look she interpreted to mean he wasn't a household pet, and if she called him *kitty* again he might be inclined to spray urine on her pillow in retaliation.

She bit her lip to stifle another laugh. "Does the sourpuss need some catnip to improve his mood? A little fresh cream, maybe? How 'bout a nice ball of twine to bat around?"

Magnus leaned forward, then licked her face with his enormous, pink, scratchy tongue.

"Ew! Bad kitty!" she laughed, pushing on his furred chest, but with a flash of light and a ripple of power, the animal was gone and the man was in its place, staring down at her with a look of barely leashed hunger in his eyes, his whole body taut as a bowstring.

Naked, and taut as a bowstring.

In a rasp of a voice, he growled, "You don't like my tongue?"

Lu thought she'd never heard anything so erotic in her entire life.

She froze. Her hands were flat on his chest, her legs open around his hips. He was breathing hard and so was she, and as they stared into each other's eyes the moment stretched out and she lost all sense of time or place, up or down, wrong or right. All she knew was that she wanted him. She burned for him. He was everything she'd ever wanted or could ever want, and it no longer mattered what happened in all their tomorrows: She needed to tell him how she felt before it was too late.

For her, this man was home.

"Actually, I *love* your tongue, Magnus," she whispered, "and every other thing about you."

It was like fitting a key into a lock.

He grasped her face in his hands and crushed his mouth to hers, kissing her with desperate abandon. His tongue was invading, demanding she kiss him back. She melted against him, her arms wound up around his shoulders, her hands tightened in his hair to pull him down deeper into her, harder against her body. They fell back against the mattress. He made a noise like an animal's, deep in his throat, as she arched against him, moving her hands to his hard ass and pulling so the hot, hard length of his erection was between her legs, separated from her aching sex by only a thin strip of fabric.

"Oh God," Lu moaned as he broke the kiss, shoved up her camisole, palmed her breast, and sucked her hard nipple into his mouth. Tongue and teeth and amazing hot wetness, his mouth went from one breast to the other, greedily sucking, and she moaned once again, loving how wild he was, loving this raw, ragged passion. As he licked her he chanted broken words that meant *so sweet* and *so beautiful* and best of all, *you're mine, angel, tell me you're mine!*

"Yes!" she cried as his teeth pressed into her skin, as his mouth ravaged her. "I'm yours! I'll always be yours!"

Another lock, another key to open it. Her answer drove him past the brink of restraint. He tore off her panties, tore off her camisole, every movement and look primal, his eyes aglow with lust. Something had snapped inside him. Now it was all about taking, claiming, satisfying the dark and awful ache they'd both felt since they'd first laid eyes on each other . . . and for years and years before that.

He licked his way down her body, biting and kissing and growling, until he put one hand flat on her stomach and cupped the other under her bottom. Then he lifted her backside off the mattress and buried his face between her legs.

She arched and cried out in shock and a pleasure so acute she thought she might pass out from it. He was as greedy there as he'd been with her mouth, and soon she was rocking her hips and mewling, her fingers clenched in his hair.

"Magnus," she gasped. Everything inside her body surged toward a high, sharp peak. "Please, please *don't stop!*"

He didn't. He pushed her legs open wider, slid two fingers inside her, and sucked hard on her swollen clit.

It was like a detonation. A brief moment of brilliant, breathless suspension, and then she was over the edge, free-falling, sobbing and jerking beneath him as an explosion of pleasure rocketed through her body, ripping her apart.

He dragged himself up her body and in one swift motion, buried himself deep inside her.

And it *hurt.*

Her yelp of pain made him freeze. Breathing raggedly above her, his expression was almost anguished. "What's wrong?" he panted, searching her face. "What happened?"

Lu closed her eyes and inhaled, willing her body to relax around the huge, hot invasion of his erection. She didn't think it would be like this. It was never like this in the books she'd read. It was always rose petals, angel choirs, rainbows, and confetti. There was never any mention of *pain*.

Through gritted teeth, she said, "You're. Big."

The tension didn't leave him. He cradled her face in his hands, forcing her eyes open. "I don't . . . I thought you were ready . . . you came . . ."

His confusion was obvious, as was his discomfort. His cock twitched deep inside her, and Lu shivered, her fingers digging into his back.

His eyes widened. Then he inhaled and looked down, his head tilted to one side and his brows furrowed together. When he looked back up at her it was with understanding dawning over his face. Understanding and dismay.

"Angel. You're bleeding," he whispered.

"Apparently it's only my dream self that's a big slut, Magnus. In this plane of reality, my hymen is—was—still intact. Stupid friggin' thing. I should've ridden more horses when I was younger."

They stared at each other, eye to eye, raggedly breathing. All at once, they both began to laugh.

"I don't think that works," he said, gasping with laughter, his head lowered to her shoulder where it rested, hot and heavy and wonderful. He pressed a kiss to her throat, and she ran her hands up his back, which made him shiver.

"Yoga? Super-size tampons?" she giggled. His body shook with laughter. He buried his face into her neck, and Lu was so happy to finally hear him laugh. It was beautiful: rich and warm as sunshine.

"God. This is so not how I pictured this happening," he groaned. He propped himself up on his elbows to gaze down at her, his eyes filled with light.

"You pictured this? Us being together like this?" Lu reached up and stroked his dark hair away from his forehead.

Like a flipped switch, his lightness disappeared and he grew serious, intense. "Every second of every minute of every day. Always."

"Gee. It's a miracle you had time for anything else, you perv," she teased.

His smile didn't return. In a quiet voice, Magnus said, "There's nothing else for me but you. There never has been. There never will be. I know that now."

Her throat constricted. Her face grew hot. "For me, either," she whispered. The enormity of it hit her, and her vision wavered as her eyes filled with tears.

Magnus made a move to withdraw, but she clutched at him, wrapping her arms around his back. "No," she said vehemently. "Don't. I want to feel you. I want you to . . . finish."

"Lumina," he said, his voice breaking, but she shushed him with a flex of her hips.

"Yes," she said, listening to his groan as he sank deeper inside her. His eyes fluttered closed, his lips parted, so she flexed her hips again, loving the feeling of power that surged through her when his groan turned ragged.

"I don't want to hurt you," he said hoarsely. She pulled his head down and kissed him, cutting off his protests.

"The only way you'll hurt me is if you stop," she said against his lips. She drew her thighs up on either side of his hips, ignoring the pinch as she did. The pain wasn't so bad now that she was used to having him there. She found herself wanting to feel more, so she put her lips against his ear and asked for it.

"Show me how to make you feel good," she breathed. "Show me how to make you come."

He shuddered, digging his hands into her hair. His throat opened on a long, low moan. His hips flexed and released in a sensual, masculine motion, and Lu encouraged it by arching her back in counterpoint.

"Yes. Like that." His voice was strained. She kissed the strong column of his throat, opened her mouth over the throbbing vein, and sucked. He moaned again, and Lu thought she might really be getting the hang of this.

Slowly, with infinite care, he began to slide in and out, controlling himself with every movement, but his arms were shaking and his face was flushed. Lu, watching him, was growing more and more excited.

"Harder," she coaxed, and smiled when he cursed.

In a swift, unexpected move, he rolled over, pulling her along with his arms wrapped around her so that he was flat on his back on the mattress and she was astride him, staring down at him in surprise.

He wrapped his big, calloused hands around her hips. "Go at your own speed," he panted. "Make yourself feel good; that's what will make me feel good, okay? That will turn me on more than anything else. I'll try and last as long as I can, but I can't promise—"

His sentence ended in a garbled low oath as Lu leaned forward, sliding the hard length of him almost all the way out of her. She sat back abruptly and took him to the hilt once again.

"Good?" she whispered. He growled his approval and slid his hands up from her hips to caress her breasts, teasing her nipples with pinches and firm strokes. She arched into his hands, supple as a cat, watching him watch her through hot, half-lidded eyes, his expression registering devotion and desire.

She began to rock atop him, slowly at first, faster when he drew his hand down her belly and pressed his thumb against the most sensitive part of her, rubbing small circles as she moved. Now it was her turn to moan because the feeling was exquisite, pressure and fullness and *all*ness, her heart pounding out songs in her chest as blood surged hot through her veins.

If her heart was singing, her soul sang louder. A song of love and possession. A song of joy.

"Magnus," she gasped as he plunged into her over and over, his breathing harsh, every muscle in his body flexed and beautiful. He was utterly engrossed, watching her ride him, and she'd never seen a man so sexy or virile or glorious.

"You okay?"

His voice was guttural, strained. She loved it. She nodded, drawing his hand up her body to caress one breast, shivering when he pinched her nipple. She drew his hand higher, and sucked on his thumb, needing something in her mouth.

He inhaled sharply. "You're so fucking beautiful, angel," he whispered. "And so . . . fucking . . . tight." A shudder wracked his body, and Lu knew he was close.

"Let me watch you," she said, breathless, lowering his hand to her hip where he grasped it, hard, sinking his fingers deep into her flesh. He took his other hand from between her legs and grasped her other hip, and then he shoved himself up into her so hard she gasped with both pain and pleasure. He registered it, slowing his pace. "No, please—as hard as you want. Do anything you want. I need to watch you."

Groaning, Magnus finally let go.

His head tipped back into the mattress. His eyes slid shut. He pumped deeper and faster, moans working from his throat, a fine sheen of sweat glistening on his chest. His abs were all engaged, each one starkly outlined against his skin, as were the muscles in his arms and shoulders, and Lu trailed her fingers lovingly over them, a thrill moving through her as he shivered everywhere she touched. His pace increased until her breasts were bouncing and his hips were jerking rapidly. Then his hips stalled and he roared her name.

He sat up abruptly, sinking even deeper into her with the motion, and Lu moaned as he fisted his hands into her hair and slammed his mouth against hers. He came with powerful convulsions, a spreading heat, delicious throbbing against the soreness inside her. His kiss devoured her. He wrapped his arms around her and held her tight against him through all the pulsing aftershocks, not breaking the kiss, until finally the convulsions calmed to random twitches and he was gently rocking into her, his kiss gentling with the easing of his breath.

Lu caressed his shoulders and neck, threaded her fingers into his hair. Her mouth and body felt bruised, wonderfully achy. He dropped his head to her shoulder and softly groaned her name.

"I'm sorry."

She knew what he meant, but she wasn't about to let it ruin the moment. "Say that again and I'll shave off all your hair while you're asleep, Seeker."

He lifted his head and gazed at her through heavy-lidded eyes, the corners of his lips curved. "You think you could get the drop on me, hmm?" He slid his hands down her back and squeezed her bottom, inhaling deeply against her neck. He nuzzled her there, trailing soft kisses along her jaw and down her throat, until she shivered. A little convulsion made her clench around the hot hardness of him, still buried deep inside her.

"Oh, definitely," she whispered, loving that little clench. She wanted another.

He chuckled in response. Dipping his head, he drew her nipple into his mouth and sucked on it, cupping her breast in his big hand. The sensation was incredible, racing from her nipple to her clit as if an arrow had been shot between them. She moaned softly, clenching again.

"You like that," he murmured, moving to her other breast, his voice full of male satisfaction.

All she could do was make a small sound of pleasure as he cupped both her breasts in his hands and lavished his tongue on each of her nipples in turn, sweeping his thumb over the one his mouth was neglecting, his touch firm, his mouth possessive. She went breathless with the sensation because he didn't stop, sucking harder and using his teeth when she responded with gasps and low moans, pushing her breasts harder against his hands. A coil of pleasure began to wind deep in her belly, drawing all her focus to that spot, to the sparks going off inside her body.

"Oh, yes," whispered Magnus against her breast. "You like that a *lot*."

Involuntarily, her hips tilted, bringing his still erect cock in contact with an incredibly sensitive spot inside her. She gasped, digging her fingers into the muscles of his shoulders. "Oh. Oh."

Speech was becoming increasingly difficult.

He pinched one nipple, nipping the other with his teeth, and she jerked, a cry of pleasure on her lips. The movement dragged him against that sensitive spot inside again, and Lu moaned, her head dropping back. Magnus made a sound like a purr and flexed his hips, and she moaned again, but this time it was broken.

"Here?" he murmured, rocking slowly into her. The answering sound that came from her throat was primal, unlike anything she'd ever made before. Her entire body quaked. Her heartbeat went arrhythmic. He flexed into her gently again, and her brain blinked offline.

"My sweet, sweet angel," he whispered, spreading his hands over her bottom. With his hands, he coaxed her hips into gentle motion, slow, small circles that kept her in direct contact with his pelvis, and kept dragging her across and around that incredible pressure point. He lowered his mouth to her nipple again, and Lu thought she would die with pleasure.

"Magnus," she whimpered. Her fingers were twisted so tightly in his hair it must have hurt, but if it did he took no notice, lavishing her with all his attention, stroking her with his tongue and lips and hands, setting an exquisitely languorous tempo of slide, rock, push, slide back, rock, push again, his entire body controlling hers.

The coil inside her wound tighter and tighter. Heat flashed over her skin and a bloom of sweat followed, her body now slick against his. She tightened her legs around his waist and her arms around his shoulders, moving faster, desperate for release, for that incredible pinnacle he was driving her toward. Writhing against him, she begged, "Please! Please!"

A growl rumbled through his chest. He was growing harder and harder inside her. He reached up and cupped the back of her neck in his hand, bringing his lips to her ear. "Give yourself to me. Give it all to me, angel. *Now.*"

It might have been that husky command that drove her over the edge, or the trigger of his own release, that throb and pulse deep inside her as he groaned and shook, but suddenly her nerves honed to a thousand shrieking exclamation points, she stopped breathing, and threw back her head on a scream of ecstasy.

She went off like a firework. Brilliant. Violent. Loud.

And the entire room around them—the bed and floors and walls—exploded into flame.

TWENTY-SEVEN

For the past ten minutes, Honor had been pacing.

Back and forth across Morgan's living room floor, arms folded across her chest, chewing her lip as if she planned to make a meal of it. It wasn't as though she could eat anything, even if she tried. Her stomach was squeezed into a horrible angry knot, mimicking what was happening to her heart and most of her other organs. She was so upset she had to keep reminding herself to breathe; there had already been one minor earthquake this morning. The colony didn't need another.

"You're sure that's what she said? A few days?"

Honor whirled around to glare at Beckett. He stood against one wall with his foot propped up against it, looking as effortlessly gorgeous as ever. Although not, at the moment, quite as smug.

"Yes, I'm sure, Beckett! My mother was very clear; they're going to *exterminate* her in a few *days*!"

"But, why, pet? What's changed? Why now?" Morgan, seated on a sofa opposite the wall where Beckett stood, was white with shock. Xander, standing beside the sofa, looked as if he was about to explode with rage. His amber eyes had turned molten, murderous gold.

"Now," Honor answered, her voice shaking, "the IF doesn't need her anymore. They've figured out how to make the medicines without our DNA."

Quiet took the room. "Which also means they don't need any of the others in the facility they're holding her in, either," said Xander. "I wondered how long it would take them."

Morgan gasped in horror, her hands lifting to cover her mouth. "No," she whispered, eyes wide.

"Yes. They're going to kill them all. Soon." Honor resumed her pacing and lip chewing.

"Magnus and Lumina won't let that happen. You know that." Beckett pushed away from the wall, his expression uncharacteristically fierce, his normally clear eyes dark and stormy. He stood in a fighting stance with his legs spread shoulder width apart, chest back, hands curled to fists at his sides. Honor thought she'd never seen him look so . . . hot.

Shit.

"I don't know anything! And neither do you! So spouting platitudes isn't going to help the situation!" Honor snapped. Could she be any stupider, admiring that jerkoff at a time like this? She wanted to smack herself. Instead she turned away from the sight of his perfect, stupid face, and said over her shoulder, "Why are you even here, anyway? Don't you have a few skirts to chase, hound dog?"

"Beckett was here when you came in, and he's always welcome in my home." Morgan's tone was gentle, but scolding. She rose and approached Honor, reaching out to touch her shoulder as she came to stand close. She lowered her voice, looking at Honor with pointed reproof. "You both are. As long as you're playing nice."

"I'm nice," she grumbled, shrugging off Morgan's hand. "*He's the assho—*"

"So what do we do now?" Beckett, loudly, cut her off. It was Xander who answered.

"We have to get word to Magnus. Honor, can you tell Lumina what's happening? You know, the way you two talk?"

"I haven't been able to reach her," admitted Honor reluctantly. "She's offline, so to speak."

Honor had been trying like hell to reach out telepathically to her sister ever since she'd awoken from the dream in which their mother told her of Thorne's plans. The news had been horrible, distressing, but Honor sensed there was something her mother had been holding back. The way she'd looked at her was so strange, both proud and terribly guilty. Honor hadn't been able to figure it out, and her mother hadn't explained. Aside from the obvious imminent threat of her death, something else caused her to turn away when Honor asked what could be done to stop Thorne from moving forward with his plans.

It was almost as if . . . as if she knew the answer, but wouldn't say what it was.

No, that can't be it. If her mother knew of any way to save herself and everyone else in that prison, she undoubtedly would have told her. The only thing that could save them now was Magnus and Hope.

She still refused to call her sister Lumina. That was like calling a golden egg a turd.

"I'll try again in a while, but I don't expect much. When Hope's being bullheaded, nothing can get through to her."

"Sounds like someone else I know," muttered Beckett, turning to leave.

"Excuse me?" demanded Honor, halting midpace to stare at his broad, retreating back. He stopped, turned, stared her dead in the eye.

"I'm sorry, were you operating under the mistaken impression that you're *reasonable*, Honor? Because news flash: You're as reasonable as a cyclone." He smiled, a grim, cheerless specimen that didn't reach his eyes. "And just as pleasant."

Her mouth dropped open. The *nerve* of him! "*I'm* not reasonable? You're the one who's being led around like a dog on a collar by your dick!"

"Will you knock it off with the dog metaphors?" he snapped. He paced forward, angry, a menacing look narrowing his eyes.

"That was a simile, genius. I know it must be hard to think with all the blood drained from your head—"

"Why can't you ever be nice, like for *one* minute? Is that too much to ask?" He walked closer, his long stride quickly eating up the space between them.

"Nice? Ha! You mean like how *you're* nice, spreading 'cheer' throughout the colony with your magical penis?" She made air quotes around the word cheer, and his face reddened.

Morgan stood from the couch, about to intervene, but Xander grasped her hand and pulled her gently to his side. He said something in her ear that made her smile.

"Pets, we'll be in the Assembly room if you need us," she said as Xander led her away.

Honor and Beckett barely noticed they'd left. His long stride had brought him face-to-face with her in seconds. She looked up at him, wishing for the first time in her life that she was over six feet tall so she could stand eye to eye with him. She felt at a disadvantage having to tilt her head back, and she *hated* that feeling.

He moved even closer, invading her personal space. He was big and imposing, radiating heat and a fury she'd never seen in him before. Blinking, she stepped back.

"You know something, Honor?" he said, his voice as hard as his eyes. "I've listened to this crap from you since we were little kids, and I'm sick of it. I'm done. Understand? I don't care if you turn me into a fucking popsicle or a giant ice cube or make the earth open up and swallow me whole, I'm not taking it anymore. Find someone else to shit on, because I'm through being your personal toilet!"

His words, his tone, his face all told her a story that made her stomach drop to her toes. "You think I would hurt you?" she whispered in disbelief.

He moved closer. She stepped back again, desperate to escape him, to escape that look, but her back hit the rounded cave wall, and she couldn't go any farther. He leaned close and stared down at her with the worst expression she'd ever seen him wear. There was anger, yes, but beneath it was pain, real pain. To think that she was the cause of it made her feel sick.

His voice as gravelly as if he'd been swallowing rocks, he said, "You've been hurting me for years, Honor. And liking it. It wouldn't surprise me if you took it one step further and did something permanent."

"I would never," she said, her voice small. "Beckett, I would never hurt you like that."

He was breathing hard. His lips were thinned. He didn't believe her. She didn't know what to do or say to make him understand, to make him realize that what she'd said was true; she'd never hurt him. She'd rather die than see anything bad happen to him. To anyone in the colony, but especially *him*.

"Why do you hate me so much?" he asked abruptly.

"I . . . I don't." Honor swallowed. This close, he smelled amazing. His skin was golden and poreless, and there were beautiful flecks of yellow in his green eyes. Why did he have to look like an angel? Why couldn't he have hair in his ears, bow legs, and bad breath?

Because he's Ikati, *that's why,* she sourly reminded herself. But even beyond that, Beckett was so beautiful it almost hurt to look at him.

So she didn't. She glanced away, hiding from his excruciating attention.

"Honor."

"What."

"Look at me."

"You're standing two inches away, Beckett. There's nowhere I can look that doesn't include having you there."

His voice gentled. "Staring at my feet doesn't count. *Look* at me." He put a finger beneath her jaw, and tipped her head up so their eyes met. He didn't take his hand away, and he didn't say anything, he just looked at her. Looked *into* her, with curiosity and the sweetest boyishness, a lovely vulnerability she never, ever saw in him. His anger had gone, and now he looked . . . open. Waiting.

For what?

Her gaze dropped to his lips. She imagined kissing him, what it might feel like—what he might taste like—and then, to her eternal horror, blood rushed to her cheeks.

She closed her eyes, hiding. Hands down, this was the most embarrassing moment of her life. The most embarrassing but also unexpectedly the best, because Beckett stroked his thumb lightly over her face, caressing the flame of heat on her skin, sending the most wonderful shivers coursing down her spine.

Then she wondered if this was how every girl felt when Beckett touched her, and her anger flared anew. She opened her eyes and glared at him.

"Okay. You want to know why I hate you, Beckett? Because you're indiscriminate. We're all interchangeable to you. Two legs, two tits, all the right parts. You don't care about any of the girls you have; you just care about getting your rocks off. And it doesn't matter which hole you stick it in which day; as long as you can have your fun and be on your way with no strings attached, you're happy. I hate you because you're a shallow, selfish *user*."

Take that, *man whore!*

"And you're a joyless, man-hating bitch," he shot back without hesitation. And it stung. Oh, it stung like a nest of angry hornets had been dumped on her head! But then he said, "But it never mattered to me."

Okay . . . what?

"Um . . ."

"You think you're so smart, Honor, let me ask you this: Why do you think I'm the only male in this colony beyond the age of twenty-five—besides Magnus—who isn't mated?"

Honor smirked. "I think we've already established that your penis has a mind of its own. Your seed-spreading tendencies automatically preclude anything so mature as *commitment*."

"Wrong," he growled, leaning even closer. "And unfair. I don't, as you so delicately put it, 'spread my seed.' You've never seen me with a female in Fever."

Well . . . he had a point. He usually avoided females in their once-annual Fever period like the plague, even though all the other unmated males in the colony became horny as tomcats around a female at that time. Usually they were kept hidden from the rest of the colony, for their own protection, as well as the males'; inevitably, fights broke out because the males' testosterone levels went off the charts.

"That speaks more to your commitment issues than anything else," Honor countered. "God forbid you get saddled with a mate and offspring—"

"That's not how it works with us, and you know it!" he roared. "We mate for life, because we're bonded and in love, and we have children out of love, not spite or tricks or to trap one another! Why do you have to make it sound so meaningless?"

He shocked her into silence. She stared up at him open-mouthed and wide-eyed, dimly aware of her fluttering heart and the pulse of heat surging between them, unable to look away from his face. His anger made her ashamed of herself, and so did his words, and suddenly her sister's plea intruded into the stillness of her shock-addled brain.

I want you to tell Beckett how you feel about him, because I think there might be something there. If I have to be courageous, you do, too.

Fuck. Fuckity fuck *fuck*!

Honor closed her eyes, gathered her courage, and said in a whisper, "I have to make it seem meaningless because it's all I've ever wanted, and everything I'll never have."

Silence. The sound of his ragged breathing, and her own. Then his hands settled on both sides of her face, and Honor opened her eyes to find Beckett staring at her with something she would have sworn was hope, had she not known better. In a whisper to match hers, he said, "Why can't you have it, Honor?"

No, those were not tears welling in her eyes! Stammering, wretched, she said, "B-because the p-person I want to have it w-with is . . . he's . . ."

Beckett's face was so close to hers. His eyes were pleading. "He's what? Say it, Honor. Tell me."

She felt her face screw up into an ugly grimace. Those hideous, traitorous tears spilled over her bottom lids and tracked down her hot cheeks. "He's a whore!" she bawled, breaking. "And he broke my heart because he wants everyone else but me, and he's been parading around like a peacock with his harem of hens since he was ten years old, and *I hate him*!"

The last part was shouted into Beckett's face. Feeling as if she would die of mortification, Honor buried her face into her hands, sobbing.

Suddenly Beckett's arms came around her. He squeezed her against the warm hardness of his chest. He stroked his hand down her back and, with a low chuckle, sighed into her ear, "Jesus Christ. It's about fucking time, woman. You're harder to crack than an atom."

Huh?

Honor couldn't respond coherently. She couldn't even think coherently. So she just kept blubbering into his shirt, hoping this was all a terrible dream she would soon awaken from, her dignity magically intact.

Courage was so overrated.

Beckett's chest expanded with his deep, slow inhalation. He nuzzled his nose into her hair and spoke in a low, soothing voice. "So. Picture the scene. Two children, a boy and a girl, playing an innocent game of Jacks. The boy is winning, until another little girl comes over and begins to watch. She keeps her distance, though, as she always does. And, as always when she appears, the little boy feels funny, like he's being tickled all over, inside and out. He can't concentrate, and soon he's lost the game.

"Because this new little girl is so spectacularly beautiful, he can't look right at her. He thinks to do so might make him go blind, like when you look directly into the sun. So he's learned to look around her, to keep her in his peripheral vision. And because he knows how to do this, he sees her smirk when he loses the game. And he feels something he's never felt before in his young life: despair. To manage it, he does the only thing he can think to do, and that is to get revenge.

"He kisses the girl he just lost the game to. His plan is successful: He sees the other little girl turn and run away, her face as white as the dress she wore."

Gooseflesh rose all over Honor's body. She fell still. Beckett was telling the story of what happened all those years ago, of the day she saw him kiss Sayer in the playroom, and her whole world came crashing down around her ears.

Because she'd always loved him. Ever since she could remember, she'd loved him.

But he wasn't done speaking yet.

"After that, the little boy felt bad, like he'd done something wrong. But the next time he saw the beautiful girl, she acted like she smelled something terrible and turned her nose up at him. All the other children laughed, and the boy felt like a part of him died. He wanted so badly for her to notice him, but the only way she ever did was when he tried to get revenge. So he began to kiss a lot of girls, and felt better when the beautiful one looked sad, and soon the only way she ever showed any emotion at all was when the boy was near another girl. And so, because he hoped in his heart of hearts that her sadness meant she cared for him, the boy . . ." his voice broke, and lowered even more, "the stupid, senseless boy set out to try and win her by making her jealous."

Her heart must have stopped beating, because her blood had stopped circulating through her veins. Slowly, Honor raised her head, looking at Beckett through tear-sticky lashes.

He looked back at her with a bottomless depth of regret in his eyes. "It didn't work, though. Years went by, and the boy didn't have the courage to change his senseless game, and by the time he realized it would never work, it was too late. The beautiful girl was lost to him, and all that was left was the game. The game that had no winner, that was a maze with no exit, only a million cold dead ends. It was the only thing he knew."

Honor stared at him long and hard, hope flaring in her chest like a Roman candle. Was he playing her? Was this part of an elaborate scheme? Was this how he did it, how he ensnared all those women, with emotional confessions that sounded too good to be true because they actually were?

"I'm not blind, Beckett. I saw how you looked at my sister," she said, grasping at straws.

"Because she looks like *you*," he replied immediately, his voice breaking. "But she's not. There's only one you, and that's the only one for me. It's always been you. You're my beginning and my end, Honor. I've been in love with you since I could walk. I'll be in love with you until the day I die, and after, whether I go to heaven or hell, I'll still be loving you. Forever. Until the end of time."

After a long time in which she did nothing but examine his face, Beckett softly pleaded, "Say something."

What Honor said was, "If you're lying, so help me God I *will* turn you into a popsicle. A big, stupid Becksicle, which I will devour after turning into a dragon. And then I'll shit you out and freeze you again and throw your frozen, chewed-up, shitty self out into the ocean, where you will float on the waves until you get eaten by fish and birds, and shit out by them, too."

Beckett threw back his head and laughed, squeezing her so tight against him she couldn't breathe. Then he looked down at her, his eyes shining, exultant. The glow appeared around his head, flaring into nimbus, warming all the dim, cool corners of the cave.

"Ah, you sweet talker, you," he said, grinning. He kissed her.

And for the first time she could remember, Honor was engulfed by happiness, bright and burning as the summer sun.

TWENTY-EIGHT

When he was a boy, Magnus adored story time. A weekly event where all the children of the tribe would gather around the great bonfire in their colony deep in the heart of the Amazon jungle, story time consisted of various elders taking turns thrilling and horrifying the children with tales of magic and adventure. His favorite story was a dark fable that starred a poor farm boy who was visited one night by an angel, who warned him he would soon face a terrible trial, and his faith was the only thing that could save him.

The angel was exquisite and fearsome, a creature of terrible beauty and awesome power, with white wings that burned with smokeless fire, painting vivid blurs of color on the air as they moved. She was a seraph, the story went, one of "the burning ones" of the human Bible, and Magnus's boyhood self imagined her so vividly she came to life for him, as tangible as his own hand held in front of his face.

Years later, still fascinated by the story, he'd looked up the term *seraph*, and was intrigued to find them described as "dragon-shaped angels" in a Christian Gnostic text dealing with creation and end times.

Now, with the room aflame around him and the roar of a conflagration in his ears, Magnus realized the seraph of that long-ago story was no creature of mystic fantasy. The dragon-shaped angels that burned with smokeless fire were *real*.

They had to be. He was holding one of them in his arms.

"Lumina!" he rasped. "Lumina!"

Her eyes drifted open. Bright-orange licks of flame were reflected over and over in their depths. Behind her, fire burned and churned hellishly bright. Superheated air lifted her hair to float around her head, a golden halo of light. A chair coasted by in slow motion, weightless, turning, along with the pillow and other suspended debris: Books. A framed picture. A pair of boots he recognized as his own.

Lumina blinked lazily, smiling as if returning from a pleasant dream. But then her eyes flew wide, wide open, and she froze, grasping what had happened.

Instantly, the fire was extinguished. The roaring flames disappeared. The floating boots and books and all the other weightless flotsam fell to the floor with a clatter and a thud, and all that was left was a strong scent of smoke and a curl of gray fume rising from the sheets.

In the silence, his heartbeat was thundering loud.

"Are you hurt?" Lumina's voice was a terrified whisper, a tone that perfectly matched the look on her face.

"No." He gazed in wonder down at her naked body, wrapped around his. There wasn't a mark on either of them. Carefully, he moved his head and looked around the room. It was in shambles, but miraculously, nothing looked burned. He looked back at Lumina. "That was new," he said, trying for a nonchalant tone. With interest, he noted he was still buried deep inside her, and still hard. "Are you all right?"

"Yes. No. Do you think the rest of the house . . ."

"I think it's probably fine, but I'll check." He paused. "In a minute. Right now I'm too busy having a heart attack."

A tiny laugh escaped her lips, verging on hysterical. "Well. We gave new meaning to the phrase *light the bed on fire*, didn't we?"

Sobering, Magnus said, "You're a miracle. Do you know that? A miracle. There's nothing else like you in all the world."

She made a sound that could have been humor or horror. "Lucky me."

Magnus took her face in his hands, and gently kissed her lips. "No," he murmured, flush with wonder. "Lucky *me*."

She returned his kiss, first tentatively, then with growing hunger. He shifted his weight and brought them both down to the mattress, displacing a soft pouf of smoke from the sheets. Propping himself up on one elbow, he ran his open hand over her skin, caressing the dip of her waist, the curve of her hip. His hand came to rest on a few words in delicate, slanting cursive tattooed on her rib cage on her right side, and he traced them with his fingertips.

I listened to the bray of my heart; I am I am I am.

"It's a quote from *The Bell Jar*, by Sylvia Plath," she said quietly. "I was a huge book hound when I was young. Still am, I guess. It kept me sane, reading those words. It was validation for me. Like, I'm here, even if no one wants me to be. Even if I'm pretending to be something I'm not. Even though I'm hiding, even though I'm unseen, I still exist. I *am*. And no one can ever take that away from me. No matter how hard the world tries to crush it, my heart just won't give in. *I* won't give in. Ever."

Magnus was gripped with fierce admiration. He leaned down and gave her a passionate kiss, his hand wrapped around her jaw. When he broke the kiss, she was breathless and wide-eyed beneath him.

"I had no idea talking books could get a man so worked up," she said, laughing. "If you like I can recite a little poetry next."

"You told me I was courageous," he said gruffly, brushing aside her comment. "But the things I do, I do to make amends. That's not real bravery. Of the two of us, you're the brave one, not me."

She looked up at him, tenderly stroked a lock of hair away from his eyes. "You don't always have to be so hard on yourself, Magnus. Sometimes just getting out of bed in the morning is an act of courage." Her fingers lingered on the scar tissue on the side of his face, and he looked away, jaw tightening.

She didn't ask, though he knew she desperately wanted to. He could feel how hard she tried to hold her tongue. It wasn't as if he would've answered, anyway, but he appreciated her restraint, appreciated how hard it must be for her to let the moment slide, to leave the question unasked, though they'd just shared every intimacy a man and woman could share. He closed his eyes and breathed, then turned his head and pressed a kiss to the center of her palm.

"I'll go check to make sure they're all right," he said, meaning their hosts. He guessed there was no imminent danger, guessed the house had taken no more damage than their room, but he suddenly needed to get away from the unspoken words that lingered between them, silent as ghosts.

What happened to you?

What, indeed.

He swiftly rose and dressed. He left her on the bed, bare and lovely, watching him with her angel eyes, and he'd never felt such desolation. Such endless, aching loss.

He already knew the end to this fairy tale. There would be no salvation by faith, no eleventh-hour reprieve. He walked, however willingly, toward his own death, and the thing that made it more than tragic was the knowledge that he'd finally—*finally*—found the thing for which he'd been searching for years.

A reason to live.

He checked on the elderly couple; they were fine, if spooked by the noise and the smell of fire. The house had taken no damage, and he assured them everything was all right. When he came back in the room he shared with Lumina, he found her dressed and waiting.

"We have to go now," she said, her voice hollow. She avoided looking directly at him.

"Why? What's wrong?"

When finally she did meet his eyes, her own were filled with dread. "I've heard from Honor." There was a long, terrible pause. "We don't have as much time as we thought."

And so they left. They rode as fast as the bikes would take them to their next stop, pausing only to recharge the batteries and wolf down some food, then were on their way once more, betting against the odds they could make it to their next-to-last stop before sunrise. They did, but barely. They were welcomed by more kind-faced strangers, fed again, shown to another cramped bedroom. They slept. And when they awoke, they made love with feverish, desperate hunger, both of them knowing that tomorrow would change everything. Tomorrow would be both an end, and a new beginning.

Tomorrow they would arrive in New Vienna, and the wheel of Fate would spin once again.

PART FOUR

TWENTY-NINE

Sebastian Thorne was a man used to getting his own way.

Even as a child, he'd been fearlessly single-minded, permitting himself only one day a week when he didn't study his beloved molecular biology. On that day he studied biochemistry instead. He'd developed an unnatural passion for both subjects and could, by the age of twelve, best his professors at school with theories so far advanced his elders merely looked at one another with raised brows and shrugged shoulders, admitting their precocious pupil was an anomaly whom they had little idea how to handle.

Knowing as he did that almost ninety-nine percent of the mass of a human body is composed of just six elements, young Sebastian Thorne became obsessed with the question of *why*. Why is a dangerous question, even for the most learned and wise of adults, but for a child with a voracious appetite for knowledge and a moral code one could only describe as *flexible*, the question of why led to a brief but intense interest in religion, and the ultimate meaning of life.

He soon dismissed religion as the tool man used to manage his existential terror of death. God, Allah, Yahweh, Satnam, whatever name you used, in essence they were all the same thing: manufactured punishment and reward systems for weak-minded people. To live without believing in God was, in Sebastian Thorne's opinion, true courage. Only cowards needed to ascribe divine power to the chaos of the universe, and he was no coward.

He was a visionary. Or so he liked to think.

So religion went by the wayside, as did anything else that interfered with his ruthless intellectual curiosity. He grew to a man, he built a successful company, he married, he had a child of his own.

Then the chaos of the universe paid him a personal visit, and Sebastian Thorne's carefully controlled world was turned upside down.

His wife fell ill. She was diagnosed with an extremely rare genetic defect that caused abrupt, coordinated failure of the major organs of the body, as if a timer had been set, and counted down to zero. Technology in the form of life support kept her functioning, but in reality his wife was dead.

Several years later, his daughter fell victim to the same malady, courtesy of her mother's genes.

It was then Thorne was gripped by a new obsession: finding a cure.

On a safari he'd taken years prior in Africa, he'd heard a local legend about creatures who looked like humans, but were stronger, faster, altogether better. More intriguing was their purported ability to change shape as they desired, shifting from animal to human to the mist that was a constant of the rainforests from whence they came. These creatures were called *Ikati*, meaning cat warrior in ancient Zulu. When his wife and daughter fell ill, Thorne remembered the story, and his search began.

It would lead him down a road that would ultimately devour what little conscience he had to begin with.

He began to play his own version of God, tinkering with human DNA. He recruited scientists and doctors and most important, hunters, whom he sent out into the world to find evidence of the mystical creatures known as the *Ikati*. He found, to his great surprise, the Church had been hunting the same creatures for millennia, using fanatical assassins who called themselves Expurgari, or purifiers. The irony wasn't lost on Thorne that he and the most powerful religious institution on the planet had such a thing in common, even if their endgames were different. The Church wanted only to exterminate the *Ikati*. Thorne wanted to put them to good use, then exterminate them.

So the godless man and the pope became business partners. It didn't work out so well for the pontiff—he was slaughtered on live television by one of the creatures with a taste for dramatic flair who'd infiltrated the Vatican. Then the Expurgari were slaughtered en masse when they landed in the Amazon the day of the Flash. Shortsighted to put all their eggs in one basket, so to speak. But the Church wasn't known for doing things by halves. Good/evil, black/white, saved/damned . . . their entire history was built on a philosophy Thorne liked to call Full Bore or Bust. You were in, or you were out. Shades of gray did not exist, and so the Expurgari went the way of the dinosaur. It wasn't as if they had an army of willing new recruits banging down their doors, either; by that point, the Church was bleeding the faithful like a hemophiliac after a bad fall.

But for Thorne, things had worked out well. He'd not only captured thousands of the creatures, including their Queen, he'd learned how to harvest their stem cells and manufacture a host of medicines that helped everything from acne to cancer.

It was far too late for his family, though. By the time he'd made the breakthrough, his wife and daughter were long gone.

It was the only failure of his life. In his darkest moments, Thorne sometimes wished there was a God, so he could curse Him, so there could be someone else to blame. But there was no one else. The blame was all his.

Regret can play strange games with a man's mind.

"What's the update on the team who went to Wales?" said Thorne, seated behind his massive desk in his massive office, staring at a massive screen on which was projected a massive image of the Smoky Mountains of Tennessee. What used to be Tennessee, the state where he was born.

Standing at attention on the other side of his desk, his third-in-command answered. "No update, sir. The signal went offline just after the distress call two days ago, and no contact has been made since."

Thorne wasn't exactly sure where Three was looking. His cast eye inevitably wandered off like some wayward pet. Combined with the ingrained habit of a former Marine to avoid direct eye contact with his superior, the walleye lent Three a furtive air that Thorne found alternatively fascinating and irritating. Topped by a thatch of wiry black hair, his head was oblong in the extreme, and his mouth was filled with an array of discolored and disheveled teeth. He had a nose that looked as if it belonged on a human-elephant hybrid. Overall, the effect was startling, and Thorne found himself wondering on occasions such as this why he'd never invented a pill to cure ugliness.

"No contact," mused Thorne, "means no survivors."

"A probable outcome, yes, sir."

Thorne strummed his fingers atop the polished wood desk. He'd read the transcript of the helicopter pilot's last transmission, and was intrigued by how quickly and dramatically the weather had changed during the flight. One minute, their equipment registered nothing. A clear day. Sunny skies. The next minute: a storm of biblical proportion.

Interesting. Also interesting was the loss of the collar's signal immediately after the pilot's last transmission. Granted, the signal had been weak and intermittent, possibly a decoy or a trap, but . . .

"Three, when was the last time we did a scan of the islands?"

Surprise registered in Three's left eye. The other eye seemed to be perusing a Blue Period Picasso on the far wall, and was indifferent. "I believe the last registered sat scan of the British Isles was six years ago, sir. It was clear; no bipedal life forms detected."

"Six years!" repeated Thorne, displeased. A lot could change in six years. Scanning technology, for instance. "Run another scan, Three," he said, rising from his desk. "Divert the satellites from the nearest assets. I want the results back no later than zero six hundred."

"Yes, sir!" barked Three. He saluted, executed a spin on his heel, and marched out of the office with a stiff-legged gait that would have made Hitler proud. Thorne tried not to roll his eyes. It was men like Three, after all, recruited from the various militaries of the world, who made such wonderfully unquestioning employees.

Men like his second-in-command, Two, who lay broken and burned in a hospital bed, fighting for his life.

Thorne sighed. Casualties, always casualties in war. Nothing to be done about it.

He leaned over and depressed the button for the intercom on his desk. "Yes, sir?" came the eager voice of his male secretary.

"Bring subject four-nine-six-two into the interrogation room, along with the Breast Ripper."

The secretary's voice didn't waver. "Yes, sir!" he said cheerfully, and Thorne congratulated himself on hiring a man to the position. He doubted a woman would have quite the same reaction to those words.

Whistling, Sebastian Thorne left his office, on his way to another invigorating chat with the *Ikati*'s formidable, and quite delectable, Queen.

Perhaps today she'd have something useful to tell him.

If not, there was always tomorrow.

"This can't be right. There's nothing here," said Magnus, frowning at the GPS coordinates glowing softly green on the windscreen display of the motorcycle. He looked up and around, and Lu followed his gaze.

They'd passed the deserted Czech border fifteen minutes ago, and were now headed south on the 6, a major north-south artery through Austria that connected with the defunct A22, which, if followed, would lead them directly into the heart of New Vienna. The GPS coordinates given to them by Nola had them navigating off the highway, however, onto a small collector road in what used to be perhaps an agricultural area, due to its parcels of flat land divided by even smaller roads than the one they'd followed off the highway. Now it was utterly desolate, with nary a leaf in sight, bald and ugly in the dim carmine light cast from the lurking cloud cover. Far in the distance, away on the flat horizon, Lu spied the glow of the grow fields outside New Vienna, and a shiver of dread coursed down her spine.

"There was nothing where we landed in France, either," Lu reminded him.

"Yes, but Jack warned me about that; I knew Nola would be coming. I thought these coordinates would take us directly to the last safe house." He was frowning, on edge, not liking the ambiguity of the situation. Lu had to agree. She felt like a sitting duck out here in the middle of nowhere.

"Well," she said lightly, squinting up at the sky, clotted as congealed blood, "maybe we'll get a sign."

As if on cue, a pair of headlights cut through the darkness, perhaps a kilometer away.

"Magnus!"

"I see it." He'd gone still as stone, his gaze sharp and calculating. "All right. There's only one car. Most likely it's the rendezvous, but just in case," his gaze flicked to hers, "keep frosty."

Lu raised her brows. "That might be more appropriate for my sister, don't you think?"

He reached out and grabbed her hand, pulling her against him, winding his arm around her back. "It's old military slang for 'keep alert.' In your case I suppose we could change it to 'keep toasty.'" He pressed a warm kiss to her neck, and she laughed, in spite of her nerves.

"That won't be too hard, if you keep pawing at me, mister!"

"You like it," he said, tightening his arms around her.

"No," she said, sobering. She pulled away to look into his eyes. "I love it."

They stood there like that for a moment, the words hanging in the air, until the car drew closer and Magnus gently pushed her behind him.

"Really? You still think I need protection?" Her tone was sarcastic, but he didn't seem to notice.

"Everything precious needs protection," he answered, gaze trained on the car. He gave her hand a final squeeze, then dropped it so he could cross his arms over his chest and glower in an appropriately sinister manner at the long black vehicle approaching slowly over the dirt road.

The car rolled to a stop. It was by far the most luxurious vehicle Lu had ever seen, and she tried not to gape too obviously. The driver's door swung open and a uniformed driver appeared, bowing and tipping his hat. A brisk, diminutive man with a conquistador's narrow black beard, he went to the back of the limousine and opened its rear door. He gestured inside.

"Sir, madam, if you please."

Magnus refused to move. "I don't have a name for your employer," he said in a soft, menacing tone. "Or a final destination for this trip. I'll need both before we get into that car, and if you don't give me what I ask for, or if you do and I don't believe you, I'll make life extremely unpleasant for you, my friend. And by unpleasant I mean painful."

To his credit, the driver barely blinked. Lu guessed he was probably used to this kind of thing.

"I understand completely, sir," he said, polite and professional as a majordomo. "However I'm sure my employer would prefer to give you that information himself." His head tipped toward the open door.

Ah, yes. Lu smelled several different scents wafting from the open door of the limousine. Tobacco and leather and expensive aftershave, the woody spice of an old scotch, and something that might have been . . . fur?

Yes, fur. There was a dog in that car, of all things. To punctuate her finding, it yipped, an anxious, high-pitched sound, followed in quick succession by a rapid-fire burst of more.

A small dog. *Wonderful.* Lu wondered what on Earth would greet them when they looked inside the car.

Slowly, Magnus approached the open door. The driver backed away, giving another respectful little bow, allowing him space. Magnus bent down and peered inside. Whatever he saw must have satisfied him, because he looked at Lu and nodded. He held out his hand, beckoning.

"We're leaving the bikes?"

From inside the car, a deep, accented voice replied, "Someone'll be along to fetch 'em, luv. You let Gregor MacGregor worry about that, so you can worry about the bigger picture."

Scottish, she guessed, by the lilt and charm of it, and by the name. Assuming he had the odd habit of referring to himself in third person, and wasn't talking about someone else. Drawn onward by curiosity more than anything else, she reached Magnus, took his hand, and bent her head to look inside the car.

There, taking up most of the wide leather seat, was a bear of a man, hale and solid, with close-cropped ginger hair, and a beard to match. He wore an expensive black suit and a gold pinky ring, and had a diamond-encrusted gold watch almost the size of the trembling Yorkie cowering in his lap. He was close to sixty, with the air of a self-made man who's come up from the gutter, and has long since abandoned denying himself any pleasure to which he feels due.

"If you're thinkin' I'm a gangster or a pimp, you're spot-on, darlin'," he chuckled, clearly enjoying her shrewd assessment of his person. "There's not a thing in this world Gregor MacGregor won't buy or sell, as long as it lines his pockets." He waved them in, giving the dog a spasm. He shushed it with coos and kisses, calling it "baby," hugging it close to his chest.

"Doesn't like strangers," he explained once they were settled on the seats across from him. "Although this particular breed is prone to shittin' themselves if they hear a bloody pin drop."

"Not much of a watch dog," Lu concurred, watching its glittering black eyes roll wildly as it shivered and whined. It wore a chunky gemstone collar Lu thought was probably real.

"Ha!" snorted MacGregor. "Tisn't! But that's what bodyguards are for, luv. Pets are just to remind you not to be so goddamn selfish. Much like women." He grinned, revealing a charming, wolfish smile, perfectly suited to the charming wolfishness of his face.

Lu grinned back. Beside her, Magnus was silent, but Lu felt the tension easing from him incrementally as they talked.

The driver shut the door, returned to his seat, and put the car in gear. They rolled quickly away over the narrow dirt road, high-tech shocks smoothing the worst of the ruts and hollows.

"How do you know Jack and Nola?" said Magnus, getting down to business.

"Don't," admitted MacGregor, stroking his thick fingers through the dog's dark fur. The dog looked as if it might be having a mental breakdown. "It's Eliana I know. We used to be in business together, back in the day. That woman is the finest thief I ever employed."

"*Eliana*?" said Magnus and Lu together, their surprise making MacGregor laugh again.

"Paintings mostly, exclusively high-end. Partial to Picasso, like me. Could slip in and out of a locked building like that," he snapped his fingers, then looked at them askance. "Well. You know how. Anyway, she was always my favorite, even if the little minx did get me shot." He reached over, wrapped his hand around the crystal glass in the cup holder in a mirrored niche in the door, raised it to his mouth, and swallowed a long, deep gulp of scotch. "Ah!" he said when he'd drained the glass. "Nothin' like a fifty-year-old Macallan to wet the whistle!"

Lu felt like she was having of an out-of-body experience, or starring in an old western where you can't tell who to shoot because the good guys and the bad guys are *all* wearing black hats. If Eliana had known this MacGregor character for years, he was undoubtedly trustworthy. And she had to admit, he had a certain rough charm. But in Lu's opinion, he was a little too far into the fuzzy, indistinct middle ground between good guy and bad guy.

Magnus was thinking the same thing. "Tell me, Mr. MacGregor, what exactly is it you do for a living?"

"Ach!" said the big man with a grimace. "My grandfather was

Mr. MacGregor. Just call me Gregor. And this is Lourdes, by the way," he added, giving the dog a brisk shake, which made it shriek. "After my mother-in-law, not the town in France where the Virgin Mary appeared to that delusional adolescent," he explained, seeing Magnus's look. "And to answer your question, I'm in the procurement business. I get people what they want. Women, weapons, drugs, art," he shrugged. "Whatever it is, I can get it. And my clients are willing to pay a premium for my services, which is what *I* want, so everyone's happy." He grinned, looking pleased with himself. "In fact, you might say I'm actually in the happiness business!"

Speaking of delusional adolescents, Lu thought. Beside her, Magnus smiled.

"Oh—before I forget." MacGregor pulled a small box from his coat pocket, and held it out to Lu. "For you, lass. Contact lenses. These are the latest technology, too; they'll even get past the new ocular scanners."

She took the box, then, worried what might happen if they were stopped by the Peace Guard or Enforcement, said to Magnus, "Won't you need some?"

"Nooo, lass," drawled MacGregor, eyeing Magnus cagily. "He wouldn'a want to cover up those peepers. Come in bloody handy, I should think, havin' death rays shootin' out your skull."

Magnus tensed. "How did you—"

"I make it my business to know, lad," MacGregor said softly. He glanced at Lu with sharp interest, his gaze roving over her in a familiar, baldly calculating way. "Tisn't anything I don't know about either of you, in fact."

"*Watch yourself!*" Magnus hissed, going from tense to furious at whip-crack speed. He lurched forward with his hands clenched, veins standing out in his neck, lips peeled back over his teeth like an animal's, and Lu thought for one horrified moment he might kill the man right where he sat.

MacGregor had the good sense to look stunned. A flicker of fear crossed his face. Then he laughed, a hearty, booming noise that had Lourdes dissolving into an apoplectic yapping fit.

"Jesus, Mary, and Joseph!" he gasped, wiping his eyes. "You nearly had me shittin' myself like the dog! I haven't had a scare like that in *years*! Bloody fantastic!"

Lu gently curled her fingers around Magnus's arm, drawing him back against the seat. He relented, but kept MacGregor the focus of his unblinking, ferocious stare, until MacGregor apologized profusely for giving offense, and sounded as if he really meant it.

"You'll have to forgive my manners, son. It's been a long, long time since I met a man gettin' his feathers ruffled over the honor of a lady. Usually he's only gettin' his feathers ruffled over the price!"

"Ew," said Lu, distinctly loud. "And totally not what I want to hear. Can we please talk about how we're going to get into the city without getting stopped?"

MacGregor looked at her. "Darlin' . . . what makes you think we're not gettin' stopped?"

The car slowed to a crawl. Lu looked out the tinted windows, and, with dawning horror, realized what MacGregor meant.

Just ahead loomed the main gate of New Vienna, lit harshly with floodlights, flanked with a double row of armed Peace Guards. One of them stood in front of the gate with his hand held out, watching the car as it slowed to a stop. Then, with rifle at the ready, he walked slowly around to the driver's side door, examining the vehicle with suspicious, alert eyes.

"Oh shit," breathed Lu, going white. "They're going to search the car!"

Across from her, Gregor MacGregor merely smiled.

THIRTY

Magnus pinned MacGregor with a murderous stare. "You fucking turncoat! You brought us right to them!"

"Oh ye of little faith," said MacGregor with a disappointed little *tsk*. "Hold your water, lad, and let MacGregor work his magic!"

Lu was breathless watching this interaction, trying desperately to check the sudden throb of heat in the palms of her hands.

The soldier tapped on the window. A threat in the form of a nasty growl rumbled through Magnus's chest, but MacGregor lifted a finger to his lips, shaking his head. He pushed a button on the door, and the window slid down several inches. The soldier and he eyed one another wordlessly as Lourdes shivered and whined in MacGregor's lap, then MacGregor fished into his shirt pocket and withdrew a small metal card, engraved with numbers.

He held it out. The soldier took it. Nods were exchanged. The soldier stepped back, without ever once glancing deeper into the shadowed car interior. The window slid up.

The soldier waved the car forward, and they were off.

"There," said MacGregor with obvious satisfaction that no one had been killed, or any other havoc had been wrought. "Dinna tell you? Magic!"

"Oh Jesus," said Lu on a shaky exhalation.

"Well, me dear departed mother thought so, but I think it's a little too formal among friends. You can jes' keep right on callin' me MacGregor," he quipped, seemingly pleased with the drama of the situation. His accent was getting murkier, sliding in and out of Scottish, veering toward Irish, and Lu wondered how much of it was for show. Like the rest of him.

"You bribed him with water credits." She'd recognized the metal card.

MacGregor nodded. "He's got a dishy new girlfriend and they like to take long, hot showers." He grinned, winking at Magnus. "Can't say I blame him; you should see the chebs on her, lad."

Throughout all of this, Magnus hadn't uncoiled from his aggressive posture, nor had his look of murderous intent left his face. "No more surprises," he said, his voice low in his throat. "Are we understood?"

MacGregor tensed, wincing. Knowing what was happening, Lu rested her hand on Magnus's arm. Softly, she said his name, and Magnus released him. MacGregor's face cleared. He drew in a breath, blinking, and raised a shaking hand to his head.

Magnus sat back against the leather seat, nostrils flared. He glanced over at her, intense and glowering. *I want to kill him for scaring you.*

And I want to kiss you for being so overprotective. Now stop it.

His lips twitched. *I'm not going to stop it if it makes you want to kiss me.*

She pressed the smile from her mouth, reached for his hand, and twisted her fingers through his. *I always want to kiss you.*

Magnus's eyes heated, sparking a little burst of fireworks in her belly. His fingers curved tighter over hers. He thought a single word, but it was enough to ignite another round of fireworks.

Later.

She nodded, thrilled by his bare look of desire and the promise that had just been made. Their look held, deepened, the air between them crackled. Her heartbeat skittered and a flush crept across her cheeks.

Gregor MacGregor cleared his throat. Loudly. Lu and Magnus looked at him.

"If you'll be pardonin' me for interruptin', lovebirds," he drawled, "but we're not out of the woods just yet."

"What do you mean?" said Magnus, stiffening.

"I mean," MacGregor answered, tilting his head to gaze out the window, and up, "that there's more than three bears on the lookout for our Goldilocks in this city."

Lu and Magnus followed his gaze. There in the distance atop St. Stephen's Cathedral, slowly rotating in brilliant yellow neon that illuminated the soaring Romanesque towers and mosaic roof, was the megascreen. Lu's picture was still plastered on it for all to see.

ABERRANT ALERT, it screamed. Wanted for murder. Armed and Extremely Dangerous.

"So keep frosty," Lu sighed, watching herself turn.

"Exactly," said MacGregor.

"Got it." Lu chewed her lip a moment, debating. Then she asked, "Gregor . . . I want to show you something, to see if you recognize it. Something we're looking for, that we need to find quickly. And you seem like a man who might know how to find . . . hidden things."

MacGregor lifted one ginger brow. "That I am, that I am. You have a picture of this thing?"

"Um, yes. Sort of."

His other brow climbed.

"Okay." Lu sat forward on the seat. "Here's the thing: The picture is in my head. I can send it to you, but I just want to make sure you're ready. You know," she glanced at Magnus, "since we've agreed on no more surprises."

MacGregor made a sound of interest. On his lap, Lourdes had begun to writhe in terror in response to Lu's movement. She scowled at the dog, and its beady black eyes went wide.

"All right. Here goes."

She reached out with her mind, feeling carefully, trying not to do anything too abrupt. She came up against a solid resistance, but pushed past it easily, like a knife cutting through butter.

MacGregor gasped, rearing back. "Holy mother of God," he breathed, his eyes as wide as the dog's.

Lu cringed. "Sorry. Is it too much?"

"No, lass, just let me," he cleared his throat. "Just give me a moment. It's . . . a little . . ."

"Intimate," said Magnus aridly, shooting her a disgruntled look.

"I'm not looking around or anything," she assured Gregor softly, holding his apprehensive gaze, "I'm just there. Okay?"

After a moment, he nodded, adjusting to the sensation of having his mind invaded. "Bugger me, that's strange," he muttered.

Into his mind she said, *All right, so, here it is. Let me know if you recognize it.*

Lu formed a mental picture of the bunker, in as much detail as she could remember from the helicopter pilot's purloined memories, focusing on the shape and size, turning it so he could see it from all sides.

"Holding cells," he said aloud. He was silent a moment, then, "Administration in the bigger areas on the top three floors, security, command center, computers. Smaller blocks from level four down are the assets. The base floor is open . . . no compartments . . . might be storage." He frowned. "It's highly secured, though. Those look like airlocks at one side. Triples." He closed his eyes, continuing on, his frown deepening as he concentrated. "And why would there be so many cameras?"

"Cameras?" said Lu, tensing.

"Those dots that look like rivets? There's a single one in each of the other cells on the other floors, all in the same position on the ceiling. But the bottom floor has cameras all over the place. Floor, ceiling, walls . . . if this space is used for storage, they're keeping a close eye on whatever's in there. Prisons don't invest that kind of mint to make sure the guards don't walk off with extra toilet paper. It's more likely that's where they're keepin' their main asset."

Magnus said, "How do you know this is a prison?"

MacGregor opened his eyes. "Been inside as many different kinds of jails as man has built," he answered quietly, looking at Magnus directly. "You get a feel for 'em. But you know exactly what I mean, don't you, lad?"

Lu was intrigued, especially by the tone of knowing in which he delivered the last part. She resolved to ask Magnus about it later. Right now she had bigger fish to fry. "We have to find this structure, Gregor. I know it's in New Vienna, underground, but I just don't know where. Do you?"

He turned his attention her way. "I surely don't," he said with real regret, and Lu's heart sank. It lifted again when he amended, "But I know someone who might."

"Can you take us to him?"

"I can," he said, nodding, "but not now."

"Why not?" said Lu and Magnus in unison.

"Curfew starts in fifteen minutes, ladies and gentlemen," he said, consulting his gigantic gold watch. "Which leaves us just enough time to make it back to my place before the Peace Guard starts sweepin' the streets. Your meetin' will have to wait."

Lu blew out a hard breath, and Magnus reached over and took her hand, knowing what she was thinking without her even having to form the thought in her mind.

Time wasn't on their side. Waiting was the last thing they should be doing, but the sun would rise, and the clock would tick, and all they could do in the meantime was count the minutes until darkness.

Gregor's "place" turned out to be a palace. Or at least a replica of one, constructed right in the heart of New Vienna, atop the ruins of a former church.

Built in the Romanesque revival style, it sported slim towers, ornamental turrets, gables, balconies, pinnacles, and copious sculptures of angels and saints, which Gregor explained with no hint of irony were his favorite parts of the property. The entire place was ridiculously ornate, and Lu told him so.

"Seriously, how much does it cost to keep this place clean?" she said sourly, eyeing the acres of dust-free carved-wood wall paneling, furniture, and screens.

"Who knows? Money isn't one of my problems, lass," said Gregor dismissively, leading them down a thickly carpeted corridor toward a suite of rooms where he'd said they could rest.

"Obviously," Lu grumbled, thinking of the years of near-starvation she'd endured growing up in this very same city, while men like Gregor—criminals!—lived in such luxury.

"Life isn't fair, princess," he said, turning to fix her with a look. "It's eat or be eaten. And I'd much rather be the one holdin' the fork and knife than starin' up from the plate."

Thanks for that fantastic visual, she thought, disgruntled. She'd never look at food the same way again.

"Here we go," Gregor said, rounding a corner and opening a door. Lu and Magnus followed, and she gasped at the grandeur that lay within. Her eyes went immediately to the enormous, four-poster bed in the corner. Just behind her, Magnus snorted.

Wanton wench.

Without turning, she gave him a swift kick in the shin.

"I'll be back at sundown," said MacGregor briskly, checking his watch. "In the meantime, I'll try and find out what I can, and set up the meeting with my contact. If you get hungry, just dial nine on the house phone; it goes straight to the kitchens. They'll bring the food up."

"They?" said Lu.

Gregor waved a hand. "The wee kitchen elves, lass. Who else?" He turned and disappeared through the door.

"Alone at last," said Magnus, his voice husky, and she turned to him with an eyebrow arched.

"And *I'm* the wanton one?" she teased.

His answer was a deep, hot kiss, his hands pinning her wrists behind her back, his body hard against hers, his passion edged with something like desperation. When he came up for air, Lu asked breathlessly, "Why did that feel like an end-of-the-world kiss?"

Something flashed in his eyes, there then gone. Then he picked her up, threw her over his shoulder, and loped over to the bed as she squealed and pounded his back in fake protest. He dropped her to the mattress, where she bounced, then stood staring down at her with eyes molten and dark.

Examining his face, she fell still. "Magnus, what is it? What's wrong?"

He gave a barely imperceptible shake of his head. "Nothing could ever be wrong with you looking at me like that, angel," he whispered.

She didn't believe him. Something was suddenly, definitely wrong. She sat up, grabbing his wrist. "Don't lie to me! What're you thinking?"

He hesitated. Then, in a voice low and infinitely dark, he said,

"I just feel like the luckiest man alive. And I want this to last forever." He knelt down beside the bed and took her face in his hands. His eyes were so tortured it frightened her. "I want that more than anything else in the world. To be with you forever."

"You're scaring me," she whispered back.

"Don't be scared, angel. Everything's going to be okay; I know it." He pressed the gentlest of kisses to her lips, her cheeks, her chin, trying to calm her, but she'd begun to tremble.

"Magnus—"

"Shh," he shushed her gently, kissing her again. He pressed her back against the bed, his kisses growing deeper, longer, his hands roving over her body. As always when he touched her, it was a sweet and wonderful homecoming, the best feeling in the world. It was so blissful, in fact, she heard music . . .

Magnus stilled. She opened her eyes and looked at him, hovering above her, his face flushed. "Is that music?" he said in a whisper, ear cocked toward the door.

"It is." And not any music. Loud music, a throbbing, pulsating beat that vibrated the floor.

They both sat up. "Where's it coming from, d'you think?" she asked.

"Downstairs? Somewhere . . . below."

Below. They looked at each other, arrested by the word.

"Are you thinking what I'm thinking?" she asked, and watched a sexy, slow grin spread across his face.

His voice dropped an octave. "Only if what you're thinking involves my face between your legs."

"Magnus!" Lu smacked him on the arm, scandalized, blushing. She couldn't believe he'd just said that out loud.

"God, you're adorable when you blush." He grabbed her, kissed her again. This time it was she who broke the kiss, when the throbbing beat of the music became too loud and distracting.

"Okay, I've *got* to know what that music is all about!"

Magnus groaned, but allowed her to drag him from the bed. Feeling like a spy, she peeked out the bedroom door, looked up and down the long, deserted corridor. "Coast is clear," she said, whispering, not knowing why but feeling like it was appropriate. "I think we should head that way." She pointed to a spiral staircase at the opposite end of the hall from where they entered, half hidden behind a huge stand of artfully arranged potted palms.

Magnus's big hands spanned her waist, reaching almost all the way around. "Your wish is my command, My Lady," he whispered, raising the hair on her arms. She straightened, and his hands slid upward, resting on her ribs, just below her breasts. When he spoke again it was against the bare flesh of her nape, exposed by her new short haircut. "Or would you rather I called the shots?"

She turned her head and his lips met her ear. "I wasn't kidding about my face between your legs, angel," he breathed, his tongue darting out to softly lick her lobe, sending her heartbeat flying. "I need to taste you again. Soon."

He slid one hand higher and swept his thumb over her hardened nipple. The other hand he spread flat over her belly, pulling her bottom against his erection, and she let out a soft moan in response. He cupped her chin and tilted her head, kissing her from behind.

"Okay. The faster we figure out what that music is, the faster we can get back to this bedroom," she said, breathing heavily, liquid fire pooling deep in her belly where he was rubbing slow, teasing circles, heading lower. She pulled herself away, smiling when he groaned in protest, and tugged on his hand. "C'mon. Five minutes."

"Five," he said firmly, following. He lifted her hand to his mouth, and pressed his teeth into her thumb. "And then you're mine." His eyes were glowing, and her smile grew even wider.

They raced silently down the hallway. They took the stairs two at a time, their feet barely making any sound as they went. They came to another floor, but the stairway kept descending, so they passed it by, gaining speed, their noses picking up the scent of sweat and alcohol, musky perfumes, a dozen different fragrances pummeling them even as the music grew louder and louder. They were getting close.

Finally the stairway ended in a long, dark corridor, its floor bare stone. At the opposite end, lights flashed bright between the slit in a pair of drawn velvet curtains. Shadows crawled along the walls. The music was almost deafening, a bold, base-heavy techno beat, and Magnus guided Lu down the hall toward the curtain. They pushed it aside, and were shocked at the scene laid out before them.

A story below, hundreds of people bounced and twisted, dancing with arms overhead or around a partner or flung wide. Lu barked a laugh at the sheer, unexpected spectacle of it all. There was a DJ booth on one wall, a bar on the other, and an old-fashioned mirrored ball dangled from the ceiling high above. The place was mobbed.

"A *speakeasy*, of all things!" said Magnus. She barely heard him above the music.

"Our friend MacGregor certainly is an interesting character," Lu conceded, watching in fascination as the bodies surged and spun. "It must be an underground thing—it's after Curfew!"

No one on the dance floor looked concerned about Curfew. In fact, there were quite a few couples who seemed far more concerned with getting a good grope in under the flashing, blinding lights.

Magnus turned his head and looked at her. His eyes glinted in the light, and the desire and intent in them was unmistakable. Her heart skipped a beat.

Not here!

No? He prowled toward her, a scant smile lifting the corners of his lips. *Why not?*

Lu stepped back, looking nervously down at the crowd below. *Magnus! Anyone can see us!*

His jaw tightened. He gave her a look of pure, possessive lust. *You think I'd ever allow another man's eyes on your body? You think I'd ever share what's mine with anyone else? Even a look?*

He kept moving forward, and she kept stepping back, assuming she'd come into contact with the wall at any moment. But then she brushed past another curtain she hadn't noticed, and stumbled into a small alcove off the main corridor, lit with candles. She realized it was a curtained balcony just as Magnus reached out his hand and curled it around her upper arm. He pulled her against his chest, staring down into her eyes with a fierce, burning need.

"I don't share," he growled. With his free hand, he ripped a second curtain hanging on a rod above the entrance around to close the gap between the main set, then guided her to the far back corner of the balcony, around a trio of high-backed chairs to a tufted velvet settee strewn with cushions. He sank down onto it and dragged her onto his lap. The music blared and thumped and throbbed, but it was quieter inside their little cocoon above the fray, and she could hear the irregular rasp of his breathing. She put both hands on his chest, felt the pounding of his heart, and smiled.

"Good," she said, leaning over to whisper directly into his ear. "Because I'm only for you. All of me is only for you. And all of you is only for me."

He kissed her then, hard, his eyes fluttering closed as a groan left his lips. He fisted his hands into her hair, devouring her mouth, then dragged his lips across her jaw and down her throat, licking and sucking, tasting her skin, ravenous and unrestrained. It excited her on some deep level, his loss of control when he touched her. She loved it.

She loved him.

She whispered it, head thrown back as he roughly unzipped

her jacket and pushed it off her shoulders, tossing it to the floor. The words were lost to the music and the sound of his harsh breath; he made no indication he'd heard, and maybe she hadn't said them aloud after all. She was reeling, breathless, drunk with him.

Her shirt came off next, then her camisole, and then his beautiful rough hands were all over her bare skin, his mouth and lips following everywhere he touched. He set her on her feet and shucked off her boots, dragged her pants down over her hips, tore off her panties. And when she stood naked before him, he looked at her for a long, silent moment, his eyes just drinking her in.

"Angel," he said, staring into her eyes with a look of rapt ardor, "looking at you could bring a dead man back to life."

"He wouldn't be looking at me if he was dead," she teased, cupping his face in her hands, "but thank you for the compliment."

She bent and pressed a kiss to his mouth, then, straddling him, pulled his shirt off over his head. He tore his trousers open to his hips, freeing his enormous erection, then flipped her onto her back in one swift, confident move, setting her down carefully against the cushion.

Maybe it was the music, or the candlelight, or the hunger in his eyes, but in that moment, Lu felt like a different person. She felt powerful, strong, and mysterious, a thread of her long-ago dream self running through her veins, urging her on.

Show him what belongs to him. Show him what's his.

Holding his gaze, she arched back against the settee, spread her legs open, cupped her breasts in her hands. He looked down at her, drawing in a sharp breath. A smile curving her lips, she slowly slid her hands from her breasts, down her rib cage, over her stomach, undulating erotically, totally unabashed, in love with the look of worship and passion in his eyes. He looked starving and brutally dangerous, hovering there above her, and what she said next pushed him right over the edge.

"I need your mouth," she said, and dipped a finger into the wetness between her legs, "here."

He complied without hesitation, pushing her hand aside to cover her with his mouth. He wasn't gentle; she didn't want him to be. He was rough and demanding, sliding his fingers inside her without preliminaries, sucking hard where she most needed it. She arched and cried out, her sounds of pleasure and his growls of desire drowned by the music. He brought her right to the edge of release, then stopped.

She blinked open her eyes. He stared up at her, her eyes feral in the flickering light.

"I think we're going to need some protection."

She didn't understand until he reached for her jacket, and pulled her gloves from the pocket.

She laughed weakly. He helped her put them on, then positioned himself above her, his arms braced on either side of her head. He eased himself inside her without ever looking away from her eyes, so she could see exactly how good it felt for him, a look she knew was mirrored in her own eyes.

When he was fully seated, he cupped a firm hand under her bottom and leaned down to whisper in her ear.

"Feel good?"

Her answer was a low moan, which made him chuckle. He slid out, then back in, deep, wringing another moan from her throat.

"Tell me," he said, husky. "Tell me how good it feels, angel."

"Better than anything, ever." Her voice was unsteady. He slid in and out again, achingly slow, and her legs began to shake.

"Tell me you love it." His words were hot and demanding at her ear.

"Oh yes, yes, I love it." Her fingers were digging into his hips and she was pulling at him, trying to get him to go faster, harder, but he stayed in control, keeping that slow, languorous rhythm.

Then, his voice ragged, he whispered, "Tell me you love *me*, angel."

He turned his face and looked at her through hooded eyes, and Lu felt as if her heart would burst wide open. "Magnus," she whispered.

"Tell me, angel. Say it," he demanded harshly, his face strained. "I need to hear you say it."

"I love you," she said, dissolving, her eyes filling with moisture. "I love you. I love—"

Abandoning all his careful control, Magnus crushed his mouth against hers. His body crashed into hers and he began to pump with hard, powerful strokes, claiming her, possessing her body and her heart and her soul. She met every thrust with one of her own, her hips taking over, both of them going crazy, grabbing, clawing, panting, groaning, all restraint thrown aside.

"God now, please now!" she begged, writhing.

Magnus must have been right there, because he moaned, "Yes!" and thrust one last time. Every muscle in his body went taut.

Lu opened her eyes and looked up at him, this man who'd saved her in so many ways, and watched him fall apart.

She fell apart with him. They stared at each other through it, both of them stunned and wide-eyed, breathless and wracked with full body shudders, glistening with sweat. He said her name, low and hoarse, the word full of wonder. Beyond the curtains, the music rose to a throbbing crescendo, and the crowd roared.

Her heart on fire, Lu thought, *I would die for you.*

She didn't know it then, but that simple, impassioned thought changed the course of fate.

THIRTY-ONE

Magnus carried her all the way back to the room. She was as bone-less as a ragdoll, worn out by their lovemaking but also by the enormity of her emotions, and the effort not to think about what might be coming next. All she wanted was a shower, and to sleep.

So they shared a bath in the ridiculously huge claw-foot bath-tub, running hot water without a thought to the credits it cost. Magnus washed her tenderly, and she washed him, and after they dried off, they fell into bed and slept like the dead.

Lu awoke hours later, disoriented and thirsty, feeling certain someone had just called her name. But the room was still, the music from before silent.

The ghost of her name came again, raising goose bumps on her arms. Carefully, silently, she rose and dressed. With a last, lin-gering look at Magnus, sleeping peacefully on his back with his arm thrown over his face, she left the room.

The mansion was as quiet as their bedroom. She wandered aimlessly through vast, echoing corridors and lavish, empty rooms, until finally she came upon the kitchen. There sat Gregor MacGregor alone at a long, wooden table, staring in silent contemplation at his hands, twisting his pinky ring around with his thumb.

He glanced up when she came in, and smiled, looking awfully pleased with himself.

"You rang?" she said, rubbing a fist against an eye sleepily.

"Wondered if that would work. Must be because you were traipsin' around in my noggin earlier, eh? Now we have some kind of Vulcan mind meld going on?"

Lu shrugged. "Beats me, Gregor. I didn't come with an instruction manual, and it's been hell figuring out how this whole contraption works." She made a vague, sweeping gesture with her hand, indicating her entire body, and its assorted bells and whistles.

He stood, lifting his bulk from the table with surprising agility for such a large man, and went to a refrigerator the size of her bedroom in the house where she'd grown up. "You hungry, lass?"

"Starving," Lu admitted. "But is that really why you called me?"

He hesitated a moment with his hand on the refrigerator door. "No." He opened the door, began rummaging through the refrigerator's contents. "But I find it's hard to think on an empty stomach, don't you?"

Lu made no comment, having had to think on an empty stomach her entire life. Judging by his size, MacGregor had never had that particular problem.

He made her a sandwich with cheese, ham, and fresh tomato, of all things, on wheat bread. When he put it in front of her, Lu looked at it as if it had just arrived from outer space.

"What?" he said, affronted.

"I saw a tomato once before. In a book."

"I have them flown in from Sardinia. I love this heirloom variety; they're so perky."

Lu stared at him. "Sardinia. *Flown in* from Sardinia."

He nodded.

"But the only flights allowed anywhere are military!"

"You think that soldier at the gate is the only man who ever took a bribe?" Gregor answered, brows quirked. "Everyone has somethin' they want, lass. And, even better for me, everyone has a price they'll pay to get it. Now eat your sandwich."

Lu picked up the sandwich, and took a huge bite. It was delicious. She swallowed, took another bite, said around a mouthful, "But . . . tomatoes?"

It was his turn to shrug now. "It's a little venture of mine. The grow light fields are adequate, but you need real sunlight for real taste. The IF doesn't keep the isotope clouds over any of the major islands of Europe anymore, or watch 'em now that they're deserted for that matter, so on Sardinia I've got a bloody great biome project with all my favorite—"

"Wait," Lu interrupted, shocked once again. "You *know* about the isotope clouds?"

"Of course," he answered, sitting across from her, calm as the Buddha. "I told you before; tisn't anything I don't know."

"No, what you said was there wasn't anything you didn't know about Magnus and me," Lu replied tartly. That made him laugh. She'd devoured half the sandwich by the time he stopped.

"Ach, how I love a woman with a memory like a steel trap! Eliana's the exact same way." His eyes grew wistful, his lips pursed. "What I wouldn'a give to see *that* one again," he mused, shaking his head. He sobered after a moment, fixing her in his shrewd gaze. "But you're exactly right, lass. That is what I said. And it's the ever-lovin' truth: I know everything there is to know about you and that man of yours. Far more than you know yourself."

He dangled it out there like a dare, and his eyes dared her, too, the offer an obvious lure. She liked Gregor, but she didn't altogether trust him, so she hesitated a long, long while before finally giving in to her curiosity.

What she said to him was a dare in its own way, too. A test. Because she didn't believe he would know, and he'd be exposed as all bluster and bullshit.

She really should have known better by now.

"All right, Gregor, if you're so smart, tell me where I was born."

"That's an easy one, lass," he scoffed quietly, holding her gaze. "Hampshire, southern England, a fancy manor house called Sommerley. Town named after it, too, hidden deep in the New Forest, surrounded by stone walls three times the height of a man." He paused, gauging her astonishment. "But you didn't stay there long."

An itch began in Lu's palms. She'd taken the gloves off for her bath, and now her hands were dangerously bare. She put down the half-eaten sandwich and slowly, slowly, slid her hands into her lap.

"You travelled by boat to another place hidden deep in a forest, the Amazon jungle just outside Manaus, Brazil. Your stay there was even shorter: less than a week, as a matter of fact. Then came the Flash. *Your* Flash. Instigated by the jealousy and total ignorance of Man, intent on wipin' out what we didn't understand."

Lu held herself perfectly still, though all her nerves screamed for action. For *something*. The animal always slumbering in her veins cracked open yellow, slitted eyes, lifting its head.

"Your next trip wasn't by water. This time it was by air." His voice was growing quieter and quieter, his attention never wavering from her face. "The flight was short, but by the end of it, you had a new home. New parents. A new life. And those new parents—missionaries they were, dedicated to spreading the word of their God—decided their foundling child should be as far away from the jungle as she could possibly get. Especially since every hunter on Earth now had her in their sights. And so that foundling child wound up in an adopted city with adopted parents who could never really figure out if she was a gift or a curse, but who loved her anyway." His voice dropped even lower. "And died for it."

A flare of anger, huge and bright, erupted in her chest. How *dare* he! "You don't know anything! My mother died of cancer!"

He was apologetic, at least. "That's what your father told you. But you were six years old, Lumina. He couldn't tell you that your mother, convinced you were a demon sent straight from hell after you lit your bed on fire the first time, opened her wrists with a straight razor."

Lu bolted to her feet, cocked back her arm, and slapped Gregor MacGregor so hard across the face he rocked back, his head jerking to the side.

She shouted, "That's a lie!"

He exhaled a hard breath, working his jaw where she'd hit him. His gaze flashed to hers. "I lie to keep myself out of trouble or make money, and make no apologies about it. But I'm not lyin' now, lass, no matter how hard you hit me. And if you want to hear more, you'd better brace yourself. That's hardly the worst of it."

Lu stared at him, her heart pounding, a burn working its way up from her palms to her arms. She was so furious she thought her entire body might ignite. "Even if I believed you—which I *don't*— how would you know, anyway? And how do you know all that other stuff about me?"

"You think a man like me would let a dangerous fugitive stay in his home without knowin' all there is to know about her?" He shook his head, answering his own question. "Eliana filled me in where she could, the rest I found out on my own. A lot of people in this world owe me favors, lass. I called in a few."

Lu began to pace in front of the table, her hands fisted at her sides. He had to be lying. He had to be! Only . . . he didn't smell or look like he was. There were no telling twitches, no sour scent of deception. And what did he mean by "That's hardly the worst of it"?

She swung around and demanded, "What else? What about Magnus—what do you know about him?"

His expression guarded, he sat back and folded his arms across his chest. "I'll not tell you if you're gonna burn down my house, after. Promise me you'll keep your temper under control."

That sounded bad. She gave him a curt nod, and resumed her pacing. Unsettled, her stomach lurched and twisted.

Gregor paused a moment, then, looking at the table, asked quietly, "Has he told you how he got all those scars?"

Lu stopped dead in her tracks, turning to look at him. She answered with a shake of her head.

"He's a strong one, your man, I have to give it to him. I've seen pretty much the worst the world has to offer and I'm still standin', but if I had to walk a mile in that lad's shoes . . ." Gregor met her eyes, and what she saw there chilled her. "Well, let's just say I don't think I could."

"What do you mean?" Hands shaking, Lu sank down into the chair across the table from him.

Gregor, twisting his pinky ring around with his thumb, asked, "How many people would you have to watch die, before you'd give up a secret? Ten? Twenty? One hundred?"

It was a rhetorical question, but Lu's skin crawled. She waited, silent, watching his face.

"How about *two* hundred? How about if they were all your friends? Everyone you loved, grew up with, everyone you knew?" His voice darkened. "And not one of them over the age of fifteen?"

Lu put a hand over her mouth, her stomach lurching violently.

"They thought they could break him," he said, admiration in his voice. "But they never did. Even when they poured acid on him. Even when they cut him. Even when they tortured and killed each and every one of the children they'd captured that day. He was captured, too, you see, the day of the Flash. Both his parents were killed. All the children were separated from the adults, taken to a different prison in Bolivia. By pure dumb luck, Magnus had heard Morgan screaming in the chaos to get everyone to the caves of Ogof Ffynnon Ddu in Wales, and he made the fatal mistake of telling one of the other children he knew where to go, if only they could all escape. Word spread: Magnus knew. And that was why they targeted him."

Gregor paused, looked down at his pinky ring. "That . . . and one other thing." He looked up at her again. "He'd seen the direction the great white dragon had flown, carrying its child to safety. He wouldn't tell them that, either."

Lu closed her eyes, sick. He'd saved her. He'd saved the new colony, and countless lives. And in trade, he'd sacrificed two hundred children. Two hundred of his friends.

Dear God.

"They brutalized him for three years in that prison, long after everyone else was dead. Then he came of age. His Gifts manifested. He slaughtered every one of the guards, and walked out breathing, but not really alive. He found his way to Wales. He began to search for other survivors, bringing them back one by one to the colony. And then he found you."

Lu opened her eyes and stared in mute horror at Gregor. She couldn't speak. There weren't any words to convey the depths of her despair, her wretchedness. Her overwhelming, paralyzing heartbreak.

Magnus. Beautiful, ruined Magnus. No wonder he was so broken. It was a miracle he'd survived at all.

Gregor asked softly, "He's saved your life twice now, lass. Don't you think you should repay the favor?"

"What do you mean?" Lu whispered, shaking.

J.T. GEISSINGER

"I mean that if he stays with you, it'll cost him his life. And he's more than willin' to pay."

The automatic *No!* died on her lips, because with awful clarity the words Demetrius had spoken came flooding back, burned like a brand into her mind.

Cogs in the machine, Seeker, all of us. You know it as well as I.

And Magnus's expression of recognition, of resignation, his fleeting look in her direction that was so foreboding she'd felt certain it was something terrible, equally certain he'd never tell her what.

Now she knew, down to the marrow of her bones. Demetrius had Dreamt of Magnus's death. He'd known it, coming here with her. He'd known it, making love to her. He'd known it all along, and had accepted it willingly.

Gratefully?

Her brain exploded into chaos. She leapt from the chair, hands gripping her head, adrenaline flooding through her veins, making her heart hammer. She couldn't let it happen. She couldn't let him die.

"What do I do?" she cried, turning to Gregor. "How can I stop it?"

His face took on an odd, calculating cast. He leaned forward over the table, intent. "You need to find what you came lookin' for alone, lass. Let him sit this one out. That's the only way you can save him."

"But I don't even know where to start looking! And I could never convince him not to come with me!" She felt dizzy. Nauseated. Heat flashed over her, and she broke out in a sweat.

Gregor stood, rising slowly, pulling himself to his full height to look at her with calm, unblinking eyes. "I told you I'd set up a meetin' with someone who might know where that prison is you're lookin' for, yes?"

Black spots danced in front of Lu's eyes, and she thought she might throw up. "Yes, yes, but Magnus will be awake any time, he'll insist on coming to the—"

"He can't insist if he's still sleepin'. And as the meetin' is right now, I think he'll just have to miss it."

Lu looked at Gregor, confused. The room wavered in her peripheral vision, and she swayed, gripped by a jolt of vertigo.

From his pocket, he removed a small cell phone. He dialed a number, waited a beat, then said, "All right then, lads. She's all yours."

Behind her, a door crashed open. Lu turned, and, as if in slow motion, saw six men running toward her from the opposite end of the large kitchen. They wore white hazmat suits with face shields, gloves, and boots, rifles slung over their backs.

Peace Guards.

Lu whipped her head around, looked at the half-eaten sandwich on the table, stared up at the man who'd fed it to her. Dazed, she breathed, "Gregor MacGregor, you son of a bitch!"

He lifted his shoulders in casual apology or agreement, but his eyes were fierce. As footsteps pounded closer, he said, barely audibly, "D'ya know why a knife needs a sheath, lass? Because the real power of a knife isn't in the sharpness of its blade, it's in concealment. Remember that. And gie it laldy."

Then the men in white suits smashed into her and grabbed her, just as the room slipped sideways, her field of vision narrowing to a swiftly closing circle of black.

THIRTY-TWO

When Magnus awoke alone, he knew with instant, bloodcurdling certainty something was terribly wrong. Lumina wasn't beside him, but there was more to it than that. He felt her absence as a raw, hollow space inside his chest, as if an organ had been cut out while he'd been sleeping.

On a small table beside the bed lay her golden dragon pendant, its red eye winking in the light.

Magnus dressed, panicked, calling out for her even though he knew she wouldn't answer, and flew out of the room, the pendant in his shirt pocket.

He searched the entire mansion in minutes. She'd disappeared.

So had Gregor MacGregor.

He stood in the middle of the vast, echoing foyer where they'd first come in, eyes closed, concentrating, trying in vain to still his mind even as his body clamored violently for action. He called for her with his mind, too, but was once more met only with silence.

When he opened his eyes again, Magnus was gone. In his place was a ravaged, monstrous thing born long ago, a thing made of blood and death and darkness that knew it could survive any horror, because it already had.

It was that thing that wrenched open the front door of the deserted mansion, stepping out into the blistering red fury of noon, determined to find the angel that had shown it the way back from hell.

Lu was being carried; by whom she couldn't see. She couldn't see because her eyes wouldn't open. They felt stitched shut.

There was more than one pair of hands carrying her, though. More than one set of arms. More than one voice murmuring in hushed excitement as warm bodies jostled around her, bumping and shoving, reckless in their eagerness to deliver her wherever it was they were headed.

At least they're not groping my ass.

She smelled cloistered air, heard the shuffle of a dozen boots over dusty stone, tasted an unpleasant, metallic tang on her tongue. With Herculean effort, she cracked open one eye, then closed it again because what she saw made no sense.

An enormous golden crucifix, suspended over an altar. A checkerboard marble floor. Soaring arches and recessed chapels and medieval paintings glowing with gilt.

Drugged. Hallucinating. Screwed.

Lu silently pronounced judgment on her situation, then sank back into darkness.

The Queen of the *Ikati* dreamt of a comet, soaring high in the icy thin atmosphere, its tail a long, sparking flare of red, shedding a bloody glow over everything on the earth beneath.

She'd dreamt of this particular comet before. Always, it was a harbinger of disaster.

Torn from sleep, Jenna jerked upright in her cot, a strangled scream caught in her throat. It was light, always light in her cell, but something dark lurked in the corners. Something awful rang in her brain, echoing. Calling.

She raised her nose, scenting the air, then froze in disbelief. In recognition. A cry of anguish slipped from her lips. "No," she whispered. "*No!*"

Jenna leapt from her cot, stood in the middle of her cell, and began to scream.

Sebastian Thorne's mind tended to run on a hamster wheel when he lay down to try to sleep, so he'd developed chronic insomnia. It was stubbornly resistant to the drugs he'd developed to combat it, though they worked like a charm on every other person suffering from sleepless nights. If he'd been a superstitious man, he might have found some unease in that, but he wasn't superstitious, ascribing that kind of whimsy to those of lesser intellect.

So he was awake during the middle of the day when the rest of the world was at rest. At the moment the call came, he was standing in front of his bathroom mirror, considering his reflection, pleased with how well the new drug to combat hair loss was working.

The green light on the phone on the wall began to blink, indicating an incoming call. He pressed the answer button.

"Yes."

"Sir! It's Three!"

Thorne frowned at the phone. Three sounded unusually breathless. Excited, even. "Yes, Three, what is it?"

There was a moment of heavy breathing, then the wet sound of gulping. "Sir . . . sir . . ."

Thorne was beginning to lose patience. For goodness' sake, didn't the man realize it was the middle of the day? Honestly, it had been over two decades since he'd first installed the isotope clouds in the atmosphere, making daylight poisonous and effectively turning the human population nocturnal. Why wasn't Three with the program yet? "You have five seconds to explain why you've disturbed me at such a late hour, and your explanation better be satisfactory. Speak."

There was a pause in which Thorne imagined Three's eyes rolling this way and that in his head, trying to decide which way to focus. Then he spoke.

"Lumina Bohn. She's been captured, sir. The Peace Guard have brought her into the facility. She's *here!*"

Though Thorne hardly believed it, Three's explanation was, indeed, satisfactory.

A slow, delighted smile spread over Thorne's face. "I'll be right in."

When she awoke, Lumina was nude, blindfolded, and strapped down to a hard metal surface that had been tilted at a forty-five degree angle, so she was neither upright nor lying down.

The better to see you with, my dear, she thought groggily, understanding immediately that she was on display.

The room she was in was pleasantly warm, so though naked, she wasn't chilled. The restraints on her wrists and ankles, however, were too tight, and chafed. Thick and unyielding, they might have been steel, or something even harder, because they gave not an inch when she tried her strength against them.

Her head throbbed. Weak and disoriented, she simply breathed for a moment, trying to center herself, and think.

She assumed it would be torture first. They'd want to know what she knew, if she had information about the whereabouts of other Aberrants, and who had helped her escape the city the day she'd burned down the Hospice. They'd undoubtedly want to know other things, too, would undoubtedly have extremely unpleasant ways of making her talk.

Magnus wouldn't talk, she thought, her heart wrenching. *Magnus would—*

LUMINA!

He burst into her mind with a roar that made her entire body jerk. She inhaled a sharp breath, then relaxed, trying to appear calm; she didn't know who was watching, but surely someone was. Probably many someones.

I'm here. It took so much effort to concentrate. To speak without speaking.

Where are you? You sound strange! What's happened?

He was panicked, frantic. She felt the enormity of his worry and his love, and behind her closed lids, her eyes filled with tears.

I don't know where I am . . . they took me . . . the Peace Guard . . . Gregor set us up.

Another roar of pure rage, unearthly loud inside her skull. She squeezed her eyes tighter shut.

Wait. Let me . . .

Lumina concentrated, recalling with as much detail as she could the images she'd seen when she'd briefly awoken earlier. The cross and checkered floor, the paintings of gilt, the sculptures. *That's all I saw, on the way here. Wherever here is.*

I know where it is, he answered in a snarl. His voice was a terrible, dark presence inside her head. Lu had never imagined a man could sound so . . . unhinged.

I'm coming! I'll find you! Just stay alive!

Lu stiffened against the restraints. Her breath hitched. *No! Magnus, don't come! I know what Demetrius saw in his Dream— don't come!*

There was an awful silence. Then his voice, still so dark, still so mad with rage. *You're my destiny, Lumina. I. AM. COMING!*

He was abruptly gone.

She moaned, and a voice spoke.

"Subject, are you unwell?"

It was a male voice, perversely solicitous, emanating from directly overhead. Through a speaker, she assumed.

"Subject? Please respond to the question: Are you unwell?"

Lu ascertained several things quickly. One: This speaker was concerned with her health. Which meant he wanted her alive and probably comfortable, at least for the time being. Two: He had little, if any, idea what her current state of health actually was. Which meant that either he wasn't entirely certain of the efficacy or power of the drug that had been used to take her down, or what its effect on her might be. And three: He was being polite, which hinted that she had value. Like the owners of expensive pets, the owners of valuable property tended to treat their possessions well.

And expend a great deal of effort making sure those costly possessions stayed in good repair.

Lu moistened her lips, trying to look as weak and pathetic as possible. In her best frightened school girl's voice, she said, "I'm very thirsty, and disoriented. My head really hurts. Sir."

She threw in the "sir" at the end on a whim, and was rewarded by the unmistakable sound of a man grunting in satisfaction. There was a prolonged silence, then the man spoke again.

"Subject, we are sending in water. Any attempt to harm the associate who brings it to you will not be tolerated. Do you understand?"

"Yes, sir. I understand, sir. Thank you, sir."

The air vibrated with that satisfaction again. Lu remembered how Lars, the Hospice head cook, used to preen when she called him *herrchen*. She'd just learned a valuable lesson about insecure men.

A door, hissing open then closed on a gust of pressurized air. Footsteps, drawing near. The feeling of a presence beside her, then a voice, so familiar she froze in disbelieving astonishment.

"I'm going to bring the cup to your mouth," said Dieter Gerhardt, *leutnant* of the Peace Guard, the man who'd warned her about the Grand Minister the day she burned down the Hospice.

Thank you, God.

Lu knew they were being watched, knew their every word was being listened to, and recorded. Though her heart thrummed like a hummingbird inside her chest, she merely nodded, and parted her lips.

He lifted the cup to her mouth. She drank deeply. It was clean, pure water, some of the best she'd ever tasted in her life. When she was finished, she turned her head and Dieter took the cup away. She whispered, "Thank you."

Dieter—listen to me.

Beside her, he jumped as if electrocuted. The voice, now fraught, shouted over the speakers.

"Lieutenant! Report!"

"Excuse me, sir, it's nothing," lied Dieter smoothly, controlling his voice. "I just wasn't expecting it to speak."

It? Thanks a lot.

You scared the scheisse *out of me, Lumina! How is this even possible?*

Lumina ignored that, cutting to the chase. *Are we at IF head-quarters? What floor am I on? Picture it in your head. I need to get to the control center, the computers! I need access to the—*

Dieter cut in, frantic. *Listen—Thorne is on his way. We've never been able to get close to him, he only allows Enforcement near, but if you can distract him long enough to—*

"Lieutenant, please remove Subject's blindfold." The voice over the speakers was mild, satisfied with Dieter's explanation, but

Lumina wasn't listening, because everything inside her had ground to a halt.

Thorne is coming.

Thorne is coming.

Lu fell motionless on the table. Everything became perfectly clear.

She felt Dieter's fingers, fumbling with the knot on the blindfold near the back of her head. She felt the fabric slide away. She opened her eyes and saw Dieter standing there above her, looking down, his own eyes widening as he looked into hers. He wore the white bio suit, but the shield on his helmet was flipped up, his face exposed.

Not brown—green, he thought to himself, distracted. *Lucent. Like an emerald held up to the light.*

Show me where I am, Dieter. That's all you have to do. I'll take care of everything else.

They stared at each other. The voice on the speaker interrupted again.

"Lieutenant, are you experiencing any kind of discomfort?"

Dieter's mouth pinched. "No, sir. None at all. It appears the subject is quite weak, sir. I don't believe it poses any immediate threat. The collar, in combination with the drug, seems to have rendered it quite harmless."

So she was wearing a collar. Lu shouted into his mind, *Dieter, show me!*

His eyes fluttered closed. Lu received a mental picture, startlingly clear, of her exact location.

She began, weakly, to laugh.

"Thank you, lieutenant. Return to command."

Dieter thought hurriedly, *The Peace Guard don't have access into the main facility; you're in processing. You're to be transferred as soon as Thorne arrives. Once you're in, I won't be able to get you out—*

Thank you, Dieter, Lu thought, smiling up at him calmly. *Thank you for everything. You've been a good friend. In fact, you might be the best friend I ever had.*

Dieter's expression registered confusion, surprise, but most of all, gratitude. To cover his emotions, he blustered, *I'm not all that great; I didn't do such a good job of keeping my eyes on your face on my way in the room.* He glanced down at her bare chest, then reddening, looked away.

"Lieutenant," repeated the disembodied voice, harder, "return to command."

"Yes, sir."

He tried to tell her something else, but Lu had withdrawn. All was silent. With a final, pleading look, Dieter turned and left the room.

THIRTY-THREE

Sebastian Thorne hadn't felt this much excitement since the day of the Flash, when all his plans had finally come to fruition, and he'd taken over the world.

Watching the thing that called itself Lumina Bohn through the one-way glass of the interrogation room where she sat calmly with crossed legs in a metal chair, reading, he admitted to himself that she was beautiful. *It* was beautiful. Whatever; the monster was attractive. Perhaps more so than any other living thing he'd ever seen.

Which was saying a lot. Thorne had been everywhere, seen everything. *God's own miracle*, he thought, allowing himself an uncharacteristic moment of sarcasm. Thorne knew God had nothing to do with anything, and never had.

"I don't recommend it, sir. It's far too dangerous."

Three, glowering beside him at the glass, stared at Lumina. In the room around him, murmurs of assent came from the gathering of his top people who'd come to witness the event.

"She's perfectly docile," countered Thorne, pointing out with his usual impeccable logic that she'd been compliant since awakening, she hadn't harmed anyone who'd come into contact with her so far, and had even expressed the quite charming desire to read a book while her vitals were recorded, her blood drawn, her body examined. From her attitude, Thorne felt almost certain that she was *relieved* to have been finally apprehended. He couldn't imagine what she'd been doing since fleeing, but it surely was unpleasant. Running, hiding . . . what kind of life was that?

Better to be here, safe with her own kind. Or *un*safe, as it were, seeing how they were all scheduled to be exterminated. But she didn't have to know that.

"Its mother was perfectly docile for years, and look what that one recently did to her doctor," said Three.

"The mother is insane," said Thorne flatly. "I'm told just a few hours ago it leapt from its bed and began screaming bloody murder for no apparent reason."

No one had a good answer for that.

"I'm going in," he announced, and went to the door, ignoring the howls of protest his decision produced. "Open it!" he ordered into the ceiling camera. Obediently, the door slid open, and he stepped into the room. The door slid closed behind him, and Thorne felt the collective held breath.

Lumina looked up at him, surprised, blinking. She closed the book, and hesitantly rose to her feet. "Um, hello?" she said softly in greeting.

Perfectly docile. And collared, to boot. Thorne smiled, clasped his hands behind his back, and paced into the room. He made a slow circle around her, looking her up and down, noting the tattoos on her ankle and wrists. *Kinky.* She wore the standard-issue white knee-length gown, and nothing else. For the briefest of moments, Thorne allowed himself to remember what delights were hidden beneath.

He'd already reviewed the recorded footage of her processing. Spectacular. He'd definitely be reviewing that again soon.

Thorne made a full circle, then stopped an arm's length in front of her, still smiling. "Miss Bohn. How lovely to meet you at last." To her obvious shock, he extended his hand.

She stared at it for a beat, then took it, shaking his hand with a firm, if tentative, grip. He released her hand and imagined the relieved exhalation from the glass behind him.

Lumina demurely lowered her lashes, clasping the book against her chest. "I-I'm pleased to meet you, sir," she stammered, "and I-I'm sorry for all the trouble I've caused. I have to admit I'm a bit embarrassed. I'm not used to so much attention."

Was that a blush on its cheeks? And it was apologizing? Charming creature! Thorne beamed at her, intensely pleased. He was expecting anything but this. Perhaps he'd keep one of them alive, after all. She—*it*—was just so . . . delightful.

In his best stern, fatherly voice, Thorne said, "Well, you've certainly led us on a merry chase, Miss Bohn."

She ducked her head, murmuring, "Lumina."

"Pardon?"

"Please, call me Lumina." She glanced up at him, shy and lovely, and his heart missed a beat.

But no. This was getting out of hand. He drew himself up and said, "I only refer to my friends by their given names, Miss Bohn. While you reside in this facility I'll—"

"Oh, but I do hope we can be friends, sir," she interrupted earnestly, her brows drawn together. "I'm . . . I . . . I don't have any friends." She took her lower lip between her teeth and gazed at him, looking a little lost.

His mouth fell open. He was astonished at his response to her, a heady mix of paternal concern and rampant lust, and he had to make a quarter turn away to manage it, hiding his face. He coughed into his hand. "Yes. Well. You've led an unusual life."

When he turned back to her, she'd sunk into the chair and was gazing at the floor. She crossed her legs at the ankle and drew them in, and he couldn't help but notice the high arches of her bare feet, the long, slender line of her calves. On his forehead, dots of perspiration broke out.

"May I please . . . if I might be frank with you, sir?"

So polite! Such perfect submission! The lowered eyes, the respectful voice, that exquisite *deference*! Thorne didn't trust himself to speak at the moment, so he simply made a vague noise of assent.

Lumina said quietly, "The Grand Minister . . ." her head snapped up and her eyes went wide, as if she'd just remembered something. Her hand flew to cover her mouth. "Oh! Sir! How is he?"

Thorne was puzzled. "He was seriously burned—as you of course know—but he's recovering nicely. Why do you ask?"

She seemed genuinely distraught. Swallowing hard, she whispered, "It was just such a shock, sir. I-I never meant to hurt him, or anyone. He just scared me so much, and I-I reacted . . . I don't even know how I did it, really, I just . . . but I swear I didn't mean to hurt him. He was just very . . . scary. I'm so sorry. Will you please tell him I'm sorry?"

It was at that moment that Sebastian Thorne, for the first time in fifty years, fell in love.

"My dear child," he said, deeply moved, "I will. And please don't concern yourself with such things. From now on, all you have to worry about is your life here."

She exhaled a quiet, relieved breath, then nodded, as if what he'd said had made her happy. He drew nearer to her, a moth to a flame.

"What were you going to say, before you remembered to ask about the Grand Minister's health?" he asked, coming closer still.

Lumina looked up at him. He would have sworn he saw a glimmer of hope deep in her eyes. "He . . . at the Hospice the Grand Minister told me I could meet my mother. My birth mother. He said if I didn't resist, I could be with her." She moistened her lips, blinking rapidly. Her voice lowered to near a whisper. "And I would like that so much, sir. That's why . . . I don't want to be a bother to you, of course, but I thought if perhaps I was good you might let me see her? Or just . . . maybe talk to her? Even if it's one time. You see, I-I never really had a mother. The woman who raised me died when I was young . . ."

She trailed off into silence, biting her lip again, looking down, and it took every ounce of his restraint not to reach out his hand and stroke her hair.

"If you give me your word you will continue to be as cooperative as you've been so far, I will take you to your mother, Lumina."

She looked up at him then, moisture welling in her eyes, and reached out and grabbed his hand. He nearly recoiled, shocked, but she pressed her soft, warm cheek to his hand, and whispered fervently, "Oh, thank you! Thank you, sir! I'm so grateful to you!"

The door slid open. Half a dozen armed men burst into the room. Thorne held them all off with a lifted hand, staring down in awe at the supplicant clutching him as if her life depended on it. She slid her cheek along his knuckles, pressed the softest kiss to his skin, then lifted her head and gazed at him in wonder as if the sun were shining right out of his head.

Dazed, thrilled, imagining in lurid detail just how grateful she might turn out to be, he said, "In fact, I'll take you to see her right now."

He followed behind her. They all did. Handcuffed, barefoot, silent, Lumina walked down a long, sterile corridor. She plainly heard the one called Three trying to quietly urge Thorne to put this off, to interrogate her before rewarding her, but Thorne wasn't having it.

"Time enough for that later," he said, and that was the end of that.

Lu wished she'd learned the craft of stroking a man's ego years ago. How much easier life might have been.

She'd left the book behind in the interrogation room. It was a laughably poor choice by the guard who'd given it to her, and she could only wonder at his motives. She didn't think he was on Dieter's side, judging by the way he smirked at her, but then again, she'd learned how appearances can truly deceive.

The book was *The Art of War*, by Sun Tzu. It contained a quote near the beginning that made Lu think long and hard.

Appear weak when you are strong, and strong when you are weak.

Much like a sheathed knife, her true power lay in concealment.

Thorne watched placidly as the doors to the suite swung slowly open, and mother and daughter saw one another for the first time.

He'd arranged to have Jenna transferred to the suite he'd built in anticipation of her acquiescence to giving him the information he'd wanted about the whereabouts of the rest of her people. She hadn't given him that information yet, unfortunately, in spite of his best efforts with the Breast Ripper and similar unpleasantries. Because she was what she was, she healed uncommonly fast, and so when her daughter first laid eyes on her, she looked relatively healthy.

If you weren't looking into her eyes, that is. Then you could really see what she was all about.

At the moment those fathomless eyes, electric yellow-green and impossibly large, were trained on her daughter.

Thorne gestured to one of the guards to release Lumina from the handcuffs. His order was promptly followed. Then the two women stared at one another in a silence that grew and stretched, becoming uncomfortably long.

Why is nothing happening? he thought, frowning. Perhaps this was their way, this stoicism? He shook that thought off because he'd seen Jenna collapse in an emotional heap when showed the video of Leander. So what was this?

Just as he was about to clear his throat and suggest that it was enough visiting for one day, Lumina ran to her mother, closing the distance between them in a bolt of blurred motion. She threw her arms around her mother's neck. They stood like that, silent, clutching one another, so similar in looks it was eerie, like seeing the older and younger version of the same person at once.

"Well," said Thorne into the hush, "I'll give you two a moment. Lumina, when you're finished here, I'm afraid there are a few things we'll have to discuss."

He turned away, leaving, but Lumina's voice stopped him.

"May I ask you a question?"

When he turned back to look at them, Lumina and her mother were holding hands. Staring at him with faint, ferocious smiles on their faces. Thorne's chest tightened with a disturbing premonition that he was no longer predator, but prey.

"Do you happen to know what 'gie it laldy' means?"

"What?" he asked, confused, irritated, struggling to push aside the growing certainty that something was terribly wrong.

Lumina said, "I heard it recently, and I didn't know what it meant. Do you?"

His response was curt and cold. "No." He turned to leave again, but Three spoke up.

"It's old Scottish slang, sir. It means, 'give it loudly.' Give it one hundred percent. Pull out all the stops, so to speak."

Lumina Bohn threw back her head and laughed, deep and throaty. It was chilling in its exuberance. Then she looked at him, smiling widely, her eyes gleaming animal bright.

Just as the hair atop his head began to lift with the first, sparking crackles of electricity, Lumina said, "Such great advice."

To his horror, the fused metal collars around both women's necks popped off simultaneously, falling with a clatter to the floor. Then Lumina waved at him, a tiny motion of her fingers that wasn't a hello.

And the world exploded into flame.

Sleeping fitfully in his hospital bed, the Grand Minister was abruptly awoken by an earthquake.

He thought it was a dream at first. The clattering windows, the jumping floor, the building groaning and shaking in a way no stationary object ever should. His eyes flew open and he stared around the room in disbelief, not comprehending what his eyes were seeing.

Screaming from the nurse's station. The overhead fluorescents flickered off and on. The data screen wrenched from the wall opposite the bed, crashing to the floor and shattering. A flare of light from the window, searingly bright. Heavy blackout shades were drawn against the hellish heat of day, but one push on the proper button on the universal remote attached to the metal rail on his hospital bed remedied that, and the shades slid silently back.

The Grand Minister was on the sixth floor of the hospital, which provided him an unobstructed view of the surrounding city through the tinted glass. Dead center of the view was St. Stephen's Cathedral, a kilometer away.

The flare of light wasn't really *light* after all. It was fire. A churning, orange inferno had swallowed St. Stephen's whole, leaving only the megascreen atop the highest tower visible. It still displayed the rotating picture of Lumina Bohn.

With his mouth hanging open, the Grand Minister watched as the megascreen listed sideways, then toppled, breaking away from the tower in a colossal spray of stone and glass, falling down to be consumed in an instant by the flames below. Then the tower itself disintegrated, and he was left staring at a writhing ball of flame, spreading out in the shape of a mushroom.

He'd seen that shape before. He'd seen that hellish mass of flame before. He'd felt the earth shake in just the same way, heard the same thundering boom of explosion.

He knew exactly what it all meant.

Magnus was in the central nave of St. Stephen's when it erupted into flame. He knew what it meant, too, because he'd seen it all before, too.

"Lumina," he whispered, sinking to his knees.

The flames swallowed him. Heat and smoke and howling wind, eddies of glowing ashes. He closed his eyes and let the fire test him, let it snap and bay at him like a pack of rabid dogs. It was hellishly hot and every breath singed his lungs, but it quickly turned cool and caressing, the flames gently licking his skin like a lover's caress.

Lumina's fire recognized him. It let him go.

He staggered to his feet. Surrounded by fire that didn't burn, Magnus pushed through walls of flame, buffeted by the wind that fire produces but not harmed. At least not by that. He called out her name again, louder, certain she was here because he'd recognized the images she'd sent, but uncertain how to get below, where he'd find her.

It made sick sense to him now. The religious oppression. The ban on the word "God." It was genius in its own way. When you wanted to establish yourself as the de facto ruler of the universe, you had to eliminate any and all competition. And if you could use the infrastructure of the enemy to your own advantage, so much the better. Almost all cathedrals had mazes of catacombs and crypts, tunnels and tombs, areas perfectly suited for hiding things. For keeping things away from the outside world.

Things like prisoners.

Thorne had constructed his headquarters and containment center for his enemies right under one of the most famous cathedrals in Europe. And Lumina had grown up within sight of the prison that held her mother.

The earth continuing to shake beneath his feet, Magnus called out to Lumina with his mind; he was answered with silence. Focused, fury pushing him forward, he didn't notice the cadre of white-suited Peace Guards that had breached the rear doors of the cathedral, pouring into the nave like a swarm of locusts.

THIRTY-FOUR

The electricity was short-circuited by the fire. The lights were extinguished; everything was plunged into darkness. The backup generators, heated beyond operational capabilities, failed. The only system that worked was the sprinklers. Inside the prison, it began to rain.

Still holding hands, Lumina and Jenna stood in the melting doorway of the suite Thorne had built, watching the fire consume him, Three, and all the other guards he'd brought with him. They screamed and writhed, trying to run, but none of them got very far, in spite of the sprinklers.

Throughout the prison, cell doors popped open. Collars dropped from prisoner's necks. The structure shook and rumbled. Cracks appeared in walls.

Humans died.

Not a single *Ikati* was harmed. Those that could Shift to Vapor did so, surging into air ducts and slipping through cracks, heading up. Those that couldn't Shift used their legs to run, preternaturally fast, for exits. Without her collar, their Queen could See them all like stars against a midnight sky. Holding hands with her daughter, she could speak to them all, as well.

Wales! Ogof Ffynnon Ddu! Go!

There was one voice that answered, and that voice Jenna had heard only once in the past twenty-five years. She jerked her head up with a cry, then looked at her daughter with eyes full of love, victory, and anguish. "Your father's waiting," she whispered.

Above the howl of the firestorm, Lumina heard the words. But she heard something else, too. Another voice. The voice she loved more than anything else in the world, calling her name.

Weakly.

A rush of terror, sharp as knife blades scraped over her nerves. Her heart like a stone in her chest. Dread married reluctance, and Lumina found herself unable to move.

Magnus! Magnus, where are you?

There was no answer.

Jenna said, "The nave—he's near St. Valentine's Chapel! He's directly above us! He's . . . he's . . ."

Her mother looked at her, falling silent, and Lumina saw what she feared most in that look: death.

"No! *No!*"

Lumina Shifted to Vapor, and was gone.

A single heartbeat later, Jenna followed.

THIRTY-FIVE

It would have been a fair fight, the Peace Guard's dozens against his one, but for the shields on their helmets. Magnus couldn't see their faces, their eyes. Worst of all, because he'd been so badly burned by the noonday sun on his way to the cathedral in search of Lumina, he could no longer Shift to Vapor, or cloak himself in shadows to become invisible.

All he had was his strength and his speed against a hail of toxin-laced bullets.

The first spray of bullets missed Magnus entirely, whizzing by his head and blasting through a sculpted marble pulpit beside him instead. He spun away as the carving of dead-eyed angels and pious saints erupted into a blizzard of jagged shards, glinting white. The flames had begun to recede in the main part of the cathedral so he was able to clearly see the flood of *Ikati* rising up with unnatural speed from the floor just in front of the main altar, where an enormous panel of marble had been shoved back to reveal a twist of stairs leading to total darkness below. The escaping prisoners were joined by glittering plumes of mist, slithering through floor vents and surging up stone walls to hang in suspension far above, some darting toward the stained glass windows only to shrink back when they felt the heat and fury of the sun beating through.

There would be no escape for them until the sun had set. They'd been set free from their cells below, but all were now trapped inside an enormous stone cage, beset by enemies all around.

Above the roar of flames, he heard helicopter blades. Enforcement had wasted no time in showing up for the party.

Another volley of gunfire rang out, and Magnus was hit in the shoulder. Snarling, he flitted from column to column in the arcade that flanked the main nave, then charged the shooter, crashing headlong into the man and sending them both tumbling to the ground. The other Peace Guards scattered like buckshot.

His injured arm didn't prevent Magnus from breaking the man's neck with one sharp twist of his hands.

He looked up just in time to see a group of enormous black animals, roaring, leap on a group of Peace Guards huddled in a side chapel. Gunfire rang out. Several panthers slumped to the ground, shot, but others surged forward to take their place. Soon the white hazmat suits were ripped to shreds, and so were the men inside them.

He took down four more, taking aim at the group near the altar. Then pain, searing, blinding white, flared through his body. For a moment, everything went black.

He opened his eyes to find himself on his back, staring at the vaulted ceiling far above. He couldn't feel anything in his lower body, his sense of smell wasn't operational, and he couldn't hear much either. The world had taken on a dreamy, slow quality—the flames arching and rolling gracefully in the periphery of his vision,

Ikati and Peace Guards running in slow motion, even the new spray of bullets streaking by, inches above his face, did so at a lazy speed, so he saw each bullet turn and wink in the light. He lifted his head and looked down. There beneath his body was a spreading stain of red. His own blood, quickly leaking from his body.

No. Not without seeing her. Not like this.

Lumina!

Magnus! Magnus, where are you?

He was just about to answer when into his field of vision stepped a large figure, clothed in white. There could be no mistaking the Peace Guard's intent; his rifle was trained on Magnus's chest. His finger was on the trigger.

A shot rang out, then another, then even more. He lost count. His body twitched with every impact, every muscle spasmed and screamed in misery. The pain was a living thing, ripping through him with a strength that left him breathless, washing over him in waves. He'd known physical pain before, though, pain far, far worse than this. And he'd known the gut-wrenching, soul-eating agony of having the blood of innocents on his hands. Those were terrible things, things that stained and warped him in innumerable ways.

But now Magnus knew true anguish, because he understood with a wrenching flare of clarity that he would never again set eyes on the woman who'd saved him from himself, who'd resurrected him from a living death, and shown him the way back to the light. He'd go into eternal oblivion without a final look at his love, his beautiful angel of fire.

He always knew he'd die alone. It was what he deserved, and right. But to do it without being able to tell Lumina that she was his touchstone, his true north, the only thing of beauty he'd ever known, seemed a fate too cruel to comprehend. He'd meant to tell her how much he loved her; why hadn't he? There hadn't been time, not nearly enough time, and now there never would be.

The last thing Magnus saw was his own face, reflected in the glass of the Peace Guard's mask. Then he closed his eyes to block out that terrible vision, and surrendered his soul to the hungry darkness that had been waiting to claim him for years.

Lumina felt it the instant Magnus died.

Her heart clenched. Gravity lurched then disappeared altogether, like a planet pulled out of orbit, everything spinning and wobbling and just *wrong*. She'd flown up into the cathedral through the main elevator shafts of the prison, moving so fast she was a streaked blur, and she'd taken human form again after slipping through a gap in the floor. The moment she stepped forward into the small marble chapel, with the first beat of her heart, she knew.

Then she saw him.

Ignoring her nudity and the war zone around her, the chaos of shouting and gunfire, flames and fighting, the stream of Peace Guards pushing into the cathedral through all the side doors and the huge, muscular animals running to meet them, she flew across the checkerboard floor and was at his side in seconds. She threw herself to her knees in a howl of banshee grief, and took his head in her hands.

All the exposed skin on his face, arms, and hands was blistered and weeping, burned by the poisonous rays of the sun. He was covered in blood, his own and others', a pool of it under his body, slick, still warm beneath her knees. There was no trace of heartbeat, no respiration, no life left in him at all.

In the inhalation that came before her scream, time stopped. Profound silence, a split second of weightlessness . . . and then the scream.

It was expulsive. There was a thundering, bass *boom*! that shook the walls and floor, the earth itself. A violent jolt rocked the cathedral to its foundations. The entire roof was ripped away as a powerful pulse of energy exploded upward, destroying in a gust of light and pressure the colorful mosaics, toppling the bell tower. The sky flared with color. Pulled with a sudden drag of winds, the red clouds were set into motion, blurring to streaks then tearing apart, dissolving. Every electrical circuit in a hundred-mile radius overloaded and shorted out, sparking and smoking. Every light was extinguished. Every Enforcement helicopter circling the cathedral dropped like a stone from the sky.

Lumina's heart was like a stone, too, hurtling through space. It collided against the reality that Magnus was dead, and shattered. She was empty. She crumpled to his chest, transfigured by misery from a person to a hollow, sobbing shell, cast adrift on an ocean of hopelessness, hopelessness like sewage, raw and rotting and utterly foul.

Blackness tugged at her, coaxing, and Lumina realized she wanted to die, too.

She didn't want to exist in a world without him. She *couldn't.*

Cradling his ruined face in her hands, dripping tears onto his cheeks, Lumina whispered hoarsely, "I can't live without you, Magnus! I can't breathe without you! You're my lungs and my heart and all the life I ever had! Please! Please don't leave me! Please . . . *you have to live . . .*"

Gasping, her body wracked with tremors that seized her, shook her, Lumina laid her cheek on Magnus's chest, sobbing.

In the stillness and silence that rose up all around, everyone, in and out of the cathedral, stared at the sky.

It was blue. A blue so vivid it was almost blinding. And right in the middle of it, hanging there like a golden, glimmering eye, was the sun. A sight not seen in a lifetime.

Lumina heard a voice, soft and caring.

"Hope."

She looked up into her mother's face. Pale and solemn, Jenna gazed down at her, beautiful as a medieval Madonna, her eyes endless, her nudity covered by a long strip of faded, dusty purple silk she'd torn from an altar in an alcove and wrapped around herself. A look passed between them, and she grasped the depth of Lumina's despair without a word spoken. All there was to know was right there in her eyes, in the tears streaming silently down her cheeks. Jenna sank to her knees beside Lumina, pulling her into a gentle embrace.

I'm so sorry. Sweetheart, I'm so, so sorry.

Closing her eyes, Lumina made a sound like an animal in pain.

Another pair of arms encircled her, strong and sure. Lumina smelled spice and smoke and that wild, nighttime scent she'd come to love so much on Magnus. When she opened her eyes again, it was to gaze into a pair that were almost identical to her own, and her mother's.

"Are you hurt?" her father asked.

Automatically, she shook her head, but then caught herself. "Yes," she whispered.

"Can you Shift?"

Now she simply nodded.

"We have to go, love," Jenna said. "All of us. Now. Your father and I will help the others—"

"I'm not leaving him!" It came out as a growl as she turned to crouch over Magnus's body, fiercely protective of him, even now.

"Bring him with you. Back to the caves. We'll take care of him there."

In the softness of her mother's voice Lumina found her meaning, and numbly nodded her head. Magnus would be buried in Wales. She wouldn't leave his body here in this godforsaken city; she'd take him back to the caves and find a spot to bury him, a beautiful spot on a hill overlooking the ocean, where she could visit him every day. Where she could mourn.

Shaking violently, an unholy howling inside her skull, Lumina rose unsteadily to her feet. She looked around, numb, heartbroken, staring blindly into faces both human and animal, all of them blinking in the first light of day they'd seen in decades. Someone in the crowd said a name in an awed murmur, and it was the same name her mother had called her:

Hope.

Lumina nearly laughed at the absurdity of it, at the sheer, colossal *wrongness* of it all. There was no Hope. The girl and the dream were both annihilated. At least for her. All that was left was a vile, pounding emptiness, ashes and bones and death.

She Shifted to dragon, ignoring the collective gasp of the crowd. She gently picked up the body of her love in her massive gold-tipped claws, then launched into the air, pumping her powerful wings hard. She vaulted into the sky through the gaping remains of the cathedral's roof. She didn't notice the throng on the city streets below her, soldiers and citizens staring in wonder at the new, harmless sky, at the red dragon soaring into the endless nexus of blue. She didn't notice the smoking remains of the Enforcement helicopters, or wonder what the future would bring.

For her, there wasn't any future. There was only the past, where Magnus—her heart, the beating pulse of her soul—lived on.

She flew, high and fast, unable in her grief to notice one other small, but vitally important, detail:

The body she was transporting to its final resting place in Wales had stopped bleeding.

THIRTY-SIX

Faces. So many faces. Every one familiar, even through the blinding haze of light. Weightlessness, the heady scent of wildflowers, a feeling of wonder. Warmth. Music.

Peace.

It was so beautiful here, wherever here was. So tranquil. He never wanted to leave.

He moved toward the light, toward the faces, happy now, at ease. Effortless motion, gliding without resistance, formless yet whole. He raised his hands in front of his eyes, and they were made of the same light as everything else, incandescent, pulsating right through his skin. He laughed, and it was music. Plashing fountains and birdsong and all that dazzling, glimmering light . . . all of it so exquisitely beautiful. So *real*.

A whisper made him pause. It was a voice . . . a woman's voice. Lovely, yet ineffably sad. The voice was familiar, but not. The name it called was familiar, but not. A puzzle. It bothered him, a little at first, then more and more as he perceived the raw note of anguish reverberating through that voice, the endless, aching pain. The pain was out of place in all this loveliness.

Looking around, he wanted to find the source. He wanted to comfort the owner of that voice. He wanted to offer solace to such unutterable longing . . .

Suddenly he wanted that more than anything else in this new, magnificent world.

He turned away from the light, and a solid resistance arose inside him as he did. It hurt to turn away, but that voice hurt him even more. It called to him, urgent, pain like a hot welter over the center of his chest. A shocking kaleidoscope of images hit with breath-stealing intensity: the dim gleam of pale skin, the curve of a bare hip. The elegant arch of a neck, lit by candlelight. Hair like spun gold, lucent eyes fringed in a curve of black lashes. Laughter like the pealing of bells, from a mouth he wanted, needed, to kiss.

A face. *That* face, even more lovely than all the ethereal beauty around him.

Fire.

Hope.

It left his lips soundlessly, but the lovely voice that had been calling out in such longing, such wretched pain, fell silent when he thought the word. Carnivorous hunger arose in him, a need to see that face, a face he loved more than anything else in the whole of his existence. A need to hear that name she'd been calling out with such depth of sorrow . . . Magnus.

His name.

With the force of a wrecking ball, it all came back to him. His past, his life, the endless labyrinth of searching for something he'd finally, finally found, only to have it ripped away from his hands.

Lumina. Hope. Two names that meant the same thing to him: love. She was his home and his home was her, not this dazzling place. It was empty without her. It was nothing without her.

He was nothing without her. He would not—*not*—give her up.

As soon as the certainty of it solidified within him, the world tilted and spun, flashing lights and falling stars and a sense of falling down, down, into nothing. Into darkness.

An eternity of darkness. And then . . .

Light again, but different this time. Diffuse. A sly, sliding flicker glimpsed through a blurry screen. Music again, too, but also different. Not instrumental, but natural. What was it? It was so familiar, he'd heard it before . . . water. Yes, flowing water, murmuring, sighing, splashing over rocky streambeds, dripping down stone walls, thundering over sheer cliffs to fall into deep, clear pools below.

He felt the same sense of peace, though. The same wonderful feeling of wholeness had followed him from wherever he'd been. It almost made up for the unholy hardness of the thing at his back. That discomfort, along with a creeping chill that accompanied it, was what finally convinced him to sit up.

When he did, Magnus was met with a scene of such impossible absurdity, his first impulse was to laugh. It was a good thing he didn't; by the look of horror and shock on everyone's faces, that would have been a bad move.

Row upon row of chairs, filled with silent people dressed in black, in a dim, rock chamber, illuminated only by candlelight. Vases overflowing with flowers, their scent perfuming the air. A burning cone of incense in a silver thurible near his feet, exhaling a sinuous fume of smoke along with spicy notes of bergamot and sandalwood. Beneath him a long, rectangular outcropping of rock, elevated a few feet above the stone floor. And on his lap, the black shroud that had covered his face and body, rucked to folds around his waist as he'd sat up.

Holy hell. He'd just interrupted his own funeral.

Into the astonished hush, he said in a voice thick and scratchy, "Well. I always knew I had good timing, but this is ridiculous."

A sound below him caught his attention. He looked down, and there knelt his love at the base of the altar upon which he sat. She stared up at him with wide open eyes, her face pale as stone, trembling hands over her mouth. She made the sound again—a high, small whine of heartbroken disbelief—and it shattered him.

Magnus reached down, dragged Lumina to her feet, and crushed her against his chest.

"How? How?" Her voice was a rasp. She shook violently in his arms.

Magnus took her face in his hands and looked deep into her eyes, smiling. "Did you think a silly thing like me dying could keep us apart?" His smile faded, and his voice became a low, vehement whisper. "Nothing could ever keep me from you, Lumina. Nothing. Not even death itself."

She burst into tears.

Then, chaos. Everyone jumped from their chairs. Cries of joy and disbelief echoed off the cave walls. They were swarmed. Xander and Morgan, Demetrius and Eliana, Christian and Ember, Hawk and Jack, Honor and Beckett and everyone else, the entire tribe, jostling and shoving, shouting and reaching out to touch him. The Seeker, returned from the dead.

Resurrected from the dead . . . by love.

"I don't understand." Lumina kept repeating it, a litany that Honor finally answered.

"You must have Gifted it to him. Like you did to me."

Lumina turned to look at her sister, still uncomprehending, her face wet, her green eyes tear-glossed, little jerking hiccups wracking her body. "Gifted it?" The words were hoarse and disbelieving, like the sound she'd made when she'd looked up at him, arisen from the dead. Honor batted them aside like one would an annoying fly.

"I told you before you left, dummy—I wasn't the one who took Caesar's immortality. That was *you*. And then you Gifted it to me. You shared it, get it?"

Lumina stared at her, frozen, *not* getting it. But a pulse of understanding went through Magnus, palpable as a fist squeezing his heart, and it was as if a door had been opened and a great wind rushed through, and he could finally see. What he saw was the future.

Ah. Yes.

Honor rolled her eyes, folding her arms across her chest. "Your greatest power isn't that you can take other people's talents, other *Ikati*'s Gifts. It's that you can *give* them away again, to whoever you want. While still keeping them yourself. Kind of like the world's best sharing software." Her lips pursed, and she gazed at Lumina with disapproval. "How do you not know this?"

"I . . . I . . ."

"Wait," Beckett cut in. He stood just behind Honor, one hand resting lightly on her waist, and Magnus knew by that simple, proprietary gesture their relationship had gone in an entirely different direction since he and Lumina had left for New Vienna. "So, what you're saying is . . . Hope can . . . she can . . ."

"Gift it to all of us," Honor finished Beckett's thought when he faltered into stunned silence. "Yes. I mean, if she wanted to." She shrugged, as if the thought had never occurred to her before, but then blinked, looking around at the crowd, who had now also fallen quiet. Her voice very small, she said, "Oh."

Oh indeed. Judging by the expression on her face, the same pulse of understanding that had just run through him was running through Honor. Their eyes met, and they shared a moment of profound silence, broken by another pulse of understanding, evidenced in the form of a ragged gasp.

"Room . . . spinning," Lumina croaked, sagging against Magnus. He caught her before she fell, lifting her easily into his arms. He felt surprisingly strong for having just survived a trip to the afterlife.

"Just out of curiosity," he said, looking down at Lumina in his arms, "how long was I dead?"

"Almost an entire day," she whispered, clutching his shirt. "We were just about to bury you."

"Hmm. In that case, I'd say my timing is better than good; it's impeccable."

Lumina rested her head against his shoulder. "I picked out a really nice spot," she whispered. "Good view. Lots of sun."

She stroked his neck, her touch reverent, and he followed her gaze. At the end of the gold chain around his neck glittered her dragon pendant, winking at him in the candlelight in its friendly, serpentine way. He knew with absolute certainty that he'd never take it off. The woman he loved more than life itself had put it there, and there it would stay forever.

Magnus brushed a kiss over her forehead. Full of wonder, his heart bursting with love, he said, "Too bad I'll never need it, since I'll be spending eternity with you."

His words produced a fresh onslaught of tears.

Then Honor said, "Um, that's not completely accurate."

Magnus looked up at her. She smiled at him with a kind of ecstatic, childlike glee. "You'll be spending it with *us*." She sent a pointed look at her sister, then made a small motion with her finger, a circle that encompassed the room and everyone in it.

The urge to laugh arose again, and this time Magnus didn't fight it. He threw his head back and gave himself over to it. The joy he felt was simple and total, bright as a starburst, growing even brighter when Lumina smiled up at him through her tears and began to laugh along with him. Then they were all laughing, rampantly happy, ridiculously, impossibly, *alive.*

Magnus began to push through the crowd, Lumina as light as his own heart in his arms. The laughter followed them all the way back to the small, spartan room he called his own.

Hours later, sated for the moment and lazily heavy in the afterglow of love, Magnus pushed to his elbow and gazed down in adoration at the woman lying on the rumpled sheets beside him. With mussed hair and a sleepy, satisfied smile, she reached up and drew her finger down his cheek, the softest caress.

"All the sun burns healed," she whispered, tracing her finger over his jaw.

He grasped her hand, kissed her fingertips. "Lucky for you, or you'd be spending forever staring at Frankenstein's monster."

Her brow furrowed. She moved her head on the pillow, getting a better look at him. "But your scars are still there, from when you were in that prison. Wonder if it's because they're from before you first Shifted—"

He stiffened. "How do you know about that?"

The words came out harder than he'd intended, but she simply smiled. "Gregor MacGregor."

A snarl ripped through his chest before he could stop it. Bizarrely, that made her laugh. She curled into him, nuzzling his throat, sliding her foot between his calves. "Who, by the way, isn't as bad as we thought."

"Not as bad as we thought? He betrayed us! He's a dead man! I'm going to track down that son of a—"

She shushed his outburst with a finger to his lips. "I admit his methods are questionable, but his intentions were good. Eliana told him about Demetrius's . . ." she glanced up at him, hesitant to speak of the Dream that had foreseen his death, even after all that had happened. "Gregor didn't tell her, but he had connections to a group of Dissenters inside the Peace Guard. He didn't know where the prison was, but he knew they would. He also knew the only way to get me inside without exposing them was to make it look like he'd found me himself, and was turning me in." Her voice turned wry. "I'm sure the enormous bounty helped in the formulation of the plan." She sighed. "So he hedged his bets. If things went badly for us, he wouldn't be suspected and neither would his allies, and if things went our way, he'd still have a giant pile of money. But he *was* trying to save you, Magnus, by sending me alone." Her voice gentled, and she gazed at him with the softest, warmest eyes. "And for that I count him as a friend, no matter what his other faults might be."

"You could've been captured," he growled. "You could've been *tortured*—"

"But I wasn't." Her voice was firm. "And in the end, I did what I went to do."

Magnus held himself still. The possibility of success hadn't occurred to him before now; he'd just awoken from being dead, after all, had just found out he'd never have to go through that particular experience again. The shock of being alive, of seeing her again, had trumped everything else. Slowly, his eyes searching her face, he asked, "So . . . you mean . . . we won?"

She lifted a shoulder, nonchalant. "Well, if by *won* you mean did I reunite with my parents, and release everyone from the prison, and not get myself caught in the process, then yes. We won." She gazed up at him, eyes shining, and Magnus was so thunderstruck he could barely catch his breath, or form words. He supposed there was only one word he really needed to speak.

"Thorne?"

Her eyes hardened. "Dead. And unlike you, that bastard is going to stay that way. Permanently."

He rolled to his back, pulling her on top of him so they were chest to chest, pelvis to pelvis, her naked body draped across his. He turned his face to her neck. "Tell me everything," he whispered, flush with awe and love, holding her tight against him. So she did.

She told him about Dieter, how he and his inside group of Dissenters had taken over command of the Peace Guard once it was confirmed Thorne was dead. She told him about the uprising in New Vienna, citizens turning against Enforcement, how quickly their reign had collapsed when the news media, freed from control and informed by Dieter, disseminated proof that Thorne's regime had been the true force behind the isotope clouds and the war that followed the Flash, *not* the creatures that had been so wrongly labeled Aberrants.

She told him how Leander had arranged transport by Thorne's own fleet of planes for all the *Ikati* who couldn't Shift to Vapor to escape the city. How he and her mother were on their way to Wales, right now.

"And the sky is blue there now, just as blue as it is here. As blue as it will be everywhere soon. Dieter accessed Thorne's mainframe computers; he discovered how the isotope clouds were manufactured and kept in rotation in the atmosphere. They're going to shut the whole thing down. No more Phoenix Corporation. No more Thorne. No more hiding."

The future was rushing at Magnus, even brighter and more beautiful than he'd ever imagined. He stroked Lumina's hair off her face and gazed up at her, his heart a mad, teeming circus of joy and euphoria and most of all, love. So much love he went hot with it, a whole body fever burn of blazing rapture.

"Magnus? Are you all right? God, you're burning up—"

He crushed his mouth to hers before she finished. His kiss was wild, devouring, and by the end of it, she was panting and laughing, her forehead pressed against his.

"I love you," he said, delirious with it. "God I love you. I love you so fucking much it feels like I invented it. Like I'm the first man who ever loved a woman in the history of the universe. Like it was me loving you that caused the Big Bang, and brought everything else into existence."

She sobered, a glint of humor in her eyes. "Yeah, I think you're kind of okay, too." She slid a hand between their bodies. Nimble fingers curled around the erection already growing between his legs. Her voice breathy, she leaned down to whisper in his ear. "But I've been told that demonstrations are more effective than conversations, so . . ."

The noise he made was part laugh, part groan, all pleasure. Then she kissed him, and showed him exactly how she felt about him, and it was more than "kind of okay."

It was flat-out, full-bore, once-in-a-lifetime love.

And it was forever.

EPILOGUE

The sunset was the most spectacular one Lu had ever seen in her life. Which wasn't saying much; it was only the third sunset she'd ever seen, after all.

"Why does the sky turn orange?" She watched in fascination as the blazing disc of the sun finally slipped below the black crags of the mountains on the far horizon. She'd never tire of seeing that sight, or the vivid sky left behind, painted an outrageous, jewel-tone array of sapphire, crimson, and gold.

With an air of authority, Beckett said, "Air molecules and air-borne particles change the final color of the light beam you see as the sunlight travels through the atmosphere. The shorter blue and green components are removed, leaving the longer red and orange hues—"

"Magic," interjected Honor, cutting Beckett off. When he pursed his lips, peeved, she rose on tiptoe and kissed him on the cheek. "Magical molecules," she amended, winding her arms around his shoulders. She grinned up at him, and Beckett's peeved expression turned into one of dazed adoration.

Leaning back against Magnus's chest, Lu smiled. Even more than seeing her sister so happy, she loved seeing a strong man brought to his knees with only a look from his woman.

You should be getting used to that by now, Magnus said silently, wrapping his arms around her and squeezing. *Seeing as how you do the same thing to me every few minutes.* He kissed the top of her head and she sighed, utterly content.

They stood together on the slope of the hill near the entrance to the caves. Birds sang in a stand of nearby trees. A cool, gentle wind stirred her hair around her face, swirled surrealist patterns in the long grass. Holding hands, her parents stood with them, silently staring into the distance with identical small smiles that looked to Lu both melancholy and mysterious, yet also glad.

All six of them were full of contradictory emotions, she knew. So much was behind them, yet so much still lay ahead. Lifetimes of adventures, still to be had.

Lifetimes spent in a new, strange, wonderful world.

"Did you see the news about that doctor from the hospital in New Vienna?" her mother asked quietly, looking out over the darkening valley. Sunset colors highlighting her long blonde hair in glinting gold, that scant, strange smile still on her lips, she turned her head to look at Honor and Lu.

Simultaneously, they asked, "No, what?"

Her mother's smile deepened, becoming almost mischievous. "The medications the Phoenix Corporation made from us had some unexpected side effects in the people who took them."

"What kind of side effects?" asked Beckett.

"Good ones." Her father drew her mother against his side with his arm around her shoulder. She rested her head there, still looking at her daughters, still smiling. "Although hardly the result Thorne would have wanted, I'm sure."

His laugh was low and wry, and Jenna angled her head to look up at him. "Funny how things have a way of working out in the end, isn't it?" she whispered.

Nodding, Leander brushed the hair away from Jenna's face, stroking a finger down her cheek. It was so strange to see them together, these two people she'd never even known existed a few weeks ago. Her *parents*. It was all still so hard to process.

Over the past few days since everyone had returned to the caves from the prison beneath St. Stephen's, Lu had struggled with her emotions. One moment she was gleefully happy, the next, she was sitting stunned on a rock in some dark corner, trying to piece it all together. Magnus would always find her at those moments. He'd take her into his arms, hold her, let her cry or rant or whatever it was she needed, letting her draw on his strength until she found her footing again.

He was her anchor now. Her center. Without him, she'd be lost.

Those strong arms tightened even harder around her. *I love you, too, angel.*

If you're going to keep eavesdropping on me, Lu thought, trying not to smile, *I should warn you that I've been thinking about a few new positions we should try. I read the Kama Sutra once and I really liked this one thing called "The Perch."*

She sent him a mental picture, gratified when a low growl of desire rumbled through his chest. *We've already done that, angel.*

Not with a mirror!

He pressed a kiss to her neck, his husky laughter muffled against her skin.

"But what exactly does that mean?" Honor prompted, impatient with their father's vague answer about the medicine.

With a look of triumph in his eyes, Leander said softly, "It means that our DNA, bioengineered to be compatible with the human body, solved a lot more problems for the patient than whatever the patient was taking the medication for. Have diabetes? Your eczema is cured, too. High blood pressure? Say good-bye to your lactose intolerance. Taking a pill for migraines? That hole you didn't know you had in your heart is now healed, too."

"Well," said Honor after a while, sounding a little disgruntled. "Bully for them."

"No, love. Bully for *us*." Leander paused, his gaze taking in the group. "Because every person who took medication from the Phoenix Corporation for the last twenty-five years has had their DNA altered. And they've passed that altered DNA on to their children, and those children will pass the altered DNA on to their children. So now, basically . . . they *are* us. Or something like us."

"Hybrids?" Beckett stared at Leander in disbelief. Everyone else stared at him that way, too.

Leander nodded. "Without knowing it, Thorne solved a problem that's plagued the *Ikati* since the beginning of time. We could never mate with humans because our genes were incompatible. The half-Blood offspring would survive until the age of twenty-five, then either Shift for the first time, or die. Only a tiny percentage were ever able to survive the Transition—"

"So that's what he meant!" exclaimed Lu, standing straighter.

"Who?" asked Honor, frowning.

"The Grand Minister! The day he found me at the Hospice he questioned me, asked if I'd ever had any health problems around my twenty-fifth birthday!"

Eyes shining, her mother reached out and touched Lu's arm. "You're only one-quarter human, and I knew how powerful you and your sister were, but I admit, the day of your twenty-fifth birthday was one of the worst I can remember. I just sat on the cot in my cell all day . . . waiting. I thought I would feel it . . . if . . ."

She swallowed, shaking her head. Leander murmured something into her ear, low and soft. Jenna cleared her throat, blinked her tears away. "But obviously I had nothing to worry about. Cliché as it sounds, we had the last laugh. The majority of people left on Earth are more like us than not. Even if they can't Shift, they have our Blood, and that makes us related."

A bird was singing somewhere out there in the twilight. High, sweet notes warbled and trilled, suspended for a long moment in the cooling air. *Lark*, Lu thought. *She'll be making her nest soon. Life goes on.*

Life goes on.

Her mother's hand was still on her arm, and Lu gripped it, overcome with emotion. Honor moved closer, and the three of them stepped together silently, embracing. Her father put his arms around them. When Lu looked up at him with tears in her eyes, he kissed her on the forehead, then kissed Honor the same way.

"We're so proud of you," he said, husky, his own eyes moist. "For everything you've done, for the women you've become, your mother and I are so proud of you both."

Lu's face was wet now; she didn't care. She smiled up at Leander, squeezed Jenna's hand, bumped her hip against Honor's. Then she looked over at Magnus and Beckett, both of them wearing huge grins, and realized with her heart full to bursting that she finally had everything she'd ever wanted. Family. Love. Home.

There was only one thing missing.

"The people you left me with," she said, looking back at Jenna and Leander. "The people I called my parents, before . . ."

Jenna's brows drew together. Leander stilled, waiting, his eyes searching hers.

Lu wasn't sure how to say what she wanted to say, only that she needed to say something to make them understand. They hadn't talked about her past yet, specifically her childhood, and at this moment it seemed important to honor the people who'd sacrificed so much for her. The people who'd taken her in as a baby, cared for her, in spite of the danger to them. In spite of how different she was. In spite of everything.

"They loved me," she said simply. "And I loved them. I . . . I'll always love them." Her voice broke, and she swallowed, looking away.

Her mother's voice was as soft as the hand she laid on her cheek. "Of course you will. They're your parents, too. And I'll always be grateful to them. Don't ever feel like loving them takes anything away from us. Hearts are big enough to fit a lot of people inside; you don't have to choose one over the other. We can all be in your heart together."

"Thank you," Lu whispered, overcome with gratitude that she understood.

Swiping at her eyes, Honor sniffled. "Okay, enough of this! My mascara's gonna run."

"You're not *wearing* mascara," Lu said.

Honor jabbed her in the ribs with her elbow. "Shut up."

"You shut up!"

"No, *you* shut up!"

"Both of you shut up!" said Beckett and Magnus, and everyone laughed. And it felt so good Lu couldn't stop for a long, long while.

"Speaking of that hospital in New Vienna," said Lu to Honor on the slow walk back toward the caves, "you and I have a little unfinished business there." She slid Honor a sideways, knowing glance, but her sister looked puzzled.

"What do you mean?"

Lu answered casually, "I mean . . . did you ever hear the old saying that if you die in your dreams, you die in real life?"

It was a moment before Honor grasped her meaning. When she did, a smile spread slowly over her face. "Oh, dear sister. And everyone thinks *I'm* the wicked one."

"Witchy, I think you mean."

"I'd rather be witchy than haggard," Honor shot back, her brows raised haughtily.

"Here we go again," said Magnus, holding Lu's hand and rolling his eyes. Beckett pulled Honor against his side, clamped his arm around her shoulders, and dragged her away.

Lu called after them, "Love you, too, sis!" to which Honor responded with a distinctive, one-fingered salute.

Magnus chuckled. "You two are unbelievable."

With a brilliant smile, Lu looked up at him. "I know."

They walked through the hole in the grassy hillside, leaving the jewel-painted sky behind.

He was dreaming. He understood that. He didn't rise to the position of Grand Minister of the Imperial Federation by being stupid, after all.

But the thing was . . . there was something wrong about this dream.

The *scent*, for instance.

He knew he'd never had a dream that incorporated smell before. He didn't know how he knew, only that he did, and it disturbed him. The scent itself wasn't disturbing—it was lovely, in fact. Lovely, dark, and deep, like an unexpected breath of springtime air in a dead winter woods. He knew this scent, but couldn't place it, and the just-out-of-reach recognition was maddening.

Floral top notes, gardenias and freesia. Something earthy and indefinite, clean like ocean breezes but woodsy like moss and beds of dried leaves at the same time. Beneath it all, a musky, exotic heart of . . . cloves? Amber? Maybe even chocolate. Mouthwatering.

Aware that his body was fully operational, and all his limbs were intact in a way they could never be when he was awake, he felt loamy earth beneath his feet, saw slanting shafts of sunlight glimmering through towering, ancient trees. This was the woods behind his childhood home, the wild Black Forest he'd played in so long ago. It was all familiar, there was no visible threat, but that sense of wrongness permeated everything.

After a moment he realized it was because he wasn't alone. There was someone—or something—behind him.

He turned with the sluggish drag of dream-speed, his body wanting to whirl about like a dragonfly, darting, but hindered by air that was thick, and time that moved like molasses. When finally he spun around and faced that dark, invisible entity, he almost laughed, relieved and ashamed by his certainty of danger.

A white rabbit wearing a fedora sat with pricked ears and twitching nose on the leaf-strewn ground, munching a carrot.

"Hello, little rabbit," said the Grand Minister, his voice echoing eerily off the trees. "You gave me quite a start!"

The rabbit dropped the carrot, sat up on its haunches, and looked at him. Its eyes glowed hellish red. From behind a nearby tree hopped another rabbit, white as the first, eyes just as red, sans the hat but with a waistcoat and pair of front teeth that seemed unnaturally . . . long.

Long, and sharp.

From its waistcoat pocket, the second rabbit produced a watch on a fob and chain. It tapped the face of the watch three times, and said in a soft, feminine voice, "Ticktock. Ticktock. Ticktock."

The Grand Minister took a step back. And another.

The rabbit in the hat mused, "I wonder . . . do you remember me?" It waited a beat, watching him, then seemed to shrug. "No? Well, maybe I'll give you a little hint to jog your memory."

It grew, stretching taller. Haunches gave way to legs, fur gave way to skin, whiskers and pink nose gave way to a face he would recognize anywhere. Even here, in his own dream, where it never should have been able to sneak in. The other rabbit grew as well, and then he was staring in horror at two identical faces, two identical women, beautiful and lethal, the most terrifying things he had seen in all his long, long years.

"You!" he hissed, skin crawling, heart pounding in his chest. "Lumina Bohn!"

The monster that had been the rabbit in the fedora laughed, advancing. Its twin merely smiled.

"No," it said with infinite calm. "My name isn't Lumina. That little mouse is gone. *My* name is Hope. And this is my sister, Honor." She gestured to her identical twin, who gave a mocking bow. The two of them kept slowly advancing with those terrible smiles as he kept stumbling back, gasping for breath, the trees crowding in all around.

Hope said, "And in regard to that question in your mind, the answer is yes."

"What?" the Grand Minister asked, breathless, choking on his own horror.

Hope smiled grimly. "This *is* going to hurt."

Without further delay, they proceeded to prove it to him.

ACKNOWLEDGMENTS

First and foremost I must thank my husband, Jay, for all his support through this incredible journey I've been on over the past four years while writing the Night Prowler saga. I never, *never*, would have accomplished this without you. You're the bedrock of my life. The best decision I've ever made was saying, "I do," on that hot July day in Vegas seventeen years ago, and I choose you again and again, every day, because you're amazing, and my best friend. I love you.

Thank you to my family, to my parents, Jim and Jean, for their encouragement, to my friends for their enthusiasm. Thank you to Marlene Stringer, my agent, and Maria Gomez and Kelli Martin, my editors at Montlake. Big thanks also to the team at Montlake and Amazon publishing for listening to and answering all my questions patiently through the years. And a big hug of gratitude to Eleni Caminis for acquiring the series, and becoming a wonderful friend. Melody Guy has provided me with incredible editorial advice on every book in this series, and I thank her from the bottom of my heart for her kind words about my work, and her insightful suggestions on how to make it better.

To my Street Team, Geissinger's Gang, thank you so much for sharing my work with your friends and being so wonderfully loyal, enthusiastic, and nice. You've become more than just fans, you've become friends, and I'm so grateful to have your support as I continue writing. A shout-out to Gang member Erin Morgan Teuton for coming up with the name Sebastian Thorne!

Finally, thank *you*, dear reader. Books are magical things, entire worlds inside a few pages, and readers are the air of those worlds, the force that keeps books alive. I write for myself, but also for you. Thank you for living inside my world, if only for a little while. I hope you'll join me again.

ABOUT THE AUTHOR

 J.T. Geissinger is an award-winning author of paranormal and contemporary romance featuring dark and twisted plots, kick-ass heroines, and alpha heroes whose hearts are even bigger than their muscles. Her debut fantasy romance, *Shadow's Edge*, was a #1 bestseller on Amazon US and UK, and won a Prism Award for Best First Book. Her follow-up novel, *Edge of Oblivion*, was a RITA Award finalist for Paranormal Romance from the Romance Writers of America. She has been nominated for numerous other awards for her work. She resides in Los Angeles with her husband.

www.jtgeissinger.com
www.twitter.com/JTGeissinger
www.facebook.com/JTGeissinger